READY OR NOT . . .

The wind chime outside danced in a wild tune, while inside the silk flattened against her and her hair blew in her eyes. A bright light flashed, and then Darius stood before her.

He was as she had first seen him. Vibrant, male, magic. Dressed in the robe and turquoise tablet and nothing else. Shards of silver sparkled about his dark hair. His hands fisted at his hips.

"Are you ready, my Isis, for our third bargain?"

PRAISE FOR KATHLEEN NANCE'S PREVIOUS NOVEL, *WISHES COME TRUE!*

More Than Magic

Kathleen Nance

LOVE SPELL BOOKS   NEW YORK CITY

For Elizabeth, Maureen, and Sandra. I couldn't have done it without you. Thanks for the advice, the honesty, the encouragement, and the wine.

LOVE SPELL®

March 1999

Published by

Dorchester Publishing Co., Inc.
276 Fifth Avenue
New York, NY 10001

ISBN 0-505-52299-3

ACKNOWLEDGMENTS

My thanks to Mary at Earth Savers, Sabina at Hové Parfumeur, and Ann and Vita at Bourbon French Parfums for answering my questions. Any mistakes and liberties taken are mine alone.

More Than Magic

Chapter One

Isis Montgomery often cut through the deserted alley on her way to the ferry, and the sudden contrast between raucous New Orleans French Quarter streets and hushed isolation always surprised her. Today, however, the silence seemed especially thick. Only her heels clicking on the rough bricks disturbed the unnatural quiet.

Shadows concealed the edges of the narrow alley, but she kept her sunglasses on in deference to the still-bright early evening sun. A gust of March breeze sent a shiver across her shoulders, and behind her a shutter banged in sharp retort. Isis started, then shook her head at her stab of nerves. Her brothers' endless warnings must be getting to her.

Dingy windows and locked doors hinted at life behind the walls, but in the daylight nothing stirred. Isis was halfway through her shortcut when a brilliant light flashed behind one window, then went off. What was that? Intrigued, Isis drew closer.

11

A hand-lettered sign was taped to the grimy window, but otherwise nothing distinguished the doorway from the other brick-fronted stores. Slowly Isis read aloud, tracing the letters with her finger: MADAME PARIS. CURIOSITIES, DREAMS, AND MAGIC.

It had been weeks since she'd been this way, so she'd never seen this place, but she had heard rumors about it, disturbing rumors. Isis peered in, shielding her face with one hand, but saw nothing. No merchandise was displayed in the windows.

The shop did not look like a place of magic.

A faint draft of air—from the store?—whispered across her face, carrying with it a whiff of perfume, exotic and alluring. Isis froze, wisps of dream memories vibrating across her skin and tickling her nose.

The perfume of her dreams?

The scent she had sought for months?

Too fleeting to tell. A frisson of excitement, tempered by wariness, skittered up her spine. "Curiosities, dreams, and magic," Isis repeated. The perfume she sought was magic to her. Dangerously alluring, sultry and intriguing—magic.

So, why the strange reluctance to go in? Because she wanted nothing to do with magic, and the prickling at the back of her neck reinforced her wariness. Isis drummed her purple-tipped nails against her thigh for a moment, throwing off the uneasy sensation. You didn't accomplish anything in this life without taking a few chances.

Besides, she needed that perfume.

She finger-combed her short, dark hair, settled her sunglasses firmly against her nose, and then pushed open the door. Instead of the common bell or rattling veil of beads, loud hisses greeted her. Two bearded dragons—flat, sandy-colored desert lizards—lurked in metal wire cages, one on either side of the door.

"Hello, boys," Isis greeted them, then strolled around the cluttered, narrow room. In the silence, her heels tapped a staccato beat on the uneven wood floor.

The shop was no more imposing on the interior. It smelled of ylang-ylang and dust, and the dim light forced her to remove her sunglasses. A crystal ball—how utterly predictable—rested atop a round table covered in shabby velvet. Tattered books were heaped on shelves and counters, in no discernable order. Magic paraphernalia, most of it the gimmickry of the stage magician, littered the store.

She picked up a deck of cards, shuffled them, then held them out in a fan. "Pick a card," she said to the silent dragons. "Ace of spades?" Isis reached into the center of the marked deck and pulled out the ace of spades, then tossed the deck on the table. "Still got the old touch. Aunt Tildy would be proud."

Her great-aunt Tildy made a living debunking charlatan magicians and psychics. Oh, not the ones who entertained, but the ones who preyed on the hopes and fears and pocketbooks of the innocent. In the past, Isis had helped her, and had picked up a few tricks in the process.

Only difference was, Aunt Tildy still believed magic truly existed, and that someday she'd find it. Three years ago, Isis had given up the search for true magic, and this place didn't look like a good candidate to change her mind.

So, where was the proprietor? Isis crossed her arms and tapped her heeled foot. If it wasn't for that faint, remembered aroma, she'd leave right now.

Her foot stilled as she spied a crystal flacon resting atop a black mirror. It was . . . not beautiful, but intriguing, with unevenly curved sides and a blood-red stopper. Fascinated, she moved closer, the muscles in her neck tightening. Even the coating of dust couldn't hide the strange scarlet marks etched into the surface.

She picked up the flacon, uncorked it, then dabbed

a tiny amount on her wrist. The true test of a perfume was how it worked on the skin, not how it rose from the bottle. She waited a moment, then sniffed.

Floral, but not sweet, with the green aromas of early spring. A head note of orange blossom was her first impression, but other, unrecognizable, spices brought warmth to her skin. The exotic scent was as complex and unique as the bottle that held it, as mysterious and alluring as her passionate dream. Unknown, yet . . . so familiar.

A memory long forgotten, drawn from the recesses of her mind by the primal powers of scent, flashed into Isis. This perfume—she had smelled it once before.

She'd been young, not yet in kindergarten, but even then the scent had drawn her when she discovered it among the perfumes cluttered on her grandmother's dressing table. Magic, her grandmother had called it, a legacy of the past. When her grandmother died a month later, Isis had searched for the irresistible perfume but had not found it.

Hope uncurled its first dormant leaf. Could *this* be the perfume of her dreams, the one she had tried for months to capture? Was this the scent she needed for Dream Scents, her aromatherapy and perfume shop?

After so long, Isis tempered her excitement. She'd been close before and been disappointed.

While she waited for the perfume to warm, she looked around more slowly. "Hello?" she called. "Anybody here?"

A repeated hiss was her only answer. Isis ambled over to the nearest bearded dragon, who flicked his tongue at her. She crouched down until she was at eye level with the beast, then mimicked the animal's hiss. It blinked and moved closer.

A sudden gust of wind shoved her against the cage. She grabbed the wires to keep herself from falling.

The lizard's tongue flicked out, touching her hand. Two hot, painful pricks, like the touch of electrified wire, coursed through her palm.

"Ouch!" Isis shook her hand.

"My pet is territorial," said a female voice from behind her.

"Your pet is also very strange. Bearded dragons don't have acid tongues," Isis answered, pushing to her feet.

"They are a rare breed." Hands folded in front of her, the proprietress advanced. She wore a long dress of spiderweb gray and dangling earrings made of turquoise. A turquoise necklace hung between her breasts, which were amply displayed by a low-cut neckline.

Heavy purple eye shadow does nothing for her, not with that silver hair, thought Isis idly. *She'd do better in Cobalt Smoke*.

"Are you Madame Paris?"

"That name will do." The woman tilted her head in study. "What is yours?"

"People call me Ice."

For some reason, that answer seemed to please Madame Paris. "Ice quenches fire," she murmured.

Oh, great, Isis thought, one of those—like that slime Benedict Fontenot—who believed the more obscure the words, the more mystical they sounded. Give her plainspoken Aunt Tildy any day.

Madame Paris looked directly at Isis, her gray eyes as hard as glacial ice. "Why have you come to my shop?"

A faint energy made the fine hairs on Isis's arms stand up. She smoothed her hands down her short blue skirt. "Curiosity," she answered evenly.

"That is why most stop," Madame Paris said. "My curiosities. They stay because of the dreams and the magic."

She's got the mysterious proprietor act down cold.

However, Isis had spent too much time with Aunt Tildy to be impressed.

"Have you found something that interests you?"

"Maybe." Isis's hand trailed across a pair of jeweled slippers, and the displaced dust made her sneeze. She picked up a deck of tarot cards, then set them down immediately, unnerved by the wash of dread that filled her when she held them.

"This is nice." She lifted a glass ball that was filled with swirling blue smoke.

"That's not what you want."

Madame Paris's slight smile, which did nothing to warm her eyes, annoyed Isis. Especially as she had the distinct impression the woman knew exactly what interested Isis. She'd probably watched from the back room or with a hidden camera.

Isis lifted her wrist to her nose. The perfume hadn't faded, all volatile top notes with no heart, no base. Instead, it had gotten richer, more exotic, more beautiful and compelling. She could identify lemon and a hint of sagelike clary in those first heart notes, scents that gave a perfume its character. Others she recognized but could not name, those elusive dream notes that would take much more to discover.

She picked up the flacon of perfume. There was such a tiny amount inside, only enough for a couple of wearings, barely enough for analysis. "Do you have more of this?"

Madame Paris shook her head. "That is the only perfume vial I possess, and I think you will find it unique to my shop."

The woman was probably right about that. Except the one time, Isis had never smelled a perfume like it, and she'd poked around in a lot of odd corners and smelled a lot of aromas.

"Who developed it, do you know? Who owns the patent?" Perhaps they would sell the formula, or be willing to work out a joint venture.

"It is an ancient perfume. The formula and the originator have been lost in the mists of time."

No patent owner, no one with the rights to the perfume? Isis's excitement rose. She could market it exclusively, *if* she could re-create it.

That was a big *if*. She had to have more perfume. Enough so she could analyze and compare until she re-created the scent.

"Do you know where I could get more?"

"There is only one way." Madame Paris hesitated for a moment. "You need to command the power of a djinni."

Isis's growing excitement sank. "A *what*? A genie?"

"They prefer to be called djinn. Djinni in the singular." The dragons hissed in affirmation. "The *only* way you will get more of that perfume is to wish for it from a djinni."

Yeah, right. "I suppose you just happen to have a lamp for me to buy."

The woman trilled with laughter. "A lamp? Surely you're not so naive as to believe the Terran superstition about a lamp?"

The back of Isis's neck tightened, radiating tension across her shoulders. As a child, she'd hated laughter at her expense, and the sound didn't grow any more pleasant with maturity. "Then how do I summon this djinni?" she asked, wondering what the woman had planned.

Madame Paris waved a hand. "To . . . summon a djinni for your bidding, you need only read the words and perform the appropriate ritual."

"I don't do rituals," Isis muttered.

"Anyone can do it. Even the powerless."

"Why don't you use it?"

"Only one from Terra—earth—can activate the spell."

This was getting too weird. "And you're not from earth?" Isis inquired deliberately.

17

Madame Paris waited with implacable calm, ignoring the question.

Okay, so the woman was probably certifiable, and the idea of performing a magical ritual again filled Isis with the ice of her nickname.

Yet, she could not walk away. There were too many strange things here—the dragons, the unsettled feelings permeating the store—to ignore.

Most important, though? Isis was absolutely certain that if she walked out the door now, she'd never find the perfume again. It would haunt her the remainder of her days, always unattainable.

"What's the price for the ritual?"

Madame Paris stared at her in continued silence. Isis regarded her back, schooling her face to reveal none of her eagerness. To hide their trembling, she rested her hands on her hips.

"A favor," Madame Paris said finally.

"What kind of favor?"

Madame Paris shrugged. "That will be determined later."

An open bargain with a woman who claimed to know magic? No way! She'd been burned before, badly, in trusting a man who professed to have magical talents, and she wouldn't repeat that mistake.

"You'll have to be more specific," Isis countered.

Madame Paris shook her head. "Not yet."

"Then I'll pass." Stalling, hoping Madame Paris would relent, Isis strolled toward the door. At the cages, she paused and pulled a compact from her purse. While powdering her nose, she cast a covert glance at Madame Paris in the mirror. Isis snapped the case shut. She tapped it with one purple-tipped nail and silently cursed. The woman wasn't going to give.

Was the ritual worth the risk and the potential cost?

Isis lifted her wrist to her nose again. The perfume

had warmed to more of its heart notes. Moss? A hint of anise? The elusive scents teased her nostrils and created ethereal images of evenings illuminated by fire and heated by passion.

It was the perfume of her dreams!

If the ritual worked, if it brought her the perfume—yes, it was worth the price.

Slowly, Isis turned back, fingering one beaded earring. "Tell you what. I'll pay you for the ritual now. If this djinni shows up, then I'll owe you your favor. But I won't do anything illegal." She picked up the flacon. "And this is included in the bargain."

After a moment's hesitation, Madame Paris nodded. "You shall pay me the sum of one thousand dollars and will owe me a favor when you summon a djinni. The favor I ask shall not be contrary to the laws of Terra, of earth."

"I'll pay you *one hundred*. Right now, all I'm getting is mumbo jumbo and this bottle. *If* a djinni appears, the other conditions apply, plus an extra hundred."

"It is done."

Isis tucked the flacon into her purse and fished out her money. When she handed it to Madame Paris, the bills vanished. Madame Paris pressed her hands together then spread them apart. Two papers yellowed and crackling with age materialized in her palm.

Isis stared incredulously, jitters dancing in her stomach. How had she done that? It had not been a magician's stunt.

Madame Paris gave her one paper. "This is the ritual you need. Follow it exactly, timing yourself to end at dawn at the time of Ostara, two days hence."

March 20th. The vernal equinox.

Isis studied the paper and grimaced. This was worse than the ritual for breast endowment she'd attempted when she was fourteen.

Why did magic always have to be surrounded with

ceremonies and placing the candle just so? A robe of solid green? Green was not her color.

"Follow this exactly?"

"Yes, exactly. And these are the words you must say." Madame Paris gave her the second paper. "With these you will compel a djinni from the realm of Kaf."

Most of it looked like total gibberish. Why did there have to be so many *foreign* words to read? Her dyslexia gave her trouble enough with her own language. "I won't know how to pronounce this." She squinted and read aloud at the end where she found a word she recognized, " 'Come to me Dari—' "

"Hush!" A clap of thunder accompanied Madame Paris's command, cutting Isis off in midsentence. "Do not speak the words until the appointed time. Otherwise the ritual will fail. As for the ones you do not know, say them as best you can. Will you do as the ritual demands?"

Isis stared at the papers. She needed more perfume, and she was convinced Madame Paris would give her no more. Though she had her doubts about this ritual stuff, though she mistrusted magic and, more, anyone who claimed to master it, she couldn't run the slightest risk that she would lose this one chance. She might feel foolish, but she would follow the ritual as described.

"Yes."

"I shall see you when I come to collect my favor." Madame Paris vanished, accompanied by a fierce blast of wind.

The last thing Isis saw was Madame Paris's triumphant smile.

Isis blinked, then glanced at the bearded dragons. "Is she always that dramatic?" she asked, hiding the uneasiness that danced up her spine.

The dragons just flicked their tongues at her.

Careful not to tear the brittle papers, Isis slipped the precious ritual into her purse. Outside, she resettled her sunglasses on her nose, took a deep breath, and then strode to the end of the alley.

A mime stood on a box across the street. He wore white gloves and a purple satin suit with a white ruffle around the neck. Stark white makeup covered his face. He posed in absolute stillness, waiting for someone to throw a dollar in the hat at his feet, when he would begin to move, wound up by the power of cash.

Isis crossed the street and tossed in a five. "What are you doing here, Marc?"

A wide grin split the mime's face. He hopped down from his box and scooped up the money and hat in one easy move. "Making sure you don't get into trouble, Ice. I saw you duck down the alley, so I figured I'd set up shop here at the other end. I do feel a certain responsibility, since I told you the street rumors about that place." He glanced back down the alley. "Find something interesting?"

"Yes."

"What?"

"That, my dear Marc, is my business. You may be an excellent personal assistant for me and Dream Scents, but the only time your mouth can keep a secret is when you're doing your mime act."

"Hey, what can I say? It's the gift of gab. Brought by the leprechauns when I kissed the Blarney stone."

"You're not Irish."

"They're equal opportunity fairies." Marc draped a companionable arm across her shoulder. "How about dinner? You can buy me a dozen oysters at Felix's."

"Sounds good." Isis glanced over her shoulder. Madame's grimy shop looked even less like a place of magic than it had before. She looked away. The bargain was made, time would tell the consequences.

* * *

Darius. He was as beautiful, as mesmerizing, as dangerous as ever.

Pari, her silver hair and web-gray robe whipping in the desert winds of the djinn realm of Kaf, stared into her blood-red crystal at Dariyavius el Zarasteya, known to most only as Darius or, more commonly, the Protector.

A man strong with the gifts of the magic. *Ma-at*, Pari corrected herself. She'd been too long among the humans, too long separated from her djinn subjects.

Her lips pressed together in hatred as she stared at the man responsible for her banishment. A man whose touch she craved, even as she despised his power.

He had a face too beautiful for a male, with golden skin and sculpted cheeks. His dark, star-kissed eyes promised exquisite joys while his clever mouth spoke cruel truths. As she watched, Darius leaned with indolent grace against the cedar tree that formed one corner of his sleeping nook and eyed the lady before him.

Pari peered closer in the scrying crystal and identified the woman. Leila. An acknowledged beauty of the djinn, a skilled seductress. Didn't she know her wiles were wasted on Darius? It was no secret that he had no intention of taking a wife, a *zaniya*. Ever. Sex and sensuality would never ensnare Darius, for he was their master.

Only *ma-at* could do that, and the events were already set in motion. The Terran woman of the prophecy had been found and set upon her course. There was no turning back.

Darius unknotted the belt of his midnight-blue robe, and Leila smiled in anticipation. The image vanished in a flash of white light, and Pari's crystal shattered.

She cursed. Darius had protective barriers she

could not guess at and her *ma-at* could not penetrate. She wouldn't be able to spy again. Darius was too strong, his *ma-at* too wild and brilliant.

No matter. Soon, Isis Montgomery would bind him, and then all the powers of Kaf could not save him.

Chapter Two

Kaf, the realm of the djinn

Darius, Protector of the *Ma-at*, leaned against the cedar tree and eyed the lady before him. Women were such pleasure. He loved the way they smelled, relished the softness of their skin and the low melody of their voices. And this lady was perfumed, polished, and dressed in her finest—and sheerest—robe. Apparently Leila had decided to conclude her pursuit of him.

"What do you seek?" he asked.

"Only to spend time with our Protector," she answered.

He held out one hand, while unknotting the belt of his robe with the other. "Then may your desires be granted."

Leila smiled and took his hand.

A small ripple of *ma-at* disturbed the protective barriers surrounding his home. Darius sought the source, but when the intrusion wasn't repeated, he decided it must be a stray remnant of a spell.

Turning his attention back to Leila, he kissed her palm, then her wrist. Slowly she pulled her hand from his and lowered herself to his pillows. The lady was eager.

He preferred to take his time, gain her satisfaction before his own release.

Unbidden, his small, but unique, telepathic talent caught a shadow of her thoughts. Discovering her desire for a diamond thread robe, Darius murmured words of transformation. Leila's robe changed from ordinary yellow to white-gold. An impossibly brilliant white-gold that hurt his eyes.

By Solomon's sands! In a blink, he muted the colors, hoping she didn't notice the slip in his control of *ma-at*.

She didn't, apparently thinking the flare was part of the transformation. "Oh, Protector," she breathed, stroking the robe, "it's beautiful."

"No more beautiful than you. And here, on my pillows, you may call me Darius."

"Darius." She leaned back, deeper into the mound of pillows, and lowered her eyes in invitation. "I've always wanted a diamond-thread robe, but I could never master the spell."

I know. He communicated not aloud, but by inserting the words into her mind.

Leila gave a satisfied laugh. Confident in her seductive abilities and beauty, she thought she had won.

She had not.

Few Protectors ever took a *zaniya*, a wife, but there had been the occasional exception over the centuries. Enough that Leila had set her snares for Darius, though he had never made a secret of his intent to remain unjoined. She was not the first to have tried and failed.

25

A triumphant smile hovered at the edges of her lips.

The smile Darius gave her in return promised nothing but delight for them both.

Ma-at sparkled beneath his fingertips, under his control this time. His robe disappeared, leaving only the turquoise tablet at his throat. Her robe and tablet he left in place. Without moving, he stroked her, not with physical touch, but with his mind and his *ma-at*. She sighed in deep pleasure.

"This is all there can be between us," he said softly, not joining her on the pillows yet. About this he would be perfectly clear. "Do not mistake and think otherwise."

"I'm just asking for this afternoon."

Like the others before her, she chose not to believe him, but later she could not say she had not been warned.

Giving her a slow smile that brought a flush to her cheeks, Darius transported to Leila's side and kissed her. Bells sounded, low and deep.

Bells? He had not created bells. Immersed as he was in her pleasure, it took several moments before the insistent sound registered in Darius's mind. Not bells; a message spell. With a curse, he rolled off Leila and glared at the shimmering yellow sphere of energy hovering in the doorway.

"What's wrong?" she asked, her voice husky with need.

"The Protector is needed."

"Can't it wait?" she whined, looking up at the sphere. "It's not red. Not urgent."

The sphere of energy chimed with an impatient tone. In seconds, Darius had lifted Leila from the pillows. He tied her new robe firmly about her waist. "Never ask that again."

"But—"

Darius laid a hand against her cheek. "All we can

share is a few hours of pleasure," he said bluntly. "For the Protector, for me, the *ma-at* comes first. Always."

"It's the Protector I want."

The Protector, not Darius. His fingers tightened briefly, then released. At least she was honest enough to use *want* and not *love*.

"I know. Now you must go." From a grain of sand, Darius formed a translucent cup holding a fire bloom, a rare blossom of sweet-scented, rainbow-hued flames. Only male djinn could create a fire bloom; thus they were prized by the females, who whispered the legend that the talent to create fire blooms signified other skills as well.

Few could sustain a bloom for more than a few minutes. His lasted for hours.

A sharp wind whipped from his fingertips, and the single bloom became an armful. More flowers spun in a circle, surrounding them with a bower of orange and blue.

Not again! How had he lost control again?

Leila giggled. "You don't need all of these to impress me."

Ignoring her gushing pleasure, Darius bustled Leila, her arms loaded with blooms, out the door. He clenched one fist and grimly stopped the multiplying flowers. When he clapped his hands, they vanished. At last, *something* had gone right.

Darius cupped the shimmering message spell between his palms. Its pulsing sent ribbons of *ma-at* down his arms. "Speak. The Protector listens."

"Message from Adept Bahran. You are needed at the school. Jared attempted a multiplying spell. On rabbits." The thin voice of *ma-at* faded into the hot sands of Kaf.

Jared. How could one djinni boy of twelve cycles be so much trouble? Most mishaps at the school were easily handled by the teachers or the Adept, but because the boy was so strong, it sometimes took a Protector's skills to rebalance his disasters. Darius chuckled. What had prompted the child to try a multiplying spell on *rabbits?*

His fingers closed about the message spell, and he murmured the words to quench it. Its power drained into his fingertips. With care, he separated his hands, expecting the forces to dissipate into the infinity of Kaf.

Instead, they shot from his palms. In an instant, Darius directed the wayward *ma-at,* toward a mound of pillows. The pillows, and the force of *ma-at,* exploded.

Multicolored feathers drifted into all corners of the courtyard. Some caught in the cedar, others in the chiming vines. A few sank in the stone-lined pool of water. One landed on Darius's nose. He blew it away with a disgusted puff.

This could not continue. His *ma-at,* the one thing, the only thing, in his life he trusted without reservation, was no longer his to command.

He knew what he had to do. First, he would deal with Jared. Then he would retest the divination. If it gave him the same answers . . . His next step would be to find the Terran woman named Isis Montgomery.

Quelling the disturbance at the school did not take long, although the strain of wielding a controlled *ma-at* exhausted Darius. Every muscle in his body ached; sweat dripped from the ends of his dark hair. He retreated into his central courtyard, a calm oasis of sand and water and greenery, where the winds that channeled through moaned soul-stirring music. This was the heart of his home. This area he kept constant, although the edifice surrounding the courtyard he changed according to his whim.

Darius dropped his robe on the sand and dove, naked, into the deep, warm pool. He swam into its depths, until the pounding of his heart forced him back to the surface and blessed air. Lazily he stroked, the buoyant water restoring his strength.

At last, cleansed and refreshed, he emerged. He laid the silk robe out before a stone-lined pit, and then sat cross-legged on the cloth, allowing the heat and eternal wind to dry him.

Darius rubbed his hands together and murmured the words for the elemental fire. A towering blaze appeared in the pit.

Solomon! He couldn't even get a simple fire right.

Heat scorched his face, while the cooler winds at his back tightened his skin. As he lowered the flames, he gazed into their blue hearts, concentrating, opening himself to the flow and ebb of Kaf. His soul was bound to her fires and to her winds. From her came his strength to wield *ma-at*. From his training and will came the ability to control and direct it.

When he had first recognized the strange, insidious erosion of his control, he had sought through all the ancient and arcane sources for a path of restoration. He had found but one, a ragged scroll and a prophecy as old as the djinn arrival on Kaf:

In the time of Chaos,
When powers run wild and free
Strong shall you grow or strong shall you fall
One unite with the line of Abregaza.
Both willing and free.
Air and fire, balanced by water and earth, will restore.

He had done a divination, asking to be shown the line of Abregaza and an answer to what he must do.

Divination didn't foretell the future. No djinni could do that. The future was too mutable. Individual choice could direct events in totally unexpected ways.

Instead, divination gave a path, a direction to take. Divination showed the way to fulfill the ancient prophecies. It was not a spell to be undertaken lightly, and the answer was often unexpected and unwanted.

Like this one.

Never before had Darius questioned and retested a divination. But with the answer he'd been given, and the strange happenings with his *ma-at* . . . he had to be sure.

The flames licked higher, their dancing colors creating an image. It was a Terran woman, with black hair cut short, full lips, and dark, intriguing eyes. Her name came to him. Isis Montgomery.

The answer was the same. He must perform the ceremony of joining, make Isis Montgomery his *zaniya*, and she must come to him willingly.

Darius pulled his gaze from the fire to stare at the distant mountains of Kaf. A twisting knot of denial formed in his stomach. A Terran!

He'd had little to do with the humans who lived on Terra, or earth as they called it; just the occasional visit to his closest friend Simon, who now resided there with his Terran wife, Zoe.

Long ago, a Terran had put the copper wrist bands of a spellbound djinni on Simon. Simon had nearly died before Zoe freed him. Because of his love for the Terran woman, Simon had forgiven her race. Darius never could.

Contrary to Terran beliefs, a djinni did not grant wishes, not unless he, or she, was spellbound. It was a fate any djinni loathed and feared. While bound, the djinni was compelled to live in lonely exile from the free djinn. While bound, he was forced to grant the wishes of any human who summoned him. Djinn history was filled with episodes of human callousness toward the djinn.

Now, according to ancient prophecy, to restore his control, Darius had to join with one from the line of Abregaza, an ancient Terran mage. This divination confirmed the path and showed him the only eligible female direct descendant.

Isis Montgomery. She was to be his *zaniya*, his wife, and she must come to him willingly!

Terran women, at least if Simon's wife Zoe was an example, were difficult—stubborn and bold. As a descendent of Abregaza, at least this Isis should be schooled in the old ways. Perhaps she would be biddable and easy to command.

Darius wanted to rant and rage and refuse, but he could not. He, the Protector, one of the most powerful of the djinn, had lost control of his very being.

Though he did not yet understand how or why, if joining with Isis was needed to restore the control of his *ma-at*, then that was what he would do.

Darius transported to Terra, emerging outside the home of Isis Montgomery while the gray of ending night still hung in the sky. It was just prior to the dawn of their vernal equinox, a most potent time for his *ma-at*, a time designated by the divination.

The air in—Darius sought the name—New Orleans was almost as warm as Kaf, but it held more moisture. He shortened the sleeves and hem of his midnight robe in deference to the stifling humidity. A neighboring dog barked at him. Darius soothed it with a low croon, then cloaked himself in invisibility.

He could not keep that state for long, for it required great effort, but he wanted to learn about this woman, this Isis who would be his *zaniya*, before materializing in front of her.

Despite the early hour, there was a flickering glow

31

from one window in her home. Curious, Darius transported inside.

She was tiny, he realized with surprise. The tip of her head barely reached his shoulder, yet she radiated energy and enthusiasm as she bustled about the small, nearly bare room. Once she paused to coo with a mourning dove, who hopped along its caged perch on one leg. A fierce-looking cat—ears scarred and notched, one eye missing—sprawled under the window, swishing its bent tail.

A blue cloth was stretched out on the floor, weighted by a circle of seven rocks, one of each of the magic colors—white, green, red, orange, yellow, brown, and black. In the background, music played at low volume. At least he thought it was music, though it was fast and unmelodic. Apparently Isis liked it, for her bare foot tapped as she lit three candles with one match. She placed the candles in a triangle at the center of the circle, and then turned out the lights.

Standing back, hands on hips, talking to herself, she studied the prepared area. " 'Choose the stones fresh from the earth.' Doesn't Madame Paris know how *hard* it is to find stones in a city that's below sea level? 'Three candles, each of purest wax.' How the hell am I supposed to know if wax is pure? Now, what am I supposed to do next?"

She picked up a piece of yellowed paper and slowly read, " 'Inside the circle of power, walk backward thrice around and chant thou the mantra of supremacy. Close thy circle and begin.' " Her eyes rolled. "I can*not* believe I'm doing this. If anyone saw me . . ."

She glanced around, as if to verify that she was alone, then stepped inside the stones. Walking backwards, she chanted, "I am the power, come to me. I am the power, come to me."

Isis was doing a magical ritual, Darius realized. Had her people retained some remnant of the an-

32

cient powers? Perhaps she would be easy to convince that he was djinn. Maybe she'd be thrilled with the opportunity he was about to give her. Her willingness should not be a difficult thing to obtain.

Darius grinned and crossed his arms. While she chanted and tried not to trip, he studied her more closely. After all, she would soon be on his pillows, close as a male djinn and a female human could be.

A fire licked across his nerves and settled low inside at the prospect.

She had dark hair, cut short, with feathery bangs. It was too short for his taste, but that could be remedied. And it did look thick and silky and lustrous, shining in the glow of the candles. A sweet, hot urge to run his fingers through it, to draw her close to him, set his blood thrumming. Still invisible, he slid forward, hand outstretched, then stopped at the magical circle. For now, he would respect her magic and not interrupt. Instead, he resumed his study of her.

She had full lips, lips that begged for his touch. Would they be soft? he wondered. Would they move beneath his kiss?

Her hands were beautiful, delicate, yet with strength in their formation. They were tipped with bright purple nails.

A robe of shimmering green was her only clothing. It clung to her, revealing a lush body, full of generous curves he wanted to cup with his palms.

Darius felt himself stir as desire and excitement replaced detachment. Perhaps the prophecy and divination that had led him to her would have their unexpected rewards.

She picked up the ritual again and shouted ancient words. Darius listened, wondering what spell she attempted.

His heart stopped in his chest. His blood thickened, grew sluggish, until he gasped for air, as he realized the import of her words.

Isis was spellbinding a djinni!

Anger, swift and hot, coursed through him. She was trying to enslave one of his people, to bind a djinni with the copper wrist bands and force the bound one to grant wishes, no matter how heinous, to whomever summoned him. To complete the binding, she needed the true name of a djinni. How could she, a human, find that?

His heart resumed its beat; the pulse pounded through his veins. Air about him crackled with lightning fury, as the words for the Spell of Reversal rose from him.

Wind plastered her green robe to her, but still she shouted, undaunted. "*Au . . . bud—no, dub . . . illahi er-Rajim!*" She stumbled over the foreign words. "In the name of Solomon, the great mage, I do call thee. *Au . . . dubillahi er-Rajim!* In the name of Solomon, the great builder, I do tie thee to me."

She peered intently at the paper, the might and fury of djinn *ma-at* beating at her, but not stopping her. "*Ash . . . hadu inna . . . illaha ash-Shaltan.* Come to me, Dar—i—ya—vi—us el Zara—steya!"

Dariyavius el Zarasteya? His name? His true name! She was binding *him!*

The summons tugged at him, pulled him to her. His arms dropped, as though a great weight wound around his wrists.

"No!" Darius shouted. "You shall not."

He materialized and gathered the swirling, pulsing, pounding forces of *ma-at*. Power, strong and invigorating, shot through him. Red, yellow, silver sparks surrounded him. *He must stop her before she finished the last word of the spell.*

"I do bind thee, Dar—" She slowed again over the unfamiliar word.

He didn't fight for control. The Spell of Reversal,

fed by anger, blasted from him and enveloped her. Then, with a deafening roar, the etheric realms sucked her spell away and scattered it to the cosmos.

The room fell silent, except for the insistent music, the madly flapping bird, and the hissing cat, who tried to scratch Darius's leg. He stopped it with a single look.

Isis blinked and slowly sank, until she sat within the circle of stones, now red hot with vibrating energy.

Eyes wide, she looked up at him. "Aren't you supposed to be bald?"

Chapter Three

The magic worked?

Isis stared at the man towering before her. Lingering traces of energy from his stormy entrance danced across her skin.

If this was a trick, it was the best she'd ever seen, and she'd seen a lot. No way Madame Paris could have faked this.

I did it! I summoned a djinni.

And the djinni she now commanded was truly magnificent.

Okay, so he wasn't the bald guy she'd envisioned, but he sure was a nicer alternative. His hair, dark as an unlit night, was thick and silky, the strands curled tighter than fleece. If straightened, she'd bet they would be longer than hers. He wasn't flabby or muscle-bound, but sleek and smooth and firm. The rich scents of cedar and myrtle surrounded him.

Right now, he didn't look happy. His fists rested on his hips in an unmistakable pose of male arrogance. His dark eyes—she'd kill for eyelashes like that—glared at her over a gorgeous nose, and his generous lips pressed together into a thin line.

Silver flashes, brighter than a Fourth of July sparkler, surrounded the djinni. Wind whipped through the room, extinguishing the candles, leaving only the pink dawn filtering through the window and the magic glistening about his hair.

"Seek you to bind me?" His voice reverberated, as if it came from the depths of a well. He lifted his arms. The sleeves of his robe fell back, and he stared at his bare wrists. As he twisted his arms, checking all sides, a satisfied, superior grin lit his face. "You have failed; the copper bands do not bind."

What did he mean, she'd failed? He was here, wasn't he? Isis rose to her feet, dusting her trembling hands on her robe, and lifted her chin. "The way I see it," she told him, "you owe me three wishes."

His robe shifted and shimmered, its color first ocean blue, then deep green, then fern silver as he advanced on her. "You dare much, foolish human."

Foolish human? Great, she'd summoned a djinni with an attitude. Isis stood her ground. She'd had plenty of experience with overbearing males and had learned her lessons well.

Never back down. Never let them see weakness.

"Three wishes," she reminded him. "It is three, isn't it?"

He paused, his head cocked as he studied her for a moment, then the grin returned. "That is the number of legend."

Isis frowned, not liking his casual assurance. This was supposed to be simple: call a genie, get wishes, get the perfume.

She eyed the man who filled her small room with sparks and arrogance. Somehow, she didn't think anything to do with him could ever be simple.

Under her scrutiny, he trailed a hand down the

black silken cord around his neck and fingered the turquoise pendant resting on his smooth chest. He shifted his hips, baring an alarming amount of masculine thigh. Never once did he take his challenging gaze off her.

Isis grew warm just watching his fluid movements.

"What's your name?" she asked abruptly.

"You already—" He stopped. His lips pursed in a soundless whistle. "You may call me Darius."

"Okay, Darius, I'm going to use my first wish."

He crossed his arms and leaned nonchalantly against the mantel. "Go ahead."

Something wasn't right. If he was a djinni, shouldn't he be more obsequious? Call her mistress or master or something?

Could she have been fooled, the victim of an elaborate hoax? Isis didn't see how that was possible, but caution tempered her eagerness and kept her from blurting out her request. She'd test him first. Wish for something small, something specific. If it worked right, she'd still have two wishes left. She only needed one for the perfume.

And if he didn't fulfill it? Then she'd know she'd been taken in by one of the best. Again.

"I wish I had," Isis said, "sitting on that table, a big bowl of sweet Pontchatoula strawberries, two toasted raisin bagels slathered with cream cheese, and a cup of steaming Kona coffee."

A mug of coffee, hot and fragrant with cinnamon, appeared in his hands. He took a sip, then held it out to her. "Would you like some?"

How did he do that? Isis tapped one foot. "Did you hear my wish?"

"I heard."

"Are you going to grant it?"

"No."

"Damn, is this some kind of a trick?"

"Trick?" His mug of coffee disappeared, and he

38

straightened. Nonchalance disappeared. The planes of his face hardened from haughtiness to ruthlessness. He had the look of a hawk, spying its helpless prey. Isis's throat turned dry as powdered shell.

Khu, the injured dove, cooed a mad warning. Vulcan, her cat, jumped into her arms, then leaped to her shoulder, hissing at Darius.

With two strides Darius closed the gap between them. Silver sparks surrounded his ebony hair, and a sudden wind wrapped her robe about her. He was so close, she caught the faint, masculine scent of cedar from him, saw the specks of starlight in his night dark eyes, heard the crackle of his anger, felt the magic to her bones. The sparks brightened, until she had to squint to see.

"*Ma-at* is no trick," Darius said, with fierce quiet.

Isis's heart beat wildly against her chest. This was no trick. He *was* a djinni.

Whoever heard of a genie who refused to grant wishes?

"This is the power of my *ma-at*." Darius pointed at the ritual lying on the blue cloth. Sparks shot from his fingertips, crackling and singeing the air with the sharp scent of lightning. The yellowed paper burst into towering flames, becoming mere ash in seconds.

"Hey," Isis protested. "You have no right—"

"I have every right," he thundered. "That spell binds a djinni with the copper bands of servitude. You would have enslaved . . . one of us."

"Enslaved? That spell enslaves?" Isis echoed, looking from the destroyed paper back to him. What had she almost done?

Anyone who summoned a genie could command wishes, that's what the legends said, but she'd never heard anything about enslavement. Her stomach twisted to a cramped ball. Of course, until Madame Paris she'd thought they lived in lamps, too.

"Did you think we answer a summons *willingly?*"

he asked. "We are a free people. Only a spellbound djinni *must* grant wishes, and your abominable spell did not bind only because I stopped it before you finished."

Which meant she had called him—a magical being, a man of magic—to her, and now she had no means to control him.

"I suppose you also believe that fiction about us living in bottles," he snapped.

Her chin came up, and her back stiffened. "Of course not. But—"

He laid a finger across her lips. "Hush," he said, the single word all the more dangerous for its softness.

Isis hushed.

At last, Darius thought, lifting his finger, *she learns.* "I am not compelled to grant your wishes," he added, very low, very deliberate.

"Yeah, I gathered that." She pulled at one full lip with her teeth, drawing his gaze to her mouth.

Heat flared inside him. For the first time in many long weeks, he had reveled in the joy of wielding his *ma-at.* He was not spellbound and he was in control. It was time to solidify that control with the Ritual of Joining.

"Look, I'm really sorry; I didn't know about the binding. I guess that means you'll be leaving." Oblivious to his plans, Isis turned toward the door. "And there's someone I need to have a little chat with," she muttered.

Darius transported in front of her, the whirlwind of his movement blowing her robe open, revealing a flash of trim leg, but he refused to be distracted. The cat on her shoulder snarled at him.

She tried to move around him. He was faster, preventing her from leaving. Finally she stopped, crossed her arms, and tapped one foot. "What do you want?"

"You will come with me to Kaf, my almost-*zaniya*."

"What's a *zaniya?*"

"That is not your concern at present. Give me your hand." Whatever he held, he could transport with him.

She glared at him and thrust her hands into the pockets of her robe.

He delved into her pocket and snagged her hand, lacing his fingers through hers. Her purple nails dug into his skin, but he did not release her. He intoned the words to transport.

Nothing happened. The muscles in his jaw knotted. In frustration, Darius repeated the spell. They did not move.

An ache settled in the pit of his stomach. His *ma-at* had been out of control, but never had it failed. Why? Why now?

The answer came swiftly. Because she fought him. The divination said she must be willing in all things before the balance could be restored. As long as she resisted him, his *ma-at* was powerless against her. By Solomon, she was a trial!

That eventually they would join, Darius had no doubt, but first he must get her willing. How? Seduction? He looked down at her. Though she held herself in rigid control, he could tell from the set of her jaw and the narrowing of her eyes that she was furious.

She batted her lashes at him. "Are we through holding hands?" She tugged out of his grip. "Either say your piece or get out of my way."

Seduction would come later. First he had to sweeten her.

To do that, he had to be near her, with her, close enough to share her every breath.

She had asked for wishes; there was something she wanted. His tension eased. Something he could provide. Something to bind her to him. Darius searched for her thoughts, trying his telepathy, ready to snatch back the talent should it flare from his control.

Instead, he detected nothing. Her mind was closed to him. Darius gave a mental curse. He'd have to do this the ordinary way. "Why did you want the wishes?" he asked.

"Doesn't matter. You said you don't grant them."

"I said I could not be compelled to grant wishes. That does not mean I cannot fulfill them. For a price."

"What kind of price?" She leaned away.

"That depends upon your wish. Three wishes. Three bargains," he offered.

Her jaw flexed. She stared up at him, her hand absently soothing the beastly feline on her shoulder. The cat vaulted down but stayed near Isis, its head butting against her calf.

"If you don't like the price, you can always refuse the bargain, my sweet Isis," he coaxed.

His pleasantry seemed to make her more wary. "I'm not your sweet Isis."

Not now, not yet, though she would be his. The sweet, however, was still in question.

Isis's eyes narrowed. "And how do you know my name?"

Darius gave her an even look. "I'm a djinni." He fingered his turquoise tablet, the source of his djinn freedom. Her willingness to come to Kaf and join with him as his *zaniya* would be the ultimate price, but, with his *ma-at* under his mastery, he could delay that pleasure.

There was something else he needed: to find out who had given her the ritual, and, most importantly, his name.

Darius made a decision. One of them must make the first move, and he wanted her trust. "My price would be to show me where you got that ritual," he said, and nodded toward the stones.

42

"Why?"

"A human sorcerer of such skill, I would like to meet."

One bare foot tapped against the floor as she scrutinized him. Darius gave her his most innocent look, but he had the distinct feeling she wasn't fooled.

"What will be your first wish, Isis?"

She let out a breath, as if reaching some inner decision. "I want you to show my aunt Tildy that magic exists."

That surprised him. A wish for another? "Why?" asked Darius, echoing her question.

She hesitated, then shrugged. "Belief in magic has been sort of a tradition among the women in my family, passed down from mother to daughter." She gave him a wry smile, the first sign of humor he'd seen in her, and it lightened her face. "Until about half an hour ago, no one ever saw any real magic. My grandmother died when I was four, my mother when I was six, and my great-aunt Tildy is the only maternal relative I have left. Tomorrow's her birthday. Can you show her your magic?"

"We call it *ma-at*," he said softly.

Isis inclined her head in acknowledgment. "Your *ma-at*."

Show the aunt some *ma-at*. Very easily could he. But Isis had wanted *three* wishes. Darius crossed his arms. "What will your other two wishes be?"

She looked away.

So there was more. Darius waited, well versed in patience.

Isis's shoulders straightened, and she gave him a direct look. "Let's leave those for later."

A skilled bargainer, she left the most important for last, when trust had been established. He nodded. "I can show your aunt my *ma-at*. Do we agree?"

"All right," Isis finally answered. "You show my aunt some *ma-at*. Tomorrow, as a birthday present,

43

but we'll have to wait until after her party, say ten o'clock, and in return I'll take you to the shop where I bought the ritual." She held out her hand. "Shall we shake on it?"

Darius reached out and fingered the hem of her robe's sleeve. The silk was warm, or maybe it was her firm, slender arm beneath that radiated the heat.

Satisfaction, pure and arousing, coursed through him. He clasped her fingers, then ran his thumb along the back of her hand. Her skin was smooth and soft, as he had imagined it. A faint perfume—languid, sweet jasmine—lingered about her.

Her breath quickened; he heard its faint rasp. The fine hairs at his nape prickled in awareness of the accelerated rise and fall of her breasts, unbound beneath her robe. His blood, in his temples and lower, throbbed in matching beat.

She was human, he was djinni. Though they would share pillows, there could be naught of more tender, more dangerous feelings between them. After the completion of all the joining rituals, after she was his *zaniya,* the path outlined by the divination grew murky. Doubtless, when his *ma-at* was once more his to claim, they must part, for he could not dwell on Terra and her home was among the humans.

Until that day came, though, there would be other pleasures to savor.

Gently, slowly, he urged her closer with a pressure on her hand. They stood, the edges of their robes, midnight blue and oasis green, whispering in contact.

"My people have a different way of sealing a bargain," he answered, his voice husky. He lifted her hand to his mouth. "With the Kiss of the Promise."

Isis felt his lips caress her palm. His kiss was warm and sensuous, despite the merest brushing of his mouth. The air around him shimmered with fleeting

colors of red, orange, and blue, and an arc of current
sped up her arm.

Was this his *ma-at?* His kiss was unlike any she'd
ever shared. Did she only imagine, with the imagination of longing, the barest touch of his tongue
against the small, beating vein in her hand?

"The hand, then the cheek," he murmured, cup-
ping his hand about her neck and leaning forward
to bestow the faintest of touches against her cheek.
"Now, you must complete the link."

Three wishes, three bargains, then he would leave,
thought Isis, bemused. It was fortunate he would not
be staying long. Not when his simple touch dissolved
her insides, when his velvet command curled her
toes. When the mere thought of kissing him set her
senses spinning.

Struggling to contain the simmering feelings inside, she kissed his hand, the strength in his grip a
competing image to his trim, buffed nails. She had
to raise herself on tiptoe to reach his cheek, for Darius only lowered his head an iota to accommodate
her lack of height.

His hand tightened about hers. "It is done. By the
powers of Solomon, the first bargain is made. May
the fates and winds preserve it."

"It is done," she echoed.

Darius's arm flexed, as though he would draw her
even closer. At her feet, Vulcan hissed, his fur standing on end, and he swiped a claw at Darius. Four
thin lines of blood, bright red against the gold of his
skin, welled up on the djinni's leg.

Darius's eyes narrowed, and the silver sparks returned, as he glared down at the cat.

"Please don't hurt Vulcan," Isis begged, hunching
defensively at her pet's side. "He's had a rough life.
He's wary of strangers. And protective of me."

Darius glanced at her, obviously startled, and then
his gaze slid down her, lingering on each curve con-

cealed by her robe, each inch of bare skin revealed by it. "I would not hurt him. His bravery does him credit." His glance reverted to the cat. "But the two of us must come to an understanding about the way things will be now. Must we not, Vulcan?"

Djinni and cat stared at one another, until Isis could swear they communicated on some level she didn't understand. Then, Vulcan gave a sharp meow. Tail high, he stalked from the room.

"You've insulted him," Isis said, a trifle miffed that this man held power over her cat as well as her. Until now, Vulcan had responded only to her.

Darius smiled. "Nay, we have just drawn the battle lines."

Deep inside, her muscles tightened with awareness. She hoped he didn't smile too often while he was here. That smile heated her, made her think about foolish things: hot nights in a garden, naked swims through cool waters, exotic perfumes and fire-bright colors, all with him at her side.

Isis drew in a deep breath. "What do we do now?" she asked.

"Go to the place where you obtained the ritual." He grabbed for her wrist.

Wary of his eagerness, Isis backed out of reach. "No."

His jaw tensed, and the silver sparks she was beginning to recognize as anger intensified. His fingers clenched, and he glared at her. "Already you fail to keep your promises, human?"

His voice was echoing again. *Inscrutable* would never be a word applied to Darius. Here was one man who had no trouble displaying his emotions.

Isis met his glare. "I've never reneged on a bargain in my life. The deal was, you meet Aunt Tildy *and in return* I'll show you the store. My aunt comes first. Tomorrow. Ten P.M."

His inner struggle showered her with silver sparks

and tangled her robe and hair. Djinni and human matched eye to eye, breath to breath, will to will, until the tension in Darius eased. A faint smile tilted his lips. Gradually, the winds died to a soft breeze, and the sparks muted to a shimmering aura.

He smiled at her, that beautiful smile he must have used before, to great effect. Even knowing, she wasn't immune. A fire ignited deep in her belly, though she tried to quench it.

His capitulation made her decidedly uneasy.

"So it will be done," he said. "The sooner begun, the sooner fulfilled." He stepped back and lifted his arms. The whirlwind engulfed him. "You called me; now we are united with ties of *ma-at* and by will of prophecy, my sweet Isis."

He disappeared into wind and flame.

Chapter Four

Now we are united with ties of ma-at *and by will of prophecy.* As if!

Isis wriggled into a turquoise bandeau before snapping shut the waist of her white linen shorts. She grabbed a comb, swiped it through her hair, and then brandished the comb at her reflection in the mirror.

"Don't trust him," she warned herself. "Or his magic." She tossed the comb back on her dresser, put on her lipstick, and then stroked gold mascara on her lashes.

Too bad he smelled so good, so . . . right.

The perfume. Remember the perfume. Isis forced herself to focus on her goal as she recapped her mascara. It was how she had learned to read despite her dyslexia, how she had saved Dream Scents. Failure was never an option.

Five years ago she'd started Dream Scents, an aromatherapy and perfume business, and within two years, she'd been poised for breakout success, on the verge of a rapid expansion.

Then everything went to hell and she lost it all.

Raised on Aunt Tildy's stories, she'd believed in magic and she'd been in love with Benedict Fontenot, a charmer who flattered and promised, offered help, and claimed to work magic. Ben helped her promote the business, although now, with the eyes of experience, Isis could see the work, and talent, had all been hers. But Ben had planned well from the beginning. He'd encouraged her explorations in the mystical, tricked her into believing her magic worked, while keeping his involvement in the rituals well hidden from public view.

Then he'd stolen her formulas and her business.

With them, and his flair for promotion, Ben Fontenot had established a national franchise that netted him media darling status, as well as several million dollars. She'd been left with one tiny shop at the remote edges of the French Quarter, a load of debts, and a humiliating reputation for flaky irresponsibility.

Isis grimaced. Even now, the memory of how she had trusted and how she'd been betrayed lingered like a sour smell. It was a mistake she would not make again.

Instead, she had studied, learned to manage the business side, not just the creative one, and hung on by a fingernail—not that she ever let anyone know that. At last, she'd put all the old rumors and gossip to rest.

Just surviving wasn't enough, though. She wanted to make Dream Scents bigger than Fontenot's Old World Parfums, and more successful than anything the high-powered, over-achieving males in her family expected from her.

A few months ago, when the perfume began haunting her dreams, she had known, beyond doubt, that unique scent was the key. It had touched every instinct, every need inside her. With that as a signature perfume, she could make Dream Scents a success and prove herself capable, to her family and to herself.

Could she get the perfume? She didn't trust the sparkling, arrogant djinni who'd exploded into her life. Didn't trust the unruly feelings he aroused inside her. That was why she had asked for the magic for Aunt Tildy first, rather than the perfume. She wanted to see how well Darius kept his bargains.

She picked up her regular perfume and spritzed the jasmine scent on her pulse points.

"That man wants something," she muttered, replacing the jasmine on her vanity table. Question was, what? She expected she'd find out when they reached the third bargain. If she couldn't duplicate the perfume otherwise, she would pay his price, no matter what it was.

After all, she'd already risked bringing magic back into her life with that insane ritual. Lord, if anyone found out about that, about Darius, she could kiss her reputation—and her success—good-bye.

She added a red, turquoise, and green Hawaiian print shirt over the bandeau and then chose a pair of platform sandals from her closet. Just as she put one on, she heard the growl of a motorcycle outside. A moment later, her front doorbell rang.

Isis stood on one foot, pulling on the other sandal, while she opened the door. "Hi, Ram," she greeted her brother, who often stopped by before his run along the levee, bringing her what he considered a nutritional breakfast.

Ram was dressed in his usual, off-work casual—faded shorts, T-shirt, and running shoes—and his hair was rumpled, as though he'd just gotten out of bed. He had a good nine inches on her height, and considerably more muscles, but, like Isis, he had inherited their mother's ebony hair and dark eyes. Although people often wondered whether she'd been left by the gypsies, they usually had no trouble believing Ram was her brother.

"Did your talk at the Zoo conference go well?"

"Standing room only. I brought you breakfast, Ice." He held up a brown sack.

"Come on in." As she let him in, Isis caught a glimpse of the ritual area still set up and winced. Maybe Ram wouldn't notice.

Ram pulled off his dark sunglasses and hooked them into the neck of his white T, then shoved his hair behind his ears. "Redecorating, Ice?" he asked, staring at the circle of stones.

"Well—"

He shook his head. "No, don't tell me. Something for Aunt Tildy, right?"

"It's complicated," Isis said, scooping up the tablecloth, candles, and stones, and shoving them into a cupboard. She sniffed. "You're wearing the sample of Winter I gave you."

He grinned at her. "You've got a hit aftershave, if my date's reaction last night is any indication."

"Ah, how much did the lady of the week like it?"

Ram ruffled her hair. "That's not for little sister to know." He headed toward her kitchen. "You got coffee started?"

"Ten months!" she called, following him into the kitchen. "You're only older by ten months."

While Ram poured coffee, Isis peered into the bag he'd set on the table and wrinkled her nose when she saw two covered cups. She pulled one out, gingerly lifted the lid, took a sip, and then grimaced. The stuff smelled like overripe carrots and tasted worse.

"Yuck, what is this, Ram? Carrot juice?"

"Partly. Drink up; it's good for you. Say, why don't you come with me on my run?"

"Run?" Isis said with mock horror, putting the lid

Kathleen Nance

back on the salmon-colored liquid. Thank God for blueberry muffins. "I swim, I yoga. I don't run."

"Your loss."

While she watched her brother stretch before his run, a thought occurred to Isis. Ram was a vet who specialized in exotic animals. If he knew where Madame Paris's bearded dragons came from—assuming they came from earth—it might give her a clue where to look for the flowers or plants that formed the base of the perfume. "Ram, have you ever heard of bearded dragons that had venom? Or acid?"

"No. What gave you that idea?"

"I saw some in a shop off Chartres."

"Did they look healthy?" Isis heard Ram's animal rights voice appearing. He grew furious when people imported, sometimes illegally, exotic pets they exploited or couldn't care for properly. Strange animals in nontraditional settings set off his warning bells.

"How would I know? Would you like to see them? I can give you directions."

Ram gave her an amused look. "The last time I followed your directions, my date and I ended up at a porno shop instead of a coffee bar."

"I meant to say turn left," Isis muttered.

"Give me the name and I'll look it up."

"Madame Paris's Magic Shop, in that alley you're always warning me against."

"Ice, you aren't getting into that magic crap again, are you?"

"Ramses—" Isis warned.

Ram winced. Her brother hated his full name, and when she used it, he knew she was annoyed.

"Don't worry, I know what I'm doing." Isis looked at her watch. "Time to go if I'm going to catch the ferry. You can use your key to get back in, if you want to shower after your run."

"Thanks. I'll walk you to the ferry."

She didn't think she'd put him off that easily.

They walked through the narrow streets of Algiers Point to the ferry. When Ram next spoke, however, it wasn't about magic. "Ben Fontenot said he planned to bid on you at the bachelor-bachelorette charity auction next month. I told him not if he wanted to keep his handsome face."

"What! Dammit, Ramses, I can handle Ben." *And damn Benedict for trying to ignore the way he'd shafted her.* He must want something, and want it badly.

They'd reached the landing. While they waited for the ferry to dock and unload, Ram leaned against the metal rails. "Do you want him to win the date with you?" he asked, ever practical.

"Well, no," she admitted. "Fontenot's a sleaze, but—"

"So, problem handled." Ram's eyes narrowed. "Anyone messes with you, Ice, they answer to me. *Especially* Fontenot."

"Down, testosterone." Isis tapped her foot. "You're my brother, not my guardian."

Ram lifted her chin with his fist. "Doesn't mean I sit by and watch someone fool with you. I didn't do a good job of protecting you three years ago. It's not going to happen again."

Isis rolled her eyes. "Go, run. Work off some of that male aggression."

"See you." Before she could say more, Ram headed at an easy lope to the levee.

Isis watched him leave with a mixture of exasperation and fondness. Her decision to keep Darius secret was the right one. Four older, overprotective brothers and a conservative father—she could guess their chest-thumping response to a man who said he was a genie, especially a man who smoldered with sensuality like Darius.

Well, keeping him secret shouldn't be too much of a problem. She expected Darius would pop in for

their three bargains, and that would be all she would
see of him.

Funny, that thought didn't give her the peace it
should have.

Darius stood on top of the Tower Lands, a wall of
mountains separating the hospitable regions of Kaf
from the whistling desert, and gazed below. The
gleaming twin spires of the school, the colorful quilt
of residences, and the white marble home of the king
were all as familiar to him as the words for transportation. Wind whipped his robe about his legs and
echoed a forlorn song in his ears. The thin air sped
through his lungs.

He absorbed the strength of Kaf; being on Terra—
away from Kaf, the source of his *ma-at*—weakened
him. While he stayed on Terra with Isis, he must
return home at least every twelve Terran days to revitalize, that much he knew. However, it seemed the
efforts he exerted to control his *ma-at* accelerated
the weakening process, for he felt as shaky as a stalk
of grain.

Or maybe it was the sheer alienness of the Terran
magic streams. That he had not expected, nor did he
like it. Gradually, though, the burning in his muscles
faded to an ache.

Alone on the isolated peak, he wondered who had
betrayed him. Isis had not known the full import of
what she attempted; her shock at his accusation of
enslavement was genuine. Someone had given Isis
his true name with the intent to bind him. Who?

Oh, he knew that he had his share of enemies. Darius gave a humorless laugh. Perhaps it was not so
much *who* as *which one?*

His telepathy would be no help. It only worked at
close range on a single individual and with great effort. He couldn't go wandering the villages of Kaf,
testing all for disloyalty.

Was it one of the djinn? Or had a modern human gotten so powerful? He would use the time on Terra to find out.

Only when the bonds between him and Isis were complete, when his *ma-at* was once more fully his, could he seek to confront his enemy. He would need his full abilities at his command to exact revenge. His fingers itched for retribution. Djinn justice was swift and unyielding, based upon the old codes of an eye for an eye.

Strength returned, Darius transported to his home. As Protector, he could not simply disappear; he had to remain available for a summons should the need occur. While he heightened the protective charms around his home so no enemy would invade his sanctuary during his absence, he added a special twist. Should the Protector be needed, the message would cross the dimensions and come to him on Terra.

That accomplished, Darius collected belongings for his stay on Terra; he had decided not to create items to meet his needs. He hadn't tested the full limits of his returning control, and he must conserve his strength while the bonds to Kaf, the bonds that gave him his power, were stretched. He shoved everything into a leather satchel.

Strangely, he found himself looking forward to a brief stay in a place where no one called him Protector first and Darius second.

There was one more thing. His enemy must have no chance to retaliate against Isis once it was learned Darius remained unbound. The Kiss of Promise had put her under his protection, but the bond would be strengthened with a physical connection.

Darius fingered his turquoise tablet a moment, then sat cross-legged on the sand, next to the deep pool of water. From his satchel he pulled another small, unmarked turquoise stone and laid it before

55

him. After surrounding the stone with a circle of five small flames, he dipped his hand into the water, then sprinkled a few drops onto the stone's smooth surface.

He pointed his finger at the turquoise, etching into its surface the rune for protection. The thin line of *ma-at* flared out of control and cut deep. Quickly, Darius withdrew it, then stared in horror at the blackened edges of the rune marking. His sweat dried in a sudden gust of hot breeze that sent a shiver of dread down his spine.

Something this basic and he had lost control. Meeting Isis had not fully restored his control as he had begun to hope.

Concentrating, he finished the rune, this time without mishap, then bored a tiny hole in the top. He threaded the stone onto a black silk cord similar to the one that held his tablet, then tucked it into a pocket in his robe.

It was time to go. Although he would make brief returns to renew his bonds to Kaf, the next time he returned to stay in his beloved home, he would have his *zaniya* with him.

His fingers dug into the strap as he settled the leather satchel on his shoulder. Never had he thought to call any woman *zaniya*. His old mentor had taught him, and taught him well, that the Protector must be free of all entanglements, free to focus on the *ma-at*, free to enjoy all the pleasures that were his due, while taking none too deeply to his heart.

Isis, his *zaniya*. For one brief moment, that sounded more precious than any of the teachings.

Darius shook off the strange feeling. She was human, a human who had tried to bind him—he must never forget that fact. He was djinn, the Protector. Darius gripped the leather satchel. He had accepted the truth of the divination, had decided Isis must be his. No distraction from his goal—restoring his *ma-at*—could he allow.

A small whirlwind blew sand into his face. Darius sneezed, and his eyes teared from the grit. Astounded, he watched a boy of about twelve cycles stumble forward. "Jared!"

The child caught himself, then stood with feet spread, fists shoved against his waist. Loose shorts and a dark wrap-tunic covered his lanky body. A scab decorated one knee, and his fingers were stained green, probably from a wayward spell.

"You are leaving!" The boy glared at the satchel Darius held. "You said you would take me with you the next time."

Darius set down his satchel. "How did you know?"

"I set a spell at the perimeter of your home boundaries."

"You set a spell on my home?" Darius's eyes narrowed, and his low voice did not conceal his annoyance at the lad's temerity.

The boy flushed, but he met Darius's gaze squarely. "It merely told me when you strengthened the barriers, as I knew you would do before you left. It just took me a few minutes to get away from the teachers."

"And how did you get past those barriers?" His voice grew even softer.

"You once said I could call you if I needed you, and you touched me here." Jared rubbed his chest above his heart. "Solomon, that hurt when you did that, but it let me come to you now."

Yes, he had done that, Darius remembered, when the boy had gotten into a particularly nasty scrape with an enraged *hamid-el-halat*. The connection had been intended so Darius could easily find Jared, however, not the other way around.

"Why were you leaving without me?" Jared asked.

Darius rarely explained himself to anyone. However, the plaintive question, one of the few times he'd seen vulnerability in the boy, formed a knot in Darius's chest. Tension wound tighter, then released. Solomon, he couldn't hurt the boy, not like this. Could not leave without some explanation.

Jared was an anomaly on Kaf, an abandoned child, found in the Tower Lands when he was approximately five cycles. In a society where children were rare, and desired, it was unheard of that no one knew who his parents were.

Normally, Jared would have dwelt with one of the many couples who had asked to raise him as their own. Jared, however, was not a normal child. Even at five cycles, his *ma-at* was strong, and his nature stubborn and combative. He'd refused every offer of a home, preferring to abide at the school.

Officially, Jared wasn't Darius's responsibility. Unofficially, he felt a kinship with the boy. Perhaps because, in Jared, Darius saw a mirror of himself.

They were both alone.

With a sigh, he settled down onto the sand and motioned for Jared to sit beside him.

"I did not promise to take you. I only said I would try." A spurious distinction to a boy of twelve, Darius knew, but it was an important one to him. Promises were sacred to him.

"Why can't you take me now?"

"Ah, that is a bit complicated."

"Where are you going? To the Fire Streams? The Wasteland?"

Darius hesitated, but between him and Jared there would be only truths. "To Terra."

Jared's eyes grew wide. "I have always wanted to go there. Why, Darius? Why won't you take me as you said? For it was almost a promise, despite what you say now."

Besides Simon, Jared was the only djinni who

used his name first, rather than his title. Even to King Taranushi he was the Protector.

How to explain to Jared what he must do? The loss of control, that no one, *no one*, must know.

"A divination has shown me a path," Darius answered at last. "And a woman I must become . . . close to."

For a moment, Jared looked confused; then his expression cleared. From the knowing look he gave Darius, the lad had learned a few things about the ways between male and female.

"Will you bring her back with you?"

"Yes."

"And will you, sometime, take me to Terra?"

"Some time, I will."

"Then I shall wait."

Darius rose and dusted the sand from his robe. "There is one other thing: While I am gone, you must stay near the school. No wandering about Kaf." At the school, surrounded by teachers and Adepts, Jared would be safe.

Jared shot to his feet, a rebellious refusal written across his face. Faint sparks shot about his dark hair, and his voice held the promise of a deepening echo. "I cannot be confined there, Darius. Do not ask it of me."

"I do ask, as Darius." His voice hardened. About this there could be no compromise. "And I demand it, as your Protector."

The boy's jaw clenched. "I'll stay," he gritted out.

Darius laid a hand on Jared's thin shoulder. The boy was strong and clever, and was apparently reaching the boundaries of what the school could do for him. "Study hard, and when I return you may train with me."

Jared's eyes widened with the promised gift. "Train with you? You mean it? I swear, I will give them no trouble."

Darius ruffled his hair. "Somehow I doubt that, but do your best. The contact between us still remains. Use the tablets."

He touched his turquoise tablet, then touched Jared's, renewing the connection. A blinding light flared, then died just as quickly. Darius clenched his fist.

Once again the *ma-at* had slipped from his control.

"Go now," he told Jared tersely.

Jared stood and raised his hands. A fierce wind surrounded him, rising with a sharp whine. Within the whipping sand, Darius saw Jared bite his lip. The whirlwind died to a safe level, then Jared disappeared.

Darius took a firm grip on his satchel. It was time to begin. It was time to return to Isis.

Heat, low and deep, curled inside him. An excitement, a challenge long missing, rose like the white sands of a desert storm, biting and stinging and changing.

"Isis Montgomery," he whispered to the vast sands, "you shall soon learn the power of my *ma-at*. You shall soon be mine."

Darius smiled and transported to Terra.

She loved this place. A surge of pride swept through Isis as she surveyed the interior of Dream Scents, pausing for a moment before bustling around the store to open. Every detail was an old friend she had selected herself. The cut-glass bottles that caught the light like crystal prisms. The soft, scarred woods of the shelves and counters. The round ceramic jars of potpourri and lotions. The small fountain in one corner.

Most of all, she loved the melange of sweet fragrances—florals, spices, musk, citrus, honey, melon, green. She loved it with the fierceness of a mother, for she had raised it from no more than a dream.

After the debacle with Ben, her father and brothers had urged her to sell, to find a steady, normal job, but she refused. She could not give up the only magic she still believed in: the deep, primitive powers of scent.

"Hey, Ice." Salem Tremaine, her head clerk, looked up from arranging a candle display and greeted Isis.

"Morning, Salem. I like the new hair color."

Salem patted the short, neon orange spikes of her hair. "Purple was too grandma."

"Then you've seen different grandmas than I have. How come you're in so early?"

Salem fingered the earring piercing her right eyebrow. "I had a vision last night—candles, plants, aromas, all green—and knew I'd found the spirit for this display. I wanted to start before I lost the image."

"Interesting use of ferns."

"Thanks. I put them near the fountain to remind them of their rainforest home, so they'll retain their inner vigor." Salem bent over, retrieved an evergreen candle from the jumble of green at her feet, and then nestled it among the piled ferns. The chains on her black leather pants clanged in accompaniment to the collection of metal bracelets on her arms.

Isis had met Salem six months ago, when the streetwise girl persisted in panhandling outside the door of Dream Scents, while offering surprisingly perceptive, if unsolicited, advice on fashion. Such flat-out gall ought to be rewarded, Isis had decided, and, on a hunch, offered her a job. To both their surprise, Salem accepted. Isis had only two rules: no drugs and keep the customer happy.

So far she'd had no reason to regret the decision, although there still was much she didn't know about the girl. She wasn't even sure of Salem's true age, although she guessed around twenty. It was a sure bet Salem wasn't born in A.D. 300, as she claimed on her employment application.

Isis headed into her tiny office. Hearing the door open, her personal assistant—a term Marc preferred to secretary—rotated his computer chair to face her. He pushed up his sleeves, revealing muscled arms, and relaxed back in his chair. "Good morning, Ice."

"Morning. Looks like I'm the last one in."

"I must note this day on the calendar with my red pen. Busy night?" Marc sounded hopeful.

"Me, the cat, and the bird—we rented a video."

"Tsk, Ice, you need a little excitement in your life."

A vision of Darius flashed before her. More excitement she *didn't* need.

"I know," Marc said, "I'll take you to this tattoo parlor—"

"No thanks. I've still got that green and blue river you talked me into last year."

"I never did see the final tattoo."

"That's because you were more interested in the tattoo artist's butt than mine."

"More's the pity. He turned out to be a very dull lover."

Isis dropped into her chair. "Mime business profitable last night?"

"It feeds the soul, but there are too many charlatans who have no concept of the nuances involved invading our street corners." In irritation, Marc rubbed a hand across his short-cropped blond hair.

"So I guess I won't be looking for a new PA soon."

"Alas, no."

It was a running joke between them that one day Marc would abandon her for the life of a street performer. Both knew it wouldn't happen in this lifetime.

Marc Delaney had breezed into her shop, and her life, on the day she'd reopened Dream Scents, insisting she needed a personal assistant. Some instinct, along with the expert knowledge of computers he displayed, prompted her to hire him, but she'd remained wary, not willing to trust any man, especially a young one as good-looking as Marc.

In time, Marc's open good humor, his wellspring of gossip about New Orleans and the French Quarter, and his talent for organization had won her over. The fact that there was no sexual tension between them—unless you counted a time or two when they both noticed the same attractive man—helped. Isis didn't insist upon regular hours, leaving him free to pursue his avocation as a mime. Only later had she found out that he'd been desperate to find a job, having been fired by a vindictive, homophobic boss.

Marc handed Isis a short stack of mail and a neat list of messages, sorted according to priority and with items not needing her personal attention already handled, then added a typed paper and neatly labeled folder to the pile. "This is your schedule for today—conference call at eight with the natural oil suppliers—and these are the financial reports you requested."

Isis glanced at the stack of papers, then gave one last look at the store. Dreams Scents would be the success she envisioned, and, for once, she would make her family proud of her.

Chapter Five

Darius chose not to return immediately to Isis. First, he wanted to visit Simon. Most djinn, without special connection such as he had given Jared, had to know where another djinn was in order to move to that locale, but because of their close friendship, Simon and Darius shared the ability to locate and transport to each others' side.

He landed in Zoe's computer workroom. Curious, Darius looked around. He had been here before, but there was more equipment now, whose purpose he could not even begin to guess. Simon had mentioned once how prosperous ZEVA, Zoe's multimedia business, had become during the year of their marriage. In one corner, Darius recognized Simon's handiwork—a carved case holding books.

Leaning one hip against a desk, he eyed Simon and Zoe. They were kissing, so in love and so wrapped up in one another, they hadn't even noticed the whirlwind of his arrival.

It had been some time since he'd seen his friend, months by human calculations, and he saw one further change: Zoe was pregnant.

Darius felt a rush of pleasure for his friend. Djinn children were rare and prized. Truly, Simon was blessed.

Immediately following the pleasure, a disturbing thought arose. If he took Isis as *zaniya*, he would never share that blessing himself. Once the ceremonies of joining were complete, he would remain joined to Isis, yet as a Terran, if she returned to her home world, she would be free to choose elsewhere.

Ignoring the hollow ache in his chest, and the unwarranted anger at the thought of Isis choosing another, Darius shoved aside questions and doubts. Since he'd never intended to take a *zaniya*, he'd never intended to father children.

Unless Isis was to stay with him on Kaf . . . No, that could not be. In the end, the Protector had only the *ma-at*.

When Simon ran his hands along Zoe's rounded stomach and levitated them both to the sofa, Darius decided he should make his presence known.

"Instructive as this is, you might greet your guest first."

Simon whirled around, shielding Zoe with protective *ma-at*, then let out an exasperated sigh. "Darius. Do you ever knock?"

"Rarely," Darius answered. He nodded toward Zoe's stomach. "My blessings to you both."

Zoe flushed and smiled. "Thanks."

The irritation faded from Simon, and he clasped Darius by the hand and arm. " "Thank you, my friend. It's good to see you. Our hospitality is yours." He wrapped an arm around his *zaniya* and pulled her close against him.

"Can you stay longer than your usual half hour?" Zoe added.

Darius shook his head. "I shall be in your city for some days, but I stay with another."

"Who?" asked Zoe, obviously surprised.

"A woman named Isis Montgomery."

"The woman who does the aromatherapy?" A crease appeared between Zoe's brows. "She's got an aunt who dabbles in magic stuff, and I seem to remember some rumors that she was interested in it, too. When I first started ZEVA, she talked to me about doing some work, but her fiancé took over the business, and he decided against me."

A fiancé? Darius's jaw clenched.

Zoe looked at him with curiosity. "I liked Isis. What have you got up your sleeve, Darius?"

Darius frowned a moment, looking at his robe. Though *ma-at* had given him English, sometimes there were odd phrases whose meaning defied the actual words.

"I meant, what are you planning?" she explained.

Darius glanced at Zoe, at her rounded stomach where she carried the child of her love for Simon. Not for anything would he bring risk to either.

I would speak privately, my friend. Darius sent the mental message to Simon.

I have no secrets from Zoe.

But I do.

Zoe looked between Simon and Darius. She had an uncanny knack for reading their faces and recognizing when they spoke in the privacy of thoughts. Her arms crossed. "Okay, what's going on?"

"I think I will partake of your hospitality," Darius said. "Zoe, would you get me a drink? Tea, freshly brewed."

She grinned at him. "Won't wash, Darius. I know for a fact you can conjure up whatever you want, faster and more to your taste than I ever could make."

Simon touched her cheek, the love evident in his

caress. "Perhaps this is something personal."

Zoe eyed the two for a moment, then sighed. "I'll have the tea ready when you finish."

A girl's voice called from the hall. "Mom! Can you help with my hair?" Zoe's daughter, Mary, appeared, part of her hair in a droopy knot atop her head and part dangling down.

She caught sight of Darius, and her eyes lit up. "Darius! When did you get here?" She ran across the room, the loose strands of blond hair streaming behind, to fling herself at him for a hug. She rose on tiptoe to kiss his cheek.

"How long can you stay?" Mary asked. "A long time, I hope. You haven't been here in *months*. Can you stay with us? Do you remember that picture I did of you? It won first place in an art show last month. I'm trying out some new techniques. Could you pose for me again?"

"Mary, let Darius answer at least one question," Zoe said, laughing.

"Pinning your hair up?" Darius asked. "You are not even eleven years yet."

Mary wrinkled her nose at him. "I'm going on twelve."

"No wonder you look like such a lady."

"Are you going to stay with us?"

Darius shook his head. "I shall be in your city, but I shall be staying with a friend."

"Okay, but I want to meet her sometime. Now, Mom, about this hair . . ."

"Let me see what I can do," Zoe answered. After casting a quick glance at Simon and Darius, she rested an arm across Mary's shoulders and followed her out of the room.

Simon waited until they were gone before breaking the silence. "So, why have you come, my friend?"

"Isis tried to bind me."

"Then this Isis shall pay," Simon said flatly. He of

all the djinn knew how cruel a binding was, how lonely was the life of a spellbound djinn.

Darius shook his head. "No retribution against Isis. She didn't know what she attempted. Someone enticed her to do it."

The sparks of anger surrounded Simon. "Who? He will not survive to enjoy the fruits of his betrayal."

"Your support warms me, but unfortunately I don't know who is behind it."

"Does this Isis know?"

"Perhaps."

"You don't trust her, do you?"

He never trusted humans. Except, maybe, Simon's family. Even though Isis had not succeeded in her attempt, he could not ignore the gnawing in his stomach at the vile thought of being bound. Moreover, he could not discuss the private matters, the loss of *ma-at*, with anyone, not even Simon.

"That is not important. What is important is finding who gave Isis the ritual."

"And who gave her your name for it," Simon added softly. "What do you want me to do?"

"Two things. Do you have any old books, any information about Terran magic?"

Simon nodded. "I gave the book that Zoe used to call me to you, but I have started a small collection of my own since then."

"Would you look in them and see if you can find anything about the line of Abregaza? Any special powers, gifts? Anything that sets them apart from other humans."

"Of course. What is the other?"

"This city is a site of great magic potential," Darius said. "It pulses with the energies of Terra, though humans do not know how to tap into them. Since you are of Terra now, would you keep attuned to her rhythms and tell me if you detect anything foreign, of Kafian origin?"

"So you can combat it? I will not leave you to fight this alone."

"The Protector must handle this."

Simon scowled at him. "Don't give me that arrogant act. You are my *friend.*"

Darius sighed. "I would appreciate your help, but you are of Terra now, Simon. If the fight is on Kaf, as I think it must be, you will not have its depths to draw on."

Simon's lips tightened, but he could not refute the argument, Darius knew, for it was but the truth. Simon's silence was the only sign of his acquiescence, however.

"I just hope the little I ask does not put you in danger. I would not bring risk to Zoe, or to your child." He gave Simon a brief smile, hoping to alleviate the tension. "She and the babe will need you, Simon. The child will have the power of *ma-at*, and you must be here to help raise it. A djinn child is too precious to receive aught but the best."

Simon hesitated, then nodded. "I'll see what I can find."

Darius was well aware that his friend made no further promises.

"Now," said Darius, clapping Simon on the shoulder, "for a time I will accept your offer of hospitality."

Tonight would begin his time with Isis.

The day passed in a hectic blur for Isis, until the front doorbell jingled during a brief afternoon lull. Heat and bright sunlight invaded her cool shop with the open door, then swiftly disappeared when it was closed.

"Isis, my dear, I have vanquished Mr. Nelson 'Knows-all' Newton with nary a whimper on his part." Aunt Tildy breezed in. Her chiffon scarf, holding on her enormous straw hat, fluttered with the force of her walk.

Aunt Tildy was small, two inches shorter than Isis and barely into the flyweight class, and her white hair belied her flawless, youthful-looking skin. Because of her age and size, the frauds she exposed tended to underestimate her.

"Had he found a secret hallway, as you suspected?"

Aunt Tildy gave a delicate sniff. "Nothing so creative. He was sleeping with the maid. I'm afraid the debunking business has gotten very plebeian these days. Criminals have no imagination. Mr. Newton was caught, very literally, with his pants down."

Isis laughed. "I wish I'd been there to see it."

"You're welcome to rejoin me at any time."

"This keeps me busy." Isis waved her hand around the store.

"I know, dear, I know." Aunt Tildy patted her hand. "And you are doing a splendid job here; your mother and grandmother would be proud. Oh, no, dear—" this to a customer picking up an aloe lotion, "with your delicate skin, you need the lighter blend." She turned her attention back to her niece. "I need more of that formula for scenting the room, the one for special evenings."

"Nocturna?"

"That's it."

Isis smiled. "A new beau? Or are you still enticing Clarence?"

"Clarence? Oh, he was at least three months ago. Before Jean Luc."

"Jean Luc, hmmmm? Will I meet him at the party?"

"Why you insisted on such a fuss with that party, I don't understand."

Isis kissed her aunt's powdered cheek. "You don't turn seventy every day."

"And I'd thank you not to remind me of that fact."

Aunt Tildy stripped off her white gloves and folded them into her pocketbook. "And no, you will not meet Jean Luc. I'm seeing two other very nice gentlemen now."

"No wonder you ran out of Nocturna."

"If you're too busy, I'll come another day."

"It won't take me long." Isis started pouring the individual oils into a small brown bottle, experience and a practiced eye telling her how much of each without measurement.

Aunt Tildy flitted about the room, her flowered dress a visual complement to the rose, violet, lavender, honeysuckle, and carnation of the perfumes. She offered a suggestion to one customer about her choice of perfume, rearranged a vase of flowers for more visual impact, and then came back to Isis.

"Are you coming alone to the party?" Tildy asked, sifting through the open bowl of potpourri.

"Yes."

She gave a tiny *tsk*. "You need a man, Isis."

Isis gave a snort as she added the final ingredient. "This from you, Aunt Tildy? Besides, I'm too busy."

"I'm talking about an affair, dear, nothing more. One can always find time for that. It keeps you young." Aunt Tildy brushed the potpourri off her hands. "For you, it must be someone special, someone who makes you feel special. A man with the power of dreams and the gifts of magic."

Isis looked at her aunt, startled by the uncanny description. That could be Darius. "Where'd you get that idea?"

"From scrying. It's a new method using mirrors and a pool of water. The fountain in my garden is perfect." Aunt Tildy leaned forward. "I'm close this time. Close to real magic."

Closer than you think. Isis couldn't wait to see Tildy's face when she met Darius.

71

She handed her aunt the bottle. "I've got a special birthday present for you, but I want to give it to you without the whole family around. Can I come by your house after the party?"

Aunt Tildy's cheeks turned pink. "You had better come before. I have . . . plans for afterward."

"Aunt Tildy!"

Before Isis could say more, or figure out how to contact Darius regarding the change, she was interrupted by the sight of an even-featured, thirtysomething blond man strolling into her shop. He stopped at the entrance and surveyed the interior, pulling a snowy handkerchief from the pocket of an immaculate white suit and patting the sheen on his face. He refolded the handkerchief with precision, then tucked it back into his pocket.

Damn and double damn. Jimmy Ray Frank.

"It's that detestable reporter," Aunt Tildy said. "The one who writes the 'No Last Names' column, and who was so unkind to you in the recent unpleasantness."

Unkind? Three years ago he'd skewered her in his column.

Jimmy Ray's three-times-a-week column specialized in no-holds-barred reporting and a scalpel-sharp wit. He never bothered with politics—claiming everybody already knew politicians were hopelessly mired in scandal—but preferred to dig for more unconventional stories of graft, greed, and gullibility. Everyone read his column, chortling over who was squirming that day and praying they would never be featured.

Three years ago, his biting prose about her forays into magic had contributed more to her downfall than the arrest had.

"Damn, what's he doing here?" Isis muttered.

"Ladies don't swear, dear." Aunt Tildy donned her gloves and tilted her hat until it shaded her face, tying the scarf into a floppy bow. The current fad for tanning was not for Aunt Tildy. She marched over to Jimmy Ray.

He tipped his straw hat to her. "Afternoon, Miz Maehara."

Aunt Tildy poked him in the chest with a gloved finger. "Young man, you have done enough damage to my niece. Do not slander her again or you shall have me to answer to." Her gaze skimmed down, then up him. "And it's too early to wear white." Head held high, Tildy left in a flurry of chiffon, the scent of her sweet perfume lingering.

Jimmy Ray stared after her, bemused for a moment, before turning back to Isis. "Do you think she will call the spirits down on me?" he drawled, pushing back the brim of his hat.

Isis braced her fists on the counter. "Don't you dare laugh at my aunt."

"I would not dream of maligning a New Orleans icon such as Tildy Maehara." His Southern gentleman persona was thick today, a sure sign he was after a story. Once she had fallen for that attentive charm and easy voice. Not again.

Her hunch was confirmed when he flipped open a small notebook. "I'm working on a new story and thought you might be able to answer a few simple questions, Ice."

"No." She smiled pleasantly as she turned away, knowing Jimmy Ray loved to annoy people because it made them talk more.

"It's about magic."

Isis hated the sudden cold that swept through her. "I don't do that anymore," she lied.

"Wouldn't you rather be the one giving information, rather than the one being investigated?"

Isis pivoted on one heel and rested her hands on her hips. "Are you threatening me, Jimmy Ray?"

"I never threaten, m'dear. I only deal in facts."

"Well, I'm busy."

Jimmy Ray grabbed a bottle without looking at it. "Why don't you just make me up some of this, darlin', a big bottle."

Avoidance always made Jimmy Ray suspicious and spurred him on to digging further. She'd better find out what he wanted, and what he knew. Isis glanced at the bottle and suppressed a smile. "You say you want a large bottle?"

"The biggest. My expenses are covered."

She began to work, wishing she could see how he would list this in his expense report.

"I've been hearing rumors about a place with some strange goings on," he said in his deep drawl.

"Strangeness is not news in New Orleans, Jimmy Ray. We thrive on it." Efficiently she put together the mixture he'd selected, looking at the bottles instead of him.

"This is different; I feel it in my gut. It's a small shop, in an alley off Chartres, but when *I* go there, it never seems to be open. You ever been there?"

To her annoyance, Isis found her hands shaking, so much that she spilled a drop, something she never did. She set the stock bottle down with a thunk, took a breath to settle her roiling stomach, and picked up another oil while eyeing Jimmy Ray with a sidelong glance.

Was he just fishing, or had he seen her at Madame Paris's? If he had, and she lied, he'd start hounding her again. The man was more persistent than a fly scenting a Twinkie.

"Never open for you? Sounds like a smart owner to me."

She mixed the last ingredients and held up the bottle. "Will this be enough?" she asked innocently.

"Make me another."

Isis raised her brows. "All right." She wrote the name of the mixture he'd chosen on a label and affixed it to the bottle, then started on another.

Jimmy Ray gave a small sigh. "I know you've been in there."

Well, that answered that question. "I stopped in a place the other day," she admitted. Since he knew she'd been there, she might as well 'fess up. Maybe it would throw him off the scent a bit. "Called Madame Paris's. It caught my eye on my way to the ferry, and you know how my aunt is always looking for frauds. I like to help when I can. That the place?"

He grunted an indistinct answer. "How many times have you been there?"

"Just once."

He gave her a skeptical look.

"That stuff doesn't interest me anymore."

"Notice anything unusual?"

"The whole place was strange."

"Did you buy anything?"

A ritual to summon a genie. If she told him that, he'd have her reputation in tatters again. However, she had no intention of revealing that tidbit. At least she didn't need to worry about Darius. He wouldn't be back until ten o'clock tomorrow.

"A crystal flacon." She nodded toward her collection of antique perfume holders. "I collect them." She labeled the bottle she'd just mixed. "That will be $49.99 plus tax."

He stared at the two two-ounce bottles. "M'dear, what is it for? Turning lead into gold?"

"It's one of our best-sellers. For impotence," she said clearly. "You just sprinkle on two drops, four if it's, um, a long-standing problem—"

For once she'd gotten to him. When he snatched the bottles from her, she simply added, "We'll refund your money if it doesn't help," and waited, allowing a slight grin, until he slapped the bills into her hand.

"If you're finished with your questions, I have some financial reports to read." Isis handed the money to Salem, who wasn't bothering to conceal her smirk. "Please get Jimmy Ray his change and receipt."

Concealing her trembling knees, afraid to look back at Jimmy Ray, Isis sauntered to her office, closed the door, and then collapsed into her chair. At least Marc was off on some errand, and she had privacy in which to collect herself.

She stared at the courtyard outside her window. Why, when she had taken the risk of doing magic, did Jimmy Ray Frank come snooping around again? The rumors he'd heard of Madame Paris had a grain of truth, for the woman wielded true magic. *I'm going to have to be very careful, not to let the rumors involve me.*

Isis lit a candle for calming, took a deep breath, and watched the palm fronds sway in the light breeze for a moment; then, with a sigh, she turned her back to the window and opened a file. She didn't need the tempting distractions of a spring afternoon. Financial reports were difficult enough with all those words and numbers. Isis propped her feet on her desk and began to read.

Suddenly, a sharp wind set the papers on her desk whirling. Her rolling desk chair slid sideways. Isis's feet caught on the side of her computer monitor. The chair, however, did not stop. Her bottom skidded across the slippery leather. Only her elbows, which caught on the chair arms, prevented her from landing on the floor in a graceless heap. Instead she was stretched between desk and chair, balancing on her heels and elbows.

"Perhaps I could teach you a levitation spell," said a melodious male voice.

Isis craned her neck to look over her toes. Darius stood before her, looking even more beautiful than she'd remembered him. He wore the same robe that reflected blue, then green, then silver. A bulging

76

leather satchel hung from his shoulder. He was studying her legs with keen masculine interest.

"Darius," she said sweetly, "enjoying the view?" She scrambled to her feet, glancing toward the door. It was still firmly shut.

He grinned. "Yes, very much. You have pretty legs." His gaze slid higher, leaving glittering starlight in its wake. "Very pretty indeed." His voice grew thick, more liquid, and the grin deepened.

To her annoyance, she could almost feel his fleeting touch, his concentration was so unswerving. Isis tilted her chin to see what fascinated him so, then groaned. The hem of her bandeau had been shoved up, nearly baring one braless breast.

Scowling at him, she pulled her bandeau into place with an irritated snap. This was not a propitious start to their association. "That's not part of our bargain, Darius. And what are you doing back here? You weren't supposed to return until tomorrow night."

"You set the time. I did not agree."

Damn and double damn. Dignity restored, Isis snagged her errant chair and dropped into it. Anxiety fluttered in her gut, and she stole another look at the closed door. What was she supposed to do with Darius?

Makeup being a sure delaying tactic, she pulled out a tube of lipstick and slicked the violet shade across her lips.

Darius leaned over the desk and plucked the lipstick from her fingers. "Why do you paint your face? I like it the way it is."

" 'Paint your face'? Now there's a retro term designed to offend every modern woman." Isis took the lipstick from him, capped it, and then picked up blusher and brushed a whisper on her cheeks. "Don't your djinn females use makeup?"

"They don't feel the need," Darius said absently,

77

reaching out and holding her chin with two fingers. He tilted her head sideways, studying her with rapt attention.

Isis pulled away from his grip.

"It glistens," he said.

"Excuse me?"

"The cheek color. It glistens when you move, as do your lashes. And you move much when you speak."

He leaned closer, and to her surprise, he slipped a silken cord over her head. His fingers trailed across her hair, then the nape of her neck, and the touch made her feel as if she glistened more than the cheek color did. His fingers slid down the cord to her clavicle while he murmured foreign, musical words. Heat, both exciting and reassuring, spread from her shoulders down her arms, until he lifted his hand from her.

Isis looked down. Dangling from the black cord about her neck was a square that looked like turquoise. She rested it in her palm to examine it more closely. A strange symbol, the edges dark brown, was etched into the surface. It was stark, simple, and compellingly beautiful.

"What's this?"

"A gift."

"We have a relationship of bargains, not of gifts." She'd been questioning the meaning of the symbol, but he'd gone to the heart of the matter.

Darius shrugged and leaned back. "Nonetheless, I wanted to give it to you."

"Why?"

"Do you always question gifts so?"

Isis gave him a rueful half smile. "Unexpected ones, yes."

"The rune is one of protection. You do not control *ma-at* like the djinn. I would not have any harm come to you."

"I don't need a man's, or a djinni's, protection."

"Then wear it because it pleases you."

She looked at him. "Are you dangerous to me?" Already she knew the answer to that one. He was very dangerous, filling her with erotic impulses, distracting her from her work, turning her bones and muscle and blood to lava with a simple look.

And if anyone found out she'd called him in a magic ritual, she'd lose everything.

"Dangerous?" he answered. "Probably. As you are to me. But that changes naught of our need for each other. Will you wear the tablet? At least until our bargains-end?"

Barely begun, and already he spoke of the end. She didn't like the idea of needing anyone's protection, and most certainly not his, but she could not bring herself to remove the amulet.

"I'll wear it," she promised, aware of a sense of both rightness and wariness in the admission.

"Good." With only a whisper of breeze, Darius was across the room, leaning against an armoire she used for storing oils and samples. "What were you doing when I came in?" he asked.

Isis rested her hand over her heart. "You've got to stop doing that. Popping in and out. Shifting from place to place on a breeze."

"It's the way I move."

"Well, try to control it. My business, and my nerves, won't survive the shock."

"What is this business of yours?"

"Dream Scents?" Isis smiled. "I've always been fascinated with perfume and scents, not just to splash on, but the way aroma affects you, your mind, your emotions, your health. Scent is such a primitive, basic sense. We barely have words capable of describing it. I do aromatherapy and blend perfumes. We also sell related items, like candles, books, lotions." Isis stopped suddenly, aware that not everyone shared her enthusiasm. She ran a hand through her hair. "Sorry. I get carried away when I talk about Dream Scents."

"Do not apologize. I am interested." Darius perched on the back of the sofa, his chin resting on his hand, his intent gaze on her. "The djinn use perfumes and incense in our rituals. We scent our homes, our common areas. It's an integral part of our lives. How do you choose a scent for someone?"

Isis explained how she questioned a customer for wants and likes in formulating each unique perfume, and then, under probing questions and unflagging attention from Darius, she talked about how she chose the aromatherapy oils, how she decided on complementary items to offer.

"This is important to you," Darius said at last.

More than he could possibly imagine. Isis ran a hand through her hair again, embarrassed about how much she had revealed. As a listener, Darius could give Jimmy Ray a few pointers.

"Yes," she said simply.

Darius straightened. "Today, you may work."

Warm fuzzy feelings disappeared in the wake of his arrogant proclamation. "That's big of you," Isis muttered. "Does that mean you're leaving?"

"I prefer to stay and watch."

She lifted one hand. "You expect me to work with you here staring at me?"

"Yes," he answered blandly.

And there wasn't a whole lot she could do about that, was there? How did you make a djinni go away if he didn't want to? She glanced toward the door. What sort of a Pandora's box had she opened with that ritual when she called him here?

A wicked grin stole across his lips. "Are you saying I bother you?"

He slid one hand across his robe, and she could almost feel the whispering of the silk beneath her skin. A shimmering aura of red surrounded him. Her mouth felt dry.

Bother? Hell, yes. Isis hauled in her errant thoughts. "Bother me? Of course not."

"Then return to your work," he said softly.

She picked up the financial report and started to read.

Darius prowled around the room, while Isis chewed on her pencil, one eye on her report, one eye on the djinni who disrupted her life, her calm, her focus. He stroked the slats on the wooden blinds as he studied the view out her windows, ran his hand along the back of the soft cloth couch, then stretched out briefly on it, tasted the French Vanilla coffee Marc had brewed earlier, sniffed the bottles of oils strewn around the room.

Once, he transported to her side, holding a bottle, and dabbed oil at the hot points on her wrists and temples. As the scent rose with her body's heat, she identified the oil. Jasmine. He said nothing, merely leaned over, inhaled deeply, and gave a satisfied sigh before returning to his explorations.

He didn't say a word, yet he made her feel like clouds and summer rain, soft, wet, and warm.

Her feeble attempt to work collapsed. The whispering silk of his movements called as seductively as a Siren.

"Can't you sit still?" she asked, irritation sharpening her voice.

In response, he came to her desk and perched at the side of it. He studied the photograph on top, picked it up, and ran his thumb across her face. "Your family?"

She nodded and pointed to each man. "My father, Royal. That's my oldest brother Thomas, and the twins, Jack and Beau. My brother Ram—short for Ramses, but don't ever call him that—is closest in age to me."

81

Isis took the picture from him and set it firmly on her desk. "Now, I really need to concentrate. There are some magazines over there you can read."

Darius scowled at her dismissal, and an array of sparks danced along the ends of his hair. The lightning dissipated as, for a long moment, they stared at one another, the only sound a faint tune from a steam calliope on a riverboat. Darius smiled. "Finish your work quickly, my sweet Isis."

"I'm not sweet, and I'm not yours."

"All right. My salty Isis."

Isis shook her head and abandoned the sparring. Darius drifted to the sofa, sat with a dancer's grace, and picked up a magazine.

After a while she heard him murmur appreciatively. "Are these the current fashions?"

"Probably," she answered, not bothering to look up.

"Then I shall clad myself accordingly."

"What?" Isis looked up from her papers.

Darius stood, casting one last glance at the magazine. He undid the sash of his robe, then tilted his head back. Softly, he began to chant. The edges of his robe fell apart.

Her fantasies were right. He didn't wear anything under that robe.

Isis swallowed, hard, the moisture sucked from her throat. Liquid metal replaced her blood, scalding her, as she stared at Darius.

He was . . . magnificent. All tawny skin that gleamed of sweat and gold and sleek, strong muscle. He radiated raw masculine power and electrifying magical charisma. Unbidden, Isis rose to her feet, her gaze never leaving him.

Darius continued to chant, while his hands skimmed along his body. Blue and silver shimmered beneath his palms. His gaze locked with hers, drawing her nearer. She was a child mesmerized by flame.

Except this hot need was none a child had ever felt.

Darius leaned closer, inviting her touch.

A sudden clap of thunder jerked them both to a halt.

Silk black boxers and a narrow, sleeveless, midnight blue T-shirt appeared beneath Darius's robe. He looked sexy and intimate, as if he'd just emerged from the bedroom to invite her in.

He'd been looking at the underwear ads.

The door to her office slammed open.

"Ice, what was that . . . ?" Salem's voice faded as she caught sight of Darius. Any questions about Salem's sexual orientation were answered by the way her eyes devoured Darius.

Marc followed close at Salem's heels. "Ice, we must talk about—" He stopped dead, his mouth hanging open.

"Who are you?" breathed Salem. "How did you get in here?"

"Oh, my," said Marc, "I think I'm in love."

"*She* is my lover," announced Darius.

Isis groaned and wished she'd bargained for a disappearing spell.

Chapter Six

Isis gave a convoluted explanation for his presence to the woman and man, Salem and Marc she called them, as she herded them out. To Darius's surprise, both took the explanation, and their dismissal, in stride. Either they were too respectful to question, or they had gotten other such reasonings from Isis and thus considered them normal, if incomprehensible.

With the door firmly closed, Isis rested her head against it. "My *lover*? I can't believe you said that." She turned to him. "How about a bargain that you leave until tomorrow night?"

Darius shook his head. "Each bargain must be fulfilled in turn."

Her lips pressed together, then relaxed, and she sighed. "In that case, we need to do something about your wardrobe." She flipped the magazine to another page. "This is what you should wear. Or this. Or this." She handed the magazine to him.

While Darius stared at the glossy page, she turned her back and waited, foot tapping. "You can change now," she called over her shoulder, "only this time do it a little more quietly."

Did she order him? With difficulty, Darius controlled his temper. Such a presumptuous command he'd refuse on principle, except for one thing. He needed her willing.

Why had the divination sent him to such an impertinent female?

Sending a brief prayer to Solomon that the *ma-at* wouldn't explode this time, he transformed his clothes into a loose, billowy shirt and soft, long pants with a drawstring waist. A few additional changes he made—he preferred a silkier fabric with reflective threads, and he kept his robe, shortening it some. "Is this acceptable?"

Isis looked him over, ignoring his sarcasm. " "Nice outfit." Her gaze settled on his bare feet. "Except—"

"No," Darius forestalled her. He refused to wear *shoes*.

"How about a compromise with sandals?"

Darius pulled a pair from his leather satchel.

Isis nodded approvingly. "Stop the popping in and out, sit here quietly while I finish, and I just might get through this." She returned to her desk, propped up her feet, and started to study a paper.

Hands propped behind his head, feet up on the sofa arm, Darius sprawled on the cushions and studied Isis. Over the next hour, she worked diligently, with intensity and with passion. Her dedication to her work was strong.

Yet she was acutely aware of him, too. That he knew from the repeated glances she cast his way, from the faint pink upon her glistening cheeks, from the tapping of her foot.

The object of his scrutiny threw the paper down on the desk, then raised her hands above her head and stretched, twisting her spine like a cat. Her elastic top lifted, enough to tantalize, not enough to satisfy. When Isis saw where his gaze lingered, she abruptly lowered her arms. "Don't you have anything else to do? Aren't you bored?"

He had been busy, although she likely was unaware of that fact. *Ma-at* requiring finesse or subtlety was often the most difficult to control. He had spent the intervening time testing himself, practicing small changes, like raising the temperature of the room a few degrees.

Unfortunately, the room now felt as if he stood on the wastelands of Kaf when the sun hung high in the sky.

"I am rarely bored," he answered, rising. "You thought I would leave?"

Her scowl was her answer.

She still did not realize how close he intended to stay.

Darius transported to her side and perched on her desk. He rested his hand next to hers, fingertips almost touching. "Don't you understand yet, my sweet Isis? You performed a ritual to summon and bind a djinni."

"I remember; it was only this morning. It didn't work."

"The *binding* did not, but you sealed our bargains."

"Your point?"

A vine, the blue of water and of sky, grew across the flat desk, spreading in tendrils that chimed a soft melody. The velvety stem wound around first his wrist, then around hers, loosely, but with a tensile strength as strong as the bonds of need and want that reached from him to her. "We are bound together until the three bargains have been met."

"By ties of *ma-at* and by will of prophecy. I remember you saying that." She shook her hand free of the vine. "I won't be bound to any man, Darius, especially not one of magic."

Darius waved the vine away, then lifted her hand and ran his thumb over her knuckles. Slowly, he traced each finger. He liked the feel of her hand in his. "You have no desire for a male in your life?"

"I grew up the only girl in a houseful of males—four older brothers and a father. Talk about chauvinism. I've lived with enough overprotection for two lifetimes."

This was a side of Isis he neither expected nor wanted to hear about. "But never to be joined as one?" He recalled the word humans used. "Never to be married?"

"Like my parents? I always thought that, deep down, my father feared that my mother had bewitched him, though he would deny it to his last practical breath. Theirs was a marriage of extreme passion but little else." Isis shrugged. "Marriage? I'm in no hurry. Right now I can't afford to take the time or the trouble."

For a fleeting moment, Darius questioned his plan and the deceit he was practicing on her. Doubt and guilt were emotions he did not enjoy, or often entertain, and he thrust away both. Unlike the way her race bound his, the way *she* had tried to bind *him*, he would give her only pleasure before she would leave. She need not even understand the import of what they did.

Isis wiped a hand across her damp forehead. "Financial reports never made me break into a sweat before. Are you hot?"

He ignored the sheen of perspiration coating his body. "Hot?" he questioned with a slow smile, letting innuendo distract her from the unnatural temperature rise. Her flushed cheeks grew redder, and she fussed with her papers.

His path was set. Too much depended upon it to change.

First, though, he had to reverse the out-of-control heat spell.

They were interrupted by a perfunctory knock at the door. Salem poked her head inside. Her curious glance took in Darius, but she said nothing. "I'm leaving now, Ice; I'll lock up on my way out. Marc said he'll see you tomorrow." A bell sounded from behind her, and Salem glanced over her shoulder, then made a moue of irritation. "It's Mrs. Grisham."

"You go on home. I'll help her."

"She'd probably insist on you anyway. Is it hot in here?"

"Afternoon sun, I guess," Isis said, following Salem out.

Darius lounged in the doorway and watched Isis draw out the difficult customer until the woman went from a sour scowl to merely a deep frown. Such unpleasantness, yet Isis remained patient and deftly combined oils.

Isis fought to keep her attention on her work and her customer. Mrs. Grisham was difficult even on the best of days, but today the frustration of trying to please her was a mere shadow of the edginess Darius's presence created. At least he'd changed from the underwear, although his attire, if decent, could not be deemed conventional.

Most men felt uncomfortable in her shop. It wasn't filled with pink and ruffles—Isis hated both—but there was an intensely feminine feel about it, she knew. Her brothers avoided it whenever possible. Darius, however, looked perfectly at home as he prowled around the room with a lazy grace.

Oh, it wasn't that there was anything effeminate about him. Quite the contrary. He seemed to be so self-assured, so comfortable with who and what he was, so blatantly male to her female, that even the feminine surroundings could not diminish that confident masculinity.

He picked up a crystal bottle, uncorked it, and sniffed. His lids half-lowered in a sexy, not a sleepy look, then he raised his eyes to her. The languid air didn't fool her. The djinni was acutely aware of his surroundings and every detail, including his effect on her. A faint smile graced his face, sending her edginess into arousal. Isis strained to see which mixture he'd picked up.

Seraglio. A mixture of jasmine, sandalwood, and clove she'd designed for its sensuality. Darius needed no aid in that department.

Her hands tingled with the memory of that soft vine binding the two of them, of the gentle stroke of his fingers. Try as she might, she couldn't control the swell of heat brought on only by thought. If he ever did anything more than smile, touch more than her hands, she'd melt faster than butter in a microwave.

At least the shop was cooler than her office, although she could still feel the late afternoon heat through the open door.

Mrs. Grisham glared at Darius. "You there, stop flitting around and distracting Isis. I'm trying to talk to her."

"Here, try this," Isis said, jerking her attention back to her customer. While she handed Mrs. Grisham a small brown vial, she watched Darius from the corner of her eye. To her surprise, he didn't seem angered by the older woman's rebuke.

Instead, he came to their side, walking instead of transporting, she was thankful to notice. With one hand, Darius fingered his turquoise tablet while the other traced a strange figure in the rock and sand garden she kept on the counter. He murmured something under his breath.

"It's marjoram, lavender, and hops," Isis said, trying to ignore him. "How does that make you feel?"

The woman sniffed, then looked surprised. "Sounds strange, but I like it," she admitted grudgingly.

"Put a single drop on your nightlight before bedtime. You'll sleep like a baby."

"Babies cry all night."

Isis laughed. "Right you are. Try it anyway. Take this sample. If it helps, you can pay me for it later."

"I'll try it." She sniffed it again, and a fleeting smile actually crossed her face. "You know, I feel better already." Before she left, Mrs Grisham paused in the doorway. "You should keep this place a little cooler, Isis."

Isis locked the front door, turned the OPEN sign to CLOSED, then confronted Darius. "What did you do?"

"Do?"

He gave her an innocent look, but Isis wasn't fooled. She smoothed the sand, erasing the symbol he'd drawn. "Don't. Don't try to make me look stupid. You know what I mean."

"My sweet Isis—"

"I'm not stupid, I'm not sweet, and I'm not yours," she said between gritted teeth.

He stilled, and the languid air disappeared. He closed the distance between them, and though he did not touch her, she felt as if he caressed each nerve, each inch of skin. He touched her mind and her emotions and made her burn.

"Stop that! Stop touching me when I can't even see your hands move. Stop using your magic on me." She wrapped her arms about her waist.

He stopped, within reach, yet still he kept his arms at his sides. " 'Tis not my *ma-at* you feel. Were I to touch you that way, you would know."

Suddenly she felt the weight of his hand stroking softly down her arm. She closed her eyes, and the whisper of his breath warmed her cheek. His lips pressed kisses down her throat. She opened her eyes, saw that he had not moved, and she groaned, turning her head from the glow about him.

Abruptly the caresses stopped, yet the fire continued, and she knew the difference. The touches came from him; the fever was from her own traitorous emotions.

She could not give in to another man of magic, especially one who was this real, this potent. "What did you do to Mrs. Grisham?" she repeated in a thin voice.

"She was in pain, was she not?"

"You noticed that? Most don't; they just think she's a sour woman. She has cancer and has trouble sleeping from the pain. Did you get rid of the cancer?"

He shook his head.

"Could you have?"

He paused for a moment. "We djinn derive our power from the natural forces around us. We do not tamper with them, or with the fundamental order of societies, without dire need, and then, only with great thought and solemn divination, for the risks are exceedingly high. Upsetting natural balances is not a thing to be undertaken lightly." He shook his head. "It is not ours to select life or death."

"So what did you do?"

"Reduced her pain. Mrs. Grisham is an elder of your society. She should be revered and tended in the end cycles of her life, not left to suffer."

Isis's throat tightened; the depth of emotion in his words surprised her. Perhaps there was more to Darius than the arrogant, sensual djinni he'd shown so far. She didn't want to see this part of him, see him as something more than his magic.

"So I just gave away my oil for nothing. All you had to do was say the magic words and the pain was gone." She laughed bitterly, defensively. "Just goes to show what a good businesswoman I am."

He shook his head. "I only enhanced the properties

91

of your oils. She will feel discomfort, yes, for she must prepare herself, but not the grinding pain." He reached out and touched her cheek. "The *ma-at* needed your talents to hold it. You are very good at what you do. Your combinations are creative, different . . . magical."

Only Aunt Tildy believed in her like that. "You sound surprised."

He gave a little motion with his hand. "Scent is not so indispensable to human life as it is for the djinn. Oh, you use perfumes and you add aromas to almost everything, but it is not . . ." He paused, seeming to search for the proper word.

"Integral?"

"Personal. It is not selected for the person, the time of day and season, the purpose of use."

"Sometimes it is, but not often enough. I'm trying to change that in my tiny corner of our universe." Isis stepped away from his disturbing nearness and keen perception and looked around the store one last time, verifying that all was neat and ready for the following day. "I'm going to succeed with this, beyond anything my family has done. But I can't do that if I keep giving away product."

She turned out the lights, leaving the two of them in shadow. The only light came through the shaded front windows. It illuminated half his face, left the other half in mystery.

"The helping is what makes your work valuable, is it not?"

"Making it a financial success will make it valuable."

"Financial success?"

"Making a lot of money."

He shook his head. "Human obsession with money. I just don't understand it." He ran a hand down her arm. "You are skilled in your craft. Is that not enough to bring reward?"

92

"That's easy for a djinni to say. You wave your hand and mumble a few words and you've got what you want. In this culture, without financial success, an eccentric craft is more of a liability than an asset."

"But—"

"I'm going to do it," she said tightly. "I know that seventy percent of all small businesses fail, but I've worked my tail off and kept afloat for two years now. I'm going to prove I'm not stupid or helpless, or a naive flake. I won't fail, not again!"

The instant they were said, Isis wanted to retrieve the bitten-out words. She rubbed a hand across her weary eyes, feeling hot and restless and washed out. "Damn, it's getting warm in here, too. Maybe the AC needs a charge. I'll call the repairman tomorrow."

"Perhaps it will be better in the morning."

Darius followed her to the street, but after that blazingly stupid admission, she felt she could not deal with him, with his solicitousness, his confidence, his too powerful personality. "I guess you'll be going back to . . . wherever you stay. There's been a change of plans. I'll see you tomorrow *before* Aunt Tildy's party. Meet me in the shop; we'll go from there." She rushed the last out, needing to get it all said and done before he could respond. "Good night, Darius."

Darius stared in astonishment as Isis turned and walked away from him. Away from him! Without asking his leave or extending her hospitality. If he didn't have to get that bedamned heat spell under control . . .

Darius relaxed and smiled. Isis was in for a small surprise. He could always find her when he needed to.

First, the heat spell must be contained; then he could point out to Isis the error in her conclusions. She would go to her home, but she would not be alone for long. He transported back inside Isis's shop.

Containing the out-of-control heat spell took longer than he expected. Darius cursed as one last remnant escaped his grasp. Sweat stung his eyes and his breath came in pants, but at last he contained the wayward spell. The heat roared its fury, a final gasp before it died, leaving behind a cooling silence.

In the following moment of stillness, alien energies from Terra bombarded him, emphasizing his trembling weakness. Kaf; he needed Kaf first. Darius picked up his satchel, lifted his arms, and transported from Isis's shop.

Isis lived in Algiers Point, an older area of New Orleans situated directly across the river from the French Quarter. She loved living there. Most of the amenities she needed were available either in the Point or the Quarter, and she could take the ferry to work instead of driving. She had a car—an old and decrepit vehicle whose only claim to glory was that she had paid for it before her ignominious fall three years ago—but she seldom used it.

Her daily ferry ride to and from work she treasured, a moment of peace and solitude on either end of a hectic day. Tonight, however, the endless flow of the river did not work its magic, nor did the short walk home through quiet streets.

I'm going to prove I'm not a naive flake. How could she have blurted out such nonsense? Her father always said she had too much emotion and too little discretion.

As she trudged up her front steps, however, pleasant pride in her home washed away the lingering self-recriminations. She'd inherited her house from her grandmother and she adored it. The old-style construction—high ceilings, intricate moldings, fireplaces, and ceiling fans in each room—reminded her of her connections to the past. She had added a lush, overgrown garden in back that gave her a sense of privacy despite the closeness of the neighbors.

Once inside, Isis changed into a tank shirt and shorts, threw together a sandwich, and went up to her third-floor workroom, chomping on the whole wheat, lettuce, cheese, and tomato. She didn't have spare time at work, so she did her experiments with new perfumes and aromatherapy mixtures at home.

All day, she'd been itching to see if she could duplicate that mysterious scent from Madame Paris. If she did, she wouldn't have to worry about whether Darius could get it for her with magic. The idea of relying on magic to get what she wanted still made her uneasy.

Two hours later, Isis admitted defeat, at least for tonight. Something or things were missing from each combination. She rubbed a hand across her nose. Her ability to distinguish scents was also fatigued. She'd try again tomorrow.

Isis stoppered the bottle and stowed it in a safe nook, then stretched and yawned. She was tired. After all, she'd been up at dawn this morning doing that ritual.

The thought brought back immediate memories of Darius, memories she'd managed to keep at bay for, oh, about a minute at a time while she'd worked. Instantly she knew sleep would be a long time coming.

The man was lethal to serenity.

A hot bath. She needed a hot bath.

A long soak in a bath scented with Meadow, her favorite scent for soothing and relaxing, did help, as did a session of petting a warm, purring Vulcan. She threw a cover over Khu's cage, then donned her old, soft, oversized Save-the-Whales T-shirt. Stretching out in bed, Isis first tightened, then released each muscle in turn to relax. Her eyes drifted shut. Sleep touched the edges of her mind.

A whirlwind blew her hair across her face and tangled her single sheet about her legs.

"Ah, so appealing," came a low, melodious voice. "Shall I join you?"

Chapter Seven

Heart in her throat, pulse racing, Isis bolted upright, scaring Vulcan off the bed, and then collapsed against her pillows. "Darius!"

He relaxed at the foot of her bed, casual and very much at home. A leather satchel sat on the floor. His black hair was damp, as though from a shower or a swim. He smelled fresh—not of soap or cologne, but simply . . . fresh. He smelled *right*, right in a way she couldn't explain, but could only enjoy.

Uh-oh. Ben had made her nose itch. His chemistry had irritated her sensitive olfactory sense. She'd ignored it at the time, but after he'd proved to be such a slime, she'd vowed never to get involved with someone who didn't smell *right*.

Darius smelled right.

Damn and double damn. Her pulse, starting to slow after the burst of adrenaline, picked up its pace.

"Are you trying to see how many times in one day you can scare me?" she complained, plumping her pillows behind her back and ignoring her previous line of thought. "Give me warning next time. Or better yet, quit popping in and out like that."

"Frightening you was not my intent."

"Word of advice then: You need to work on your technique."

He laughed. "Few have complained about my technique."

"Have there been many?" Isis could have bitten her tongue for asking the question.

"Some," he murmured, "but perhaps not as many as you guess. I am selective." He fingered the turquoise tablet that rested on his smooth chest. His gaze moved across her with slow interest, but he made no move toward her.

Vulcan, who had sniffed at the satchel and then at Darius, jumped back on the bed. He pressed against Isis's leg, purring loudly, his rear end turned pointedly toward Darius.

Vulcan's actions broke through the mesmerizing moment. "You're not supposed to be here until tomorrow," she said, deciding the best defense is a good offense.

"You keep making assumptions about me, my sweet Isis. We are bound—"

"By the bargains. By bonds of *ma-at* and will of prophecy. I've heard the refrain. It said nothing about sharing my home."

"Where else would I stay while we await the fulfillment of the bargains? I have no pillows on your world."

"A hotel has plenty of pillows."

He raised one brow. "You would turn out a guest? Are your customs of hospitality so barbaric?"

Isis recognized manipulation when she heard it. She also recognized stubborn male, despite his relaxed stance. "No, but—"

"Perhaps you would rather await the time at my

home on Kaf?" he suggested with some eagerness.

"Kaf?"

"The realm of the djinn."

"And spend my day lounging around like you do? I have too many responsibilities, even if you don't."

His lips tightened. From the faint sparks, Isis knew she'd hit a nerve, but exactly which one she couldn't tell. She decided not to press the issue further. "You can stay with me."

As soon as she said it, she bit her lip. The words could sound like an invitation, and Darius was too sensual a being not to realize it. To her surprise—or disappointment?—he didn't pounce upon it.

Instead, he inclined his head. "I thank you for opening your home to me, and I shall guard it as my own."

The formal words, perhaps a custom with his people, had the odd effect of reassuring her. Her nerves, taut as a tightrope, relaxed. "You can use the third floor, if you don't mind my workroom on one end. The other is sectioned off with a bed and an armoire."

He held out his hand. "Show me."

Isis didn't take his hand immediately; she had no reason to trust a man of magic. "If you stay here, no one must know you're a djinni."

"Why?"

"It would complicate things for both of us, in a lot of different ways."

"I shall take care." He extended his hand again. "Show me," he repeated.

Isis placed her hand in his. His strong, smooth fingers closed about hers in a sure grip.

As they left, Darius gave one last glance at Vulcan, who gazed at them with unblinking feline displeasure. Darius crooned something low, or maybe he purred it, for Vulcan tucked his paws beneath him and his green eyes drifted shut.

Isis led Darius up one flight to the floor above her bedroom. With each step, a voice of caution insisted she was entering dangerous territory, allowing a djinni, a man of magic, to become part of her life.

Another equally strong voice insisted she was the fool of a lifetime for putting him in a bed other than her own.

The next morning, during her ferry ride, Isis found it impossible to focus on the day's mental to-do list. Last night, when she'd left Darius in his room, she'd expected at least a minor pass from him and had had her arguments and defenses all mixed and ready to go. Instead, he'd simply echoed her good night, then kissed her hand. The sensual look he'd given her while bent over her hand was hot enough to make toasted marshmallow of her insides.

She'd retreated—there could be no other word for it—and this morning she'd been no braver. She'd thrown on an oversize Dream Scents shirt, below-the-knee bike shorts, and red Keds, slicked on makeup, and then left—snuck out, to be honest—before he'd stirred. Darius, fresh from sleep, and bed, would be a potent assault on her good sense.

The breeze off the Mississippi ruffled her hair, and a drop of sweat stung her eye. She lifted her chin and sucked in the humid air. March was a fickle month in New Orleans. Two weeks ago it had been chilly enough for jackets, but today was warm, the prelude to the stifling heat and humidity of summer.

Isis leaned against the ferry rail and watched a tree limb float toward the shore. When the morning sun glinted off the gray-brown Mississippi, she slid on her sunglasses and gazed at the lapping water.

The wind gusted, blowing her hair in her eyes. Within the foam created by the ferry's wake a colorful, translucent image of Darius's face appeared, as if her thoughts has conjured the hallucination.

She blinked, then laughed and turned around.

Darius leaned against the railing a couple of feet away. His loose pants and tank shirt were pearlescent gray this morning, but the robe was still the changeable blue. "I did not wish to startle you again."

"Thanks for the warning." She looked around, but no one on the sparsely populated ferry seemed to be paying attention to them. Darius's sudden appearance had passed unnoticed. Thank goodness she'd picked an isolated corner. "You can't keep appearing out of the blue, Darius. People will notice."

"Then I could not have brought you this." A cup appeared in his hand. Steam curled from it, carrying the scents of green tea and honey. He handed it to her. "You had only burned bread to break your fast," he said scornfully.

So, she hadn't snuck out at all; he'd seen her hasty gulping of toast. "Thanks." She took a grateful sip.

Grapes followed the cup. He plucked one from the bunch. "Eat," he said and held it to her mouth.

Isis bit into the sweet, juicy fruit. His fingers brushed her sensitive lips before letting go of the grape.

Definitely better than "burned bread."

He fed her another one, then took one for himself. "Now, today—"

"I'm a working girl, Darius." Success didn't come to those who sat around waiting.

His lips tightened, but before he could say anything, a pulsing orb of pale yellow light appeared above his head. Isis's eyes widened as it chimed, low but insistent. Darius scowled, annoyance stamped across his face. He held up his hands, and the orb drifted down until it rested in the cup of his palms.

He spat out a single word. The orb responded with a mechanical-sounding voice, although Isis couldn't understand a word it said. It didn't even sound like a recognizable language.

Darius listened in silence. When the voice died, he closed his hands on the orb and it disappeared, just as the ferry jerked onto its mooring. When he opened his hands, a faint, satisfied smile crossed his face, and then he turned to her. "I must leave. I shall see you this evening, before your aunt's party."

"Wait! You can't just—"

With a lift of his hands and a whirl of wind, he disappeared.

Isis looked around, but fortunately the other passengers seemed more intent on disembarking than on a disappearing djinni.

Darius and she definitely needed to come to an understanding about that disappearing. Ben wanted something and he wouldn't hesitate to pounce on any perceived weakness. Jimmy Ray was sniffing about, and if he discovered she was experimenting with magic, her reputation, and the reputation of Dream Scents, wouldn't withstand the drubbing he'd give her in print.

She would just have to be very careful. This time, she'd do things right.

While Isis selected candles and aromalamps for tonight's party from the Dream Scents collection, an attractive woman, vaguely familiar, with curly brown hair and the rounded stomach of early pregnancy, came in. "Isis Montgomery?" she asked.

Isis nodded. "How can I help you?"

The woman smiled. "I think maybe I can help you." She held out her hand. "Zoe James. We met a few years ago, when you thought about hiring my company, ZEVA, before your, ah—"

"Before my arrest and fall from grace?" Isis forced a smile and shook Zoe's hand. Once, she'd hoped to use ZEVA to promote her aromatherapy business, but Ben's thievery had stopped that. "Yes, I remember. I might need ZEVA's services in the future, but right now—"

"That's not why I came." Zoe looked around the busy shop, then leaned forward. "Darius," she whispered conspiratorially, "is a djinni."

Isis's knees buckled, and she grasped the counter in astonishment. "How—?" She bit off the question. "Come in my office. Salem, can you handle things?"

At Salem's nod, Isis ushered Zoe James into her office and carefully closed the door. Zoe settled herself into a chair.

"How do you know about Darius?" Isis asked, leaning against the door. "What do you know about him?"

"That he's a djinni, and the most arrogant male you'll ever meet. But he has a beautiful voice."

"He smells good, too," blurted out Isis.

Zoe laughed. "Trust a perfumer to notice that."

Isis sank into her chair, unable to believe her ears. How much did this woman know? What did she want?

"Why are you telling me this? How do you know?"

"How do I know?" Zoe let out a breath. "Darius is my husband's best friend."

"He's—?"

Zoe nodded. "Simon is also djinn." She leaned forward. "And you won't tell a soul that fact. I will not have him hounded by crackpots or those who would exploit his powers."

"I won't," promised Isis, struck by this woman's fierce devotion and love. "I don't want anyone to know about Darius, either."

"I didn't think you would," Zoe murmured, relaxing back in the chair. "I must admit I wondered when Darius said he was staying with you. Djinn can't live on earth, you know, not permanently."

"No, I didn't. Your husband lives here, doesn't he?"

"Simon is an exception. There were . . . extenuating circumstances. Other djinn must return to Kaf every few days to revitalize. Darius is worse than most." Zoe grinned at her. "We can never get him to stay more than a couple of hours. What's your secret?"

"It's complicated," Isis said.

Zoe nodded in understanding. "It usually is with djinn. I came because I thought you might like someone to talk to. I have good friends who know; I thought maybe you could use one, too. We women—we humans—need to stick together. Besides, I was curious."

"About what?"

"About the human woman who has captured Darius's attention. That's quite a feat, you know. He's like quicksilver—beautiful, shiny, but impossible to hold."

Isis sank back. "Tornado and lightning in human form."

"Good description."

The ferry horn sounded in the distance, reminding Isis of his quicksilver appearance that morning. "Does he always just sort of pop in and pop out like that?"

Zoe laughed, a warm, pleasant sound. "Always. And generally at the most inconvenient time, too."

Isis fingered her turquoise tablet, unsure why she continued to wear it but compelled to do so nonetheless. "He's intriguing, but I'm not sure I trust him."

"Listen to your instincts; don't risk your emotions. Darius has always attracted women and is well versed in the ways of passion, but he knows little about gentler feelings."

The soft warning sent a shiver down Isis's spine. "What can you tell me about him?"

"Not a whole lot, to tell you the truth. Darius doesn't talk about himself much." Zoe thought a moment. "He's so damned beautiful, so charming, he can steal your breath and your heart and you don't even think to question. Even I wasn't immune to his appeal, and I was in love with Simon."

Isis's muscles grew fluid as Zoe's words recalled his charm, his kiss, his touches. She looked out the window. The spring heat baked through the pane of glass, and for a fleeting moment she blessed the fact that the AC had decided to work properly this morning. "I don't trust him, but I can't ignore him."

Zoe hesitated a moment, as if deciding whether to tell Isis something, then drew in a deep breath. "Simon once told me that he and Darius schooled together, until Darius was removed for intense, individual training. Apparently, Darius's instructor was a cold, emotionless man, strong in *ma-at* but weak in compassion."

"How sad," Isis whispered, aching with sympathy. Before her dyslexia was diagnosed, she'd had a teacher who'd been determined Isis wouldn't leave her class unable to add. Unfortunately, the woman's determination wasn't tempered with compassion, tolerance, or understanding for her pupil's unique needs. It had been the most miserable year of Isis's life.

"I would trust Darius with my life—he saved my husband's once—and he is a loyal friend," Zoe continued. "But he's distrustful of humans, with some cause. His parents were killed on Terra; an accident, no one's fault, and when my husband was bound—"

Zoe broke off abruptly, but Isis needed no help in filling in the blanks. She remembered Darius's horror at the ritual she'd attempted.

Zoe laid a friendly hand on Isis's arm. "Be careful, Isis."

"I will. Don't worry; growing up with four older brothers taught me a lot. I can handle one djinni."

"They can be tricky," Zoe smiled softly, "but there are rewards, too, and maybe you're what he needs. Just remember"—she laid a business card on the desk—"if you want to talk, you can reach me here. Otherwise, I'll just wish you good luck."

After Zoe left, Isis tapped the card on the desk a moment, then propped it against her lamp. She had a hunch she might need it in the future.

Zoe's story and warning only served to intrigue Isis, not scare her. Overbearing, haughty males were a challenge, one she'd met all her life. And that Darius attracted her in a very fundamental way could not be denied. Yet, briefly, she'd glimpsed the man behind the arrogant exterior, and that gave him a depth that was damn near irresistible.

She would have to be very careful that it went no further. He was djinn; she was human. There could be nothing more.

Darius took care of the problem reported by the message spell in record time, a simple matter of a djinni using *ma-at* for gain at the expense of another's well-being, a misuse of the talent. The miscreant was punished with a sentence of five days' labor without the benefit of *ma-at*.

While one corner of his brain pronounced sentence, the other contemplated how he could get more time with Isis, an irritating problem that stayed with Darius all day. How was he to woo her if she was too busy for his seduction?

He still hadn't come up with an acceptable solution when he transported back to Isis. The shop was closed, and she was alone. This time he sent the aromas of cedar and sandalwood on the whirlwind as a warning of his presence.

She spun around, and he materialized.

"Are you ready?" he asked.

"We're supposed to meet Aunt Tildy in twenty

minutes, and I have to change for her party there."
She tilted her head. "Maybe you could just zap us
over to her?"

"Zap?"

"That thing you do, moving from place to place."

"Transport?" He shook his head. "I can only go to
a place if I hold its image here," he pointed to his
temple, "or have been given image and direction.
And I can transport to the side of certain people."

Isis wrinkled her nose. "That's the way you find
me, I suppose. Part of that 'we are bound' bit. Well,
it wasn't a good idea anyway." She tapped a scarlet-
tipped nail against her hip. "You will show her your
ma-at?"

"I made a bargain, Isis," Darius said quietly. "I take
promises very seriously. Your aunt will experience
my *ma-at* in the time and manner of your choosing.
On this you can trust me."

"I don't, you know. Trust you or your magic."

"Why?" The question was as soft as the wind.

Isis looked away. "Once, I trusted a man who
claimed to know magic, and he took everything from
me. I learned then how unreliable magic, and the
people who claim its power, can be."

"In time you will trust me," he said, ignoring the
hollow ache inside that told him she was wise not to
trust.

Her eyes searched his face for a moment. "After
you show Aunt Tildy the magic, would you like to
come to the party with me?"

She had made a small step nearer to him, both in
body and in trust. Wise or not, satisfaction and a
sense of rightness filled him. "I would," he answered,
then lifted her hand to bestow a faint kiss on it.

Her hand rested easily in his, as though she had
accepted his touch as natural. A small spurt of ela-
tion ran through him. She was sweetening toward
him. Soon Isis would be his *zaniya.*

107

"That has got to be one of my more harebrained ideas," she muttered, pulling away from his light grasp and running her hand through her hair. "Just behave yourself, okay? No transporting, no magic, no genie stuff."

"I shall be as discreet as a houbara in a sandstorm."

Isis stared at him, then swore. "Damn, I'm in trouble."

So much for sweetening.

Chapter Eight

Aunt Tildy's house needed a coat of paint, Isis noticed when she pulled the car up to the curb in front of her aunt's Uptown shotgun. Guilt stabbed her. Aunt Tildy had helped give her a second chance with Dream Scents, co-signing a loan and supplying her with additional funds. *I'm going to repay every penny.*

What if she used one of her bargains with Darius for money? Enough that she could repay Aunt Tildy five times over and never have to worry about Dream Scents going bankrupt.

Enough that the IRS would have her locked in a cell for the rest of her days.

Besides, that bargain wasn't what she wanted. Wishing for money wouldn't prove she was capable of making Dream Scents a success. If anything, it would prove just the opposite, that she couldn't accomplish anything on her own. It would be giving up, and if she did that, she might just as well go back to the life her father wanted for her: hostess for his social events, charity work for the approved causes, marriage to a suitable man.

Her success with Dream Scents must be hers, and hers alone.

Aunt Tildy—dressed in her best dress of lavender chiffon and wearing pearls and perfume—opened the door at the first knock. "Isis! Come in." She opened the door wider, and her smile of welcome shifted to amazement when she caught sight of Darius. "My dear, introduce me to your young man."

"This is Darius, Aunt Tildy. He's your birthday present." Isis followed her aunt inside, with Darius right behind her.

Aunt Tildy stopped short, then eyed Darius with decidedly more interest, while he smiled back with warm attention. He did not, to Isis's relief, seem to take offense at her aunt's open admiration.

A man who looked like him, she supposed, was used to it.

Isis didn't like the clutch of almost jealousy that squeezed her heart into skipping a beat. His lovers—past, present, or future—meant nothing to her.

"Birthday present?" Aunt Tildy gave her a mischievous look. "That's very thoughtful of you, dear, but I think I'm too old to handle the likes of him."

Darius laughed, and the deep sound filled the corners of the small house. He picked up Aunt Tildy's hand, wrinkled with the first vestiges of age despite her faithful use of creams and gloves, and kissed the back of it. "I think, madame, you could handle anything you chose."

"I like your young man, Isis." Aunt Tildy led them to the tiny garden in back, where they settled into floral-cushioned wrought-iron chairs. A fountain burbled in the center. With water and the shade of the enormous, overgrown greenery, the garden remained cool even on the hottest days of summer.

"He's not my man. He's your present, or rather his magic—"

"*Ma-at,*" corrected Darius.

"—*ma-at* is." Isis took a deep breath. "Darius is a genie—djinni—Aunt Tildy, and I summoned him. Magic does exist, just like you always told me. He is the proof."

Aunt Tildy rested a hand over her heart. "Oh, dear, Isis."

She's thrilled. I can tell.

"I thought I'd trained you better than that. How could you be fooled again?" Tildy turned on Darius, her expression fierce. "How dare you take advantage of her like this?"

Isis gaped at her aunt. Aunt Tildy didn't believe her!

What else should she have expected from a professional debunker?

Darius crossed his arms. "Her words are true. What proof do you require?" Before her eyes, he seemed to grow bigger, and a faint glow surrounded him.

"How about a cup of hot Earl Gray tea and a bowl of sliced bananas?"

"Very well." Darius picked up a loose rock from the garden. "Transformation is easier than creation," he said, then added with a smile, "and perhaps more telling for the skeptic."

As he cupped the rock, it slowly changed, becoming first soft, then molten, although Darius held it in his hand without difficulty. He spread his hands, dividing the mass between his two palms. The colors shifted and swirled from gray and brown to white, pink, and green. Darius never took his gaze from Tildy, as though he pulled the image of what to form from her mind.

The liquid reformed, becoming delicate china with a rose pattern. In his left hand a cup, in his right a bowl. As the insides solidified the left filled with hot tea, the right with white, even slices of banana.

Isis watched in awe.

Darius leaned forward and placed cup and bowl on the table beside Tildy. "Drink," he said, his voice breathless, as though he'd just run a race. Aunt Tildy took a sip, while Isis nabbed one of the bananas. It was sweet and just the right firmness. It was, in fact, the best banana she'd ever eaten.

Aunt Tildy watched him warily and closely. "It's good," she said, "but it's no secret that's my favorite afternoon snack."

"Have you ever seen a fire painting?" Darius rubbed his hands together in a circular motion, and this time his unswerving gaze fell upon Isis. Blue and red and yellow exploded from his hands, crackling and dancing like a sheet of flame. The colors swirled, forming the picture of a desert land filled with undulating sand, cool green oases, and stark blue mountains—a place of uncompromising beauty.

He was painting, Isis realized, painting the air with fire. It shimmered with heat. Was this his Kaf?

Her breath caught in her throat. Flames seemed to lick across her nerves and rise to her cheeks. She touched the turquoise amulet he'd given her, and the picture expanded until it enveloped her.

She was in a courtyard, where a deep pool invited her to swim and chiming vines called her to dance. Beautiful, rich scents of cedar and myrtle and sandalwood filled her. Under the hot sun above, she grew languid and weak. An overwhelming urge to stay and never leave whispered across her senses.

She struggled against it, looking around for a handle to normality. Her breath came in short pants. At the edges of the courtyard, she could still see Aunt Tildy and the garden. Her aunt gazed wide-eyed at the sight before her. Closer was Darius. Sweat formed upon his forehead and the tendons in his neck stood out slightly, as though he fought an internal fight. Or fought her struggle. It got hotter, and Isis labored for breath.

"Hypnosis," snorted Tildy.

Her aunt's skepticism sliced through the image, and it exploded with a sharp bang. Tiny dots of color swarmed around the garden in a riotous rainbow. Isis shot to her feet. She had to get out of here.

"I'd better change for the party," she gasped, saying the first thing that came to mind.

"Do not go!" Darius grabbed her hand.

His fingers trembled, very faintly, and a muscle twitched in his cheek, giving her the impression he had worked to capacity. Was he not as strong as she had first guessed?

Isis's heart skipped a beat. She sympathized with those who struggled beyond expectations. After all, she herself had been labeled *not too bright* at one time because of her dyslexia. Maybe Darius also struggled; maybe the mentor was a special tutor, like she'd needed. The thought that perhaps he was a rather minor djinni was comforting, made him and his magic more approachable.

Fear left her, and she stayed.

Darius sat motionless, arm outstretched, holding her hand. Gradually, the colors slowed and drifted to the brick, then winked out. Letting go of her hand, he turned to Aunt Tildy.

"As final proof of *ma-at*, I grant you one wish. Whatever you ask, but ask now, so there can be no thought that I prepared ahead. Three limits: I cannot bring the dead to life, nor can I foretell the future or travel in time. One warning: The powers are best used for personal choices. Changes forced upon natural rhythms or the nature of man often have unwanted results."

"No other conditions? No special setup? No atmosphere needed? No hedging?"

"None."

Tildy tilted her head to eye him. "I'm almost starting to believe you."

"Then ask your wish."

"I've never told anyone this before, but I've always wanted to visit the Incan ruins of Machu Picchu. Can you take me?"

"Not if he hasn't been there before," interjected Isis.

Skepticism returned to Tildy's face. "Hedging, Darius?"

Darius shook his head. "As a matter of fact, I have been there. When I was very young, my mentor took me there." A shadow passed across his face, and for a moment Isis wondered just how unhappy his memories of the place, and the mentor, were. "I still remember how to get there." Darius looked at Isis. "We will be a short time. I shall get your aunt to the party. You may change and go ahead of us." He held out his hand to Aunt Tildy. "Shall we go?"

"Let me get my hat and gloves."

As they disappeared on a whirlwind, Isis called, "Be sure and wear a suit to the party, Darius."

"You're late, Isis. Did you get lost?" The unspoken *as usual* hung between Isis and her father, Royal Montgomery, despite his quick hug when she arrived at his house.

"No, I didn't get lost."

"There was one time—"

"One time, Dad." Her sense of direction, of right and left, was poor, part of her dyslexia. One time, because of construction on I-10, she'd been forced to take an unfamiliar route to her father's Old Metairie home, and she'd ended up on the Causeway, a twenty-six-mile bridge across Lake Pontchartrain with no place to turn around. "One time, and you've never let me forget it."

"I worry about you, Isis."

That was the problem. It would be much easier if they didn't love each other. Part of his uncompromising attitude was because he loved her, worried about her, yet never trusted her to meet the expectations he had for the rest of the family. Part of it was because he simply held very old-fashioned ideas about women. Part of it was because she had failed miserably the first time with her aromatherapy, getting involved with magic, believing Fontenot's claims. And there was that little brush with the law afterward.

He just didn't believe she'd learned. Thinking of Darius, Isis wondered if he was right.

"I'm late because I was swamped with work, and I went by Aunt Tildy's first."

"Where is Tildy?" Royal looked around.

"She had . . . an errand to run. She'll be along soon."

Isis declined to mention exactly what Tildy, and Darius, were doing. Her practical father hadn't built his construction business into one of the biggest in New Orleans by believing in magic. If he found out she'd done a magical ritual again, she'd lose any chance of gaining his confidence in her abilities.

"I only agreed to host this party for your aunt if you were here to supervise the caterers, the way your mother always did."

Isis stashed her purse in the hall closet, feeling the acid in her stomach churn. If she wanted to prove herself capable, this was not a good start.

Quickly, Isis conferred with the caterers about the food and setup; then, assured things were well in hand, she toured through the rooms where the party would be held. The scented candles she'd brought needed to be lit and the potpourri in the washrooms refreshed, but otherwise everything seemed in order. She paused before the massive cabinet at the end of one room, like someone unable to stop prodding a sore tooth.

The cabinet was filled with athletic trophies, academic medals, commendations, and awards. All in the names of her brothers. She'd never won an athletic event—too klutzy—or a spelling bee. She hadn't made honor roll or gone to college. She had nothing to add to the collection. Once, Isis remembered, she'd set a picture she'd drawn amid the gold of the plaques. Her father had taken it down, saying that wasn't the place for it.

The ache in her stomach had faded and her secret tears had dried, but the hollow sensation inside rose as easily now as it had then.

No trophies, just Dream Scents and the elusive memory of an irresistible perfume, a legacy from the women of her family.

"Wine, Isis?" Her father held up the bottle from the bar setup. Isis shook her head.

"Hey, Ice!" Her oldest brother, Thomas, strode into the room. In some ways, Thomas reminded her of a tank—solid, dependable, and unswerving. "Glad to see you're here already. How's business?"

Deliberately, Isis turned her back on the case. "Fine, Thomas."

Her brother gave her a crushing hug, his arms and chest strengthened by years at construction sites, and then straightened his mussed tie.

"Heard you got a contract to do repairs on the bridge," she said. "That's quite a plum to land."

Thomas nodded. "It's going to require a lot of night work, when traffic's low, but we'll pull it off."

"I'm sure you will."

Beau and Jack, the twins, followed Thomas in, their blond hair gleaming in the candlelight.

"Evenin', Ice."

"How's things going?"

"Fine." She gave them each a peck on the cheek.

116

"Don't you two look fashionable tonight."

They were dressed in chalk-striped suits, identical except for two details. Jack wore a blue-striped tie, while Beau had chosen red, and Jack had a faint, rakish scar that ran down his forehead and into his brow. For some reason—a twin thing, perhaps—Beau and Jack often ended up dressing like the identical twins they were, a fact that annoyed them both. However, unlike what any sensible woman would do, they never bothered to call each other first before dressing for a mutually attended event. They preferred to take their chances and scowl at each other when it didn't work.

"I haven't seen a paper in a couple of days," Isis said. "Did you win your case, Beau?"

"Of course. We nailed the bast—bum. He got life."

Her brother worked in the D.A.'s office, second in command. He was being groomed to take over when the current D.A. left office.

Of course, if his flaky sister was linked with magic again, it wouldn't help his campaign.

"Is business good, Ice?" Beau neatened his tie and tugged his shirt cuffs to a precise half inch below the sleeve hems. "One of the partners in my firm is ready to pay top dollar for that site. It's too off the beaten path for a business, but it would be great for a house."

"I'm not going to sell."

"I'll handle the paperwork for you. No fee."

"I'm not going to sell. And if I were, I can afford to hire a lawyer, Beau. I don't need pro bono work."

"I've never understood the allure of aromatherapy," Jack, ever practical and blunt, said. "I mean, it's just scent."

"If you'd set foot in the door since my grand opening, you might know the answer."

Her brother had the grace to flush. "There's no scientific basis for it. I'm just afraid it's going to be a flash in the pan, a fad, and that you'll lose everything." He patted her shoulder. "I worry about you, Ice."

Of all her brothers, Jack understood her the least, and vice versa. With an M.D. and Ph.D. in biomedical engineering, Jack looked at things as a series of facts and equations and materials to be understood and manipulated. She worked on instinct and intuition. They didn't fight; they just didn't speak the same language.

"Think about Beau's suggestion," said Royal. "Your shop isn't in a safe location. A woman was raped not a block over last week. And break-ins all around you."

"I'm not going to sell," Isis repeated tightly.

Beau strolled over to the bar setup and poured himself a splash of Scotch. "You really should, you know. Opportunities like this don't come along too often. Besides, you'll be getting married one of these days, and your husband'll take care of you."

"Philip Beauregard Montgomery, what a chauvinistic thing to say. I'm surprised they've let you into the twentieth century."

"Hello, all." Ram came into the room, his suit coat draped over his arm. Only for Aunt Tildy would Ram don a suit. He came over and kissed her cheek. "I'm glad you braved the den," he whispered. "Dad is, too, though he won't say it." Then, in a louder voice, "Isis is getting married?"

"No, I'm not getting married! Besides, why should I be the first one married? You're all older."

"You're a woman."

"Geez, Jack, you're as bad as Beau."

Her brother shrugged, unrepentant. "Just telling you my experience of women. They want to be married."

"You've been with the wrong women," Ram answered.

"I still think you should sell," repeated Thomas. "The building is your best asset."

"My sweet Isis has many assets."

As one, the Montgomery men turned, looking first at Isis and then at the owner of the deep, melodious voice that came from the doorway.

Darius lounged against the doorjamb, next to Aunt Tildy, who, Isis noticed, was beaming, despite mud on one shoe and a tilt to her hat. She held a bird-of-paradise bloom, the biggest Isis had ever seen.

"Who the hell are you?" asked Ram bluntly.

Darius didn't bother to answer. He strolled into the room and headed directly for Isis.

Isis pressed a hand against the bridge of her nose. She'd told him to wear a suit. She should have been a bit more specific.

He'd given the masculine uniform a unique interpretation. Long, loose, gathered pants in a pearly gray, a poet shirt of glistening eggplant purple, and the ever-changing robe—at least he'd shortened it to suit-coat length—flowed about him. His version of a tie was a turquoise pendant on a black silk cord. And he'd kept the sandals he'd chosen when she insisted on footwear. Surrounded by suits and ties, he was totally out of place.

He was also infinitely compelling. Self-assurance and command radiated from him. In this room filled with masculine power and strength, he demanded his place at the top of the order. Even in a room of hundreds, Darius would stand out. And not just because he refused to wear a normal suit.

When he reached her side, he kissed her hand. There was nothing overly sexual about the gesture, yet it felt as if he had stamped her with a male heat that brought a flush to her cheeks.

He lifted his head and stared into her eyes.

Do not worry, my sweet Isis. They will grow used to me, slowly.

119

Isis's jaw dropped open. Had he just spoken to her without words?

She swallowed hard. "Are you telepathic?" she breathed.

He lifted a hand, his thumb and forefinger about an inch apart, an easily recognized symbol.

The heat that had begun to fade rushed back with a vengeance. How many of her thoughts—? Had he caught the one about lying naked on a beach? Oh, damn!

Your face speaks your thoughts, sweet Isis. I can only speak to you, not hear you.

That was a relief! Sort of.

"Who are you?" Royal repeated Ram's question.

Darius turned from her and gazed evenly back at the five sets of masculine eyes glaring at him. "You must be Isis's brothers and her father. I have seen the images she keeps on her desk."

Isis found her voice. "This is my friend, Darius."

"A close friend," added Darius.

She wished he'd stop trying to help.

"Friend?" repeated Beau.

"How close?" asked Jack.

Ram stepped closer. "Isis hasn't mentioned you before."

"I haven't seen you in town," added Thomas.

"I am newly arrived," explained Darius.

"Let me handle this," hissed Isis to her infuriating djinni.

"From the East," added Aunt Tildy. "Morocco."

Royal gripped the lapels of his suit. "What do you do?"

"Do?" asked Darius, puzzled.

"Do you have a job?" asked Ram.

"Of course he has a job," answered Isis, although she doubted her own words. Djinn didn't work, did they?

"On Terra?" asked Darius. "No. No job."

Thomas gave a snort of disapproval, his gaze skimming across Darius. "Not another one of your strays, Ice?"

Darius's eyes narrowed, and she could see the beginning of angry sparks about his head.

"Not a stray," cut in Isis quickly. "Darius is very good at what he does."

"And what is it Ice thinks you're so good at?" Beau asked with deceptive quiet, twirling the Scotch in his glass.

Isis thought desperately. "He's a model."

Darius ignored her. "I am a djinni. Protector of the *Ma-at*. Or magic, as you call it."

"*A genie!*" This from her four brothers; her father merely turned to stone!

"*Magic!* Ice, are you nuts?" Ram turned to his sister. "Didn't you learn anything with Fontenot three years ago?"

"God, not again," said Beau.

"You really screwed things this time." Jack.

"Isis, how could you?" Thomas.

"This is intolerable, Isis Elizabeth." Liquid nitrogen held more warmth than her father's voice.

The front doorbell rang.

"Party's starting," chimed Aunt Tildy. "This is going to be fun."

Isis threw one glance at her family, then hastened to the door. This was going to be a disaster.

Chapter Nine

"Machu Picchu was wonderful, Isis," Aunt Tildy said, waving the bird of paradise flower.

With the demands of hostess, Isis had not had a chance to talk to her aunt earlier. Now, with the party in full swing, the caterers keeping the food replenished, and the aromalamps keeping everyone mellow, she took a second to relax and ask about the unusual trip. "Did you see the ruins?"

"Oh, yes. It was evening, and we had the ruins to ourselves. It was such fun. Darius showed me so many things and told me about Incan beliefs and customs, knowledge I know isn't found in any of the books."

"How did he know so much about it?"

"He was there, when the Incans lived."

Isis, just taking a sip of her champagne, choked. "Aunt Tildy, that was how many years ago?"

"Five hundred. Of course, he was quite young at the time, I gathered, and was taken there by a new mentor." Tildy frowned. "Some of the Incan rites were . . . not genteel. Not at all the thing for an impressionable child."

Isis glanced at Darius. He was surrounded by a knot of women, as he had been the entire evening. "He certainly is spry for being over five hundred years old."

"Oh, djinn age differently than we do," Tildy announced with an airy wave, the bird of paradise bloom dancing in the air, "and time passes differently on their world."

"You're an expert on djinn, now?" Isis asked with a laugh.

"We didn't just talk about ruins," Aunt Tildy answered with a prim sniff. "You know, dear, Darius only had to take me there and back to prove his *ma-at*, but he didn't."

"I know," agreed Isis, grateful for the kindness he had shown Tildy.

"Oh, there's someone I must speak to. Excuse me." Aunt Tildy patted Isis's hand, then, chiffon rustling, bustled away.

Unable to help herself, Isis cast another covert glance toward Darius and the women. He listened mostly and gifted them with that slow, killer smile. Although the women flirted outrageously, challenged by his faint aloofness, so far, he didn't seem inclined to accept any of the offers. His restraint shouldn't have pleased her so, but it did.

At least he wasn't flitting about or using his *ma-at*.

While she watched, he reached toward the nearby dessert table and a chocolate mint flew into his hand.

Oh, damn. A drop of champagne spilled from her glass. Isis set the crystal flute down on a nearby table and put a hand to her chest, an ineffectual gesture to stop her suddenly racing heart. Had anyone seen what he'd done? Apparently not. Perhaps because his hand had been close to the sweets, and the women around him seemed more focused on his face and mouth.

Isis took a resolute step toward Darius, but a firm hand on her arm stopped her.

"Long time no see, Ice."

Her stomach churning at the sound of the cultured voice, Isis tried to break free of the man's grip, but he held her fast. Unwilling to make a scene, Isis turned and glared at Benedict Fontenot.

"Let me go, Ben," she hissed. "How did you get in here?"

"No kiss for old times' sake?"

"I'd rather kiss a swamp rodent." She shook off his hand and started to turn away, noticing that Darius had moved away from the women and was examining the stereo system.

"Jimmy Ray Frank came to see me," Ben said casually. "I didn't tell him anything, but I can always call him back."

Wanting to leave but knowing she had to find out what he was up to, Isis picked up her champagne flute. It was a flimsy barrier, but it gave her something to use to hide her shaking fingers. Feigning nonchalance, she rested one hip against the sofa. "You have nothing to tell him. Nothing that isn't stale news, anyway."

"Doesn't matter. I'm sure I can find something new to interest him."

Was he threatening to manufacture some dirt? "What are you saying? Are you threatening me?"

"Threaten? Come, Ice, you're being irrational." Ben laid a hand on her bare arm, making her flesh tighten beneath his cool grip. "I just want us to be friends. I miss you, Ice." He ran his fingers down to her hand. "It was good between us."

Isis moved away from his touch. "Good for you, maybe, but not for me, Ben." As she spoke, the music stopped abruptly, and her words hung in the wake of dying conversations.

Fine time for Darius to find the volume knob.

Fascinated, Darius nabbed another of the rich sweets—chocolate, someone had called it, a tiny taste of bliss, he thought—and examined the source of the music for the party. A machine, not musicians. So, how did one get music that was pleasing to the ear? He turned one knob to the left. In the ensuing silence, surprised conversation died. Except for one voice, which reached him easily.

"Good for you, maybe, but not for me, Ben."

His Isis sounded annoyed.

He turned from the music device to search her out. The party was larger than he'd expected, filled with relatives and friends, yet he had no trouble picking her out of the crowd. Her red dress—short and lacy— claimed his senses more surely than a flame. Did she know red was the color for djinn celebration, the color they would wear when they joined? When he had first seen her in that dress, he'd envisioned it beneath his touch—the textured lace, the silk beneath it, and her smooth skin under that—and he'd wanted to savor all.

Even had she been dressed in a robe of mud drab, however, he would have found her. Male djinn became acutely aware of their chosen mates—subtle nuances of expression and emotion, the identifying scents of their femininity.

To his surprise, Darius found himself increasingly territorial when he thought of Isis. It mattered not that he was frustrated at being trapped into this joining by the divination, nor that she was human. Primitive instincts did not recognize mitigating circumstances.

Right now, that djinn brand of possessiveness was directed to this "Ben," the dark-haired man standing beside Isis. Darius did not like the man in the least. Not the cool, superior smile, nor the glossy shoes, nor the way the man's hairline came to a point in the middle of his forehead. Darius especially did not like how close the man stood to Isis, who sat on the broad arm of a divan, one foot bracing her, while her other foot swung back and forth, a barrier between the man and herself.

The blackguard's fate was sealed when he placed a hand on Isis's arm. Such boldness was not to be tolerated.

Not bothering with the dials, Darius turned up the music and then walked the short distance to Isis's side. He draped an arm across her shoulders.

Ben stroked his small beard with one finger, while his thick brows lifted in challenge.

Darius gave him a smile no other male could mistake. The smile said, "Back off. She's mine."

"Stop sparking," Isis said, so low only he heard.

Ben saw the warning and must have thought better about continuing the confrontation, for he leaned back. "Somebody should have told your friend to dress for a formal occasion," he said with cool amusement.

Darius's eyes narrowed. He cared little what humans—Isis excepted—thought of him, but insults to the Protector he would not tolerate.

"I happen to like what he's wearing," Isis answered.

There was nothing wrong with his clothing, Darius knew. He was more comfortable than any fool man in the room. Before he could respond, though, Ram and Thomas closed in on the trio. Their gazes went first to Darius's arm around their sister, bringing matching frowns, and then to Ben. Frowns turned to outright distaste.

"Ram, Thomas, no need for the cavalry." Darius heard the warning note in Isis's voice.

"Hello Ramses, Thomas," Ben greeted them.

"Fontenot," said Ram, ignoring the man's out-stretched hand. "Who invited you?"

Ben pointed to a woman across the room. "One of Tildy's grateful clients."

"You've overstayed your welcome," Thomas said.

"But Ice and I haven't finished discussing business." Ben slicked a hand down and up Isis's arm. "She was an excellent pupil, in many things. I thought it time to resume our . . . studies together. She would find it rewarding."

The slimy insinuation was obvious. And insufferable.

"You're delusional if you think I'd trust you again," Isis said.

Suddenly the name, the currents of unexpressed emotion, the few comments Tildy had made while they were in Macchu Pichu made a picture as clear as a fire painting for Darius.

Ben Fontenot was the man who had wronged Isis three years prior, who had made her so wary of magic, and thus of him.

Ben Fontenot had a lot to answer for.

Darius scratched his chin, contemplating a fitting retribution. Nothing so childish as turning the doomed man's clothes to stinging ants or hanging a visible cloud of gloom above him.

Keeping an eye on Ben, Darius gave Isis a tiny kiss behind the ear. The silky ends of her hair tickled his cheek, and for an infinitesimal moment he nestled against her softness; then, with the barest of voices for her ear alone, he chanted ancient words.

Ben dropped his hand from Isis's arm, as though she had become too hot for him to touch. He rubbed his fingers together. "Not even for Whispers?" he asked Isis.

Isis stilled. "Damn you, Ben," she said, so low Da-

127

rius barely heard her. His eyes narrowed, and his power filled the words he murmured.

"Come by my office and we'll talk about it." Ben clasped Isis on both shoulders. She shrugged, as if to shove him away, but Ben had already sprung back. Panting, gasping for breath, he rubbed his frost white hands together.

Thomas slapped him on the back. "Hey, man, are you choking? Do you need the Heimlich?"

Ben shook his head frantically, sticking his hands beneath his armpits.

Isis looked over her shoulder at Darius. "What are you doing?" she asked softly.

I do not tolerate insults to you, he told her.

"Stop it. This is not a good idea."

The power continued its easy flow despite Isis's protest. Apparently her displeasure only affected him when the *ma-at* was directed toward her person. Interesting and useful to know.

Like the change of clothing, the fire painting until Isis had refused it, and the trip to the now ruined site of the ancient fortress of the Incans with Tildy Maehara, he wielded the *ma-at* with deft finesse. It felt *so good*.

To you, she will be as the Ice you call her. Darius inserted the thought into Fontenot's mind. The fool looked around with wide-eyed terror. *Any part of you that touches her shall freeze, cold and brittle*. Fontenot flinched, as though gut-punched, and his pinkening hands fluttered protectively over his groin.

"Stop. Please," hissed Isis.

Abruptly, Darius stopped. His point had been made. Fontenot took an overdramatic deep gasp of air. He had been in no danger, Darius thought with scorn. His breathing had been unimpaired; only his tongue was rendered inoperable briefly from the cold.

While Thomas clapped the choking Fontenot on

the back, Beau, a woman on his arm, joined them.

"Isis, dear, I've been meaning to come by your little shop one day," the woman purred. "Hello Ben, Thomas, Ram." She held out her hand to Darius. "Monica LeBeau. I don't think I've seen you in town, and I'm sure I'd remember if I had."

Darius dropped his arm from around Isis's shoulder, leaned forward, and kissed the back of Monica's fingers. "The pleasure is mine."

Beside him, he felt Isis tense. "Monica, this is Darius. He's . . . a model, and a friend."

She had claimed that earlier, that he was a model, and though Darius had no idea what she meant, he decided, for the time, to allow the fiction. He was enjoying too much the faint scent of jasmine carried by Isis's warmth and the sight of the gently swaying delicate bones in her foot to gainsay her.

Monica lifted one thin brow. "Just Darius?"

"Just Darius," he answered.

A cat smile tilted Monica's lips. "I've always liked men with continental manners. Where are you from, Darius?"

Isis tensed again, and her brothers' wary gazes turned to him. Even without telepathy, he could hear the question—would he claim to be djinn?

"I'm newly arrived. From Morocco." The collective Montgomery sigh of relief was almost audible.

"Then you'll need someone to show you the sights of New Orleans."

In many ways, Monica reminded him of the djinni seductress, Leila. Oh, she was blond and blue-eyed, where Leila was dark, but he recognized the look well. Polished, perfumed, and predatory. Two days ago she might have attracted him. Two days ago he might have considered accepting the invitation radiating from her.

Two days ago he had not met Isis and made the choice that he would follow the divination and that she would be his *zaniya*. Now, Monica's practiced charms paled beside Isis's freshness, directness, and energy. He stayed planted firmly beside his *zaniya*-to-be.

"Isis has already promised me that," Darius said smoothly, capturing Isis's hand and settling it in the crook of his arm.

"Pity." Monica turned to Isis. "Dreams Scents is generating some positive spin as an up-and-coming place to shop."

"If she's given up the magic," said Fontenot.

"Have you?" Monica lifted arched brows.

Isis's hand tightened around Darius's arm. "Walking the straight and narrow these days, that's me. Aromatherapy and perfumes, but no magic."

Monica cast a malicious glance between Ben and Isis. "I never thought to see you two in the same room again."

"Oh, I don't know," Ben said smoothly, "Ice and I may be mending some old fences. Now, Monica, suppose you let me freshen your drink." Before Isis could answer, he led Monica to the bar, pausing just once to call over his shoulder, "Word of friendly advice, Darius. Whatever Isis promises, get it in writing."

Beside him, Isis swore and took a deep slug of champagne. She took another swallow, and then heaved a big sigh. "After three years, I finally saw Ben Fontenot again and I didn't rip his eyes out. That was an accomplishment. I can't say it was a pleasure, but at least it's over."

"I can't believe he had the gall to come here, after what he did to you, Ice," said Ram.

"Gall was never something Ben lacked," she replied.

Puzzled, Darius asked, "What did he mean, 'get it in writing'?"

There was a moment of utter silence; then Isis

said, "Ben won the rights to all my formulas by show-ing the judge my notes."

"I don't understand."

"That judicial idiot decided no one who wrote like me could have the brains to create those perfume formulas, so he awarded them all to the slime." Her voice was bitter, and she finished her champagne in one gulp.

"Dyslexics have trouble spelling," Thomas ex-plained, at Darius's continued perplexity.

Darius tilted his head to Isis. "What is dyslexics?"

"It's a learning disorder," Beau said after a mo-ment.

Isis's lips tightened. "I have trouble with sequenc-ing, left and right. Words and letters get turned in-side out, upside down." She lifted her chin. "Reading is a challenge, and when I write something, it's al-most unreadable, because I spell terribly, write the wrong words, or make up new ones."

"Is that all?" Darius dismissed her problem with a wave of his hand.

"Is that all? Do you know how hard I had to work just to read required texts and squeak by in school?"

"Reading and writing are but one form of com-munication. Did your school not use other methods for you?"

"Eventually, but we're still a written-word society."

Darius shrugged. "That is a limitation in your so-ciety, not in you."

Isis stared at him for several moments, then let out a long breath, as if ridding herself of tension, and smiled. "Very few people recognize that fact." She turned and gave Beau a regretful look. "Sorry about Ben appropriating Monica."

Beau straightened the handkerchief in his pocket. "That's okay. She'll be back, and I've got a few more hands to shake tonight." He strode over to a nearby group of suited men.

"Would you like to see the gardens?" Isis asked Darius. "My father is noted for his azaleas."

"I would enjoy that." Now that he had completed his part of the bargain, he was anxious to have Isis complete her half, but a walk in a candlelit, fragrant garden with Isis was something he could not resist.

Thomas and Ram immediately fell into step on either side of them.

"I meant alone," she told her brothers with a smile.

"Been a while since I've seen Dad's azaleas," said Thomas.

"Because you're allergic."

"You know, Darius," began Ram in a conversational tone that did not fool Darius in the least, "I've been wondering exactly when you first thought you were a genie."

"And what you meant when you said sweet Isis had many assets," added Thomas.

Isis's hand tightened around his arm. "No third degrees, guys. We're at a party."

"Do you not think she is sweet?" asked Darius.

"Of course. We're her brothers," answered Thomas. "Doesn't mean we appreciate your saying so."

As they talked, they left through the double sliding doors and came onto a stone porch. Three steps down was the garden. Burning torches in metal cages were set at intervals throughout, creating a mix of warm light and mysterious shadow. In the humid night, the flowers emitted a sensuous perfume, although it could not compare to the scent of jasmine-and-Isis in its power for sheer arousal.

Isis took a deep breath. "Oh, the lilacs and lemon blossom are fragrant tonight."

Her brothers were not deterred, if that had been her intention. "And we want to know a hell of a lot more about you than a claim to be a genie from Morocco."

"Ram! Leave it!" Isis sounded annoyed.

Darius stopped at the foot of the steps. As he wooed Isis, he did not want obstacles and objections thrown in the way by her protective family. Besides, he sympathized with their attitude, not that it would change his path. *I shall be good*, he promised.

"Why do I doubt that?" she muttered.

Ah, but I can be very good, and he sent her a wicked look. With a flush, she fell silent.

"Do you believe in *genies?*" Darius asked Ram and Thomas, with faint amusement.

Thomas snorted.

"Of course not," said Ram.

Darius shrugged one shoulder. "I must have been joking when I said that, no?"

Ram and Thomas looked doubtful but nodded slowly.

"Then you have your answer." He stepped away from them, Isis on his arm, onto the dew-damp grass.

"What *assets* were you referring to when you said Isis had many?" asked Ram, not being left behind.

Isis jabbed Ram with her finger. "Does it ever occur to you that some men look beyond busts?"

"You mean you do not know?" Ignoring Isis's comment, Darius was astonished at their blindness. "I find her fascinating, brilliant."

"Brilliant?" Thomas and Ram chorused.

"The formulas she creates in her shop are marvels." He ticked off the next points. "She works hard, is creative, and has beautiful hands." He looked at the three Montgomerys—Isis included. They gaped at him as if he'd hit them with a stun spell. He couldn't resist adding, "She also has very soft lips. Now, Isis and I must be leaving."

Isis shook her head. "I can't. I—"

"Our bargain," Darius reminded her, gently but firmly. "I have kept my part."

Isis's mouth snapped shut. "I need to make a few arrangements first."

She hurried off, but Thomas and Ram lingered at his side.

"You have some interesting notions about Isis," began Thomas.

Jack and Beau passed by the glittering windows and caught sight of them. In a moment, Darius found himself surrounded by a wall of male Montgomerys.

He leaned one shoulder against a rough-barked tree and crossed his arms, curious. What would they do—and ask—next?

"Just so you don't get too many notions," warned Ram. "She's been hurt badly before."

"Ben Fontenot? I would know what happened between them." The voice was low, but the Protector's command backed it, and even the Montgomerys were not immune when he reinforced it with a Truthspeak spell.

"Despite his misgivings, Dad staked her in the aromatherapy venture, using funds he would have spent on college for her," Thomas began after a momentary pause. "She'd have been a disaster in college."

Beau took up the story. "She got really crazy then, into strange chanting and crystals and claiming she could work magic."

Jack stuck his hands in his pockets and jiggled his coins. "When we were growing up, Aunt Tildy used to fill us with stories about magic. Isis was the only one who believed."

"Later, she said Fontenot encouraged her in it—he'd joined her in the aromatherapy business—but none of us ever saw it," Beau continued. "At least she was never stupid enough to get involved in the druggie scene, but she was naive enough to get intimate with Ben."

Darius grew cold at the thought. He leaned forward. "How intimate?"

Beau's face hardened. "She never told us the whole story."

"All we knew was that while Isis was dabbling in rituals, Fontenot was expanding the business," Jack said.

"Upshot was, after two years Fontenot dropped her flat, saying she and her magic rituals gave him the creeps," Ram said.

"That was bad enough," continued Thomas, "but shortly afterward, Fontenot started his own perfume business and it became wildly successful. Isis went ballistic, claiming he'd stolen and patented *her* formulas; that her aromatherapy was magic and the spell she'd cast over the scents should have stopped him from making any money from the theft."

"Made a big splash in the papers," added Beau. "Her business died overnight."

Darius leaned back against the tree and crossed his arms again. "And did you believe her?" he asked softly.

The four Montgomerys avoided his probing gaze.

"Isis had been interested in scents and aromatherapy for years, but she'd never marketed any perfumes," Ram said.

"She was pretty flaky in those days," Jack offered.

"There was no proof of any wrongdoing," said Beau. "In fact, it looked like Ben had done all the work on the business."

"The Fontenots have as much clout as we do in this town," Thomas added. "More, because their family's been here longer."

"And how could a woman who could barely read develop anything as special as a successful perfume?" said Darius, even softer, saying what he knew, now, must have been at the back of their actions. He could see it clearly. Brilliant Isis, wronged by a man she trusted. The magic she'd grown up with, but never truly understood or had the capability to use, failed her. Her family as judgmental as the rest. Disgusted, he stopped the questioning and the Truthspeak spell. "You should have known her better."

The Montgomerys blinked, as though awakening.

"We got the charges dropped when Fontenot had her arrested for breaking and entering!" said Beau. "She claimed she was just getting back what was hers."

Darius laughed. "Ah, my Isis is a determined one."

"Your Isis?" asked Thomas softly.

Jack eyed Darius with suspicion. "Why are you so interested in all this?"

Ram's fists tightened. "We may not have done all we could have back then—in hindsight, I'm willing to admit that—but that doesn't mean we'll allow her to make the same mistakes again."

Darius straightened. "Isis is a woman grown now, who has matured through fire and adversity. The choice is no longer yours to make for her."

"At last, a voice of reason." Isis's voice came from behind them. Darius turned with her brothers at the sound. Her red dress gleamed within a halo of white light cast from the room behind her. One foot tapped against the stone steps, while her scarlet nails brushed her hair behind her ears. "I'm no longer a child, boys."

"That's what we're worried about," said Ram dryly.

Isis laughed and strolled over to them. She gave each of her brothers a kiss. "I know, but wrong or not, they were my choices then, and they're still my choices to make. For once, guys, have a little confidence in me, okay?"

"Are we really that bad, Ice?" asked Ram, and Darius could hear the tenderness and concern in his voice.

"Sometimes," she admitted, then hooked her arm through Darius's. "Ready to go? To *walk* out?"

"Walk, we shall." Darius paused before leaving, addressing her brothers, who had watched over his Isis, though they had not understood her in the least. "Do not worry; she is safe in my care."

"Oh, heavens," groaned Isis. "Not you, too."

As they left, Darius glanced at the line of Montgomerys staring after him with suspicion. A trifle annoyed with their questions and doubts, he could not resist just one tiny spell. He sent flowers of jasmine twirling about them, like a flurry of soft, sweet snow, allowing the petals to drift to their feet only after he and Isis had made their escape.

Chapter Ten

Bowing to Isis's insistence that they not transport, Darius settled himself, with some difficulty, into the tiny box she called a car. Why she preferred this inconvenient and odorous means of transportation, he could not fathom. Fortunately they did not drive far before Isis found a place to abandon the vehicle. "Parking inside the Quarter's a pain," she told him. "We'll have to walk from here."

"Is it far? This place where you found the ritual?"

"A few blocks, but the store won't be open this late."

"It does not matter." Locks not made of *ma-at* posed little barrier to him.

They started down the narrow streets. Despite his eagerness, Darius shortened his steps so Isis could keep pace. While they walked, he looked around with curiosity. His time on Terra had been limited, but this New Orleans was interesting. He didn't care for some of the smells in the occasional odd nook, but

138

he appreciated the heat of the air. On Kaf, djinn homes were fluid, changing with the desires of the ones who resided there. Human homes were fixed, immutable, but these had odd angles, rough textures, and curling decorations that intrigued him.

Pulsing energies rose from Terra, flowing around him like the soft murmur of a stream. They were foreign, drawn from water and earth rather than air and fire, but no less powerful than those that anchored him to Kaf. While he stayed on Terra, her forces continually weakened his bonds to Kaf, until he needed to return home for revitalization. For the moment, though, the strangeness was tolerable, if uncomfortable.

How Simon had taken such alien forces as his source of strength and magic, Darius could barely understand. If *he* were to reside on Terra—Solomon be benevolent and prevent such a tragedy—he would have to strip himself of all *ma-at*, all connections with the powers of nature just to survive.

No, that would not be survival. It would be a living death.

There were a lot of people around them, too many for his taste, but with his *ma-at*—a *ma-at* that remained under the exquisite control he had once taken for granted—he kept the crowds from intruding too close. Using so much *ma-at* on Terra had him aching with fatigue, but the next time he transported he could go briefly to Kaf and revitalize. The important thing was that, despite the tiredness, today he was in control.

While they walked, Isis talked. "I don't know what you did to Ben," she said, "but you don't need to fight my battles."

"We are united, my sweet one. I do not fight for you, I fight with you."

"Fight with me? Yeah, we've had a few disagreements."

Darius scowled. She had mistaken his meaning. English was so devious at times, and he detested having to explain himself. "I meant that your fights are mine, now."

Isis paused in front of a narrow alley. "And are yours mine?"

The question startled him. He was the Protector; no one asked to fight his fights. In fact, only once in his life had someone intervened on his behalf. Harbad, his mentor and the previous Protector, had deflected a deadly, traitorous blow of *ma-at* aimed at Darius. Harbad had died as a result.

And are yours mine? The simple question curled itself around his heart. His *zaniya*-to-be kept surprising him.

A faint breeze ruffled the short ends of her hair, feathery as a fern. Jasmine, her sweet scent, wafted to him on the steamy night, bringing arousal with its touch. Darius pushed back a strand of hair that fell across her eyes, then traced a line along her high cheek and set jaw. There could be no possibility of her, a woman without the power of *ma-at*, standing against whoever had tried to bind him, of fighting his fights. The thought brought a shiver of fear he did not expect or like.

Yet the simple fact that she would ask, and would expect to make his fights hers, flowed inside him like the life-giving waters arising from the depths of Kaf. The ebb filled a hollow in his chest that had been with him so many, many years that he had forgotten its existence.

"It's not that hard a question," Isis said, reminding Darius that he stood and watched her. "Yes or no?"

Did she fight his fights? She was soft of skin and voice, but beneath was strength and determination. She would be offended if he said "No," would turn from the trust growing between them. As long as she wore his turquoise tablet, however, his strength would protect her.

The thought of her at his side was a sweet image, as irresistible as the honeyed flow of *ma-at*. He touched the blue stone nestled in the hollow of her neck. "While you wear this, you face my fights, too."

Temptation, always near, always drawing him to her, grew too strong to resist. Other than the Kiss of Promise to the cheek and hand, they had not kissed. Only the kisses of his fantasies had tasted her lips. His fingers slid up the black silken cord to her neck. Her pulse fluttered and raced beneath his fingertips. With his thumb, he tilted her head up.

"I would much rather make love to you than fight."

Her dark lashes swept down briefly, then she looked directly at him. "Kiss me, then." Her voice was husky with need, a need that matched the heat coursing through him. Darius grew hard with the wanting.

Slowly, with a patience as threatened as his control, Darius bent to her lips. They were soft, as he had imagined, and so willing. With the barest touch of his tongue, she opened to him and he took possession. Yet she took possession of him as well. The cool taste of her mouth did nothing to quench the fire ignited by the sweep of her tongue. He skimmed a hand across her hip. *Closer*, he urged, with his mind and with the faint press of his hand.

She obeyed, until she could not mistake the need he had for her. His touch roamed across the red lace and silk of her tiny dress, the thin fabric no barrier to the heat of her skin, while her fingers tunneled through the strands of his hair.

Normally, Darius first thought only of the woman's pleasure, his own needs always well under control. With Isis, however, those desires were as unruly as his *ma-at*, spreading throughout him with no containment or control. Her low moan of pleasure drew forth an answering growl from him. Evidence of djinni emotions sparkled and crackled around them.

Drawing back slightly from his mouth, she smiled against his lips. "You make me feel—Whoa, what's that?" Her voice held amazement, not fear.

Darius opened his eyes. Around them, sparks of red and pink and yellow shimmered and snapped.

"Djinn emotions," he explained with a small smile. "Sexual excitement."

"Oh—"

He rocked against her, and the pleasure of that small movement exploded around him in a shower of blue.

"Oh, my," she breathed, eyes wide.

On the other side of the street, a man staggered past them. At the sight of the sparks, he stopped and sloshed a plastic go cup to his lips. "Fireworks? Hot-diggity, Fourth of July." He stared, waiting for the show to continue.

"Go on about your business, old man," said Darius gently.

"The fireworks are over," added Isis.

"Over? Sh-eeee-t, I allas miss 'em." With one last regretful look, the man wove away.

"The fireworks are over?" Darius lifted Isis's hand and nipped at her fingers, setting off a sparkle of red. "I think not."

Isis chuckled. "I think we need a bit more privacy." She backed up, until she no longer stood on the street, but in the darkness of the narrow alley where they'd stopped. Darius followed her, preparing to transport them back to her house. Their first coupling would not be standing against an alley wall.

As soon as he stepped into the alley, however, an insidious sense of *wrongness* crept inside him. Darius froze. What was it he felt? Taking a deep breath to quell the parts of his body clamoring to touch Isis, to take her and make her his, he fought for the inner calm he needed to sort out the uneasy sensations creeping under his skin.

As Protector, he was highly sensitive to the energies of Kaf, which gave him power, and to the disquieting streams of Terra, which stole from him. There was *ma-at* here. Not Terran magic. Djinn *ma-at*. Twisted djinn *ma-at*.

"Is this where you got the ritual?" he asked, his voice pitched low.

Drawing away, Isis nodded. "At a shop down this alley. What is it? What's wrong?"

Darius just shook his head. "Show me."

Darkness shrouded the alley. Darius rested a hand at Isis's waist, ready to guide her should she not see as well as he, but her steps remained steady. He moved soundlessly; the only noises in the isolation were the faint click of Isis's heels on the hard bricks and the gentle flow of her breath. The enveloping humidity lessened, no match for the chill invading this place.

"This is it." In the silence, Isis's voice was an eerie, wavering sound.

Any doubts about whether someone was actually intent on his destruction evaporated the instant Darius read the sign outside the shop. Sights, sounds, heat, all receded.

Not Madame Paris. Madame *Pari*. Isis had read the words wrong and missed one small item—the apostrophe. The shop was Madame Pari's Curiosities, Dreams, and Magic. Because of that misread, and her slight mispronunciation of the name, he had not realized until now whom he dealt with.

Pari.

That explained so much.

Flashes of cold memory blinded him to his surroundings. Pari had trained with him, had endured with him the crushing demands of the previous Protector, his mentor, Harbad. Both of them knew they competed, ultimately, for the position of Protector, and Harbad had fostered that competition at every turn. The result would be either an unbreakable team or a bitter rivalry, and Pari had made it clear from the beginning that she alone would prevail.

Under the relentless tutoring, Darius had grown in his *ma-at*, until his mastery matched and heightened his innate power. Pari had grown strong, too, although not quite as strong as he, and that fact ate at her. She had not allowed herself other pleasures or diversions—like the release to be found in the pleasures of the flesh, of which he had availed himself. Most important, she had no friend—as he had had with Simon—to keep her sane.

She had made plans, plans for domination of the djinn, when she became Protector, and had tried to kill her rival, Darius. She had come very close, for she was nearly his equal even when he had full mastery. Only the intervention of Harbad had saved him from the unanticipated betrayal, and in the melee Harbad had been killed instead.

For her treachery, Pari had been banished from the company of djinn for the remainder of her days— a punishment second only to complete stripping of the powers of *ma-at*, for murder was an abominable crime. She had vowed to return and take her revenge.

Questions whirled inside him. Did Pari know of his weakness? He did not see how, for he had hidden it well. If she did, then why did she not move against him? Did she seek out Isis to prevent his restoration? Why had she not harmed Isis outright? Or did her *ma-at* also not work to harm Isis, as his did not? Maybe she had sought only to bind him, choosing Isis simply because of the prophecy, an ironic twist that he would lose his freedom—and his Protector status—to the one woman destined to be his *zaniya*.

144

Pari knew such a binding would be intolerable, unforgivable to him.

He tended to believe the latter. It would have appealed to her perverse nature; even among the flamboyant djinn, Pari was noted for grandiose gestures.

Like now? His focus sharpened and narrowed, until only the shop existed. He searched the exterior of the store, not only with eyes and ears, but with tendrils of *ma-at*, seeking diabolical traps.

He detected none, but traces of Pari's tainted work lingered. Why had Pari established the shop? To find Isis? To toy with the humans who came under her spell? Or had she had another, deeper purpose? He peered inside the grimy windows, fixing a spot to transport in his mind. He would go inside, look around, but doubted there would be much to find. Obviously Pari didn't care if he knew who had given Isis the ritual.

If only he knew where the treacherous djinni hid!

She must be waiting to move until she was confident of success. For if she lost a second time, the punishment would be permanent severing of her bonds to Kaf. She would be forever separated from her *ma-at*.

Darius shuddered, despite the heat. For a djinni, death would be preferable.

When would Pari begin her return? The answer came swiftly. She would return at Mingara, the festival of gardens, the anniversary of her banishment. One Terran month hence.

Darius looked at Isis. He had one month to woo her, win her, make her his. One month to restore his control.

What had caused Darius to go so utterly still? Isis wondered. Even the faint breeze did not disturb him.

She laid a hand on his arm. "Are you all right?"

He looked at her then. His dark eyes, normally bright with emotion—anger, humor, pleasure, desire—were a black abyss. The planes of his face were hard and cruel. The Darius she had first met, the Darius of wind and emotion, had not frightened her. Much. This one scared her down to her heart and soul. This one was the dangerous man of magic.

"Darius? Do you want to leave?"

"Wait here," he commanded and disappeared.

Dust eddied in his wake, then settled. Isis looked around, the silence and chill of the alley making her decidedly uneasy. She peered in the window and saw nothing at first; then Darius appeared and glided around the inside. She tapped at the window, but he ignored her.

Well, she'd kept her end of the bargain. There didn't seem to be any reason to hang around. She'd just turned to leave when he reappeared before her, preceded by a faint rainbow shimmer of warning. Isis halted.

"This shop has been enchanted," he said, his voice hollow, "though only faint traces remain."

"Enchanted? How?"

"It tugs at your deepest dreams, brings them to the front of your mind. Is that what happened to you, Isis?" He tilted her head to look at him.

The wisp of perfume she had smelled. Isis nodded, filled with the ghosts of dread.

"What was the price for this dream?"

"Two hundred dollars, half still owed."

"And?"

"A favor. To be determined later."

Darius closed his eyes, and a soft sigh escaped his lips. "Humans! You have no idea of the costs, the dangers, when you flirt with the forces of magic." His eyes opened, and their endless black held her captive. "A bargain made is a bargain that must be honored, regardless of cost, and you can be sure the price Pari extracts will be high." He touched her turquoise tablet. "Not even my power can protect you should you fail to keep your bargain."

"Pari?"

"A djinni. A devious, traitorous, dangerous female djinni, and the proprietress of this shop."

Isis looked at the sign. Damn, she'd misread it, not that it would have made any difference at the time.

She'd been an absolute idiot to make that bargain. Isis swallowed, trying to add moisture to her arid throat. Hadn't she learned not to trust magic and anything or anyone connected with it?

What would the favor be? Or what would the penalty be if she were unable to meet it? The questions skittered inside her. Pari had not looked like a kind woman. Isis crossed her arms, warming her suddenly icy hands. Regret was a wasteful emotion; she'd learned that long ago. When threatened, or faced with her own limitations, Isis never considered failure, but sometimes a strategic retreat was in order to regroup.

She scowled at Darius, unwilling to admit that maybe, just maybe, her hunger for success, her need for that perfume, could be dangerous.

Then another thought struck her, and she brightened. "Since I didn't bind you, does that void the bargain?"

"What exactly did you agree to?"

Isis tried to remember. What had she said? "That if I summoned a djinni, if one showed up, I'd owe her the money and the favor."

He spread his arms.

"I guess you showed up. But I don't command you," Isis pointed out.

"Only because I stopped you before you finished."

"Oh, yeah, right." And, now that she thought about it, his appearance was damned convenient, too. She glanced back at the sign. Isis wasn't good at logic, but she was good at intuition, and revelation smashed into her.

"It was a setup! She used me to get to you, didn't she?" She jerked from his grip and stomped down the alley, her heels tapping an angry beat. "Damn and double damn. When will I learn never to trust anyone with magic? I've had enough of these bargains. I'm going home."

Suddenly Darius loomed before her. He grabbed her hand in a grip that wasn't painful but was absolutely unyielding. "Good. That's where I'm going, too."

The alley disappeared, and Isis felt herself sucked into a whirling vortex of howling winds and searing heat.

Chapter Eleven

Before Isis had time to draw a breath, the blast of heat receded, without so much as singeing her, and the violent whirling steadied. She felt as if she was sliding down a long, slick tube, like the water slide at Blue Bayou, except this was made of air, not plastic. An instant later the whirling returned for a brief, disorienting moment, then all sensation stopped.

Isis blinked and looked around. They were back in her house, on the third floor, between her work area and his sleeping quarters. She pulled her hand free of Darius's and pressed the bridge of her nose against the dizziness.

"Whoa, what a disconcerting way to travel. Is it like that every time—"

"You will not turn your back on me."

Isis's head jerked up.

Sparks radiated from Darius in a dazzling display. His voice echoed, as though at the end of a long tube, while his fists rested on his hips, and he glared down at her. "And you cannot refuse the bargains before the appointed three."

Returning anger cleared away the final remnants of her dizziness. Isis glared right back. "I will turn any way I damn well please, and before I agree to any more of these bargains, I have a few questions."

Arms folded across his chest, Darius glowered at her. "Such as?"

"Have you been reading my mind?"

Why, of all the things she needed to know, did she start with that? Probably because she wanted to know how embarrassed she should be.

Darius gave an annoyed huff, but the sparks around him lessened. "I told you I could not. Djinn can send their thoughts to another, insert words into the mind to be more specific, though the receiver always knows where they came from. Because it takes a great deal of energy and focus, we prefer speech. We cannot—well, most of us cannot—read thoughts that are not chosen to be given to us."

"Most of us?"

He examined one buffed nail. "I have a small, very rare talent for telepathy."

Isis sank into a convenient chair. "How small?"

"Thoughts stirred by emotion are sometimes sent to me without my leave or the sender's knowledge."

"And?"

"With control and concentration, I can find another's thoughts, whether they send or no."

"Which of my thoughts have you heard?"

"None." There was a world of disgust in the single word, leading Isis to believe he spoke the truth.

"All humans or just me?"

He gave her a studied look, then answered, "Just you."

"Why can't you read mine?"

"I do not know."

That, and his obvious irritation about the deficiency, cheered Isis immensely; she was even willing to forget the fact that he had obviously tried his telepathy earlier.

"I can see that pleases you." With one of his impossibly quick moves, Darius perched beside her on the broad arm of her chair. "It is almost worth it, to see you smile like that."

"About this Pari—"

"Do not concern yourself with Pari. She is mine to stop."

"I owe her a favor—and from your description, this is one woman I do not want to be in debt to—and now you say don't concern myself? Forget that, Darius." She shook her head. "Why was I so lucky as to go into that shop just as Pari decided she needed a pawn? She must have been crowing like Peter Pan; a perfect sap dropped into her lap."

"A sap? From a tree?"

"A dork, an idiot, a gullible fool."

"You are none of those, my sweet Isis. Forget Pari. Think only of this."

The touch of his finger upon her jaw lifted her gaze to his. A faint shimmer, fiery red, hovered above his smooth golden skin. His black eyes held the languid invitation she recognized, for it compelled an eager response inside her.

He wanted to complete what they had begun outside the alley.

So quickly he switched from anger to lust; so quickly his touch aroused her.

He bent to her lips, nipping them lightly before settling to his task of pleasure. Isis softened under his expert kiss, feeling her insides become fluid. Cedar, myrtle, man—his so-right scent surrounded her.

She ached to touch him. Were those vibrant djinn emotions as electric as they appeared? Yet she resisted the urge to run her hand through his dark curls and find out how long they were and if they were as soft as the light shimmering in their depths. Talk of a vengeful—a scorned?—djinni made her wary.

Too many times the men in her life had dismissed her or tried to shield her. She could not tolerate it with this man, who touched her so carefully and intimately. She could not bear that he would be like the others.

With difficulty she shifted scant but important inches away. "Pari, and the favor, *are* my problem, Darius," she said, trying to bring her breathlessness under control. "Kissing you isn't going to change that."

"It makes it my problem," he said softly, "as is everything about Pari. You do not know what you face with her."

"Then tell me."

"Why? You are not capable of standing against her."

You are not capable. Isis froze, and her head fell back against the chair. Her eyes squeezed shut, containing the pain caused by those blunt words. She should be used to them: You're not capable, you can't do that, just give it up, Isis. It didn't matter that they were true this time; that just made them all the worse.

Darius lifted his head, obviously sensing her withdrawal. "Isis?" he inquired gently. His hand cupped her cheek, urging her to look at him.

She shoved to her feet, needing to be alone until she could rebuild the walls of bravado and outer assurance he'd breached. Blindly, she walked to the door.

Again, he appeared in front of her, in the familiar pose of irked djinni. "Where do you go, woman?"

Woman? Isis tapped him on the chest with her forefinger, glad for an emotional outlet. His smooth skin—more like warm silk than electricity—momentarily distracted her. She folded her hand against the urge to stroke him.

"Point of information on modern females, Darius. We do not appreciate being addressed as 'woman.' It's barely one step above 'wench.' Now, get out of my way."

"Where do you go . . . sweet Isis?"

"To get my car. It'll be towed by morning, and it costs a fortune in this city to get your car out of the pound."

"Out of the pound?" He shook his head. "Never mind. I will handle it." With that, he disappeared.

He'd be back before she even got to the ferry. Isis swore and kicked the doorjamb, earning herself a sore toe. "Damn you, Darius," she spat as she massaged the ache she could reach. "I thought you were different."

Returning to her shop from her refuge on Kaf, Pari knew at once that Darius had been there. In his arrogance, he hadn't bothered to conceal his invasion. She had expected him to come, had wanted him to know who was behind his binding. She had not expected him to be able to cross her barriers.

Sparks, wild and brilliant, showered her. He was free, unbound; otherwise he would be exiled from the company of djinn and unable to enter the premises.

Gray robes whipping about her, Pari stormed around the room, heedless of how her fury tore pages from ancient books, shattered glass, and created a shambles. Her pets, the Kafian dragons, hissed in matching rage.

Stupid human! She must have bungled the spell. Humans couldn't be relied upon for anything but annoyance and occasional amusement.

If only she had destroyed the human when she'd

first found her. But, no, she'd been too delighted with the idea that Darius would be spellbound, and to the woman who, according to some prophecy Harbad had known about, could be his salvation. Instead, he was free and had the woman in his thrall and under his protection. For the moment Isis Montgomery was safe from her fury.

Now she'd have to come up with a new plan, for she was not ready to meet Darius. Not unless . . .

The sinister forces? Did she dare allow them to give her strength?

Pari stopped pacing and fingered her turquoise tablet. It was said that when the sinister forces took hold, the turquoise tablet was shattered and replaced with one of blackest onyx. That the will was no longer that of the djinn, but of the greater, evil forces.

Pari shook her head, abandoning thoughts of using those powers. She would do this on her own. She would be the master over all the djinn and owe allegiance to no other.

Darius had to have some weakness to exploit. If only she knew what it was! She would consult with Harbad's diaries again.

She'd stolen a few before her banishment, not as many as she would have liked, but as many as she could obtain. Unfortunately, Harbad was as maddeningly cryptic in his writing as he'd been in life, but from the diaries she'd discovered he had been concerned about a prophecy and a choice that one day would be forced upon Darius. A choice Harbad himself had once made to increase his power. Somehow the choice involved the line of Abregaza, and that information led her to Isis.

Exactly what that choice entailed she did not know. How this woman was involved and why the line of Abregaza, she didn't know either.

She had tried to find out. This shop, which she had begun merely to amuse herself in her exile, became a means to search for arcane relics of Terra, which might tell her more about Abregaza and the prophecy. Pari had been patient, waiting for the information and the woman.

No more.

Isis Montgomery was the key to bringing down Darius, Pari was sure of that, although she couldn't see how a powerless human could impact on a djinni's strength. Somehow she would find out how best to use her.

Pari stood before the cages of her dragons. She bent down until they were at eye level with her. "Ah, my pets, if Darius is with her, the woman Isis still owes me a favor." She smiled then. "That I shall demand it, do not doubt, but it is a single advantage. I must choose very carefully when and how to wield it." She rose and picked up the two cages. For a moment she looked around the room. It had been fun for a while, playing with these puny humans and their petty dreams. Now that Darius knew of it, she could no longer risk staying here. Pity.

"Now, my pets, we must go and prepare for the time of my return."

As the time lengthened and Darius did not reappear, Isis's flash of temper burned to ash. After all, what had he done besides tell her to stay put and tell the truth about her capabilities against his magic? He was just a convenient target for the people she was really angry at—Madame Pari, yes, but mostly herself for not listening to her instincts about the dangers of magic.

She wondered if maybe her family had been right all along.

Was she incapable of success? Was her insistence

on doing things her way a subtle sabotage of herself?

Tonight she had no answers, and she didn't want to face the questions.

Isis changed out of her red dress into one she always thought of as her comfort dress. The loose, soft cotton allowed easy movement and the feline print always made her smile at the cats' antics. She lit the candles at her worktable, and then picked up the strange flacon. This perfume would give her the answer. If she could duplicate it, and if it was the success she predicted, then she would know she was right to trust her battered instincts.

And if not? Then she would also have an answer.

Carefully she unstopped it and sniffed. Although little of the perfume remained, the essence of it so pervaded the ancient container that she could still smell it.

The aroma was beautiful, as always, but different. How? Puzzled, she dabbed a tiny amount on her wrist and sniffed again. This time, it was a joyous scent, one to cheer a sorrowful spirit. It smelled of new sea grass and hot sand and sunwarmed air. Instead of erotic nights, an ocean beach came to mind.

Isis immersed herself deeper in the image, for that was how she often created her new perfumes. Waves lapping. Brine and fresh air. How to capture fresh air in a bottle? She drew in a long breath. Water, deliciously cool and foamy. Her mind drifted further. Swimming, the wet slide of sea across heated skin.

And then Darius was there, swimming at her side, his strong strokes easy and sure. Even here, in her fantasy, he mastered. She could not escape the sweet flash of awareness and the tension coiling in her belly. Her imagination knew what her mind would not admit, for next he was inside her, his strokes there just as sure and even and strong, and infinitely more pleasurable.

Tremors rippled across her sensitive skin. The breath she held was released in a shuddering wave. Abruptly, Isis put the stopper in the flacon. The images faded, but the memory, and the lingering arousal, did not. She shook her head, trying to quell her clamoring heart. What magic allowed him to take over her fantasies?

She glanced at the other, still empty, half of the floor.

Darius was of Kaf, could not live here, and she did not belong in his world, for she had no magic.

Those sure facts were like a cheap cologne that faded as soon as applied next to the splendor of his kiss and a single memory held in her heart.

He thought her, and her perfumes, brilliant.

Resolutely Isis turned her back to the bed and got to work.

She could not replicate the formula. An hour later, Isis admitted she had failed. Every combination she tried was missing the magic.

She stared thoughtfully at the tiny amount left. Decision time. Should she keep trying to figure out what was in it by trial and error or should she send the remaining perfume to a lab for analysis?

Isis looked at her scratched notes. Madame Paris's words echoed inside her. *The only way you will get more of that perfume is to wish for it from a djinni.* A gut feeling told her the woman was right—that was why she'd risked the ritual—but she had to know for sure. Gas chromatography was a form of scientific magic. She'd try that first, before resorting to the uncertainty of magical bargains.

Carefully, Isis poured the remaining perfume, all but a few drops, into a sturdy vial, then wrapped it for transport, planning to call FedEx in the morning for a pickup. She'd used the lab before and knew them to be quick, accurate, and trustworthy. She should have her answer in a couple of weeks.

It was late, but Isis prowled around the workroom, straightening and organizing. Intense concentration, the wait for Darius's return, two days of roller-coaster emotions—she should be exhausted. She was exhausted, but too on edge to sleep.

Isis plopped back down at her desk. Maybe it was time to perfect that new formula, the one for calming.

Nude, Darius stretched facedown on a velvet rug beside his pool. The setting Kafian sun and the arid breeze dried the droplets of water left from his vigorous swim.

It had taken him only minutes to conjure Isis's car from the place she had left it to the street beside her home. Darius chuckled to himself, remembering the astonished expression of the man who had stood beside the car, attempting to attach a metal hook to it. AL'S TOW had been emblazoned on the side of his yellow truck, and Al had been greatly surprised when his tow had disappeared under his nose.

Afterward, Darius had lingered in Isis's wild garden. Sweet lemon blossom had perfumed the damp, warm air, and on another night, with his *zaniya* at his side, he might have enjoyed it. Instead, he'd watched the flickering candlelight burn in the upper windows and tried to calm the chaos inside him.

It didn't work. Even the shadow of Isis Montgomery disturbed him. Her silhouette moved in a sinuous flow that brought his unruly body to instant arousal. When he closed his eyes, he still remembered how her lithe body felt against him.

At that, he'd transported to Kaf, hoping the distance would lessen her impact. He needed revitalization, but more than that, he needed the connection to who and what he was.

Intense concentration on a difficult spell, a strenuous swim—neither had forced her from his thoughts. Instead, he had marveled at how the *ma-at* was returning to his command as he spent more time with her, and had wondered whether Isis enjoyed swimming and would find pleasure in the pool of water as he did.

From there it had not been too great a leap to imagine her beside him, laughing as she kept pace with his strokes; then his imagination had carried him inside her. Moaning in pleasure, here, too, she kept pace.

With a grunt, Darius turned over. The remembered fantasy, and the arousal it brought, made lying on his belly too uncomfortable. Hands stacked behind his head, he forced himself to relax without release and allowed himself to think of her.

She had family. That simple fact perturbed Darius, for it forced him to view Isis beyond his needs for her.

For him, she was the desirable, infuriating woman who would be his *zaniya* and who would, in some way he had yet to find, restore fully his control over his *ma-at*.

She was also a daughter, a sister, an employer, a worker, a friend.

For the first time, he wondered if desire could be enough to overcome all the ties that held her to Terra.

Darius bolted upright. When had that idea—the notion that Isis might linger with him on Kaf—taken root in the recesses of his mind?

When he had seen Simon and Zoe, he realized. When he had witnessed love between djinn and human and recognized that his friend's loyalty now lay first and foremost with his human family.

159

Put bluntly, he wanted Isis. In his bed. But . . . in his life?

Darius shook off the thought. It could never be. They were of two different worlds, djinn and human. Besides, ultimately, the Protector must stand alone with only *ma-at*.

Protector, may I enter?

Leila. Darius lay back down, ignoring her request for the moment as he had ignored the multitude of others that had beset him since his return. None had required the skills of the Protector. They had only wanted the honor of his presence, and he felt no necessity to oblige.

Protector, I seek to thank you for the gift of the fire blooms.

He closed his eyes. *Leave. I wish to be alone.* His words were blunt, he knew, but he had not the patience to temper them.

If you insist, Protector. Her irritation was clear, and he almost heard her flounce away.

Darius smiled. He couldn't imagine Isis ever flouncing.

Isis. Regardless of her ties to Terra, he must take her as *zaniya*. Though his control improved, according to prophecy it would not be complete until he had joined with Isis. With his obligations to his people, with Pari hiding in the shadows ready to strike, he could do nothing else.

Darius looked down at his arousal and gave a rueful grin. All honorable arguments aside, the simple truth was, he wanted Isis, and he was not willing to give her up.

He would have her. No power of Kaf or Terra could stand between the might of the Protector and his chosen *zaniya*, regardless of how that choice had been made.

As long as she was willing. Darius sighed. Which meant he must figure out why she had denied their passion just before he left. What had brought the pain to her eyes, had turned her from him? He had wanted to hold her, pet her, kiss away the dampness from the corners of her eyes.

His rebellious flesh—which grew more unruly, the more his *ma-at* returned to his control—sprang to life again. Darius groaned in frustration.

A flurry of sand prickled his skin. Did Leila dare to return? "Leila, I told you I would be alone."

"In that condition you sent Leila away? Has your brain gone the way of your blood, my friend?"

Darius opened one eye. Simon, dressed in his preferred jeans and T-shirt, stood there, grinning and eyeing his friend's obvious erection.

"Did you not see the stones of privacy outside?" Darius grumbled.

Simon's grin grew wider. "I just ignored them, as you do mine. So, why did you send Leila away? Why force yourself to see to your own relief, when the woman is willing?"

"Leila is not the woman I want."

"Ah," replied Simon knowingly.

"Ah, indeed." Darius waved a hand, and a pile of plump cushions materialized. Without further invitation, Simon seated himself. Darius rose and donned his robe. At least talking with his friend was shifting the blood back to his brain.

When he clapped his hands, tiny cups of strong brewed tea and thin slices of flat bread drizzled with honey appeared. "Would you like some refreshment?"

"Thank you." Simon nabbed a cup of tea, took a sip, and then set it down. He rested back on one elbow. "So, Isis resists your legendary charm."

"What makes you think 'twas Isis who had me in that condition?" Too restless to sit, Darius paced beside the pool.

Simon gave him an incredulous look. "Which

female djinni would refuse you? Besides, I married a Terran woman. I know how contentious they can be. I've been in that condition a few times myself," he admitted, then took a slice of bread and studied it intently. "Zoe visited Isis and warned her about you."

"What! Simon, can you not control your woman better than that?"

Simon snorted in disbelief. "With that attitude, it's no wonder you can't get to first base with Isis."

"First base?"

"A Terran expression. You know Zoe. Well, according to her, Isis is even more fiercely independent. She had to be, if she didn't want to get swallowed by that family of hers."

Darius stopped his pacing and sank to a rock beside the pool. Her family, her brothers. They had been so surprised to find he thought her brilliant. He remembered the too casual way she'd described her dyslexia.

His last words came back to haunt him. *You are not capable of standing against her.*

He dropped his forehead to his palm. Oh, Solomon, his thoughtless tongue. It had been his fear talking, his fear for what Pari would do with the power she held over Isis, but Isis would not have heard it that way.

"Simon, I have been as blind as a camel with both eyelids shut."

"That bad? Does this mean a big-time shift to apology mode?"

"What did you say?" Darius snapped.

Simon gave a rueful grin. "Sorry. I hear so much of the casual Terran speech, some of it has become my own. I meant, it sounds as if you owe an apology to Isis."

Darius leveled a steady gaze at his friend. The dress, the speech. If he had needed any confirmation that Simon was no longer of Kaf, but a djinni of Terra, he had just heard it with his own ears.

They would always be friends; that would not change. He could still trust Simon with his life, but their paths ran very differently now.

And he was alone on his path, as the Protector always was.

He had known it was so, but this night the lonely way did not seem an appealing one.

"Yes, I must make amends with her."

With knowing eyes, Simon watched Darius's pacing resume. "And I keep you from her." In an easy movement, he rose to his feet. "But first, I forget the purpose for which I came." He retrieved a paper from his back pocket. "This is a fax of a copy of a page—" He stopped when he saw Darius's puzzled look. "Never mind. It's from an ancient clay tablet found in the ruins of Susa. Humans have not deciphered our ancient language, but you should have no trouble with it."

"What does it say?" Darius glanced at the blurred figures.

"You'll want to read the original words, but in essence it is the legend of Abregaza, a female mage—"

"Female! I should have guessed."

Simon chuckled. "At that time in Terran history, djinn still resided on Terra, for we hadn't made our transition to Kaf. Some humans were also gifted in their magic. The legend says Abregaza was one so talented. When a male djinni tried to make her his own, she cast a spell protecting herself against his *ma-at*."

"An insane spell," muttered Darius.

"The clay was broken there, but there were other shards. You can see, only a few words are legible." Simon pointed to the copies of fragments at the bottom of the page. "Something about balance and willing, and a warning that the spell lingers through eternity to her descendants. It's not even clear if those fragments were part of the original tablet."

"They were."

Simon tilted his head. "What's going on, my friend?"

"Pari's involved."

Simon cursed, fluently and colorfully, under his breath. "That witch tried to bind you?"

Darius nodded.

"Pari returns for her revenge, doesn't she?"

"At the Festival of Mingara, I think."

Simon fixed Darius with a stare. "And you need the line of Abregaza to defeat her?"

"In a fashion."

"Will Isis be hurt?"

"She should not be, not through my actions." He would make sure their joining brought her only pleasure. The results of her own stubbornness would be another tale, beyond his telling.

"Then I will leave you to your preparations, unless I learn more. And I shall keep Zoe from interfering. Call on me should you need help."

"Thank you." With one hand on Simon's shoulder, he gripped his friend's elbow with the other. "Go in strength and peace, my friend."

Simon mirrored the action. "May the sun light your way and the sand bless a firm path beneath your feet."

With only the faintest tightening, Darius released his friend. "Go now, return to the warm bed of your *zaniya*."

Simon laughed. "And how long do you think your blood will stay with your brain?"

Darius echoed his laughter. Already, with the thought of returning to Isis's side, excitement danced across his skin. "About five minutes, my friend. Long enough for an apology."

The two djinn disappeared in a whirlwind of sand and searing heat.

Chapter Twelve

A faint, plaintive tune brought Isis to groggy awareness. The candles had long since been doused in their wax, leaving only the fitful moonlight as illumination. Something rough and wet licked her cheek. Fur tickled her neck. Isis blinked in confusion, reorienting herself as she awoke.

She'd worked until letters and numbers had blurred to indecipherable sticks and circles. And then? Weary to her bones, she'd dragged herself to the bed in the opposite half of her workroom before allowing sleep to overcome her.

That bed was now Darius's.

Another rough lick dampened her cheek, and a rumbling purr sounded in her ear. Vulcan had come out of his sulk and braved the upstairs.

The snatch of tune played again, followed by a now familiar whirlwind. Darius had returned, this time announcing his sudden entrance with music. How could the man be so annoying and so thoughtful at the same time?

Vulcan hissed and sprang from the bed. He didn't leave, but stood like a sentry at the edge of her work space. His swishing tail told clearly of feline annoyance. Darius might have invaded half the upper floor, but that side the cat still claimed.

Her djinni appeared before her. He'd abandoned his earth clothes for the long robe again. With his dark hair and unreadable eyes, he appeared more shadowy than the surrounding night, more warlock than djinn, more magic than human.

"Your car is here," he said. The melodious voice soothed, but his mere presence was sufficient to chase away sleep.

"I know. I looked out the window."

"It was faster for me to go."

"That's true."

"Al was about to hang a metal hook on your vehicle."

"You were just in time, then."

He let out an exasperated breath. "You are not going to make this easy, are you?"

"Make what easy?"

He transported next to her on the bed. Isis sat up, but he laid a gentle hand on her arm to restrain her from leaving. "Do not go. Listen to what I have to say."

His voice held command rather than entreaty. Had she expected anything different? Yet she could not find the power to move away. "I'm listening."

He glanced away, hesitating, as if trying to find the correct words, then looked back, his dark eyes luminous. "Pari is a dangerous djinni. Only *ma-at* can defeat her. That you do not have those skills does not lessen the talents that lie here," he touched her temple, "or here." He touched her chest, right above her heart. "You cannot do *ma-at*. I cannot make perfumes. I meant nothing more than that by my ill-thought words."

167

He reached into his robe and pulled out a small jar, which he handed to her. "I noticed you had a collection of these in Dream Scents. This is old, made by one of our artisans. It is for you."

Isis turned the narrow jar over in her hands. She'd never seen one like it before. Surprisingly heavy for its size, with a narrow neck and flaring body, it was made from a burnished metal, golden in color, but harder than gold. Circling the rounded body were brilliant cloisonne pictures of mountains and streams of red fire and green oases. Kaf, she presumed. The colors were bright and the detail intricate. She pulled out the stopper. Inside was a very faint scent of sandalwood.

"Darius, it's unique, beautiful," she breathed. "Thank you. I shall treasure it, but you didn't need to give me this."

"Yes I did."

She tilted her head. "Why?"

"Because I do not want us as two snarling tigers. I offer a new bargain. I would spend time with you, the two of us together."

Vulcan gave a cat growl and crouched to pounce position. Darius glanced at him, then back at Isis. "*Just* the two of us."

"Why?"

"Why? Why? Always why," he snapped. "Is this not reason enough?" He leaned forward and kissed her.

For just a moment Isis resisted before giving in to the thrill. Tension radiated from him to set electricity dancing across her skin, reaching from her fingers to her throat to the bottom of her feet. It seemed as if he held her, caressed her everywhere at once, when the only physical touch was his mouth on hers. Her bare toes curled with sheer excitement.

Despite its engulfing power, the kiss was soft—delicate pressure on her lips, lazy strokes of his tongue, infinitesimal nips. His fingers tunneled through her hair, as if to hold her in place, though Isis had no desire to move.

Oh, yes, the man could kiss. If he ever progressed to touching her more intimately . . . she'd be lost. Always before she'd resisted being overwhelmed by the sheer brilliance and drive of the men in her life. Now, her own passion threatened to rob her of both will and fortitude.

"Do all djinn kiss this good?" she gasped.

"No," he answered, "and do not attempt to discover elsewise."

Before she could respond to the arrogant, possessive answer, he'd captured her mouth and her common sense again.

I like you here on my pillows, Isis Montgomery.

Oh, the images that exploded in her fevered imagination! From her or from him or from both, she couldn't tell. His muscles bunched with lithe grace as he shifted position, and suddenly Isis found herself beneath him on the soft bed.

She didn't remember it being this soft.

"Stay," he urged against her lips, his hand stroking down her side. "Stay."

One drop of sanity remained. This was too fast, way too fast. Too magical.

Isis found her breath, which seemed to have departed with her reason. "No," was all she could manage.

He stopped. "You are unwilling?"

"Yes."

"You are sure? You are unwilling?"

"Yes."

To her surprise, that was all she needed to say. Darius groaned and buried his head in the pillow beside her. His ragged, warm breath tickled her ear. That he was very aroused she had no doubt from her position beneath him, but he held himself quite still. She heard him muttering under his breath.

"What did you say?"

"Quiet, woman!"

Isis opened her mouth to protest, but he forestalled her.

"Unless you wish to resume, do not interrupt. I recite mantras for solitude and centering. Their complexity diverts my need."

"Oh," Isis said in a small voice.

She lay beneath him, listening to the monotonal chant, which, from her perspective, didn't seem to be making much difference in his arousal. It sure wasn't doing much to cool hers, either.

Apparently, he reached the same conclusion, for he rolled off her with a curse. "Do I but switch one uncontrolled energy for another?" he muttered.

She didn't understand what he meant, but at least, for the moment, the seductive wildness had passed.

With difficulty, Isis sat up, the bed shifting beneath her. To her surprise, she found herself lying in mounds of green foliage. Not grass; it was softer and had such a beautiful fragrance, like honeysuckle and sage. She looked around. She was still on the third floor of her home, but this half had been transformed.

Glittering silver rocks surrounded her, while sheer blue covers, as silky as water, tangled about her feet. Gnarled tree trunks formed the posts for the bed, and from somewhere she heard a rushing waterfall.

"What? How did you—?"

Darius rolled to his side and propped up his head with his hand. "Do you like my bower?"

Isis looked around in wonder. Vulcan, his cat curiosity apparently overcoming his jealousy, abandoned his post to sniff the strange greenery.

"It's beautiful. What do you call the grass?"

"*Sha-hei-la*. It means . . . feather grass is the closest I can come."

She grinned at Darius. "Modern tip number three.

You should set the scene *before* I get too preoccupied to notice."

He laughed. "I shall remember that."

When Vulcan meowed and tilted his scarred ear, Darius nodded in solemn acknowledgment, adding a low croon. Vulcan circled a mound of *sha-hei-la*, pawed it a moment, and then settled into the center. His purr was one of pure ecstasy.

That quickly her cat abandoned his opposition— for a pile of grass. Remembering how she'd felt beneath Darius on that same greenery, Isis couldn't argue with Vulcan's capitulation.

"Did you make this up?"

He shook his head. "This grotto is a special place on Kaf. It is cool and green, with a waterfall and a pool of refreshing scarlet water. Would you like to go there? The most exquisite flowers shade its glade. There is one flower—"

"No more. Don't tempt me. I'll stay right here on earth." When she lifted a hand, Isis realized her dress had bunched up about her waist. She tugged it down only to discover the undone buttons in front. She gave a sigh of exasperation. The man definitely worked fast.

Isis began to redo the buttons, but Darius slid a hand up her front, leaving a trail of heat and a row of refastened buttons. He kissed the side of her neck. "Someday you shall see Kaf, my Isis." He shifted to his back and propped his hands beneath his head. "I like to lie and watch the leaves," he said, "the patterns of color and shade. They are nature's lace."

"Nature's lace. What a pretty thought." She was so tempted to lie beside him, to gaze at the green and inhale the fragrance, but she resisted. So easily could he overwhelm her.

"Now, about this bargain—"

"Ah, yes, the bargain."

"You wanted us to spend time together. Okay, but

171

that doesn't mean I'm ready to go to bed with you."

"I can wait."

He'd misinterpreted, perhaps deliberately, acting as though it was not a matter of *if*, but *when*.

Ah, who was she fooling? It was simply a matter of when, but that didn't mean the time was now.

To bare her body would bare her soul as well to this man, and she needed to know that he wanted more, saw more in her than just a romp in the grotto, sweet smelling though it might be.

"I just don't understand why. Why me? Surely there are plenty of other women who would be willing bed partners."

"I want more than a bed partner." He picked up her hand and kissed each fingertip. "And the others are not the one I want."

To be told by this mesmerizing man of dreams and magic that he wanted only her almost broke the last barriers of her resistance. Only lifelong habits of steely determination kept her from giving in.

That, and the fact that he was evading her question about why her.

Lying on this decadent bed wasn't helping. Isis regained her feet, and then leaned against the tree trunk. She eyed the djinni stretched out nonchalantly before her.

"And if I say no sex?"

His long lashes shadowed his half-closed eyes so she could not see their expression. "I want you, Isis, make no mistake about that. I want to kiss you and lie with you and join with you and share all the pleasures, the variations, the treats a man and a woman can share."

Just listening to his soft words brought dangerous images to mind and weakened her resolve to stay away from that decadent bed. Isis willed her feet to stay planted.

"However, that is not why I ask the bargain," he

continued. "I want to learn about your Terra."

"I thought you didn't like earth."

He shrugged one shoulder. "That does not mean I do not wish to learn more about her, and I think you would be an excellent teacher and companion for my explorations." The lashes lifted, exposing her to the full force of his liquid gaze. "Most important, you intrigue me, Isis Montgomery. I desire not only your body, but your company, your wit, and your smile."

Oh, God, she was a goner. She hoped he was telling the truth about that telepathy thing, because otherwise he'd know she'd give in on this bargain with nary a concession on his part.

"How much of my time?" she managed.

"All of it?"

"I can't," Isis sputtered. "My store, my work. I can't—"

He grinned at her. "Shhh, my sweet one. It was worth asking, but I did not expect it. Your evenings, I want. When the front door is locked, then your . . . time belongs to me."

"And my nights?"

"Shall be according to your wish and our mutual desires."

"You're expecting a lot, Darius."

"Then ask much in return." He gave her a self-assured smile, one that said he could dream of no trouble with whatever she asked.

"Give up your *ma-at*."

"What!" He bolted upright.

"No *ma-at* during this time."

"Absolutely not." He transported from the bed and began pacing about the room. His long robe billowed about him, its shifting colors reflecting agitation. He stopped, hands on hips, and glared at her. "I will not give up my *ma-at*."

She leaned against the tree, trying to look casual. "Your *ma-at* is causing me a lot of trouble, both with

173

my family and with the store. So that's the bargain, take it or leave it."

His jaw clenched, and the sparks showered him in silver. "I cannot just stop my *ma-at*. It is my breath, my blood. It is what I am. Can you stop your nose from smelling each scent it encounters; can you stop inhaling?"

"But you can control it."

"That's a matter of opinion," he muttered, so low Isis doubted she heard right.

"How about a compromise? No *ma-at*, not even so much as a nose wrinkle, while there are others around. And none of that popping in and out. You never know who might be with me."

"You expect me to *walk*?"

"Or take a very fast course in driving."

"But I must be able to return to Kaf, and I can get there only by transporting."

Zoe had said something about his needing to revitalize. "Okay, you can transport to Kaf and back. Just don't do it where others can see."

"And I can use my *ma-at* while on Kaf?"

"Of course. What you do on Kaf is your business."

"Your bargain said others, not humans."

"Okay, no *ma-at* when there are humans present."

"Except you."

"Except me."

"For how long?" he asked.

Isis thought a moment. How much time could she spare? "A week?"

He ran a hand through his hair. "Not enough time," she thought she heard him mutter; then he countered, through gritted teeth, "Three weeks."

"I can't give up that much time to spend with you!"

"If I can give up my *ma-at*, you can certainly put up with me for that time."

"Two weeks."

His breathing sounded harsh in the ensuing silence. The set of his shoulders, the tight neck, the dazzling sparkling about him all spoke of frustrated djinni.

"It is agreed," he finally spat out. "Your evenings from the time of closing *and* one day of your Terran weekend. In return, no *ma-at* on Terra when other humans are with us."

"And no transporting except to Kaf and back."

He gave a sharp nod. "I accept."

"And so do I."

"Then I claim my Kiss of Promise," he said roughly. In a single stride he was at her side. Grabbing her hand, he pulled her flush against him. He was wiry, not muscle-bound, yet to Isis he felt as hard, as fit, as any bodybuilder. He lifted her hand, kissed the back of it, then leaned over to kiss her cheek.

"Kiss me," he commanded. "Seal this infernal bargain."

Isis complied and wondered who would regret the bargain first.

She did. At precisely six o'clock the following evening, Darius strode into Dream Scents. Why had she bothered to stipulate no transporting? His entrance was dramatic enough, heralded by the scents of cedar and man. Chatter ceased as feminine eyes devoured his loose, easy movements.

Apparently he'd spent part of his day studying earth fashions. She'd never seen a man whom the bad-boy, biker image fit so well. His black pants looked like supple leather, loose enough for his fluid stride, tight enough to tantalize. If she didn't know that his black T-shirt had to be new, she'd have sworn the shirt had undergone a thousand washings to give it that soft, faded drape across his chest. A pair of mirrored sunglasses rested atop his dark curls. The only incongruous notes: his ever-present

175

robe—short now—the turquoise tablet at his throat, and sandals instead of boots.

Darius headed, without a single hesitation or diversion, to her side. Isis flushed. She smoothed suddenly damp palms down her short purple skirt, and then tugged the hem of the black satin camisole she wore beneath a sheer flowered overblouse. The gestures did nothing to still the trembling in her abdomen, and Isis quit when she realized she was fussing.

In defense, she turned back to her customer. "You have to use more because this year's oil is less potent," she said, answering the woman's previous question.

The woman wasn't listening anymore. She stared with rapt attention at Darius, a bottle of oil dangling dangerously loose in her hand. Isis plucked it from her slack fingers and set it safely on the counter.

"Because natural oils aren't supplemented with synthetics to standardize them, the potency does vary," Isis persisted.

The woman didn't even look at her.

Darius had reached Isis by now. "It is time, my sweet Isis," he crooned to her. "You are mine for the evening."

The customer gave a long sigh.

"I'm busy—"

His lifted brow cut her off before he turned and smiled at the customer. "You do not mind that I take Isis from you?"

The woman shook her head, all power of speech apparently robbed by that devastating smile. That smile was lethal to feminine common sense, and even Isis found she wasn't immune, as Darius gently herded her toward the door.

"I'll close up," Salem called.

Isis dug in her heels. Never again. Never again would she allow a man to ride roughshod over her, not even this one. Isis found her voice. "I'm not through, Darius—"

"Is it not your time of closing?"

"Yes, but we still have customers to finish up with, the cash register to close, some straightening—"

"The bargain was for the time of closing and then your time would be mine." He gave her a scornful look. "Do you humans not honor your promises?"

"That was a cheap shot."

"I *walked* here. You are the one who does not fulfill."

When was she going to learn to listen a bit more closely to those bargains? "Ten minutes. Just ten minutes to go over a few things with Marc."

Darius paused, then nodded and crossed his arms over his chest. "Ten minutes."

Marc was in her office, busy at the computer. "Ice, sweetie, you've been writing checks again, haven't you?" He turned in his chair to face her. "How many times have I told you, you simply must stay away from the computer."

Isis grimaced. "What'd I do this time?" she asked, looking over his shoulder.

He pointed to the screen. "That check was for $912, not $192. Played absolute havoc with our petty cash balance this month."

"Did we overdraw?"

"No. This has been a solvent month, but it was close."

Isis held up a hand. "I promise, I'll stay away." They discussed a few other matters; then she braced her hands on the monitor, rested her chin on them, and gave Marc a grin. "Since you want me to stay away from the numbers, you won't mind closing out the register and making the night deposit for the next two weeks. I'm going to be leaving on the dot of six."

Marc leaned back in his chair and pushed back the sleeves of his Dream Scents shirt. "You're leaving early? There must be a delicious story behind this. Oh, do tell Marc all."

The door banged open and Darius filled the doorway. His hands rested on his hips. "I have finished waiting."

Marc chuckled. "Say no more, Ice. If I had him that eager, I'd be out of here, too."

"I—"

"Shoo, shoo." Marc waved his hands at her. "It's about time you took a vacation, even if it is for only an evening." He eyed Darius with interest. "Though I doubt you will find it restful." He sighed. "I do envy you."

Darius scowled at him, then took Isis's hand. "Come. Our bargain."

Had Darius been offended by her PA's blatant admiration? Often she'd found the more heterosexual the man, the more threatened he felt by Marc, and there was no one she'd ever met who exuded more heterosexual charisma than Darius.

"Don't mind Marc," she said, as Darius hustled her to the door. "His mouth is usually several seconds ahead of his brain."

"Mind him?"

"Some men feel uncomfortable because he's gay." Darius looked puzzled.

"Because he prefers men," Isis clarified.

"The djinn make no judgments on such matters." His eyes narrowed. "However, we have definite preferences, and mine do not run that way."

"Big surprise," she muttered.

None of the remaining customers had left yet. Isis had the sinking feeling they were waiting until the Darius-and-Isis floor show played itself out. Please, just let nothing else happen.

Pleas like that were doomed to failure.

Outside, they had both paused to don sunglasses

178

when Isis heard her name called. With dread, she turned.

Jimmy Ray Frank strolled down the sidewalk, still wearing his trademark white suit, still annoyingly immaculate. Isis stifled the urge to run in the other direction. It did no good to evade Jimmy Ray. He found you anyway, or found what he wanted elsewhere, and was just that much more wicked in his column as a result of the extra effort.

Besides, she was tired of running from him. It was time to try a new ingredient in the old formula.

"Who is that?" Darius asked with irritation.

"Jimmy Ray Frank. He's a reporter. Please, Darius, just let me handle this."

Darius frowned but said nothing. At least he was under the vow of no magic, Isis thought. If only he didn't start sparking.

"Hello, m'dear." The reporter drew even with them. "I expected to find you toiling amid your soaps and perfumes." Jimmy Ray glanced at Darius, who rested his hand at Isis's neck.

Isis didn't bother with introductions. "Evening, Jimmy Ray. Who you dragging over the coals tomorrow?"

"Read my column and find out."

"Still working on that magic story?"

"Oh, off and on."

His casualness didn't fool her a bit. He was still bulldogging the subject.

Jimmy Ray brushed an invisible speck of lint from his lapel. "One of my many sources, a bartender, offered me an interesting tidbit this morning. Seems a tow truck driver in his establishment claimed he was about to tow a beat-up red Ford when it disappeared in front of him. You own an old Ford, don't you? Red?"

"So do probably a hundred other people." Isis

burst out laughing. "You think I made a *car* disappear?"

"She has not this capability," said Darius.

Isis jabbed him with her elbow, hiding the motion from Jimmy Ray. "The man was probably drunk, Jimmy Ray."

"Not when he came in. Neither was his partner."

Two witnesses. Damn and double damn.

"I also had coffee with Benedict Fontenot this morning," he added. Despite his slow drawl and casual smile, Jimmy Ray was studying her reactions, Isis knew. She gave him back only mild interest. "Said someone took a bottle of the new perfume he's going to unveil at the auction next month. The thief tried to get the formula but didn't. He says he's not going to the police because he thinks the culprit is someone he's fond of."

That slime! He was setting her up again. "You're slipping, Jimmy Ray. I thought you were a better reporter than to take anything from Ben Fontenot at face value."

"Did I say I was believing everything?" Jimmy Ray asked softly. "However, it seems like I remember you claiming he stole several formulas from you."

She'd been so naive then, thinking Jimmy Ray was a sympathetic ear, when all she'd gotten from her own family was disbelief. It had taken one read through his column to make her get cynical real fast. Hiding the clutch of her stomach, Isis crossed her arms. "That was three years ago. I've grown up since then."

"Not planning a little revenge?"

"Nope. I'm too busy with my own business."

"Well, if you think of anything to tell me—" He stuck a business card in her breast pocket.

Isis felt Darius shift against her, closer, as though he didn't care for even that faint touch from another.

"Just to show my good intentions," continued

Jimmy Ray, glancing again at Darius, "here's a little tip: You'd be wise to prepare your alibi for last night, Ice, around 2 A.M."

"I was home, in bed."

"Alone?" He eyed Darius with crude insinuation.

Gusts of heat emanated from Darius, and she thought she heard the crackle of lightning. Oh, damn.

"We have endured your insolent questions long enough," Darius said with lethal softness. His hand shifted to her shoulder, and a faint pressure urged her to turn her away.

Although she hated to let Darius dictate when and how she left, she didn't want to treat Jimmy Ray to a juicy argument. Besides, she'd had enough of the reporter, too.

"No answer?" Jimmy Ray's drawl grew more prolonged. "Does that mean you weren't alone?"

"My private life is just that: private." She pivoted and strode away. Darius, hand still on her shoulder, kept pace.

"So, Ice," Jimmy Ray called, "who were you with? Did Ben Fontenot reject you again? Is that what this is all about?"

"That slime?" Isis threw over her shoulder. "As if."

Darius stopped and then faced Jimmy Ray. "She was with me all night and is now under my protection. You will cease this."

Isis groaned. She'd almost gotten away.

Amusement was stamped on Jimmy Ray's face, and the reporter held out his hand. "I don't think we've met. Jimmy Ray Frank."

Darius made no move to shake the outstretched hand.

"This is my friend, Darius." Anyone who'd been at Aunt Tildy's party would tell Jimmy Ray that much. And probably already had.

Jimmy Ray withdrew his hand. "Doesn't talk much, does he?"

"Only when he has something worthwhile to say. Unlike some men of my acquaintance."

Do you release me from our bargain, my Isis? This man's insolence should not go unpunished.

Isis shook her head in emphatic negation.

Pity. Darius then spoke aloud. "Do not bother her again. There is naught she can tell you."

Darius did not know reporters. It was the worst possible thing he could have said. Jimmy Ray would not hear the menace, only the challenge.

Isis glanced over her shoulder as they left. Jimmy Ray was staring at Darius, a faint smile on his face, as if he'd just swallowed a sweet treat.

Damn and double damn. Why hadn't she realized? She'd bet her last bottle of absolute jasmine that Ben had also mentioned Darius in the morning chat.

That's why Jimmy Ray had come. Not because of Ben or the missing perfume. Today's little visit wasn't about her. It was about Darius.

Chapter Thirteen

Already he regretted that infernal bargain. Darius stalked down the French Quarter street, shortening his strides only when he discovered that Isis did not keep pace. Instead, she strolled, enjoying the warm spring evening and the myriad street performers.

He did not like crowds. The rudeness of the surrounding humans—jostling, the occasional elbow, one even stepped on his foot!—only fueled his frustration.

Were it not for that outrageous bargain, he could have prevented such discomforts. He could have silenced that inquisitive "reporter." The questions had distressed Isis, and he had been powerless to protect her from the man's probing curiosity.

Darius's fists clenched as he fought the urge to use his *ma-at,* even now. But a bargain was sacred, and he could not.

Not yet.

"No *ma-at,*" he muttered, then stopped suddenly,

waiting impatiently for Isis to finish watching a dancer, whose heels clicked a rapid tune.

How was he to judge the return of his control and regain his lost mastery if he could not use his *ma-at*? Solomon, whatever dervish had possessed him while he made that bargain? He shook his head and turned to Isis, who finally came to his side.

"Just one small spell," he coaxed.

"Trying to weasel out of the bargain already, Darius? You didn't have to agree."

Oh, yes he did. He needed her wanting and willing, but Darius decided it was wiser not to mention that. "Weasel?"

"A flexible carnivore that's reported to suck eggs and leave the shells intact."

He frowned. Was that the insult it sounded like?

"It's an expression," Isis explained. "Means trying to get out of an obligation."

"Why no *ma-at*?" he asked. "Do you like these crowds, the raucous noise"—he sniffed—"the smells? I could easily banish the unpleasantness."

Isis gave him a bland look, then started down the street, as though *she* had been waiting for *him*. Darius had no choice but to follow, his jaw clenched.

"Actually, yes, I do like it," she answered finally. "Not all the smells—stale beer I'd never choose for a perfume—but the crowds, the music, the foods, the artists and tarot readers, yeah, I like it all."

He shook his head, not understanding. "You *liked* being questioned by that reporter? You *liked* his insinuations?"

"Well, no, that part I didn't like."

"Jimmy Ray Frank was fortunate not to find himself hip deep in a pit of Oxus slugs," he muttered.

"Eeeuw, that sounds gross." She cast him a curious sidelong glance. "Would they have harmed him?"

"They are not dangerous, but their touch is highly unpleasant."

"Oxus slugs, huh? I may have to remember that one." Her cheeky grin said she was not taking this seriously.

Darius took her hand. "How am I supposed to protect you when you render me as impotent as a tuskless mammoth?"

"I've been meaning to talk to you about all that 'I must protect' and 'my Isis' stuff. Modern point number four, Darius. Earth women take care of themselves. We belong to no man. It's called independence."

Darius stopped and, since he still held her hand, Isis did, too. "Being called mine—is that as bad as calling you woman? Or wench?"

"Not quite as bad," she whispered.

With his free hand, he brushed a strand of hair behind her ear and felt her tremble at his touch. "Would it really be that unpleasant, Isis?"

After long seconds, she answered, "I'm not yours, Darius."

Not yet. He was careful not to send her that thought.

"And if I were to marry one day, I wouldn't be my husband's possession either."

Darius lifted his brow. She misunderstood. "I speak not of possession but protection. That urge is strong in a male," *especially toward his chosen mate.* "It is so among my people. Is it not among yours?"

"Even when a female djinni has strong powers of *ma-at?* I mean, it's not like she needs testosterone-induced brute strength to fight off the saber-toothed tiger. She can do it with a flick of the hand."

"Even then. Perhaps especially then, for she will have strong powers to pass on to her children, and she must be kept safe in the hopes she will one day bear a child. We do not think of women as lesser—

185

our women are free to choose their own mates and their own paths—but we do believe them different. Often they possess different skills in *ma-at*. The skill of protection, of guardianship, is, generally, a male's."

There were exceptions, but too often those created problems of unbalance and chaos. Like Pari.

Isis grinned at him. "Well, I think I like our system, but when you talk like that, you might singlehandedly set women's lib back a couple of centuries."

She resumed their walk. After a few minutes, when he'd begun to wonder if they had a goal in mind, she asked, "Have you thought about how you'd like to spend our evening?"

He'd had plenty of thoughts, but the no-sex stipulation had eliminated quite a few of them.

"Frankly, I'm starving," she added.

"What would you like? I can—" Darius halted. He could not. He could not use his *ma-at*, and there were no wild groves of oranges or fields of bulgur or hives of honey to provide for basic needs.

Darius scowled. This bargain was even more bothersome than he had anticipated. He should have suggested something else, done something else. But he had not, and now he must comply with the bargain that was.

"Do djinn have restaurants?" Isis asked.

"We have those who's cooking skills are renowned, who specialize in creating meals without the aid of *ma-at* and are willing to trade those talents. I myself have enjoyed their creations." He'd enjoyed some of the feminine chefs' other talents, as well, but he didn't think it necessary to share that fact.

"Well, New Orleans is a food town, so let me treat you to dinner. Seafood, I think." She gave him a mischievous smile. "You up for some boiled crawfish?"

"Is it as good as your chocolate?"

"Well, nothing beats chocolate, but it's pretty darn good."

Darius stared in consternation at the tray the waitress set before him. Mounded on it were piles of bright red crustaceans. Such a surfeit of food, if he could figure out how to eat them. Crawfish, it turned out, had shells, claws, and antennae.

Isis had taken him to an area she called Bucktown, where blocks of squat buildings clustered amid the pungent aromas of fish and hot peppers. Inside the noisy, crowded restaurant, Isis ordered two all-you-can-eat specials, a beer, and a cola. At Isis's urging, he had tasted both drinks and had chosen the cola.

Isis must have seen his confusion. She picked up a crawfish. "You're supposed to suck the heads and pinch the tails."

Darius stared aghast, as she twisted the crawfish in two, separating head from tail. She took the head part, sucked at the end, and then tossed the shell into an empty tray.

"Do you eat its brain?" His stomach roiled at the thought.

"Nah, just getting the juice it was boiled in, with a little of the fat. It's very spicy. The tasty part is the tail. You pinch down here," she held the end of the tail, "and eat." Her white teeth closed around the other end and tugged, pulling out a piece of pink and white meat no bigger than his little finger. Isis gulped it down.

Darius looked at the heaping tray before him and sighed. "Such a lot of work for such a little morsel." He picked up one, then looked at her, his Isis who barely reached his shoulder. "However, I find I've acquired a recent taste for troublesome morsels."

Isis flushed. "Try the potatoes and corn."

* * *

187

Some time later, Darius discovered, to his amazement, that his tray was empty and a mass of shells was piled beside him.

The crawfish had been good. His people enjoyed spicy foods, and these had definitely been a flavorful combination of sweet meat, hot spices, and rich broth. Like Isis, he had just kept eating, one after the other, intent not on the numbers consumed, but on the bursting flavors and the intriguing conversation of the woman with him.

Isis leaned back and patted her stomach. A dot of red pepper remained on her chin. He leaned over and wiped it off with a paper napkin. She smiled at him. "I'm full. Do you want more?"

Darius shook his head. "How did you eat so much? You got a second trayful, where I merely finished my first."

"It's not polite to tell a lady she eats too much," she teased, then glanced at the shells beside her, the pile twice the size of his, and laughed. "But, in this case, I'd say you're right. Crawfish are a weakness of mine. I can spend the day peeling tails."

Her laughter sounded rich, full, and relaxed. He had not heard her laugh so, he realized. Just as she had never talked to him with such ease before.

Before, she had been wary around him. He was so used to respect, deference, and even touches of fear in others, he had not seen it. He only noticed it now because of its absence.

Had some good come from that bargain? Had she so distrusted his *ma-at*?

The thought should be more troublesome. Yet he could not think when he had sat with a woman and simply talked and enjoyed it so much. Women desired either his boon or his body, his power or his prestige.

Isis wanted nothing, but perhaps his presence.

To be wanted for simply Darius, not Protector. It

was a strange feeling, but not an unwanted or an unpleasant one.

The next morning, Sunday, Isis awoke early, even though it was her day off. The habit of early rising was a hard one to break for just one morning. Besides, she treasured these first moments of a fresh day, when she didn't have to rush to work. It was a favorite time for preparing herself for the challenges of the coming week.

Dressed in an orange terry-cloth jumper, she sat on her back steps, sipped a glass of apricot juice, and listened to the faint strains of Pachelbel's *Canon* coming through her opened window in accompaniment to the tinkle of her wind chime. Vulcan batted at a hanging lilac bloom. A chirping Khu perched in his cage, which hung from a porch hook. She took slow, deep breaths, inhaling the citrusy bergamot steeping on her aromalamp.

The tightening of her spine as much as the soft rustle behind her told her that Darius had joined her. Silently, he sat beside her. Resting one foot on the step below, he braced his chin on his knee and stared out at the garden.

His eyes were half closed, attesting to his recent awakening and, although his hair could never be said to be messed, it did have a softer, more tousled look in the morning sun.

He was barefoot. She'd never really looked at men's feet before, other than to notice they were a lot bigger than hers, but Darius's were nice—strong and long and lean, just like the rest of him. He wore a brief pair of navy gym shorts and a tank top, this one emerald ribbed. Of course the turquoise tablet and the blue robe completed the outfit. Dark hair dusted his arms and legs.

He was a picture of masculine grace and power.

He turned his head to look at her but said nothing at catching her staring.

Isis felt her heart stumble. He was beautiful in the dawning light, a fantasy too mercurial to touch, much less hold. As if sensing something of her thoughts, he leaned over and kissed her neck, a kiss as delicate as a cat's whisker. As quickly as it began, the kiss ended, and he was gazing back at the trees and shrubs.

"I dreamed of you last night," he said.

The murmur of his voice flowed through her like the ceaseless tide. She waited, but he did not elaborate.

"A good dream, I hope."

A faint smile played across his lips. "Very."

If his dream had been anything like hers, he'd woken up hot and unsated. Isis took a sip of her apricot juice, then held the large glass to him. "Thirsty?"

"Thank you." He took the glass, turned it so he drank from the same spot as she, and then handed it back, again turning it so her lips would taste after his.

Isis leaned one shoulder against the newel and closed her eyes. Every gesture, every word of his struck deep chords within her. He was like that long-sought perfume: filled with layers—some blatant, some hidden—all exquisitely perfect and so *right*.

Silence lengthened between them, a comfortable silence neither felt compelled to fill. The tensions, the awareness were there, too, but the warming sun diffused them.

How many men of her acquaintance would be content simply to sit on a porch step, sharing a glass of juice, and enjoying the morning peace, not rushing to the next task? Not many.

"Tell me about your world," she said, opening her eyes.

He leaned his back against the other newel. "What would you like to know?"

"Whatever you would like to tell me."

After a pause, he began. "Kaf is a beautiful land, as least we think so, though I suppose humans would deem it harsh. Deserts, high mountains, patches of water and green that shine with life. It is hot there, as hot as here, but much drier. Legend has it that Azazel, our leader when we left Terra, chose a spot that would remind his people of their abandoned home."

"The djinn were once of earth?"

He nodded. "We preferred to be masters of our own world, than be between the humans and angels in this. But that's why we can transport here."

"You can't live here, can you?"

"Our souls, our powers, are bound to Kaf, to her fires and her air. Those bonds must be replenished, without them our *ma-at*, and thus our souls, shrivel and die. We die."

"Can humans live on Kaf?"

He looked at her then. "Yes. Human bonds to Terra are not as strong."

"I don't know. I think many of us have very strong bonds to earth. Perhaps not in magic, but in family, in our place here, in love."

He looked away. "Perhaps." In the distance they heard a horn honk, and a plane buzzed overhead. "When I am here, one thing I particularly miss is the solitude and silence on Kaf. There are not many djinn. I have difficulty with your crowds."

She was surprised to hear him admit a weakness. "Then why do you stay?"

He hesitated a moment, then rose to his feet in a lithe motion, his muscles bunching and flowing. "Because for the next two weeks we fulfill a bargain."

She had the distinct impression he'd debated saying something other than that nonanswer. There was still so much mystery about Darius, little pockets of unease that compelled her not to trust him fully.

There was also so much about him that was magical; little things beyond his *ma-at,* like the way he seemed not to notice human divisions of class or race, or the way he delighted in small pleasures. He wasn't chasing after power or prestige or wealth, but treasured nature and life. Something in him called to her as powerfully as a dream. Already, Isis knew his inevitable departure would be a painful loss.

Darius held out his hand to her, and Isis placed hers in his keeping. He pulled her to her feet, but he did not let go of her hand. Instead, he urged her closer. "This is our day. How shall we spend it? If you have no ideas, I have some."

Isis heard a metallic click, but as mesmerized as she was with thoughts of what they might do, she ignored it. Instead, she stepped closer to Darius. His free hand circled down her spine in a graceful spiral.

The low, masculine whistling coming from her garden did register. Someone had opened her back gate, someone was coming, but she was too boneless to move.

Until the whistling stopped. "What the hell?"

"Good morning, Ram," said Darius without looking away from Isis.

Isis tore her gaze from her djinni to her brother.

The early hour, the rumpled dress, the intimate pose. She knew Ram saw it all and drew his own conclusions, all correct except for the technical fact that she hadn't yet slept with Darius.

Rapidly, Ram closed the gap. He halted at the foot of her steps and opened his mouth.

"Don't say a thing," warned Isis, forestalling the lecture, the questions, and the offended brother. "Not unless you're giving me permission to meddle in *your* life. I'm three years over twenty-one, and I know what I'm doing."

"Are you through?" asked Ram mildly.

Isis gave an emphatic nod.

"I just came by to offer you a ride to the volleyball game. You do remember Dream Scents is playing today?"

"Oh, uh, yeah." No lecture? No questions?

"I've got breakfast." Ram held up a paper bag.

"Thank you. We have not yet broken our fast," answered Darius for her.

"Thanks, Ram, we'd like a ride. On one condition—" She looked pointedly at the paper bag. "You stop and get beignets on the way."

Chapter Fourteen

To Isis's surprise, during the ride out to the Lake-front, Ram said nothing about the early morning intimacy he'd witnessed. Instead, she found herself ensconced in the back seat with her bag of sugary beignets while the two men shared the front seat and Ram's breakfast concoction. Ram questioned Darius, relentlessly and not too subtly. Why was Darius here? Had he been modeling long? Did he have a job lined up? How long was he staying? Were the hotels all booked up?

Darius, in turn, was his usual charming, and evasive, self.

By the time they'd reached the Lakefront, Isis was ready to consign them both to a rowboat without oars.

Ram parked in the lot near West End Park and the Municipal Yacht Harbor at Lake Pontchartrain. On Sunday morning the lot was nearly empty; the surrounding seafood restaurants were shuttered and quiet. Isis started with Ram toward the volleyball sand to watch the current game, but when Darius drifted in the opposite direction, toward the lake, she followed him onto the concrete sidewalk.

With a muted roar, waves rolled across the rocky shoreline. Colorful striped sails dotted the horizon; the Sunday sailors were out enjoying a pleasant morning. The warm spring sun heated her skin, while the light breeze cooled it.

"Is it an ocean?" Darius's voice held a touch of awe.

"Lake Pontchartrain. Not nearly as big as an ocean, and the water's fresh, not salt."

Darius traversed the jumbled rocks to the water's edge and scooped up some in his palm.

"Don't drink it," Isis warned. "There have been remarkable efforts to clean it up, but I still wouldn't drink the water on the shore's edge."

"Can we swim in it?"

Isis shook her head. "We swim in pools or go to the Gulf beaches in Mississippi, Alabama, or Florida."

"Pity," he said. "We have water in Kaf, but few large bodies like this. They are sacred places to my people." He let the water trickle from his hand.

"We enjoy it in our own way. I like coming out here, or by the river, just to sit and watch and listen. People boat, jog, picnic. Do you like to swim?" At his nod, she continued, "Some time I'll take you to the beach—a day of sun, sand, and surf."

Darius turned and smiled at her. "I would like that."

"Hey, Ice," Ram called, "we're up."

Their opponents were slathering on suntan lotion and warming up on the sidelines, while the small crowd of fans and players—assembled on the tier of bleachers or the surrounding grassy levees—cheered the game in progress. Darius and Isis joined the Dream Scents team.

"Darius, you've met Salem and Marc. This is Joel Samson." Isis introduced the tall, muscular black man. "He's a friend of Ram's, a fellow vet. Joel, this is Darius. He's, uh—"

"I am a friend of Isis's," Darius supplied.

"Nice to meet you." Sun glinted off Joel's gold tooth, gold earring, and shaved head as he shook hands with Darius.

Funny, Isis thought idly, Joel looked more like her one-time image of a genie than Darius. "Where's Everett?" she asked, looking for the sixth member of the team, a lawyer who consulted for Dream Scents.

"He called and said he couldn't make it this morning. He knew we could pick up an extra player." Salem nodded toward the bleachers.

"How about Darius?" suggested Joel.

"Oh, I doubt he's ever played." Isis shoved her sunglasses onto her nose.

Ram looked at Darius, lifting one brow. "Have you?"

"No." Darius studied the ongoing game, then eyed Ram, before turning to Isis. "But I am a fast learner."

Marc clapped him on the shoulder. "Then you're elected."

In a low voice, Isis ran down the rules, while the others got ready to play. "Six people on a team; our team has three hits to get it over the net; place it in bounds, but where they can't return it; the team only scores points while serving; fifteen points wins."

"What is the purpose of this?" Darius studied the players with grave intent.

"To win."

"And then?"

"You slap hands in victory and play again."

"But what is the purpose?" he repeated, turning his attention back to her. "Does it train your skills? Sharpen your hand and eye? Teach you control? Do the losers owe one day's labor?"

196

Isis stared at him. His confusion was genuine. "It's a game, that's all. We play to win, but the only thing at stake is our pride. We're here just for fun."

"Ah." He sounded surprised at the concept.

"Don't you djinn ever just goof around?"

"Goof?"

"Let your hair down, fool around, relax, have fun, play."

"We have games." He looked away. "But I have not been part of them in a very long time," he said softly, almost to himself.

Isis's chest tightened. No games, no play? What kind of a life had he led? She grasped his hand. "Well, today you play." She looked him up and down. "The shorts and tank top are okay, but you'll have to ditch the robe and sandals. We play barefoot. And no *ma-at*," she added in an undertone.

He gave her an offended look. "I honor my bargains."

The Dream Scents team had the first serve. Ram slammed the ball across the net, but their opponents recovered and spiked the ball back, right at Darius.

It hit him on the top of his head and dropped into the sand.

"Change serve," called the other team.

Darius looked so astonished, Isis had to laugh. When he glowered at her, she laughed all the harder. "It's just a game," she reminded him. "Have fun."

"Fun," he muttered, but his tension receded.

The other team served, a bullet right at Darius. Apparently they sensed where the weak spot on the Dream Scents team stood. Darius stuck out his hand and the ball slapped against his palm, back toward Salem. She two-fisted it toward the net, a perfect setup to Darius.

He, however, was staring at his palm and missed the ball.

"One-nothing," called the other team.

"I guess I should have told you it stings when you hit the ball." Isis giggled. "It's best to hit with the heel of your hand or fist."

Darius rested his hands on his hips. "Is there aught else you forgot to tell me?"

"Things will come up, I'm sure."

Since he was staring at Isis, he missed the next serve entirely.

"Two-nothing."

"You two gonna play, or are you gonna stand around having a *conversation?*" Ram called out.

"Play," answered Isis, grinning at Darius. "Right?"

"Play," he answered with both word and grin.

Darius was, as he said, a fast learner. He was also agile and coordinated and moved with a quick, lithe grace that soon took him from the status of liability to asset.

Dream Scents lost the first game, the score close and hard fought. Darius, she discovered, was also competitive and did not like losing, any more than the others on the team did. They demanded a re-match and this time won on a spike from Joel, set up by Ram and Darius.

Neither team pressed for a tie-breaker.

As Isis and her friends sprawled on the grass outside the chain-link fence, drinking the 10-K Ram retrieved from his cooler and wiping sweat off with towels, Joel gave Darius a friendly cuff. "Good smash on the tenth point. No way they were returning that."

"It would not have been so easy had not Marc given me that pretty floater."

The spring sun had warmed the ground. Sitting slightly above the others on the levee, Isis rested her chin on her knees and watched Darius's easy interactions with her friends.

He looked as though he had been a part of them for years. That simple fact spread the warmth at her back to a place deep in her gut and to her heart. His charm was not all sexual, for even Ram and Joel were not immune. Her brother's wariness, though not gone, had lessened. He could rib Darius about those first shots, then laugh heartily when Darius tartly reminded him about a serve Ram had sent straight into the net.

When Marc added a comment to the male ritual of insults-as-bonding, Darius tilted his head back in easy, shared laughter. Isis took another gulp of the 10-K, then pressed the cool bottle against her fevered cheek. His laugh lodged deeper inside her than any of his smiles had.

In their short acquaintance she'd never heard him laugh like that, unfettered and joyous. It was a sound she would risk much for, just to hear it again.

Part of his appeal was that Darius listened, Isis realized, watching him turn to Joel. He listened with intensity and attention, rarely turning a conversation to details about himself. The latter was frustrating to a woman who wanted to find out more about the elusive djinni. Delve deeper and you hit a crystal wall whose surface glittered and shone but relinquished few secrets.

Salem flopped down beside her. "Man, it's hot here. Hey, Marc, you bag of bones, throw me another 10-K," she yelled. He tossed her one. She downed half, then tilted her head to look at Isis.

"Y'know, Ice, I had my doubts about Darius at first. I mean, he just sort of appeared. But I like him." She grinned. "And he's got one bad case for you, you know. 'Course you do for him, too; your eyes devour him when he's not looking."

"How do you know he's got a 'bad case' for me?" asked Isis, curious and determined to ignore her own telltale behavior.

"I'm a good reader of body language, and his shouts, 'Hands off, she's mine.' A bit retro, but kinda cute, too." She tilted her head toward Isis. "One

199

thing's got me curious: He's living with you, but you're not sleeping with him. Not yet, anyway."

Salem did tend to be blunt. Isis's scarlet-tipped nail tore at the paper label on her 10-K. "You can tell just by looking?"

"I've seen a lot of people with that look of sex. You don't have it." Salem raised her brows. "Besides, if you were doing the deed with him, would you be *here* working up a sweat?"

Isis flushed and took another swallow of drink. She sometimes forgot how astute Salem could be, but the girl hadn't survived the streets by being unobservant.

"Hey, I didn't mean to embarrass you, but I worry about you, Ice."

"You worry about me?"

Salem shrugged. "You're smart and a good boss and all that, but you've been kind of sheltered."

Isis choked on her 10-K. "Sheltered?"

"Compared to me." By Salem's standards, and experience, Isis supposed she *was* sheltered. "How much do you know about Darius?" Salem continued.

Isis looked at the djinni. "A lot. But not enough."

"Do you trust him?"

Darius's gaze flickered toward Isis. He'd done that several times, she realized, as though he, too, needed to renew the contact between them. He gave her a fleeting smile, waiting until she returned it before resuming his conversation.

Thoughtfully, Isis stroked the turquoise pendant he'd given her. "Yeah, I guess I do."

"That's okay then," answered Salem. "You've got good instincts."

She *did* trust Darius, or at least she had started to, Isis realized. His *ma-at* was as innate as breathing to him. It would have been so easy for him, automatic almost, to float the ball a little higher, to tug an errant serve so it landed inside the lines instead of out, to add power to his hits. Yet, despite his competitive nature, he had done none of that.

Not even when he dove for the ball and ended up sliding along the sand. The resulting abrasions on his cheek and arm had oozed blood, and he'd grimaced, as if surprised by the blood and the pain. Isis had seen him start to chant something under his breath, then he had tensed and abruptly stopped. He'd shot her an irritated glance before wiping his cheek on his shirt and going back to the game.

He'd honored the terms of their bargain. He wasn't like Ben.

Darius glanced at her again. Something of her thoughts must have registered on her face or maybe she was broadcasting them to his telepathic brain, for he quickly excused himself from the men and strode over to her. He dropped down beside her, lolling on the grass with casual grace. It was a very masculine pose—legs spread, one arm extended behind him for maximum space, the other resting on her shoulder.

In some ways djinn and human males were very much alike.

"Are you ready to go, Isis?" he asked.

Salem got to her feet and dusted off her hands. "I gotta run. See you tomorrow, Ice. And probably you, too, Darius."

Isis acknowledged the Dream Scents team's adieus, but most of her mind, and all of her body, was fully occupied elsewhere. One of Darius's fingers delved beneath the strap of her shirt and traced whorls of heat across her shoulder. Her skin tightened with the touch, making her breasts tingle and her insides ache with a swelling desire to be touched as well. "I was missing you," he said in a low tone.

"I was right here."

"Ah, but you were not where I could do this." His

little finger traced the line of hair on her nape, an area Isis had never realized could be classified as an A-1 erogenous zone. Until now, that is. Her breathing quickened.

"If I cannot stroke you with my *ma-at*," he continued, his voice soft as spring air, "then I want to touch you with my hand, my lips, my body."

"In public?"

"In public I will not stray beyond your society's sense of what is proper. In private I will not stray beyond *your* sense of propriety."

"You know these boundaries?"

"I think you would tell them to me. Do you trust me on this, my sweet Isis?"

She looked at him then. Despite her insides feeling like sun-heated lotion, his only touch on her was a chaste hand at the shoulder. "I trust you on this."

A smile crossed his lips. "Then how shall we spend the rest of the day?"

"How about the beach?"

Ram joined them, just in time to hear their final exchange. "A day at the beach. Sounds like fun. Let me call Rachel to pack her swimsuit—"

Isis shook her head. "Ram, I doubt Rachel wants a double date with your sister."

Ram opened his mouth. Isis stared at him. He shut it.

At least, Isis thought, *one of them is learning.*

Too bad it wasn't the djinni.

How long could one endure an incessant mix of frustration and contentment? Over the next week, Darius asked himself that more than once.

Each evening, he and Isis explored a different part of the city. They listened to hot jazz by Coup de Fire, saw the jaguar exhibit at the zoo, watched sharks swim at the aquarium, paddled canoes down one of the bayous. He had especially enjoyed the traveling exhibit of Persian art at the museum. The curator responsible for the exhibit had been most knowledgeable, and they'd had a fascinating discussion about the meaning of certain hieroglyphs. Isis had waited patiently, he remembered, with a faint, contented smile.

One night, when they got hopelessly lost because of Isis's poor sense of direction, Darius learned to decipher human maps, but generally he let Isis choose and lead. He didn't care where they went, as long as he was with her, and she seemed pleased that he didn't demand to take over the guide role.

Tonight they'd opted for a late-afternoon picnic at one of the city's parks. The sun was still up, for the days grew long this time of year, but the broad emerald cover of leaves shielded its brilliance. Others were taking advantage of the daylight: a group of young boys kicked around a black-and-white ball, a mother jogged by pushing a child in a wheeled seat, four older youths lounged on a wooden table and sucked on thin white tubes that had smoke coming from them.

Feeling lazy, Darius rested on the cool ground, leaning against a massive oak tree while he watched Isis spread out their repast. "Do you need help?" he asked, making no move to her.

"Naw, just sit there and vegetate."

Darius was content to listen to Isis humming along with a distant radio, which competed with the swans honking in the bayous, and to feast on the grace of her brisk movements. She wore yellow today, bright as the sands at Hilaku, a reflection of the energy she brought to even this simple task. He liked that in her, her enthusiasm.

A wasp buzzed around Isis's ear, and she flinched. Darius leaned forward and trapped it between his cupped palms. He released it, sending it in another direction, away from her.

"Thanks."

"You are welcome." He resumed his relaxed pose.

When had he ever simply enjoyed being with a woman, without sex and without *ma-at?* Never, Darius realized.

For this short time, the ease of these evenings with Isis—with no demands beyond enjoying himself and no responsibilities beyond arriving at her store at closing—filled him with a contentment he'd not known before and hadn't even realized he was missing. He was well aware that the threat from Pari had not vanished—part of his days he spent unsuccessfully seeking her—and soon he must resume the responsibilities of Protector, but, for now, for the first time in his life, he was simply Darius. Not the Protector, not the Protector's apprentice, not the one who must learn, at any cost, to control and wield his power. Just Darius.

It was an odd feeling. One he savored as a unique treat, but one that, in the end, did not sit naturally upon him.

Being unable to wield his *ma-at* at his choosing should have been a loss more painful than the sharp bite of a tiger. Often he was forced to stop responses that came as automatically to him as a heartbeat. Without *ma-at,* he never felt . . . complete.

Isis made the void bearable, though, her delightful companionship taking the edge off his need for his *ma-at.*

It also helped that, during the day, he returned to Kaf, where he could readily explore his returning mastery and could feel the *ma-at* flow through him, pure and strong and controlled, almost as it had been before. Only rarely did it slip from him, and that would be remedied as soon as Isis became fully his.

Isis handed him a round sandwich, then bit into her own. "How you can eat a muffuletta with only cheese and olive salad. I'll never know," she said around a mouthful.

Earlier, she'd been indignant when he'd insisted the meats be left off his, but she had given in to his demands. Isis, Darius decided with some smugness, was challenging and fascinating, a pleasure to be with, and compliant when necessary.

She would make him a worthy *zaniya*.

His gut tightened. And therein lay the ever-present frustration. He still wanted Isis, with a hunger that deepened each night, but he had decided he would not take her until the second bargain was fulfilled. Until he was once more complete. Until she could be his by all the rituals of the djinn.

Waiting, however, was harder than taking a breath in a sandstorm.

A black-and-white ball bounced against his glass of juice, tipped it over, and then rolled through the spilled liquid.

"Sorry, mister." A dark-haired boy, about the equivalent human age as Jared, ran up.

Darius wiped the sticky ball clean on the picnic cloth before handing it back. "There is no harm."

"Thanks." The boy ran back to his friends.

Isis tilted her head. "You do that a lot, you know."

"Do what?"

"Little things. Little acts of kindness. Like wiping off the ball."

"I like children. We have few on Kaf."

She shook her head. "It's not just children. You notice when something's not right and you fix it. I think it's almost second nature to you."

"I'm not a kind person, Isis," he felt compelled to warn her.

"You're arrogant, yes. Aloof, too. But not deliberately cruel."

Darius shifted, uneasy with her grave praise. "I can be if I must."

A tiny shudder rippled through her. "Yes, I suppose you could, but I've never seen you use your talents to exploit the weak."

"That would misuse the gifts of air and fire."

Would she think his plans for her exploitation? Something told him she might. Under her admiring gaze, unfamiliar guilt bit into him.

Could he tell her why he had come? Isis cared about others; she would understand his need to protect his people. The Isis he had come to know this past week would surely agree to the ritual. The urge to tell her all—his role on Kaf, the prophecy, the full import of the ritual he would ask of her, even the loss of control—swept through him, strong as a cyclone.

"There is much you don't know about me and the djinn," he began. "I'd like to show you my home, Isis."

"That might be fun one day." She looked away and started shredding the remains of her bread.

"When? Shall I take you now?"

"No transporting, remember? There are people about." She nodded toward the youths lounging against the table and the lads finishing up their ballgame.

"Then soon." He touched her cheek. Her skin was so soft; almost involuntarily he rubbed his thumb against her lips. "It is a beautiful place."

"I'm sure it is." She brushed the bread crumbs off her hands and into the grass. "I've got too much to do here right now to take off to some foreign dimension. The business, keeping Jimmy Ray off my back, figuring out what Ben wants, a charity bachelor auction, volleyball."

Darius tilted her chin so she looked at him. "Those sound like excuses. Are you afraid you wouldn't want to leave Kaf?"

She laughed, but the sound was hollow, not mirthful, and her lips trembled beneath his touch. "Look, I'm sure it's very nice, and I admit to a certain curiosity. I'd like to visit, but I wouldn't stay long."

"Why?"

Her gaze darted about, refusing to meet his, then she shrugged and looked directly at him. "Because everyone there does magic."

He waited in silence, one brow lifted in question.

"While I was growing up, I always felt less capable than everyone I knew. Everyone could read but me. I refuse to go back to that, to feeling like the dunce. Voluntarily staying in a place where everybody can do magic but me? I learned to read; I can't learn magic."

With that, his faint, fragile notion—almost unvoiced, born when he had seen Simon and Zoe together—of his *zaniya* at his side, of children, crumbled to dust and blew away under the harsh breath of her words. She would never stay on Kaf; he had known that from the beginning. The divination said they must join but said naught of anything beyond. Darius's hand stopped caressing her face. His insides tightened, trying to contain the unexpected sense of loss.

Earlier she had told him she had no desire to wed or join with a man. Why would he think she would agree to the ritual if she knew its full import?

He could not tell her, could not risk that she would refuse and he would be left with a *ma-at* beyond his control. He was Protector. His responsibility and his loyalty must go to his people, and *ma-at*. He could not risk both to satisfy his own need.

He could not tell her. He could not trust her.

The urge for honesty gave way beneath the cold inflexibility of necessity.

Unaware of the turmoil inside him, Isis rolled to her stomach and propped up her chin with her hands. "You're right, though; I don't know a lot about you. One thing I've been wondering: Physically, you're strong, Darius, and very fit." She gave him another admiring look, which, to his consternation, sent a flush coursing through him. Why did she still have this effect on him?

"But *ma-at* doesn't require a lot of physical effort, does it?" she continued. "Are all djinn like you, or is it because you have to work harder at your *ma-at*?"

Darius answered automatically. "*Ma-at* springs from the strength of mind and will, yes, but the physical body is its conduit. With disease, or if the body is not at full physical harmony and health, the power does not flow." He stopped abruptly as he realized what she had said. "What do you mean, I have to work harder at my *ma-at*?"

She flushed and rolled to her back, breaking eye contact. "Nothing. Forget it."

Darius planted a hand on either side of her shoulders and loomed over her. *"What did you mean?"*

Her tongue moistened her lips. "Before this bargain, I saw how much effort it took for you to generate spells. Like at Aunt Tildy's. I just figured you were kinda low on the Richter scale of magic."

Low on the Richter scale of magic? He didn't understand the reference, but he certainly understood the meaning. The efforts he'd expended to control his raging, pulsing *ma-at*, the fight against the impact of alien Terra—she'd taken those as weakness!

She laid a comforting hand on his shoulder. "Don't worry. I like you that way; it makes you more human."

More human! That was supposed to soothe him?

"I know what it's like to be considered slow," she barreled on, oblivious to his rising heat. "It gives us a common ground."

Darius was unsure whether to laugh or to demonstrate just how wrong she was. Only the constraints of the bargain kept him controlled. She thought him, one of the most powerful of the djinn, to be a minor djinni!

She would learn otherwise. They would complete this bargain, and then he would demand her willing participation in the ritual. She would be his *zaniya*, and he would show her exactly how high on that Richter scale of magic he was.

Hesitantly she touched his hair. "You're sparking. Remember, no magic with this bargain."

"That is out of my control. Even we weak djinn spark and our voices echo when angered."

"Why are you angry?" Then her face softened. "I understand. My brothers get angry, too, rather than admit a weakness."

He glared at her. In the receding light beneath the tree, her face was shadowed, and only her wide eyes could he see clearly. They were alone, or nearly so, in the park.

Forces of *ma-at* battered him from inside, demanding release. He resisted by substituting something that called to him as powerfully; he leaned over and kissed Isis.

Anger could not withstand the rush of passion.

This kiss was not like the balmy, unsatisfying kisses he'd endured this week, kisses that gentled her but did not tempt his *ma-at* to break its imposed fetters. This kiss contained desire and blatant need and all the surging powers of an aroused djinni. This kiss claimed what was his and whatever else she would give.

With a soft moan, Isis opened beneath him, allowing his tongue and his breath to sweep inside. Her fingers gripped his arms as he followed her down. The fire of his desire met a raging river in her passion, and it seemed as if steam billowed inside him, beyond his control. The magic of Terra, alien streams of power, rose in response.

She shifted beneath him. The ground at her back

209

must be uncomfortable for her. He wanted only her pleasure, not a hint of discomfort.

Never releasing her lips, he twisted, sitting upright and pulling her into his lap. He cradled her in his arms, wondering at how right she felt there.

His arms tightened about her, and the explosion of scalding steam inside him settled into a softer, gentler cloud. The demanding *ma-at*, roused by his anger, quieted under her caresses and became a rich flow of sweet power.

Even the magic of Terra accepted it. With a gasp, Darius broke off the kiss. What magic had she worked?

The chaotic question, however, would not be answered at this time.

An impudent human poked him with a shod toe. "Hey, dude, how about us taking a turn with your old lady?"

The four youths who had occupied a neighboring table surrounded them. The harsh words faded in the silence of the darkening, empty park.

"Go away," said Darius, the sound of command automatic in his voice. He turned his back to the youth.

A rough hand grabbed Isis and pulled her away from Darius; then a booted foot kicked him in the ribs, knocking him backward. To Darius's astonishment, a sharp pain pierced his chest, robbing him of breath and motion.

Isis sprang to her feet. "Leave him alone." She thrust her backpack at the nearest leather-clad youth. "Here, take this. It's all we've got."

The one who had spoken first grabbed her shoulder. "I don't think so. Me and my friends figured we'd show ya a good time."

All the Protector's training and the djinn's dislike of humans fused inside Darius. *Ma-at* swirled through him, burying the alien energies of Terra in a maelstrom of power and fury. It spread to his hands, his fingers, and only at the last minute did Darius pull it back.

That bedamned bargain! He had made a solemn promise.

Instead, panting, he rolled away from another swing of the foot. Ignoring the burning agony of his ribs, he grabbed the boot and swung up. Ancient techniques of combat, studied through long, agonizing hours to tone the body and to give him control over each movement, returned to him as easily as they had to the first warriors who had fought without *ma-at*. A motion of the hand, a swing of the foot, and one of the attackers lay moaning on the ground, clutching his abdomen.

He was vaguely aware that Isis also fought, with a kicking motion strangely similar to his own, and just as well placed, bringing down a second, who was apparently too startled by the unexpected ferocity of such a small woman to resist.

Darius attacked the third.

"Enough," snarled the leader.

Isis screamed.

The leader had grabbed her hair and used it to twist her head to the side, holding her immobile. A metallic object, clutched in his other meaty fist, pressed against her neck.

The third attacker went down. Pain shooting throughout him, Darius strode to Isis, ready to finish this.

"No, Darius," she moaned, "he's got a gun."

Darius stopped. "What's a gun?"

"This, mother!" The leader turned the metallic object toward him. There was a blast and an acrid smell, followed by silence and numbness.

Darius looked down and saw blood, his blood, spreading out across his robe from a hole in his side.

Agony, unrelenting and debilitating, followed and filled every cell of his body. Darkness fought for supremacy.

Darius fell to his knees.

Chapter Fifteen

Sight and sound ceased to exist for Isis. Her ears rang from the blast of the gun, and the hurricane roar of fury drowned out all else. All she could see was the bright red stain spreading across Darius, his golden skin turning ashen.

She twisted her head, ignoring the pain that flashed down her neck and shoulder from the unnatural angle, and tried to sink her teeth into the arm of her captor, but she couldn't reach it. An elbow to his gut, however, followed by a well-placed kick, did work.

Cursing, the punk doubled over, and his grip on her hair loosened. Isis yanked away, tears coming to her eyes from the sting of several hairs being ripped out. She stumbled forward. She knelt beside Darius, trying to lift him to his feet while she frantically worked to staunch the flow of blood. "We need to get out of here!"

He grabbed her chin with a bloody hand. "Release

me," he commanded. "Release me from the bargain."

Their bargain! My God, the damned bargain! If he'd been able to use his *ma-at*, he wouldn't have been shot.

"I release you from our bargain. Willingly, I release you." Isis rushed the words, prayed she was not too late.

Darius drew in a deep breath. Color returned to his face, then radiated outward, encasing him in a golden glow. Around her, the air felt like a hot night filled with dry lightning.

From the corner of her eye, she saw the punk struggle upright, recovering from the kick to his groin. "Darius," she shouted.

"I see him," he answered calmly. His hand shot downward, behind her back, from her head to her feet.

The gun fired.

Isis jerked, expecting a shot in the back.

The bullet fell harmlessly to the ground.

The punk stared in wide-eyed horror.

Darius's outstretched arms rested on her shoulders, and he intoned something undecipherable in a low, cold tone. He clenched his fists, then thrust them open. Power—unseen, but felt to her bones—exploded from his fingertips.

Behind her, the punk screamed as the gun in his hand turned red hot, then twisted into molten steel.

The fires of *ma-at* raged across Isis from where Darius's arms rested against her. She laid her hand on his arm.

"Do not burn yourself, my djinni," she whispered.

Subtly, the *ma-at* shifted. A cool whispering, like the rustle of leaves, joined the inferno. The *ma-at* still flowed, still as strong, but not as wild.

The punk dropped the gun and watched, with fear-glazed eyes, as it melted into an unrecognizable lump. Breathing hard, seemingly frozen in one spot, he stared at Darius.

"Hey, man, I'll just be going." He backed up.

Darius's reply was a smile, a smile that sent a chill straight to her gut. He had been right. He could be very cruel.

"Do not forget to take your friends with you." Darius wrapped one arm around Isis's shoulders, holding her close, while he waved his other hand in the air. He chanted something foreign, something he didn't bother to hide under his breath, and then he picked up two handfuls of dirt and leaves and tossed them toward the three punks struggling upright and their leader. Just as the leaves fell to earth, he shouted something.

The four punks disappeared. Only heaps of leather and dirty cloth and oversized sneakers remained.

"Did you kill them?" Isis wasn't sure what she wanted his answer to be, now that the danger had passed.

"No. Djinn do not kill."

"Then—" She heard a tiny squeak, and saw four brown field mice poke trembling noses between blades of grass. Her eyes widened. "You turned them into mice?"

"It is an archaic spell and one not easily mastered. Even mine will only last about an hour of your time. But perhaps they will remember what it feels like to be small and timid."

Isis twisted until she faced Darius. "I'm so sorry. If it wasn't for that stupid bargain—" She hugged him fiercely.

Darius winced.

"Your wound!" She tore at his robe, stiff with drying blood. "Are you still bleeding? We need to get a bandage on it. Get you to a doctor."

He gripped her at the wrists, stopping her. "The missile did not lodge." He let her go, then peeled back the robe and shirt. "See, it is healing."

Isis gaped at the wound. It had stopped bleeding and the edges met in a ragged seam. Although still red and inflamed, the scar seemed to fade a bit as she looked. "But you lost so much blood." Gently she touched the wound.

He winced again. "And thus I am still sore and weak."

"Your *ma-at* can do this? Are you immortal?"

"No. We can be killed by accidents, sinister *ma-at*, spells gone awry. If it had been a more grievous wound, or if the missile had lodged in a vital area like my heart or my head, I would have died."

Isis closed her eyes against the ripping agony of the thought of losing this vibrant djinni who had exploded into her life with wind and fire. Lose him she must when they went their separate ways, but not to the finality of death.

"Let me get you home."

She helped him rise, but he did not immediately go toward her car. He looked at her, no hint of his thoughts in his dark eyes. "It would be easier for me to transport."

The bargain between them was finished, yet he asked. Something inside of Isis dissolved, a last barrier to trust and caring. This past week she had felt relaxed enough with him to see beyond the *ma-at* to the man beneath. And the more she liked the man, the more she missed that spark of *ma-at* within him.

He was djinni, a man of magic, yes. He had also kept his word at great cost to himself. He could be cruel; he could also be kind. And, for now, he was hers.

Without even looking to see if anyone watched, Isis said, "Take us home, Darius."

Being coddled was a new experience for Darius, and he found he enjoyed it. Especially when it was Isis doing the coddling.

She settled him on a divan downstairs with plenty of pillows and brought him iced juice to drink. She insisted upon bathing his wound with healing scented water. Although it was unnecessary—his body healed well on its own—her soft hands held such caring that he did not have the will to deny her. He craved her touch, both in womanly concern and feminine need.

He would have healed faster on Kaf, drawing her strength as his, for Terran energies still nipped at his abilities, but Darius could not bring himself to transport away.

Drowsiness stole across him. He felt the pillows sag as Isis sat beside him and laid a cool hand on his forehead.

"No fever, it seems. That is, if your body temperature is similar to ours."

"I think it is close, perhaps a degree or two higher," he answered without opening his eyes. He felt her muscles bunch as she prepared to stand, and he reached out for her hand. "Stay beside me. Lie beside me."

She hesitated, then stretched out beside him. Darius wrapped an arm around her and snugged her tight against him. He buried his nose at her neck. "I love the scent of jasmine," he murmured and fell asleep.

They spent the night nestled together, and when they awoke Darius knew he could not wait another week to make her his *zaniya*.

His hand trailed slowly up her front, from her abdomen to her chest. Deftly, his fingers undid the buttons on her nightshirt, then delved beneath for a goal he had long sought. She was bare, as she should be, not wearing that idiotic contraption human females called a "bra." He cupped her breast, his thumb resting on the nipple, then he stopped, savoring the tex-

217

ture of her silky skin, the lingering jasmine scent of her, the weight of her breast in his palm. He knew the instant she awoke and recognized the intimacy of their embrace, for he felt the bud beneath his thumb grow tight. Yet he did not start a deeper caress, even when she stirred, pressing herself more firmly against him. Instead, he moved to the other breast and delighted in it as well, while he pressed faint kisses against the back of her neck. She sighed in pleasure, reaching behind her to stroke his leg.

With a slight touch of *ma-at*, he shifted their positions, so she lay beneath him and he was settled between her legs. He cupped her head between his hands. Her eyes were wide, questioning, and filled with the sparkle of desire. If he wanted to take this further, she would be willing, he knew with sharp masculine instinct.

No, their first mating would be that of *zani* and his *zaniya*. He didn't question the deep-honed instinct.

And, if truth be known, he was still a little rankled with the realization that she preferred him without his *ma-at*. The djinn joining ritual was filled with the solemnity and power of *ma-at*. Only after she saw him then, in his strength, with his control fully his, would he become one with her.

But first he could not resist just a taste. He bent down and sipped at her lips, sweeter than fresh orange juice. She sighed, her breath ragged, and tunneled her fingers through his hair. Desire rose like a wave between them, and it took all his control not to be engulfed. To wait.

Reluctantly, Darius lifted, before the kiss became more, became what they both wanted it to be. He laid a finger across her lips, slightly reddened from his kiss. "Do you not have to go to work this morning?"

She paused in nibbling at his finger, blinked, nodded.

"I shall see you at six then." He lifted his hand.

"What?" The glaze of desire still filled her eyes.

Darius smiled at her. "You released me from the bargain; I did not release you. Your evenings are still mine."

Her eyes narrowed as desire faded.

He laid the finger back over her lips, stilling her. "If you were a djinni, I think you would be sparking right now," he told her gently. "Tonight, I think, shall be our third bargain."

Her gaze beneath his silencing hand roamed across his face, and her expressive dark eyes closed, shielding her emotions from him. Too bad his telepathy continued to fail with her. Slowly she nodded.

"Tonight," she whispered.

5:30. Sitting amid the clutter of Isis's workroom, Darius gave in to temptation and dabbed her jasmine perfume on his wrist. Her scent would linger on his skin as well as in his memory.

He looked at the clock once more. 5:32.

He closed the bottle, then sat back, thinking, his fingers steepled.

After Isis had left that morning, he had slept for a time, before awakening refreshed and healthy. He'd spent the remaining hours restless and bored, waiting to return to Kaf until he had Isis with him.

He had turned on the device Isis called a television. For a while the sounds and colors fascinated him, but he'd soon turned it off. It did not include the scents and touches of djinn stories, and he could make no sense of a tale where people jumped up and down and screamed for a car. He'd scrounged through Isis's cupboard and found a true treat, a chocolate cake labeled with the unlikely name of *Ding Dong.*

Eventually he'd ended up in the part of the house that was so quintessentially Isis, her workroom.

219

There he'd been content to sit and plan what he would need for the ritual of joining.

5:36.

Darius got to his feet. Enough of this. Isis could leave early on this most special of nights. She would name her price, he would fulfill it, then she would be his.

He pivoted and saw the shimmering energy of a message orb forming in the air before him. Not now! Then he froze, as it gathered its energy close. By Solomon, it was red and chiming with the persistence of a watcher giving alarm over a blinding sandstorm. High urgency!

Sands of Hilaku! Had he misjudged Pari? Had she begun her move early? Had his fascination with Isis endangered his people?

Darius held out his hands, and the message spell shot into them. "Speak. I, Darius, Protector of the *Ma-at*, do listen."

"Djinn from the edges of the Wastelands report strange forces at work. The waters turn sour and the storms gather."

Pari. It was Pari. Was she making her move or just testing his defenses? Either way, she must be stopped.

The message spell wasn't finished. "Jared is missing," it continued in a thin, emotionless voice. "It is suspected he seeks the cause."

The message spell faded, and Darius returned its energy to the cosmos. He could not even glory in the fact that his control had not deserted him this time.

Pari had begun her attack. And she had Jared.

While he dallied with a Terran woman, Jared had been put into danger. Coldness engulfed Darius, erasing the contentment of the day. He had failed, utterly, in his duty as Protector. Exacting training—emotionless and powerful—took over.

He shed all trappings of Terra, keeping only his

220

cleaned robe and his turquoise tablet. He stroked the glyphs of strength on his tablet, drawing their essence inside himself.

He was the Protector.

He intoned the words of connection, the words that would take him to Jared's side, and then Darius, Protector of the *Ma-at*, lifted his hands and disappeared.

"I don't suppose you know anything about this, m'dear."

A folded newspaper slid on the counter in front of Isis, who'd taken advantage of a lull to inventory her natural oils. She looked up.

Jimmy Ray leaned one elbow against the pale wooden counter and pointed to a headline. NUDES ARRESTED IN CITY PARK. WITCHCRAFT TURNED THEM INTO MICE.

Isis crossed her arms. "No."

"But you haven't read the whole article." Jimmy Ray read aloud in a slow drawl, and in spite of herself, Isis listened.

Unfortunately for the punks who'd attacked her, the spell had worn off just as a police car was patrolling through the park. Their scampering as mice had taken them far from their clothes, and their post-transformation daze had made them easy to subdue. Surprise, surprise, the police hadn't believed their story about being turned into mice, especially when urine tests had revealed traces of illegal drugs.

When he finished, Isis shook her head. "If you think I had something to do with that, aren't you worried I'll change you into a toad?"

"Your car was found nearby, illegally parked overnight."

Damn! She'd forgotten to get it back, and now it was probably in the Carollton tow lot. "Not that it's any of your business, but I had trouble getting it started, so I took a bus home and then collapsed into bed."

Marc came out of the office and, seeing Isis with Jimmy Ray, sauntered over. "Why, hello, Jimmy Ray. Have you discovered an abiding interest in aromatherapy? Our last preparation do the trick?"

Jimmy Ray ran a finger around his collar. "Isis, or her friend Darius, knows something about this." He stabbed the newspaper.

Marc smiled smoothly and leaned one hip against the wooden counter. "Ah, Darius; now there is a fine figure of a man."

"Of whom no record exists. Not with Customs, not with Interpol, not with the Morrocan government."

Isis hid a grimace and decided to offer no explanation.

Marc scanned the article, then burst out laughing. "You think Isis is a witch who goes around turning people into mice?"

"Do you really think magic exists, Jimmy Ray?" Isis braced her hands on the counter and stared at him. "Because if you think I did this, then you must ascribe some pretty strange powers to me."

"Not you, m'dear, your friend. I think you might be desperate and using him for a little revenge."

Isis wrinkled her brow in puzzlement. "Desperate? Revenge?"

Under his arm, he carried another folded section of the paper, which he set in front of her. She had no trouble reading this headline, or recognizing Ben Fontenot's snaky smile in the picture. "Old World Parfums releases 'Whispers,' a scent for the ages," she read in a tight voice, crumpling the paper in her fist.

Whispers had been the last perfume she'd created with Ben, the last formula the judge had awarded him. It was a tribute to the strong women of her family, a scent that was exotic without being overpowering, and the best one she'd ever done. Only the elusive, alluring perfume she now sought, the one she'd begun to call Magic, rivaled it.

Damn and double damn him! She'd hoped he'd have enough sense of honor not to use it. She should have known better.

At least now she knew what he'd hoped to gain when he'd crashed Tildy's party. Whispers was the last of the formulas he'd stolen. He needed a perfumer to continue to create new products, because if Old World Parfums didn't keep up a flow of new scents, it would eventually fade.

Had she really thought she was so stupid that she'd go back to him? Had she really thought his charm was so great that she'd forgive and forget? Yeah, he probably had.

Damn, she was tired of having people think she wasn't too bright, of cowering before people like Jimmy Ray Frank, afraid of what they might say about her.

Isis handed him back the newspaper. "So, what are you going to print, Jimmy Ray? That I'm a practicing witch who goes around turning people into mice? Or that I'm a crazed woman who's carried a grudge against a sleazy ex for three years? Either one would be a sure winner when you go to negotiate your next contract with the paper. Especially when I sue you for slander."

"You'd sue for libel," offered Marc. "Libel is the written word."

She nodded. "Thanks. Sue for libel." She waved a hand around the room. "This is what I do, Jimmy Ray. There's nothing magic about it, just hard work. And a lot of it, so if you have nothing more to say, leave."

She waited, and Jimmy Ray gave her a speculative look as he left.

Marc gave her a peck on the cheek. "I'm glad you're

finally standing up to him." He returned to his beloved computer.

Isis lifted the newspaper and picked her way through both the articles; then she dropped the paper and swore.

Ben Fontenot was planning to expand his business—skin care products, bath oils, even aromatherapy. Old World Parfums was being renamed By Nature. He was going to challenge her on every front, with Whispers as his signature scent. And he was bigger, better financed, and could flood the area with advertisements and promotions.

He could bury her.

Fingernails digging half moons into her palms, Isis fought against the old feelings of inadequacy, of failure, of being less than capable. She wouldn't give up on this. She wouldn't!

She had to have that mysterious perfume, something that Ben Fontenot could not compete with. The report from the gas chromatograph had come today. Everything they'd identified in it was expected, duplicatable. But there was something else there, an anomaly noted at the bottom of the report by the technician. A peak that seemed to move, to appear and disappear and reappear. Something unknown to human science.

That was the ingredient Darius would give her.

That was the ingredient that would make her perfume magic.

And tonight she would get it.

Four hours later, however, when she sat alone, in a dark and silent shop that had been closed for well over two hours, Isis had to admit an undeniable fact.

Darius wasn't coming.

Chapter Sixteen

At the farthest reaches of the Tower Lands, Darius found Jared sitting on a rock next to a pool of water. An acrid scent arose from the water, tainting the air and turning the surrounding rocks a dull gray. Swollen, unnatural dark clouds tumbled across the barren desert and collected at the jagged mountaintop. Lightning flashed across their black bellies, releasing a distant echo of thunder.

Jared sat hunched over, his arms wrapped around his legs, his cheek resting on his knees. His shallow breaths sounded rough and his face looked flushed.

"Jared," Darius said softly.

The child looked up, and Darius saw a darkening bruise on his jaw. Tears had left tracks through the dirt on his face.

Fury raced through Darius. He had no doubt who was behind this, and Pari would pay for using the child, pay dearly. He fought deep instincts that bid him run to Jared, embrace him and take him away,

225

for the Protector recognized the trap calculated to evoke just that response. A barrier of *ma-at*, nearly invisible except for a faint green sheen, lay between them.

"Protector, I'm sorry," Jared gasped. He swiped a hand across his cheeks, obliterating the telltale signs. His shoulders straightened. "I thought I could find out what was going on and tell you. I wasn't going far, but I met this djinni, and she seemed so nice and she—"

"Shhh," Darius soothed. The child's disobedience in leaving the school could be discussed later. Pari's banishment was nothing more than history to the child, a history the djinn rarely acknowledged. Jared would not have recognized her or the danger she represented. "My only concern right now is taking you home. Are you well?"

"It's getting hard to breathe, but I don't know how to get past the barrier."

"Breathe shallowly, slowly, while I see what she has done. I will get you out of this, Jared."

While he spoke quietly and soothingly, calming the boy, Darius studied the barrier. Pari would be watching, he knew, for this was a test. A test of how he had grown in strength over the years.

Getting Jared free would be difficult, and if his control faltered, if Pari saw the weakness, she might choose not to wait for their confrontation.

"Solomon," he breathed, "let me be strong. For Jared. Let my powers stay under control."

Darius approached the barrier, until its energy pulses ruffled the hem of his robe. He held up his hands, palms just inches away from touching it. Jared got up from the rock and placed himself opposite Darius.

"Tell me what to do, Protector, that I may weaken it from this side."

Darius hesitated, then nodded. The boy needed

226

something to keep his mind off the foul air, and his abilities, though untrained, might help. "You were wise not to touch the barrier."

"It seemed dangerous."

"It is. Take great care that you do not touch it until I say you may. She has used the poisons of the death beetle."

"A death of paralysis?"

Darius nodded. The poison of the death beetle was absorbed quickly through the skin. If he had followed his first impulse and run to Jared, he would have been dead by now, and Jared would have suffocated slowly.

"I shall be careful." Jared's eyes skimmed over the nearly invisible barrier. "There is an element of dragon venom as well, is there not?"

"Good, you recognized it. We must first combat those two additions before we can collapse the barrier. Here's what we must do."

While Darius recited the words to speak and led Jared through the steps of the ritual, he watched the child closely. His breath grew more ragged, and the flush on his cheeks more pronounced. Yet Jared was strong, in *ma-at* and in will, and he stood steady beside the barrier.

Darius wanted to race ahead, to barrel through the noxious creation, but to do so would be more dangerous, more surely fatal, than the foul air. He forced himself to work slowly and calmly, keeping Jared as quiet as possible, using the child's absolute trust in the Protector as reassurance.

Under the spell Darius wove, the center of the barrier darkened to a lizard green; then, slowly, the green spread to the edges. Beginning in the center, it faded to yellow, then winked out. The death beetle poison was gone. Darius drew in a deep breath and rubbed his tingling fingers together. The *ma-at* had stayed under control, had flowed through him with strength.

"Solomon be praised!" cheered Jared. "What next?"

"You will need some water. Do you have anything with you that can carry it? You should not put your hand in the pool."

Darius stared, astonished, as Jared emptied out his knapsack. A rock, a stubby red candle, a silver mirror, a scroll that he thrust hastily out of sight. Darius knew he'd have to find out what ritual was on *that*. A small toad, another rock, some glittering sand. Finally, Jared held up a battered bronze cup. "Will this work?"

"That will do."

While Jared scooped up the water, Darius cupped his hands and collected some from a stream seeping out of the mountains. Even this was tainted, and it burned his palms. Darius ignored the discomfort; he would be finished before it could dissolve past the first layer of skin, and his reddened flesh would heal later.

"When I count to three, fling the water upon the barrier and shout, '*Khal-eh-adun Ism-el-Azam.*' Ready? One, two, *three!*"

Both djinn flung the water. "*Khal-eh-adun Ism-el-Azam.*"

Wherever the water struck, pricks of red shone like bright dots of blood. Darius chanted the words of power, spreading the red across the barrier, neutralizing the poison. Ah, the *ma-at* felt so good! It shimmered and flowed and energized.

"Can I come through?"

"Almost."

Then, almost imperceptibly, the red darkened and the barrier stopped dissolving. Pari! Pari was counteracting him!

Hastily, Darius halted her spell. It changed. He

matched. The red brightened again and resumed its spread across the barrier. Only a few more seconds and it would reach the edges and dissipate into the air, taking the barrier with it.

It stopped, no more than the width of a lizard's tail from the edge.

From the corner of his eye, Darius saw Jared drop to his knees. "I don't think . . ." he gasped.

The fumes from the waters were winning the battle. If the barrier wasn't down in a few minutes, Jared would succumb to the fumes and die.

No! It would not be so! He pulled energy from Kaf, shot it through, his body a mere conduit.

"Hold on, Jared, hold on."

The red quivered, then darkened to a dull, muddy black and grew stronger. Behind him, the clouds boomed their anger. Pricks, like dots of acid, attacked him.

By the great magician, it could not be! Not even Pari was that far lost. The barrier thickened. She was. Pari was using the sinister forces of *ma-at*.

Sweat poured down Darius's body as the new enemy fought him. His *ma-at* grew, straining to jump from his control. He had to keep it concentrated, focused on the barrier, but it began seeking a wider release. Solomon, not now!

A tiny amount slipped out and hit the barrier with a shower of sparks, but the dull, flat red moved. It brightened and moved toward the edges.

Darius whipped the belt off his robe. Six knots. Six knots to contain evil. A maelstrom of wind flung gravel and sand in his eyes, but he did not need sight to feel the *ma-at*.

One knot. "Be gone."

Two knots. "Be gone."

Three knots. "Be gone."

Lightning flashed about him; wind howled in his ears. *Ma-at* slipped further from his control, explod-

229

ing a rock and pelting him with its shards. The water at his back began to steam. Sparks crackled about him.

Four knots. "Be gone."

Still his *ma-at* grew, but it raced from him. He was losing it. The barrier began to tighten.

Darius lifted his arms. Could he retain enough focus until the last two knots were in place?

A whiff of jasmine brushed across him. The scent of Isis he had put on just before leaving. Solomon, he didn't need to be distracted by her. Not when all his concentration must be here.

The jasmine brushed across him. Isis. Something inside him, something cool and rustling, flowed out to join the lava of his *ma-at*. The power gathered in, back at his command.

Five knots. "Be gone."

The red brightened again.

Solid temper my fire. Cool embrace my power. Unbidden, the strange words arose.

Ma-at flowed pure as a sweet river, strong as a blazing fire. It was his, dancing with airy joy, solid and strong.

Six knots. "Be gone."

He thrust the belt forward. "Be gone from this place!"

The red turned as bright as the inner sun, shot from the barrier, and enveloped him. He could feel the sinister forces tearing at him, seeking a place to take control.

"Be gone. I am air and fire. Earth and water are at my command. You have no power."

The barrier exploded and, with a deafening crack, the evil forces disappeared. The stench from the pool of water rolled over Darius, gagging him. With a flick of his wrist, he sent a mighty wind to suck it away. The dark clouds evaporated to nothingness. He chose a sparkling rock and tossed it into the pool.

White vapor billowed from the water, then vanished.

Pari's test was finished.

Darius raced to Jared's side. Blessed Solomon, the child still lived. Hugging him, Darius transported to his home. As he did, the words of the prophecy returned to him.

Air and fire, balanced by water and earth, will restore.

Pari sprawled face down on the rocks. The hard ground beneath her was a minor discomfort compared to the pain invading her body. Ah, Solomon, she had not felt such pain since Harbad had died. It ate at her guts, set every nerve ajangle.

Slowly she pushed herself upright. She sat and rested her head in her hand, feeling warmth stripped away by the invading forces she'd unleashed. Darius had been stronger than she imagined. She had hoped the years had made him soft. They had not.

Yet, she *had* almost won. Victory, close and tantalizing, had almost been hers. Something had happened, making him vulnerable, but not vulnerable enough. Not even turning herself over to that siren call from the sinister forces had stopped him. Instead, in the end, from somewhere, he had found strength.

She would have to find out the source of his weakness and whence his well of power came. What had he tapped that was strong enough to turn back her power? Power she could feel growing inside her, replacing her ties to the soul of Kaf.

She had time to find out. For now, the test, the changing to the sinister forces, had burnt her out. She would be unable to use *ma-at* beyond the simplest of spells until her strength returned. But when it did, she would be far stronger.

Pari lifted her arms, wincing at the burning that shot through her chest. She would use her time to find out why he had faltered and what had given Darius his last burst of strength. The first she could exploit, the latter she would find a way to neutralize.

By the sacred sands, she would bet that woman was involved somehow. So far, she'd been unsuccessful in finding out more about Isis and the prophecy. She would have to seek harder.

Fingering her tablet, now blackest onyx, Pari got to her feet. "Come, my pets. We have some tasks to do." She made her way to her solitary lair, the two dragons following behind.

By the Festival of Mingara, she would be ready. Next time, she would be unstoppable.

Darius went first to his home. There, after he had assured himself of Jared's well-being, they swam and refreshed themselves. The subject of Pari, and Jared's disobedience, was delayed until Darius was reassured that the boy had suffered no lasting ill effects.

"Is Pari responsible for that bruise?" he asked once.

Jared grimaced in irritation. "No. I tried to get away from her when I realized what she intended. I used the invisibility spell. Did I tell you I'd achieved that? Adept Bahran said *fortunately* most don't get it until at least sixteen cycles, and I'm only twelve. How old were you?"

Darius smiled. "A month before my twelfth cycle."

Jared made a face. "Next step I'll do sooner than you."

"How did Pari stop you if you were invisible?"

"I tripped on that rock. Hit my chin, then my forehead. I was dizzy, so I lost the invisibility, and she slapped the barrier around me." He sounded totally disgusted with himself.

As Jared finished the last honey and sesame roll, Darius set down his cup of tea. "You disobeyed a

232

direct order of the Protector," he said quietly. "You were to stay at the school until I returned."

Jared looked away, then met his gaze squarely. "What will be my punishment?"

Darius was proud of him for that, as proud as he would be of a son of his body. No excuses, no evasions. The boy had made a mistake, but he admitted it and was ready to accept the consequences.

Unfortunately, that didn't mean Jared would necessarily obey the next orders. Darius couldn't be assured that he wouldn't wander about again. Jared had to be put somewhere safe. If Pari didn't know where he was, she wouldn't be able to transport to him. But it had to be somewhere that Jared wouldn't immediately start seeking methods to escape.

There was only one place he could think of. "Pack a bag," Darius told him. "You're going to spend some time on Terra."

Mary Calderone, Zoe's daughter, was sitting at the kitchen table when they arrived at Simon's home. Her tongue was caught between her teeth, while she industriously used gray pencils to shade a picture she was drawing. Two round black circles, connected by a black band, rested over her ears, and she bounced back and forth to an inner beat, oblivious to their arrival.

Darius walked over to her and picked up one of the black circles. "Mary."

She shrieked, then collapsed back into her chair when she saw who it was. "Geez, Darius, don't you know not to startle someone wearing headphones? I've got a few years left, and I'd like to keep them."

There were times when it was very clear, even as young as she was, that Mary was a Terran female, as outspoken as her mother or Isis.

Darius picked up the headphones and listened to the blaring sounds.

"Cowboy Mouth," Mary said. "Pretty fine group, huh?"

Darius declined to answer.

"Hey, who's that?" Mary eyed Jared with interest.

Jared, who'd been looking around with wide-eyed interest, thrust his hands against his hips. "My name's Jared."

"Are you a djinni?"

"Yes. Are you?"

"No, I'm an artist."

"Are your parents available?" Darius asked. After the last time he'd interrupted Simon and Zoe, and seeing Isis's reaction to his sudden arrivals, he'd decided perhaps he should transport to a common area, rather than directly to their side.

"Mom! Simon!" Mary screamed without getting up from her seat. "Darius is here."

Darius winced, but the method of communication seemed effective. Within moments, Simon and Zoe came into the kitchen.

"Darius? Jared!" Simon said. "What are you doing here?"

"I need to speak with you both," Darius said. "In private," he added, eyeing the children.

"Mary, why don't you take Jared and show him your new computer game?" Zoe suggested.

Mary looked from one of them to the other, then hopped out of her chair. "Okay. C'mon, Jared, you ever play *Treasure Trove?*"

"I have sought treasures in the Tower Lands and Grand Oasis."

"Really? Cool. Well, this is a bit different. I'll show you, while you tell me about these Tower Lands."

"It is a dark place . . ." Their voices faded as they left.

Simon, his arm around Zoe, faced Darius. "What's going on?"

Briefly Darius told them about Pari and her attack

on Jared. He omitted the loss of control and the strange manner in which it had returned, but he did tell them that Pari had called down forces no djinni should use or could hope to control.

"Is Jared all right?" asked Zoe, her voice concerned.

"Yes."

"Physically, maybe, but there could be other, more subtle reactions from a horrible experience like that."

"Perhaps," Darius admitted, "but Jared is resilient."

"Do you want us to keep him?" Simon asked.

Darius hesitated, then nodded. "I must prepare to meet Pari, and I cannot give Jared the supervision he needs. I fear, if I leave him on Kaf he will get into trouble again. He has always wanted to come to Terra. I think he will stay here, and I don't think Pari will follow. I took care to conceal our path here."

"We'll keep him," Zoe said.

Darius glanced toward her stomach. "I do not want to bring you risk, but . . . I did not know where else to go with him."

"We shall keep him." Simon repeated Zoe's offer, in a tone that brooked no questions.

"Thank you. Now, I'll say good-bye to him."

Darius found Jared in Zoe's computer room, sitting on a chair next to Mary. Both of them stared at the computer screen.

"The gnome has the first key," Mary said.

"No, it is that dragon," answered Jared.

"You think so? Hey, you're right."

Jared sat back in his chair, a satisfied smile on his face, and crossed his arms.

Bringing him here was the right thing to do. Not only for protection, but for other things. For home and family.

"Jared, I must go now." Darius spoke in the language of the djinn, rather than English.

Jared sprang to his feet. "You're leaving?"

"I must."

"You go to meet Pari. Because of me."

Darius shook his head. "Pari and I were destined to meet; events long ago decreed that. The time has come now. In the meantime, you will stay here. I must have your absolute promise on that, the word of a djinni, not to be broken. And you can use no *ma-at*. Not even transporting, except to revitalize."

"No *ma-at*?" Jared sounded horrified.

"No *ma-at*. I will not give Pari anything to trace to you. *Ma-at* on Terra she could recognize."

"For how long?" wailed Jared.

"You can remain here for twelve Terran days before you must revitalize. At that time, return to me on Kaf and we will discuss it. Before that time, no *ma-at*, no Kaf. If something needs my attention, Simon can notify me. I must have your promise on this, Jared."

"Twelve days." Jared sighed and his shoulders slumped; then he straightened. "I give you my solemn promise that I shall stay on Terra, with no *ma-at*, for twelve days."

He leaned forward and gave Darius a light kiss on the cheek and hand to seal the promise. Darius returned the gesture. "It is done."

Jared, however, did not step away immediately. Instead, he flung his arms about Darius and hugged him tightly. "Take care, Darius. Come back."

Darius hesitated only a moment, then hugged the child back. It was a strange feeling, a sweet feeling, knowing that someone cared whether he returned or not. Others had worried whether the Protector would be defeated and would leave them undefended. Other than Simon, no one else had worried about Darius, and Simon had been in exile for most of the years he was Protector.

Darius released Jared. "I shall see you soon."

It was time to return to Isis.

Isis! He had promised he would meet her at six. And it was now nine.

Two questions kept Darius company on his brief transport to Isis: How had he brought his power back under control? Would Isis also care whether he came back or not?

Chapter Seventen

For once the calming scents of sweet orange, ylang-ylang, and marjoram failed her. Yoga wasn't working either. With a disgusted oath, Isis unwound herself from the lotus position and blew out the candle in her aromatherapy lamp.

Where was Darius? It was nine P.M. and he was three hours late. Her initial frustration had turned to anger, but now it was laced with worry. *If he isn't seriously injured, he will be if he doesn't come up with one darn good excuse.*

She shoved aside the front curtains to look out at the night, lit by the yellow glow of streetlights and moon, then gave a short, humorless laugh. Was she really expecting to see him bounding up the steps? Not Darius's style; he was more unconventional than she was.

Was that one of the things she loved about him?

The curtain dropped from her hand. Damn, damn, and triple damn. In love with Darius? No!

Yes. She turned away from the peace of the night and began to pace, her insides churning.

How had she fallen in love with a djinni? He was everything she *didn't* want. He had no ambitions, a minor djinni among a powerful race. *Stable* was not a word that remotely described Darius. Fascinating, mercurial, exciting? Definitely yes. He was like fireworks—beautiful and sparkling, but soon gone, leaving only smoke.

He was a man of *ma-at*, a master of magic and illusion. He jumped in and out of her life. Literally. He disordered all her plans, made her question her goals.

Perhaps catching a bit of her agitation, Khu stirred sleepily on his perch, and Vulcan nudged at her, demanding his nightly roam. After she opened the back door for him, she leaned against the porch post, her foot tapping.

Night jasmine hung heavy in the air, and the cicadas chirped their tune. A light breeze set the wind chime above her head tinkling. The chime, a mix of bells and crystals, was a gift from Aunt Tildy. According to Tildy, the harmonies welcomed the spirits, and maybe there was a truth in the claim, for, as Isis stood there, a spirit of calm did seep inside her.

She'd never run away from a problem before and she wasn't about to start now.

When had she fallen in love with Darius? From the very first, she supposed, although she had been too wrapped up in mistrust to recognize the warning signs. From the time he had kissed her, with the Kiss of Promise, and had lit a fire inside that refused to die. If she believed in those things, she'd almost say it had been ordained. From the first, she'd known he smelled just right, and he did not judge her as other men in her life did. Later, as she saw the man of generosity and honor, her shield of mistrust and doubt had faded, leaving only love.

And frustration, too, darn him. Why had he left her this morning? She'd been willing. More than willing, she'd been downright eager. Why had he touched her with intimate care, then left with the promise of tonight? And why had he failed to show up?

Tonight. Isis released a soft sigh and sat down on the upper step. The bargains were to be concluded tonight, and then he would leave. Of that fact she had no doubt, and she faced it squarely. When the bargains no longer tied them, he would be gone. Isis leaned her head against her knees and fought both tears and the dull ache tightening her chest. She never cried, and she never gave up.

Despite his actions, Darius wanted her, that she knew, even as inexperienced as she was. Couples maintained bicoastal relationships. She and Darius were from two different dimensions; maybe they could have a bidimensional affair.

Vulcan returned from his rounds and curled up beside her. Isis stroked his soft fur. His low purr rumbled against her leg in a soothing vibration.

"No," she softly told the cat, "a sometimes affair is not for me. I never did like to share." Better a heart that was alone than one that waited and watched the magic disappear.

In the distance the ferry horn sounded for its last cross over the river. The end of the day. The start of dreams. But which dreams?

When Darius returned, she would ask for the perfume. Whatever the cost, she would pay it. With the newest threat posed by Ben Fontenot, she needed that perfume for Dream Scents. Her business would sustain her when Darius had left; success had always been her goal and that dream did not change. In fact, after facing her love for a djinni who would be gone, perhaps by morning, it was even more important. It would be all she had.

"I won't be a failure; I simply can't accept that. I'm

240

going to prove I'm as capable as any of them. But you know, Vulcan, maybe I've been going about it the wrong way. On sheer size, I can't compete with Ben." *Not yet, anyway.* "Finance-wise, I can't out muscle him. I'm barely making ends meet as it is."

Vulcan nudged her with his head, then rolled over, commanding her to rub his belly. With a gentle laugh, Isis complied. "You're right, Vulcan. I never was too good at acting the straight businesswoman. So, what have I got? I've got some good people working with me. I've got myself. Maybe a little magic, a little uniqueness, isn't such a bad thing."

Oh, not the magic that she'd tried before, with the rituals and the robes.

But there were other kinds of magic. Like her perfumes. Like that special perfume she called Magic.

"Something tells me I need Magic for more than just Dream Scents," Isis admitted to Vulcan, not caring that his only answer was a louder purr when she scratched under his chin. "I need it for me. I think that perfume is some kind of a legacy."

Somehow it was connected with the women of her family. Why else would her grandmother have had it? Why else would it have haunted her dreams for so long? In her drive to emulate the male Montgomerys had she disregarded the instincts that came from the women?

It was an interesting thought.

"What do you suppose Mom would do in this situation?" she asked Vulcan as she picked him up and went inside. "Aunt Tildy? How about Grandmother? I remember how she used to sprinkle glitter in my hair and we'd pretend I was a moonbeam. Women want dreams, whimsy, fantasy. That's what I'll give them."

It was as though the admission, the acceptance of whimsy and magic, lifted a veil inside her mind. Other than Winter, the aftershave she'd made for

Ram, she'd created nothing new these past three years since her debacle with Ben. Tonight, ideas flooded through her in a wave of creativity long absent. She'd felt scared when she opened Dream Scents, Isis realized, but she hadn't felt this excited in a long, long time.

"That perfume, Magic, is going to be big, I can feel it," she told Vulcan, locking the back door. "And how about that line of natural cosmetics, or those classes I've had in mind? Wouldn't that be a switch, *me* being a teacher!"

Vulcan purred his agreement. He was a good sounding board. Isis suspected she'd be talking to him a lot in the future.

Yes, when Darius reappeared, she'd ask for the perfume.

And her love for him? Her love would be there, too, not that she'd ever tell Darius that.

Isis looked down at her outfit—silk tap pants, camisole, and short robe, all a brilliant red—and grinned. Add jasmine in a few strategic places, light the sandalwood candles, and her djinni would not be sending her off aroused and unfulfilled by a chaste kiss. Not tonight. Not as sensual as Darius was. Before he left, she would have memories to cherish.

Tonight she was going to seduce him.

Maybe, after the bargains, they could go away for the rest of the weekend. Impulsively, Isis dialed Aunt Tildy's number and got her aunt's answering machine.

"Aunt Tildy, this is Isis. Can you take care of Khu and Vulcan for a couple of days? Remember, you told me I needed a man with the gifts of magic and the power of dreams? Well, I think I've found him, and I want to make this weekend one to remember."

A weekend to cherish, Isis thought as she hung up the phone. That is, if the infuriating, mercurial djinni ever returned! Isis fingered the turquoise tablet she still wore. Where was he?

The wind chime outside danced to a wild tune, while inside the silk flattened against her and her hair blew in her eyes. Vulcan leaped from her arms and raced up the stairs. A bright light flashed, and then Darius stood before her.

He was as she had first seen him. Vibrant, male, magic. Dressed in the robe and turquoise tablet and nothing else. Shards of silver sparkled about his dark hair. His hands were fisted at his hips.

"Are you ready, my Isis, for our third bargain?"

That was it? No "Hello, how are you?" No explanation for being over three hours late? No bleeding wounds and plaster casts to explain his absence?

Isis leaned forward, her hands shoved against her waist, her foot tapping. "Where have you been? You said six o'clock." She tapped her watch. "It's past nine."

"You cared whether I came back?" he asked softly.

"Of course I cared; I was worried! Besides, you kiss me, get me all hot, then set me aside and don't come back for fourteen hours?" Oh, damn, she hadn't meant to say *that*. "Sure, I cared," she muttered, looking away. "We've got another bargain."

That quick, he was at her side, so close. She knew, not by hearing him move or feeling a touch. His scent, his warmth, the arc of awareness that shot through her told their own story.

He turned her face toward him. His slow, heated smile reached all the way to the depths of his midnight eyes. "I do not think it was thoughts of the bargain that made you 'hot,'" he murmured.

"You haven't told me where you were," she reminded him, hoping her vulnerability and love weren't visible in her eyes.

"No, I haven't."

Isis waited a moment. "Well?"

243

His finger stroked from the corner of her eye to her lips, leaving a trail of heat across her cheek. "Already the *zaniya*, a worthy *zaniya*" he said, so softly Isis doubted she'd heard him right, for she didn't understand what he meant. Lightly he traced the outline of her lips, and then he cupped her nape. One finger rubbed her tender skin. "I am sorry," he whispered, the first time she'd ever heard those words from him. "I was on Kaf. I was summoned and had no choice but to answer."

So djinn had demanding bosses, too. "Are you on your own time now?"

He looked at her, puzzled.

"Are we apt to be interrupted?"

"Not tonight." His gaze swept across her. "What are you thinking of tonight, my sweet Isis?"

"Isn't your telepathy working?"

"Not with you. I suspect it will never work with you."

"Well, bless St. Valentine for small favors."

Darius laughed softly, then dipped his head and kissed her. His hands slid across the silk of her robe, coming to rest at the small of her back. He kneaded gently, urging her closer, but allowing her to make the next move. His tongue traced her lips.

Clutching his lapels, Isis sighed, opening her mouth in invitation. She shifted closer, leaning against his powerful, lean body. Darius's arms tightened. He gathered her close, enveloping her in cedar, heat, and glitter.

My sweet Isis, my zaniya, *I want you so.* His words sang in her mind, while he deepened the kiss. No prelude to a slow simmer this kiss, but rather heat for an instant boil. It demanded and overwhelmed, and she met it with her own passion.

Every sense clamored in response, as she wound her arms around him and speared her hands through the soft, tight curls of his hair. Her palms tingled, as

244

did her breasts, belly, and thighs where she pressed against his smooth skin. The rightness of his scent filled her. Blue sparks surrounded them in a crackling, bedazzling display. He tasted of sweet honey.

They were both gasping for air when their lips parted. Isis rested her cheek on the warm silk on his chest. His heart pounded against her, and her heart beat in a matching rhythm. Darius's arms, his heat and scent, surrounded her, and amid the passion she felt both protected and cherished.

They stood that way, Darius stroking her hair, while the conflagration returned to a contained fire. The final bargain would come first; it had to be that way.

"Are you ready?" Darius asked.

Isis nodded. "The bargain—" she lifted her head to look at him—"and then we finish this."

Darius shook his head. "Then we begin this."

Isis smiled at him. "What is it you want, Darius?"

"Twice, I have told you first. I think it is your turn, my sweet Isis."

It was a very scary thing to admit openly a heart's desire. Reluctantly, Isis disentangled herself from his arms. "Come upstairs with me. To my workroom."

Hand in hand they climbed the two stories. In her workroom, Isis handed Darius the crystal flacon.

He turned it over, and his finger traced the scarlet markings etched in the glass surface. " 'To my lost love, a final gift of my only love.' " Suddenly he stopped, and his fingers tightened about the flacon. " 'Harbad,' " he breathed.

"Are those letters? You can read that? What does it mean?"

Darius ignored her questions. He lifted the blood-red stopper and sniffed at the perfume. "What is it you want, Isis? What is your final bargain?" He did not look at her.

245

Isis took a deep breath. Even with only drops left in the bottle, the exotic perfume swirled around her and wrapped her in rich velvet. "I want to duplicate that perfume. I want to bottle and sell it. It's going to be my signature perfume for Dream Scents. It will make my fortune."

"And that is what you want? Bigger and richer?"

"Yes."

"Not the satisfaction of helping one by one."

"They're not mutually exclusive."

He merely shrugged, as if he didn't believe her. Why should he, when she didn't believe it herself? But a career of hanging on by her fingernails was not going to prove a thing.

"That's what I want," she repeated a trifle belligerently.

"This was what you asked Pari for?"

"She said only a djinni could get it for me. I bought the spell so I could call a djinni and wish for the perfume."

"Ah, but it did not happen as you planned."

"No." Isis waited a minute. "Can you do it? What's your price?"

He looked at her then, stoppering the flacon. "Pari misled you. No djinni can duplicate this scent."

The taste of disappointment was not bitter but dry, Isis discovered. As dry as the dust of old dreams and lost hopes. She swallowed hard. When would she learn? Why had she pinned her hopes on something *magic*? "So, there's no bargain to be made."

"I did not say that." Darius handed her back the flacon.

Isis gave him a sharp look. "You said I couldn't get the perfume. What's there to bargain for?"

"I said the perfume could not be duplicated."

With care, Isis set down the flacon; then, with her forefinger, she tilted Darius's chin down until their eyes met. "Now is not the time to be enigmatic, my dear djinni. Can I get that perfume or not?"

"It is a complicated story."

Darius took her hand and led her to the pile of pillows that made up his bed; the fantasy grotto was now gone. Isis sank down and rested against a soft blue mound. He sprawled next to her, still holding her hand. His thumb traced random patterns across her skin while he spoke.

"The essence of that perfume I recognize. It is from a *halifa* flower. The flower of dreams, the djinn call it. For each person its fragrance is different. And perfect."

"What do you mean?"

"Those who smell the *halifa* think it beautiful, the ideal scent, but when asked to describe it, they all use images, not words like 'woodsy' or 'citrus.' And the image, or dream, varies from person to person and from time to time."

"A hot sandy beach. A rumpled bed. A fragrant garden," Isis said softly.

"I would describe it as a cool spring breeze that slides across hot skin, or silken pillows beneath my lover while she lies under me." He reached out and brushed her hair behind her ears, tracing the sensitive curve of her ear. "A fire that burns with white-hot pleasure but does not consume."

Isis closed her eyes as his words wove a sensuous spell about her. The seduction would not start after the bargains, for it had never stopped. She opened her eyes and cleared her throat. "So, the *halifa* is a very special flower."

"It was created by Harbad—"

Isis sat up. "That was the name on the flacon!"

He nodded. "Harbad was the most powerful djinni our race has ever known."

"Was?"

"He died. Caught unawares by a djinni he trusted. One of the many things that died with him was the secret of the *halifa* flower. No one has been able to duplicate it, or its essence. Many have tried; our strongest have not succeeded. If I were to duplicate the perfume by *ma-at*, it would have all the other ingredients, but I cannot give you the *halifa*."

"And that's what gives it its magic."

"Yes."

Isis leaned back against the pillows. Her interest in Darius's story had momentarily pushed aside the disappointment, but now it returned in full force, settling inside her like a double order of hush puppies. She closed her eyes against the heavy ache.

"Although the *halifa* cannot be duplicated, it still thrives on Kaf. In a remote grotto, known to very, very few."

Isis opened one eye. "That grotto you created in here? You know where it is?"

He nodded. "The *halifa* blooms but once every hundred cycles. When it blooms, it is possible to collect the essence of the blossoms. Less than a drop of the oil would it take in each bottle; the supply would be sufficient for many years."

"You said the flower bloomed every hundred years. When is it next due?"

"Soon. Very soon."

Isis's eyes widened as she took in what he said. She could do it! She could get the perfume! Between that and the plans she'd formulated earlier tonight, Dream Scents would be the success she envisioned.

It was all within reach. The elusive perfume. Everything she'd worked for. With a whoop of joy, Isis sprang up and flung herself on Darius. "I can get it. I can do it."

"Yes, you can." Laughing, he fell backward beneath her onslaught.

Isis sprawled atop him, leaned down, and kissed him—nose, cheeks, chin, mouth. Desire, dormant not extinguished, flared again. Darius's arms tightened around her. His robe had fallen open and through the thin fabric of her camisole, she could feel the heat of his skin. Lower, through the double layers of silk robes, she knew she aroused him.

Before she lost all sense again, Isis lifted her head. "And what will be your price for this perfume? What is your bargain?"

She held her breath, awaiting his answer.

He cradled her head between his hands, gave her a quick kiss. "Come with me to Kaf. I need you to perform a certain ritual with me."

Isis stilled. "What kind of ritual?"

He hesitated, as if debating something within, and then said, "It is a balancing ritual."

"Why do you need me?"

"A human is required."

Though he met her gaze squarely, Isis sensed there was more to this than he told her. So, what else was new? She often had that feeling around Darius. Yet had he not shown he was a man to be trusted?

"It won't hurt?"

He gave her an indulgent smile. "Actually, I think it shall be quite pleasurable."

This was it, then. The exquisite pleasure of loving for a few short days, the perfume, the ritual, and then he would be gone. Isis fought back the hollow echo of that final loss. She had best make the memories last.

"All right. We'll wait here until the flowers bloom— I've got some things I want to get rolling—then—"

Darius laid a finger across her lips. "The ritual will be done tonight. You shall stay with me, on Kaf, until the flowers have reached their peak."

The rush of words caught in her throat. "Why?" was all she could manage.

"That is my price."

"How long? Should I bring a change of clothes?"

"Time flows differently on my world, but when you

return"—he lifted one shoulder—"it can be to any time after we leave. Moments, if you so desire. As for clothing"—he gave her a wicked grin—"you need bring nothing."

Her pulse fluttered wildly. So, she would go with him, love him, get the perfume, and return a few minutes after she left, with no one aware of her absence.

As if the interlude had never happened. But she would know. She would remember, forever.

If that was the price he asked, it was one she would pay.

"I agree. I'll come with you and perform your ritual."

"Willingly," he interjected. "You come willingly and participate in the ritual of your own free choice."

She nodded. "I shall come with you and perform your ritual willingly. When the flowers bloom, you will help me collect their oil, then return me, and the oil, here."

His lips tightened for a moment, then relaxed. "Agreed. Now, we seal with the Kiss of Promise."

Darius shifted subtly, and Isis found herself lying beneath him. His body, sprawled full length over her, pressed her into the pillows, but his bed was so soft, so laden with pillows that she welcomed his weight. He laced his fingers through hers. "You first."

She lifted their joined hands and kissed the back of his. He turned his head slightly, and she kissed his cheek. Darius mimicked her actions, with a kiss that truly seemed one of Promise. He did not lift his lips from the kiss on the cheek. Instead, he trailed tiny kisses to her mouth, where he settled in with a soft sigh, as a thirsty man welcomes the spring of an oasis.

Isis found her other hand entwined with his, and he pressed her deeply into the pillows. He teased and tasted, until she moaned and demanded more.

"Take me," she whispered. "Take me to Kaf."

Darius rose and, with a deft move, lifted her into his arms. As the world spun around her, Isis wrapped her arms about Darius's neck and buried her nose against his chest to breathe in his familiar scent. She closed her eyes and felt a rushing blast of wind. Heat replaced air-conditioning, and the dizzying sensation subsided.

Isis opened her eyes. The leaves of a cedar tree swayed above her in a gentle breeze, the woodsy scent mixing with clean air redolent of myrtle and sandalwood and orange. On earth it was night, but here, hot sun baked her skin. In the distance she heard a strange sound, part rustling leaves, part tinkling bells. Sparkling sand spread out before her and a deep clear pool of water lay at the corner of her vision.

It was beautiful, sensuous, and totally foreign, just like the djinni who cradled her close to his chest.

The bargain had begun. She was on Kaf.

Chapter Eighteen

As she looked further, Isis saw a white barrier—it seemed to be the exterior of a building, but it didn't seem solid enough to term a wall—enclosing the sandy courtyard where they stood.

"This is beautiful. Where are we?"

"My home," Darius told her. Although his voice was solemn, Isis could hear the note of pride.

He lowered her to her feet, then walked around the perimeter of the courtyard, bending down at each corner. Once it was to place a green rock. Another time a tiny fire burst into life at his fingertips. A third time a short column of whirling sand rose, and the fourth stop was at the pool of water, where he dipped in his hand, and then sprinkled droplets of water in to the air. The white barrier shimmered and seemed to gain depth and solidity, until it sparkled under the desert sun.

He returned to her side, picked up her hand and kissed it. "No matter what happens outside these walls, tonight we shall not be disturbed." His dark gaze burned into her. *Not during the ritual, not afterward.*

When he spoke like that, directly to her thoughts, the intimacy of it always startled her. "Do we start the ritual now?"

"We shall wait until nearer sundown. The ritual must end at the point of transition, when day turns to night."

"I see."

"In the meantime," Darius continued, "I have a few things to prepare. You should rest"—he caressed her, smoothing back her hair—"for you will not get much sleep this night, my Isis."

The words—so simple, so full of promise—sent heated images through her and shattered her tenuous calm. Her stomach knotted, and her palms began to sweat. "How about a nice hot bath?" she asked with a bravado she didn't feel.

"If you wish." His fingers tunneled through her hair to her nape, where he cupped her head in his palm, holding her steady for his kiss. He lingered, until she was breathless and weak. Though his touch was gentle, power and resolve radiated from him. Isis saw it in the glow about him, felt it in his strong hands, sensed it spreading through her. There would be no holding back, of his magic or his passion. There would be no turning back.

Tonight, in this setting, she was reminded forcefully that he was not human, but djinn, and she was on his home turf. He was a man comfortable with *ma-at*, with ritual and illusion, and in a very short time she would share in an unknown ritual with him, and then . . .

For a moment, Isis's courage failed her. Could she do this? Could she give herself over to his commands in the strange rites of his people? Could she love him and then leave?

His hand tightened, as though he sensed her fear. "The bargain, Isis; you have willingly promised."

She took a deep breath and gave him a tremulous smile. "I have, and I won't fail you."

"Good. Now, come with me."

There was that increasingly familiar rush of hot air during transport, and then Isis found herself standing in a room more sybaritic than any she'd ever imagined. No harsh edges or abrupt corners here. It was round, as best as she could tell, but the walls shimmered like rainbows in clouds, making the exact edges blur. Sheer fabric of palest orange, attached to nothing that she could see, billowed around a mound of plump pillows.

Music played, so softly that it created an atmosphere of sensuous delight while the tune remained elusive. The ambient light in the room, from what source Isis could not determine, faded as Darius passed his outstretched hands in a circle and dozens of candles, of different thicknesses and heights, but all in shades of red, flared to life.

Darius indicated the pile of pillows. "Sleep now, my sweet one. You will be awakened at the correct time with instructions as to what you must do."

"And arrangements for a hot bath?" Isis asked, lying down on the heavenly mound of pillows.

Darius smiled. "And a bath." He leaned over and kissed her warmly and tenderly on the mouth, although he made no move to deepen the caress. "Until sunset." Then he was gone in a whirlwind.

Isis thought she would not be able to sleep a wink, but as she burrowed into the pile of pillows, as they supported her and warmed her, her eyes drifted shut and sleep overtook her.

Sometime later, how long she could not say, a soft chiming roused her from her restful sleep and her vividly erotic dreams of Darius. To her surprise, she awoke clearheaded and aware of where she was.

She looked around for the source of the chiming and saw a shimmering orb of purple light hovering above her head. It drifted down to eye level and chimed again. Remembering when she'd seen a similar orb with Darius on the ferry, she lifted her hands. The orb settled into her palms. Like a soap bubble, it had no substance, but when it touched her hands, instead of popping, a thin voice came from it.

"Isis of Terra, woman of the line of Abregaza, prepare."

One of the curtains surrounding the bed drew back, and the shimmering walls of the room parted, like the curtains on a stage being drawn back. The orb lifted, and she followed it into a bathing room unlike any she'd ever seen.

The candles were lit here, too, again the only light. The bath was huge, more a pool than a tub. The faint scent of jasmine wafted from the water. A line of alabaster jars sat at the edge of the pool. Isis dipped a hand into the water; it was the perfect temperature. She gave a soft sigh of bliss. To her mind, a scented bath was one of life's greatest pleasures.

She doffed the silky camisole, robe, and tap pants she still wore, laid the turquoise tablet on top of them, and then stepped into the bath. The lining appeared rocklike, but no rocks ever felt so soft beneath her toes, nor did they add to the sweet jasmine fragrance in the air with each step as she lowered herself into the silky water.

Isis swam over to the alabaster jars. The crystals inside looked like grains of sand, but when she poured a little into her hand, they foamed like soap. She washed her hair and body, then floated in the water, reveling in its soft play across her skin.

She could have stayed longer, except that the purple orb began its chiming again, a cue, she assumed, to get out. When she did, she looked around for a towel, then realized she didn't need one. A warm breeze blew over her, drying her body.

Her clothes had disappeared. Was the ritual carried out in the nude? She hadn't thought to ask too many details, Isis realized, drawing a deep breath. She could do this. She'd given her word, and it wouldn't be much longer before there was nothing between her and Darius, not even a layer of silk.

The orb drifted toward the opening. Isis followed, but it stopped before they left and gave an impatient chime, as though reminding her of something she'd forgotten. Isis looked around. The turquoise tablet Darius had given her still lay on the rock. She slipped it over her head.

Apparently that satisfied the orb, for it preceded her from the bathing room.

A red robe lay on her bed of pillows. The orb waited above it. Okay, apparently the ritual wasn't done naked.

Isis picked up the robe. It felt like silk and satin in one: soft, smooth, and warm. When she donned it and wrapped it around her waist, there were no fastenings that she could see, but she pressed the two layers together and it stayed in place. It was sleeveless, with a *V* neckline that stopped just short of being revealing. When she moved, the floor-length fabric swirled around her legs like cool, scented smoke and rustled with a sensuous call. The fabric wasn't pure red, she realized. Woven into it were threads that glinted as if they were made of thin, flexible diamonds.

The orb chimed once more, an approving sound, and the walls separated. Stomach fluttering, Isis stepped through. The walls closed, and the orb winked from existence.

She stood in the courtyard. At the opposite side stood Darius. He too was barefoot and wore a red robe, although his was long-sleeved and a shade darker than hers. His hair and eyes were as black as the night to come and his face remained in shadow. Behind him, the sun hung above the horizon like a massive red ball. Isis swallowed, trying to moisten her dry throat, and clenched her sweating palms into fists. She took a step forward, and more candles flared to life.

Darius met her halfway, moving with quiet grace. His gaze brushed across her, and he gave her a satisfied smile. "You are beautiful," he said, "both on the outside and in your soul. The divination chose well."

Isis smiled back, not fully understanding his words. Tonight, however, she would not question. Tonight was his, and she would trust him. She would give herself over to the man with the gift of magic.

With that decision, the fluttering in her stomach settled, replaced by an expectant excitement and a sense of rightness. Darius picked up her hand, but this time he didn't kiss it as he often did. Instead he led her over to two scarlet and blue rugs, placed before an iron brazier containing rocks that glowed red with heat.

"Kneel," he said. His deep voice sent a thrill through her.

Isis knelt on the left rug and Darius on the right. Often sand was hard, but where she knelt the sand beneath the rugs was soft as a meadow of thick grass.

He handed her a parchment and a brown chalk. "You must write your name, then the words I tell you below it."

Isis looked at him, stricken. "I can't."

His eyes narrowed.

She took a deep breath, realizing he'd misunderstood and thought she was reneging at the last moment. "My dyslexia. I have trouble writing. The letters get all mixed up." She lowered her eyes. "Ben used to laugh at my notes. If it has to be perfect for the ritual, I . . . can't promise that." She thrust the parchment toward him.

He laid his hands over hers. "Whatever, however, you write, it will be accepted. Put your thoughts with the words, and it will be all I need."

"You're sure?"

Darius nodded. "How you write matters nothing to me."

Isis stared at him for a moment, then smiled. He spoke the truth. Her problems with reading and writing meant nothing to him. He judged her not on her deficiencies, but on her strengths, strengths only he seemed to recognize. If she had not loved him before, she would have for that gift alone.

Her teeth worrying her lip, Isis wrote her name. She managed that fine usually—except for the *g* in her last name, which, when she was particularly tired, could look like a *b* or a *p* or even a *j*, or so she'd been told. She rarely noticed the difference. Tonight, however, she thought she got it right.

Darius repeated a series of strange-sounding words, speaking slowly as she wrote.

"How do you spell—?"

"It does not matter," he assured her. He never hurried her, never commented on what or how she wrote.

At last the ordeal was over. Darius took the parchment, laid it on top of another one—one he'd written before, she guessed—and rolled the two together. Then he picked up a small crystal pitcher containing a myrtle-scented oil. He sprinkled a few droplets on the brazier, and the fire rose to new life.

He threw the parchments on the fire. "Repeat the words again with me."

Following Darius's lead, she spoke the words she'd written.

"The old of one is gone," he said when they'd finished. "The new of two begins."

He turned on the rug and faced her, nodding for her to do the same. He held out his hands, palms up, and Isis placed her hand in his keeping. His fingers closed, holding her tight.

A glow shimmered about Darius. The heat of the fire grew, and a sheen of sweat coated his smooth skin. Reflections of flames danced across the gold of his skin and brought a light to his dark eyes. The sun grew bigger and redder. Beads of moisture dotted Isis's forehead and slid down her spine.

His eyes, deep and black, mesmerized her. Sun, courtyard, fire, all faded behind the glow surrounding him. She felt as though she fell into him, into his scent and touch. Around her, pinpricks of color twirled in the air, forming pictures against the orange glow of the sun. Isis barely had time to recognize the scenes before they became symbols she could only guess at, for she saw them only at the edges of her vision. Her attention remained on Darius.

My sweet Isis, come thou to me.

She shifted forward, until she was on his mat. He spread his knees apart and dropped her hands, resting his fists on his knees. *Come, Isis.* She knelt before him, between his legs.

Place your hands upon my shoulders. Isis complied with the commands, her eyes never leaving his. The colors became brighter, twirled with greater abandon. Myrtle and jasmine strengthened and combined to a perfume of uncommon richness. Though she could see his hands resting upon his knees, it felt as though Darius's hands moved up and down her back. It was his *ma-at*, not his skin, that touched her. Yet she felt embraced and cherished.

He surrounded her, although he had not moved a muscle.

This was his *ma-at*, his magic. Isis took the knowledge inside her and saw him anew with eyes of love and trust. Never had he looked so foreign or so powerful to her.

Never had she loved him more.

My sweet Isis, my zaniya.

"Yes, my sure *zani*," she breathed, voicing words that arose, to her surprise, unbidden.

He nodded once, as if that was the answer he needed, and picked up a length of scarlet ribbon, which he tied around her upper right arm. "Bind thy *ma-at* to mine. Let our fires burn together. Do thou do this of thine own will?"

The solemn words struck deep in Isis, like the base note of a perfume that lingers with resonant accord. Awe, passion, trust completed the heady mixture.

"I do."

He turned her hand and placed the tips of her fingers against the turquoise tablet at his throat. Then he did the same with his hand.

Something—electricity, the power of *ma-at*—flowed between them. From tablet to hand, hand to tablet. It danced inside Isis, a fairy leaving stardust in its wake. Then . . . it changed.

Stardust became the eternal tides of the ocean. The roar of the fire contained the faint rustle of meadow grasses. Because Isis was watching him so closely, she saw Darius blink, as though the change had startled him.

"Let the balances be restored," he intoned. "Air and fire. Water and earth."

"Water and earth. Air and fire. Let the balances be restored," The ritual seemed to reach deep inside her, drawing forth the proper responses from buried ancestral knowledge.

The sun lowered and began to dip beneath the horizon, its orange glow darkening.

"I desire now to be one with thee," Darius continued.

Isis hesitated. This seemed so much more than a spell of balance as he had said. Yet, the words also seemed so very right to say. "I desire now to be one with thee."

"By Solomon, the vow is sealed."

"By Abregaza, the vow is sealed," she said, ancient instinct giving her surprising words.

The sun was nearly down. Darius lifted her hand from his shoulder, kissed the back of it, then replaced it on his chest. Isis could feel the satin heat of his skin and beneath that the beat of his heart. He leaned forward and kissed her cheek, his lips lingering a moment.

"*Zaniya,*" he whispered.

Isis picked up his hand from his knee and kissed it, then placed it above her breast, over her heart. His fingers flexed slightly, and when she leaned forward to kiss his cheek, his hand slid with her movement, until he cupped the weight of her breast in his palm.

The beauty of the ceremony, the night, the man before her filled her. "*Zani,*" she said, her voice husky.

A flare of satisfaction lit his eyes. His hands encircled her waist—his hands, not his *ma-at*. He leaned forward and kissed her on the lips. With a final streak of orange, the sun dipped below the horizon and disappeared into the night.

Darius lifted his mouth from the kiss.

"Mine," she thought she heard him breathe.

The candles extinguished, and they stood, Darius's hands still at her waist. In the darkness, Isis could see nothing beyond the faint glow that surrounded him. "The ritual is complete?" she asked.

"It is complete."

"The balance, whatever it is, is restored?"

"I shall see, but yes, I think so."

"Then it worked." Isis smiled. "I think that's the first magic ritual I've done that actually worked."

Silence fell between them.

Isis bit her lip, wondering what to say, what to do next. They both knew what they wanted, what they intended, but how did they get from this point to sharing a bed? It wasn't as though she had a lot of experience in the etiquette of this. Did they make a little chitchat, have a bite to eat first? Did he expect her to stretch right out on that red-and-blue rug?

What would he ask of her? Oh, Lord, she hadn't even thought about that. Was the djinn version of making love the same as humans'? Maybe they did it with robes still on. Maybe they just did that talking thing with their minds. If so, tonight was going to be a pretty one-sided affair.

She should have realized Darius would have no such questions or doubts. He gathered her close. "Such troubles cross your face, my sweet one. Tonight, let them all fade."

Isis rested against his lean strength, content to abandon her doubts. The muscles in his arms bunched when he pulled her nearer. His breath whispered across her ear while he intoned a faint chant, the hot whirlwind surrounded them, and then they were back in the room where Isis had slept earlier. At least she thought it was the same, for it contained the mound of pillows and the multitude of red candles. The rainbow walls were faded, however, and she could see beyond them to the courtyard. A cedar tree made a canopy over the pillows. It was like being in a translucent tent, open to nature, yet private. A world inhabited by only the two of them.

Isis took a long, shaky breath.

Darius loosened his hold on her, not to release her,

but enough that she could see his face when he leaned back. His hips pressed against hers, and she could feel his growing arousal.

"I want you, my *zaniya*. I think you know that." His hips slid lightly across hers, and the first embers of desire began to burn away the fears.

"What does that mean? *Zaniya?*"

He hesitated, looking away until she thought he might not answer; then his wary gaze returned to hers. "It can mean 'dear one.' "

" 'Dear one.' I think I like that." Perhaps Darius had feelings for her, feelings beyond desire and need. No, she wouldn't delude herself with that hope.

His hand stroked her hair. "You are as skittish as a newborn fox; I can feel you tremble. There is no need to be nervous, my Isis. You have not changed your mind, have you?"

"No. I want this, too."

"Good."

"But . . . You're a djinni. Maybe you do things differently." The words tumbled out.

"Oh, I think the basics are the same," he said with faint amusement.

She'd seem him naked, knew he was built like other men. Well, to be honest, like everything else about Darius, there seemed to be *more* than other men. He moved his hips again. It sure felt like his reactions were similar to those of earth men. And he'd kissed her and touched her, so maybe things weren't so different.

He gave her a slow, heated smile. It brought such beauty to his face that Isis's breath caught in her throat.

"I wish only your pleasure tonight. We shall do nothing you do not want." His hand dipped inside her robe to cup her breast, and his thumb rubbed lightly around her nipple, until she ached for his

263

touch. He bent over, nipped lightly at her lips. "Do you like that?"

"Oh, yes," she moaned. "I guess the basics are the same."

He laughed, low and resonant. "Perhaps when we get to the advanced levels, we shall find a few differences, but I promise you will not be disappointed by the comparison."

"That's okay. I don't have anything to compare it to."

Darius stilled.

"Don't stop now," Isis grumbled.

He tilted her chin upward, so she looked at him. "What do you mean? Have the men you've known taken only their own pleasure and given you none? Have they been as clumsy, as hurried, as the camel spying an oasis in the desert?"

Isis laughed. "What an awful image."

"Well?"

She sighed, knowing Darius wouldn't leave it alone. Why had she said anything? "I don't have any comparisons because I haven't made love with anyone before."

His hands dropped to his sides and he stepped away, utterly quiet, and stared at her. Isis had thought of reactions he might have—delight, surprise, satisfaction—but stupefaction wasn't one she'd entertained.

Isis crossed her arms. "Gee, don't look so thrilled. I don't suppose your reaction is because it's your first time, too, and you're wondering whether one of us knows what to do?"

The gold of his skin tinted a faint pink. "Ah, no."

"Didn't think so." Isis tilted her head. "I didn't take you for one of those guys who gets annoyed at the thought of breaking in a clumsy virgin."

"Solomon, no!" The denial burst from him. "I am the clumsy one here. I am . . . honored. It's just, you seemed . . . more experienced. I had thought—"

Darius broke off abruptly and rubbed a hand across the back of his neck. It was the first time Isis had ever seen him looking remotely flustered. Apparently, it would be a night for many firsts.

"Go on. You thought what? Honest answer, now."

He gave her a wry smile. "I had been entertaining some ideas about those, ah, advanced levels. But, now—"

His voice faltered as Isis gave him a slow smile.

"I said I hadn't done it before. Doesn't mean I don't know what happens. Ignorant naivety hasn't been my style for years. Books and movies are pretty explicit, and I grew up with four older brothers. They talked, when they didn't realize I was listening." She stepped closer and ran a hand down the lapel of his robe. "There are a few things I've always imagined trying. So, shall we get on with it? The better to get past beginner."

Darius laughed, and with a quick motion swung her up in his arms. "Ah, Isis, only you would order me to 'get on with it.' " In two strides, he was at the pillowside. He dropped down, and Isis clutched his neck at the sensation of falling.

The thick pillows caught them, and they floated gently into their soft embrace. With a lithe movement, Darius rolled over and trapped her beneath him.

He lifted his head slightly to look at her. "Why me? Why choose me as your first?"

"You smelled right."

He laughed again. "Ah, the answer of a master perfumer." Gently, he stroked her cheek. "You make me laugh, sweet Isis. You lighten my heart. I don't remember ever feeling like this with a woman."

She traced his dark brows with one finger, her gaze fixed on his mouth. "I won't ask how many others there have been, Darius, but answer me one thing: Is tonight any different for you?"

She held her breath, waiting for his answer. She didn't expect him to actually say she was like all the others, but if she heard a lie in his voice or saw it in his eyes, she didn't know if she could get past the pain.

His hand cupped her cheek, and she met his eyes. "Tonight is very different, very special, and very new to me, sweet one. You are Isis, my *zaniya*, and I have called no other woman that, nor will I. The gift you give me tonight is one I treasure."

She saw the truth in his eyes, heard it in his voice. His words were like a refreshing spring that quenched all her doubts.

"Come with me, now, and be mine."

"I'm yours."

A wealth of emotions buffeted Darius at the sight of Isis, now his *zaniya*, beneath him on his pillows. Her dark hair against the white of the pillow, her soft skin blushing beneath his touch, her eyes bright with desire. The erotic scent of jasmine arose from her heated skin, making him as hard as an alabaster column. For so many days he had imagined her here.

Isis delighted him, even beyond his imaginings. During the Ceremony of Joining her very being had balanced him: fire and water, air and earth. The seeds of the great Abregaza still lived inside her.

He'd ached to tell her the ceremony's true purpose; he wanted her to share in the majesty and joy it brought him. Guilt had eaten at him when she'd asked the meaning of *zaniya*. Only at the last moment had he remembered her aversion to joining, to Kaf and his world of *ma-at*. If it had just been him and his control at risk, he would have told her, but he was Protector and he could not deny his duty. No matter the loss or pain, he could not place his own

266

needs above the well-being of his people. In the end he had told Isis the truth of the meaning, but not the whole truth.

Now he ran his hands down her sides, and her diamond-thread robe disappeared. Tenderness, protectiveness, possessiveness all welled inside him. Each word, each action of the ceremony had bound them together and filled long-empty parts of him.

He stood, and Isis stretched out on the pillows, watching him, welcoming him as she had welcomed no other. With a single wave of his hand, Darius doffed his robe. Pleasure, and a certain male pride, arose in him when her eyes widened at the sight.

"You are so beautiful," she whispered.

"Nay, you are the beautiful one." A deep satisfaction billowed inside Darius. By all djinn custom, ancient and new, she was now his *zaniya* and he her *zani*. He ignored the small voice that said she had not accepted him as husband according to human custom.

He sank down into the pillows beside her, and she hugged him close. Ah, the feel of her skin against his. It was silk, satin, velvet, yet beneath she was strong and supple. Her feminine strengths were so different, yet so complementary, to his male powers.

He rolled over until she was beneath him again; then he kissed her as he had longed to do, slow and deep. His tongue touched the edges of her lips and she opened readily to his invasion. She tasted sweeter than honey.

Her hands ran up and down his back. She moaned with pleasure and pulled him closer. "Ah, Darius, my djinni." Each stroke of his tongue, each caress of his hand, she matched him. When he bent and took her breast with his mouth, suckling and teasing, swirling his tongue about her taut nipple, then treating the other to the same, she caressed him from head to shoulders to back, then cupped his behind.

He wanted to go slowly, to savor each lingering moment and bring her such pleasure first, but Isis would have no delays. For a virgin, she was knowledgeable, as she said. In typical Isis fashion, she demanded all of him with her fierce passion. She held back nothing, and her desire fanned the flames of his need. If she had any doubts, she let none of them sway her from her course.

His Isis. How could he ever let her go?

Darius stroked her everywhere, with hand, with mind, with *ma-at*, with all that was in him until the need in him shouted for release. *My Isis, my sweet, sweet, Isis.*

My sweet, sweet, Isis. The low croon resonated to the deepest parts of Isis. The air around her crackled and sparked. Where Darius touched her with hand and mouth, blue and green and red swirled about her. She felt the stroke of his smooth fingers and the deeper caress of *ma-at*. It was a dazzling assault on all her senses. She could see only Darius, smell only him, taste only his kisses, feel their mutual need. His hand trailed from her breast to the curls below, and a sparkling, bright as diamonds, followed in his wake.

Isis lifted her hips. "Now, Darius."

"You are so ready for me," he said wonderingly as he tested her with one finger. He nudged her thighs apart, then settled himself between them. Isis felt his manhood throbbing against her, ready to join with her.

Darius kissed her on the nose and pressed into her the smallest amount. "I wanted your first time to be slow, wanted you to be prepared."

She gave a short laugh, trying to draw him farther in, but he held them both firmly in place. "Darius, any more of your preparation and I'd shatter before you have a chance to join me."

He stopped. "Really?" He reached down and stroked her, touching her most sensitive spot, but the trembling in his fingers and the sheen of sweat coating his body told of the effort it took for him to maintain his control. "Shatter, Isis, and then draw together so you can shatter again."

Pleasure, hard and fast and deep, raced through Isis. She bracketed his face with her hands. "No, this first time will be with you. With all of you." She pressed down, feeling him move farther inside her. But not far enough. *"Darius!"*

"So be it. I cannot wait any longer. I want to feel you shatter, and I want to be inside you when it happens." With one determined thrust, he broke her virgin barrier and was inside her. Isis sucked in a deep breath.

Darius held his lower body very still while he leaned over and kissed her. Sparks raced from her lips to her lower femininity, filling her with a magical thrill.

"You are in pain?" he asked softly.

The stretched feeling changed from one of invasion to one of exquisite pleasure. Isis shook her head. Movies and overheard conversations had kept a few secrets. She twisted experimentally beneath him. Oh, my, she'd missed a lot.

She'd missed nothing, for no other time would have been with her djinni.

Darius gave a long, satisfied sigh, and then started to move. Sensuously, determinedly, expertly.

They sunk deeper into the cloud of pillows. Isis gripped Darius's shoulders. Trying to contain her feelings was like trying to hold on to a dream or to capture a moonbeam, so she didn't even try. Love, joy, perfection surged through her, a blaze sent out of control by a whirlwind.

Then it was as he promised. She did shatter, bursting into glittering shards as brilliant as the djinni emotions that crackled and sparkled around them, and from his hoarse shout of triumph, she knew that her love joined her.

A sharp bolt leapt between them, from turquoise tablet to tablet, fusing hearts as bodies joined.

I love you, Darius, her mind called.

My sweet, sweet Isis, my zaniya.

Chapter Nineteen

"What is this?" Darius lazily traced the wavy blue lines that decorated Isis's behind.

Isis, sprawled face down in the pillows, didn't even raise her head to look. "A tattoo," she said, her sleepy voice muffled. "Marc talked me into it."

"It looks like a river."

"It's supposed to."

He rubbed a bit harder. "Why does it not come off?"

"The ink's permanent."

"It's pretty." Feeling drowsy, sated, and more contented than he remembered being in his adult life, Darius outlined the stylized design. He might have felt a twinge of jealousy that Marc had seen her bared bottom had he not just shared an incredible interlude with Isis. As it was, he could not raise the energy.

During their first mating, had he heard her mind whisper *I love you, Darius?* Or was it just his imagination, fueled by longing? He knew little of love—the Protector could not afford to be weakened—but something inside him had grabbed at the words. He knew only that she was part of him now, as he was part of her. *Nothing could change that, nothing could take that away,* he thought fiercely.

"Did you say something?" she murmured.

"No," he answered, wondering if he had unknowingly sent his thoughts to her. Darius frowned, not liking that idea, but he had other things on his mind right now. His hand moved to the dip in her waist.

After that first time, they had roused to swim in the pool of clear water in the courtyard, where they had made love again, slow and languid at first, with the surrounding water making their bodies slick against each other. As before, though, slow soon gave way to undeniable need.

For a woman new to lovemaking, Isis embraced it with an honest, uninhibited passion that fueled his own.

Afterward, the night air had dried them, and then, still naked, they returned to his pillows. It was there Darius noticed the strange marking and asked Isis about it.

His tracing finger moved up her side, along her outstretched arm, and captured her fingers with his. Physically she fit him perfectly: her hands in his, her curves to his hollows, her head tucked under his chin.

How well did she fit inside his *ma-at?* She had accepted him tonight. Had he begun to overcome some of her fears of his powers? Had this night brought him back the control he sought? He supposed he could rise and begin the 1001 Circles of the Adept, a series of increasingly difficult spells that would give him the answer.

Later. There would be time for that after the customary three days of privacy, in which the newly joined couple was left strictly alone, and after the final Ceremony of Closure. He was confident his control was fully restored and the Circles would verify it.

The thought raised his curiosity, however, and he could not resist a small experiment. With his *ma-at*, he stroked down her spine, one vertebrae at a time.

A tremor rippled through her. "What are you doing?"

"Nothing." He leaned over and nipped at the back of her neck, then kissed the tiny sting, while his hand still held hers.

Isis sighed. "It sure feels like something."

"Shhh," he soothed, "let me give you this pleasure." As his *ma-at* massaged her, the air about them haloed Isis with a glittering rainbow. The power, so perfectly controlled, set his skin tingling and raised the fine hairs along her arms. He stroked her in places visible by eye and by imagination, not to arouse—although it was having that effect on him—but to relax and please. He touched her with hand and mouth, skin and mind, and always with *ma-at*.

It danced at his command, as delicate or as strong as he wished. The sparkling flow filled him with a bliss he had found only one other place—in the arms of Isis, his *zaniya*.

"Oh, Darius, that feels *so good*," Isis purred.

"It is my *ma-at* that gives you the pleasure."

She shook her head, the strands of her hair sliding on the silken pillows. "*Ma-at* is nice, but you give me the pleasure, not it. Without you, the *ma-at* is meaningless."

The *ma-at* is meaningless? His stomach clenched at the thought. No, he was his *ma-at*, always and only. It defined his soul, his existence. She had to understand.

It was best to show her. He shifted to a sitting position, and pillows moved to support his back.

Isis turned her head from the pillows and eyed him, her lids half closed. "You know, this is the most unusual bed I've ever been on," she murmured. "A hundred pillows that move just where and how they're needed? They aren't alive or anything?"

"Not exactly."

Her eyes widened. "What do you mean, not exactly?"

He bit back a laugh. "Isis, I am trying to seduce you with my *ma-at*. Now is not the time to discuss my pillows."

She relaxed. "Don't worry, you're doing a fine job with the seduction."

Ah, maybe she did understand. He held out his arms. "Then come here."

Isis squirmed around, the pillows giving her a faint boost upward, until she nestled against him, her back to his front, skin to skin.

Darius wrapped an arm about her shoulders, a strange sense of protectiveness and peace coming over him. He rested one hand on her flat belly, holding her against him. "Once you told me I should 'set the stage' first, before we made love. Tell me your fantasy, Isis. Where would you want most to make love?"

She arched one brow. "Again?"

He lifted his hips in answer, pressing his hardness against her, then hesitated. "Unless you are too sore."

She gave him that slow smile, which set his insides hotter than the Fires of Baharshan.

"Tell me your fantasy," he urged. "Would there be moonlight or sun? A hot stillness or a cool breeze? Your wish is my command."

"Genies don't grant wishes," she told him primly.

"Tonight this one does." He moved his hand in a caressing circle on her soft skin. "Tell me. What do *you* want?"

"I'm not used to someone asking me that. Usually

they just tell me what they think I need."

"I'm asking."

She hesitated a moment, then said, "There'd be water, water I could hear, like a brook or a waterfall."

Darius waved his hand and a fountain appeared. The water tinkled from rock to rock in a merry melody.

"Yes, that's it." She leaned her head back to rest on his shoulder. Darius kissed her exposed throat, and a shiver ran through her. "It would be nighttime, no lights except a sky filled with stars and a full moon," she whispered. "Warm, with just the hint of a breeze to keep it from getting too hot."

The walls of the room faded away and they were outside, on a night just as she described.

"Music," she said softly.

A breeze rustled through, setting the chiming vines astir.

She grinned at him. "Something faster."

He remembered a tune he had heard her humming once and set it to the rhythm of harp and drum.

Isis giggled. "Not the Buster Burger theme! I heard that on the radio the other day and couldn't get it out of my mind. Drove me nuts."

Darius scowled. "How can I fulfill your wish if you insist on laughing?"

She touched him lightly on the cheek. "Laughter feels good, too. I love it when you laugh."

Right then, Darius resolved to laugh more with her.

"How about this?" She hummed a tune.

He remembered that one—about loving truly, madly, and deeply. It was one human song he liked. The harp music changed.

"Nice," she murmured. "And there must be perfume. Orange blossom and sandalwood."

He complied.

"Chocolate?" she asked hopefully.

A tray appeared, holding candies of rich cacao—sweet with a hint of bitterness for interest. Darius held one up and teased her mouth with it before feeding it to her, then taking one himself.

"Mmmmm." She licked her lips. "A crackling fire."

Darius's hand circled across her belly, until the air crackled from his internal fire. The setting, the scent of her, the feel of her satiny skin, all roused him to aching hardness. He longed to bury himself deep within her to assuage the need, but he held back, for this was her fantasy and she would command.

"Kiss me."

He kissed her. Lips, cheeks, nose, jaw, neck, breast.

Isis moaned. "These pillows. You. Show me."

"I thought you would never ask." With a swift motion, Darius rolled them both over, until Isis lay face-down, with him on top of her. The pillows adjusted to accommodate them. Isis wiggled, as though to turn over, but Darius held her gently in place.

"Are you ready for one of those more advanced levels?" he whispered, kissing her shoulder and commanding one of the pillows to plump beneath her hips.

Isis stilled. "Oh, yes."

Three days later, Isis explored Darius's home while he bathed. It wasn't an easy task, she discovered, for the walls and rooms were not fixed. Walls became mere shimmers of energy. Rooms changed size. Doors moved. It was a disconcerting experience, even for her, to get lost on the *inside*.

She was about to abandon her curiosity—soaking her pleasantly sore muscles in the pool with Darius was an enticing alternative—when she spied a carved cedar cabinet. Opening it, she discovered a treasure trove, hundreds of vials of essential oils. Eagerly, she pulled out bottles, sniffing each one, marveling over the purity of the scents. When she found the delightful myrtle, she thought of Darius.

He'd given her much these past days. He was an inventive, generous lover who made her feel so alive. Isis swore a glow radiated from her, she was so happy. She felt wanted for who she was, not some image of what he thought she should be.

And when they weren't making love, they talked. Not about the big things, but about the tiny pieces that made up the notes of their lives. She had learned that he had a sweet tooth especially for chocolate, that human prejudices about color or class or physical limitations were unfathomable to him, that he collected ancient and arcane oddities, that he loved to be touched by her.

Isis sat back on her heels, fingering her turquoise tablet. She wanted to give him something, and now she knew what.

She searched through the cabinet. Did he have myrrh? She had her head buried in the cabinet, looking, when a chiming interrupted her. One of those orbs of light—this one crystal white—appeared above her.

"You looking for me?" she asked it, reluctantly setting down a vial of frankincense. The light chimed once, then drifted away. Isis dusted her hands on her shorts and followed it.

It, at least, appeared to know the way through the maze of movable corridors. It led her straight to the courtyard, where Darius was levering himself out of the pool.

Droplets of water clung to his golden skin and glistened under the setting sun. He flung back his head, lifting his face to the light, and ran his fingers through his hair, shaking off the last of the moisture.

Isis's heart twisted in her chest. He was so magnificent, but the physical beauty would have soon paled for her if she had not discovered so much more beneath that. Arrogant, yes, but caring, too. Despite the sometimes vigor and, uh, creativity, of their joining, he took care that it was never uncomfortable for her, that they never crossed the bounds of mind-shattering pleasure. He didn't laugh much, true, but she thought he was learning what it meant to relax and enjoy. Although he spoke little of his past, she had the feeling that he'd not had much vacation time in his life.

There was another white orb in the courtyard. The two combined into one and chimed once. Darius glanced over, first at it, then her. He smiled, not the sensuous smile she'd seen often, but a smile of genuine pleasure, which she'd seen too rarely.

"If you seek to join me in my bath, you have come too late."

Isis snapped her fingers. "Too bad. Think I could persuade you to reconsider?"

The orb chimed again, and Darius sighed. "I fear not. Duty calls." He held up his hands, and the orb drifted down to them.

Isis looked at it, and then dissolved into laughter. "I've figured it out! That's the djinn equivalent of a beeper!"

Darius gave her a quelling look. "It is a message sphere."

"Like I said, a beeper. You being paged back to work?" Oh, she hoped not. She wasn't ready to give up exclusive rights to him. Isis ignored the fact that she would give up all rights when the *halifa* flower bloomed.

"Something like that," he said dryly. "It is from my king."

Isis lifted her brow, impressed. The orb spoke in a low tone, although Isis didn't understand a word it said, and when it was finished, it disappeared. Darius stayed still, staring into space and rubbing the back of his neck.

"Well?" she asked.

"The king needs to see me," he answered without looking at her, "and he insists I bring you."

King Taranushi was an immense djinni dressed in a brilliant white robe, who had a booming voice and a crushing grip. After changing into loose pants and robes, both a midnight blue, they'd transported directly to the king's receiving room, a square of white marble covered in intricate tapestries. The king clasped Isis about the forearm, grinned at her, and said something, a greeting, she supposed. When he released her, she looked at Darius for interpretation.

"He is pleased to meet you," Darius said.

Isis inclined her head. "I'm pleased to meet him, too."

He reached out toward her, but something Darius said stopped him. The king clapped Darius on the shoulder, said something else, and then laughed, casting an arch look her way.

Isis stopped herself from rolling her eyes, not wanting to offend his king. Male humor needed no interpretation.

With an excess of motion and a spate of incomprehensible words, King Taranushi beckoned her to a plush chaise.

"He also asks your indulgence while we consult."

Isis inclined her head in understanding.

King Taranushi sprawled into the matching chaise beside her and waved his hand. Trays with steaming tea and honeyed sweets floated next to her, and a third chaise appeared for Darius. With a graceful movement, he reclined on it and began to speak with his king.

While the two djinn talked, Isis thoughtfully nibbled one of the sesame wafers, her attention on Darius. When the king spoke, Darius listened intently, and then he answered at length. The king nodded, as though Darius had given him a needed bit of advice. The exchange was repeated twice more.

Perhaps her assumption that Darius was a minor djinni was just a wee bit off.

That uneasy thought was reinforced when something the king said drew a flash of irritation from Darius. He argued, it seemed, but the king just laughed it away.

Darius turned to Isis. "He insists I—we—stay a few moments more. There are . . . reassurances needed."

"Reassurances? Is something wrong?"

"A disturbance of the *Ma-at*. They wish to know things are under control."

"So that's why you needed the balancing ritual? Sure, we can stay. I'm not going anywhere."

King Taranushi rose and strode to the door, calling out to unseen listeners. He clapped his hands twice, and the chaises disappeared. Unfortunately, Isis wasn't expecting it, and she landed with a thump on the hard marble floor.

Darius, evidently not caught by surprise, extended a hand to her. "Sorry," he murmured. "I forgot to warn you."

Then, although she could see his hand holding hers, she felt it also caressing her sore bottom.

Does this make it feel better?

"Stop that," she hissed as other djinn swarmed into the room, the wind of their separate entrances setting the massive tapestries swaying.

He gave her an unrepentant grin, but he stopped the intimate caress and was soon surrounded by the newcomers. They greeted Darius warmly and gave him rapt attention when he spoke. A few of the women cast her vexed looks, but no one approached her. From politeness or lack of interest, she didn't know.

Feeling out of place, Isis drifted out of the melee, rested one shoulder against a wall, and watched a subtle change come over Darius. The aloof, haughty djinni she'd first met had returned. He stood with his arms crossed, hands tucked in the sleeves of his robe, listening politely, smiling with practiced appeal. It was as if the humor and natural warmth she'd seen in him was a veneer that had been erased. Or was this arrogance the veneer he donned? Which was the real Darius? She'd thought she knew, but now doubts crept in.

One woman, beautiful and sleek, appeared to remonstrate with Darius. Isis heard that word, *zaniya*, again. It was the only word she understood. Darius quickly cut the woman off. Her lips were pressed together in anger, but she obeyed the command.

All around Isis, the air in the room sparkled. A fire roared to life in the corner fireplace that had not been there five seconds earlier. Djinn appeared and disappeared. *Ma-at*, powers she could not share, surrounded her.

The knot in her stomach grew tighter as a long buried memory swamped her. Her first day in second grade. Each child had been forced to read aloud to determine his or her reading group placement. The words had swum before her eyes, totally unrecognizable. She'd failed, utterly and miserably, unable to read a single word.

That same feeling of being different, of being something less, threatened her now. Taking a deep breath, Isis battled back old feelings of inadequacy. They would not rule her again.

Darius had not minded her lack of magic.

The woman recovered from Darius's dismissal when he bent his head back and laughed at something she said. She laid her hand on his arm, cast a superior look toward Isis, and joined his laughter.

Isis crossed her arms, clutching her robe with sweating fingers, and hid fear beneath a practiced pose. Her bare foot tapped the hard floor.

The children in second grade had laughed, too, and one had told her that she needed to go back to the nursery reading group. Isis had kicked him in the shin and spent her first day of school in the principal's office.

Now, she throttled the urge to kick the gorgeous witch in the shin. Catfights over a man were too utterly tacky, and jealousy was not her style. Instead she traced a finger around her turquoise tablet and returned the adult version of a kick in the shins—a knowing, satisfied smile.

Of course, the fact that Darius subtly moved out of the woman's reach helped.

Isis's spine stiffened, and she moved away from the wall. Enough of this stupid cowering. She'd seen the curious glances sent her way. It was time to meet them head on.

"Hi, I'm Isis Montgomery." She held out her hand to the nearest djinni, a handsome male, who looked a few years older than Darius. Isis figured the man wouldn't understand her words, but some gestures were probably universal.

They were. He smiled, inclined his head, and pressed his palm against hers, instead of grasping and shaking it.

Okay, so some gestures weren't universal.

"Arsaces," he answered. Isis assumed that was his name.

She gave him a brilliant smile. "Well, Arsaces, it's a pleasure to meet you."

He tilted his head, then a pleased light came into his eyes, and he bent over and inhaled near her neck. Apparently, he liked the perfume Isis had dabbed on earlier.

"You like that?" Isis asked.

Arsaces held up one finger and asked something. Isis shrugged in response.

He placed his index fingers on her temples, one on

each side; suddenly he stopped and glanced at Darius on the other side of the room. Darius was watching them, eyes narrowed. Isis got the distinct impression that Darius said something with that mind-talk thing, for Arsaces backed off at once.

With gratifying haste, Darius extracted himself from the feminine knot of djinn and strode to Isis's side, his blue robe flaring out behind him. There were protests, it seemed to her, but Darius quelled them with a single look and a few words, mild in pitch but uncompromisingly commanding.

Minor djinni? Not in this lifetime.

He gave Arsaces an unsmiling look, then picked up Isis's hand and kissed it. "Are you ready to leave, my *zaniya?* I find myself eager to be alone with you."

"Well, the conversation has been scintillating, but I'll tear myself away." She was more than ready to leave this foreign gathering.

He laughed and kissed her cheek. "Then come."

"What did you say to them, to Arsaces?" she asked as the familiar whirlwind enveloped her.

"That I insisted on extending the customary time alone with my *zaniya.*"

Customary time? Isis got the distinct impression she was missing something here. Something important.

Chapter Twenty

Beside the pool of water in his courtyard, Darius stretched facedown on a green velvet rug. Overhead, the cedar tree shaded him with fragrant coolness. He gave a soft, drowsy sigh and reached for Isis's hand.

She wasn't there. Darius shot upright. Where was she? Had she gone? How had she gotten back to Terra without him?

She could not. He settled, remembering she had said she was going inside, although she hadn't said why.

He frowned and lay back down. This panic at the thought of Isis leaving confused him. Soon, he knew, their idyll must come to an end, but not yet. When the *halifa* bloomed, she would leave, but until that moment arrived, he would keep her close.

Darius had known pleasure before in making love to a woman, but he had never discovered it could be fun. Not until Isis lightened his heart with her enthusiasm and her wit. Nor had he known that it could be followed by a sense of contentment so profound it almost made him weep.

He'd spent hours sharing pillows with women, but never days, and always he'd grown sated and a trifle bored, losing interest in feminine charms for the siren call of the mysteries of *ma-at*.

He had been with Isis for the past four days, barely straying from her side except for basic needs and that one near disaster yesterday when King Taranushi had insisted on meeting the Protector's *zaniya*.

Darius had not wanted to go, but the king's summons was the only one a Protector could not refuse.

The three days of privacy had ended at sundown yesterday, and they'd been summoned to the king immediately after, for King Taranushi was curious to meet his Protector's *zaniya*. If that had been the only reason for the summons, Darius could have delayed, but there was more.

Since his return, Darius had sensed the discordant ripples in the *Ma-at* from the sinister forces gathered by Pari. King Taranushi had begun to feel them, too, and a vague unease crept across Kaf. The djinn wanted to know what was happening; they wanted reassurance. He had gone to the king, and he had given them that reassurance.

In return, he had insisted that he and Isis not be disturbed again until after the Ceremony of Closure, until he chose to revert the stones of privacy about his home to those of welcome. Yet he could not bring himself to do so. Four days, and he still had not satisfied his need for her.

Sometimes, when he lay at her side in the dark of night and watched her gentle breathing, this need for Isis frightened him. He could not allow it to weaken him.

So why had he not begun testing himself with the 1001 Circles of the Adept?

Why had he stopped Arsaces from teaching Isis the

djinn language yesterday? Why had he not taught her himself, though he wanted to?

Darius gave a rueful laugh. Those questions were easy enough to answer. He did not want her to find out what *zaniya* meant, or what the ritual had meant. He had an uneasy feeling that Isis would be very angry when she learned, so he kept it from her despite the prick of conscience. Out of custom, the djinn would not approach Isis unless she approached them first—both her status as a new *zaniya* as well as being the Protector's mate assured that. And since she did not yet speak the language, he had thought himself safe for a few more days.

He had not counted on Isis's innate friendliness.

With the luck of Solomon, she would not find out before the *halifa* bloomed, and they would have at least these days together.

When she left, this aching yearning would fade, and he would be back as he was: the Protector, in full control of his *ma-at*.

In the meantime, he would make love to her again. And he would hold her close in the dark of the night.

"Ready." Isis came tripping out from the interior, carrying a jar. Darius propped his head on his hand, enjoying the sight of her bright smile and the sunlight gleaming on her dark hair. She had twisted several gauzy flowered scarves together and then knotted them at her waist, creating a belt that fluttered in the light breeze and snugged down her thigh-length purple cotton shirt, which had the added advantage of outlining her full breasts in a tantalizing fashion.

In the privacy of his home, Darius felt little need for clothes. Although Isis seemed comfortable in the nude, she was, by her own admission, a "clothes-horse." He was not exactly sure what that meant, other than the fact that she had been delighted when he created an array of garments for her, styled from the magazine pictures he'd seen, the needs of the hot Kafian climate, and his own tastes.

He did not mind if she dressed. It just gave him something to take off.

She knelt beside him and set the jar on the sand. Her admiring eyes scanned the length of him. "You are like a beautiful, golden god," she whispered, touching him lightly on the chest. "Every time I look at you, it takes my breath away."

His unruly sex reacted at once to her touch and her regard, and he reached for her.

A gentle shove to the chest pushed him to his back. "Later."

"Later?" he complained, plucking the knots at her waist.

She batted his hands away. "Later. You're a very generous person, Darius, so I wanted to give you something back."

"A gift?" Darius lay back, intrigued. He often gave gifts to women, but to be the recipient of one was a new experience.

"Yes, but what, I asked myself, could I give a djinni? I mean, you can conjure up anything you want, right?"

The scarves and purple shirt dropped to the sand, right beside him. Darius's smile grew wider.

"So, I got to thinking," Isis continued. "I couldn't give you any *thing*. It had to be something you couldn't do yourself."

She straddled him at his hips, squirming a little in a highly erotic stroke. Solomon and sands, what movie had she seen that in? Darius reached up one hand to stroke her thigh.

Firmly, she took his hand and replaced it beside his head. "Your hands stay there."

What was the little fox planning? Anticipation coiled in his belly. Isis could be unpredictable, but she was never disappointing.

"As an aromatherapist, one thing I learned to do, and do quite well if I do say so myself, is massage."

Massage. Darius closed his eyes and allowed the primal powers of Kaf to flow through him to her as he stroked her belly.

"Stop," she said.

The *ma-at* cut off abruptly; he was still unable to work magic on her if she was unwilling. "I thought you liked that." He stacked his hands beneath his head for a better look at her.

"I do, but not right now," she answered.

She was nude, gloriously nude. The sight of her breasts, brown-tipped, tight-nubbed, shining from the sun, distracted him. "Is this better?" He circled his palm across a nipple and thought about sitting up so he could take its well-remembered sweet taste in his mouth.

Isis thrust her fists against her waist. "Darius, has anyone ever told you, you have an annoying habit of taking charge?"

Offended, Darius dropped his hand. "Never." The Protector was always in control; no one thought to question it.

"Well, you do. Most of the time I tolerate it, but not now."

Darius looked at her face. Her lips were pressed together and her eyes were narrowed. She was truly irritated, and he was not exactly sure why. "What do you want me to do?"

She shifted, until she knelt beside him. "I want you to roll over, then just lie down and accept. Do nothing. No touch, and especially no *ma-at*. Relax. Turn yourself over to me."

A beating panic rose in Darius. No *ma-at*? Control to her? He almost started to protest, but at the last moment he caught a faint quiver about her lips. His actions had hurt her, and that he did not want.

Without a word, Darius rolled onto his belly and laid his head down on his arms.

She straddled him again and dropped a light kiss on the back of his head. "Thank you. Now that wasn't so hard, was it?"

She had no idea how difficult that one simple movement had been.

He heard the jar open; then, a moment later, a rich, complex perfume, one he'd never smelled before, wafted to him on the hot desert breeze. It was a scent that curled inside him, deep and satisfying. "What is that?"

"Do you like it?"

"I do. Very much."

"That's your present. At least part of it."

Her hands, warm and fragrant with the perfume, began to massage his back. A solid pressure, and a muscle he hadn't known was tense relaxed. A series of pats, and his skin started tingling. Isis was right. She knew how to massage, and the oils she used enhanced her sensuous touch.

"I noticed you had some essential oils," she said between strokes across his shoulders, "and I found this empty jar. I hope you don't mind my taking them, but my supplies are on earth."

"I do not mind. What I have is yours," he murmured.

"I wanted to make you a signature cologne, one that would be only for you."

"You made this for me?" The thought delighted him.

"Yes."

What a talent she had! The scent was one that pleased him and filled him with a sense of being perfect for him, yet had he tried to describe it, he could not have. "What is in it?"

"Hazelnut oil, cedar, a little rosemary, a touch of myrrh, a few other ingredients. You can use it on the brazier to scent your rooms, in your bath, for massage, however you like."

"Isis, this is a wonderful gift you have given me."

Her hands stopped their pressure. "You're pleased?"

"I am well pleased. Thank you, my *zaniya*."

"You're welcome."

As her hands moved across him, working down his legs to his feet, and the special scent seeped into his pores, Darius felt himself relax. He gathered his *maat* and his desire inside and simply felt.

Darius was so content, his mind at rest, that he barely noticed the gust of wind that signaled the arrival of a djinni.

Perhaps I should return at a less intimate time. Simon's amused voice touched Darius's mind.

Simon, here? And Isis was—

Darius spat out the needed words and clothed them both in robes; then with an impossibly quick movement, he rolled, grabbing Isis to prevent her tumbling off.

"What—?" she protested. "Darius!"

Darius lifted his head to glare at his friend.

Simon leaned against the cedar tree, nibbling on a date, looking upward. "Can I look again?"

"Who—?" Isis squealed. "Oh, damn!"

"Did you not see the stones of privacy?" Darius asked Simon, jumping to his feet, and then holding a hand out to Isis.

"Seems to me I remember asking you that very same thing a few times," Simon answered.

Isis clutched the lapels of her robe together. "Let me guess. You're Simon."

Simon gave her a bow. "And you must be Isis." He strode forward, picked up Isis's hand, and kissed the back of it. Isis smiled in return. "A pleasure to meet you at last, Isis Montgomery."

Darius crossed his arms and shifted closer to his

Isis. "You had a reason for coming?" A sudden thought struck him. "Jared! Is he—"

Simon waved a negligent hand, his attention still on Isis. "Jared is fine, safe. He's taking to Terran customs quite well."

Darius frowned. That was not exactly the reason he had sent Jared to Terra. "Then why have you come?"

Simon gave Darius a speculative look. *Why are you with this woman when the ribbons of celebration for your joining cross your doorway, my friend?*

Isis is now my zaniya.

"Your what?" Simon blurted out. "You said you would never take a *zaniya.*"

At least Simon had the sense to switch from English to the djinn language so Isis did not understand. Or maybe he was just so astonished that he had reverted to his native tongue.

"Things changed," Darius answered.

"She's human."

"You married a human."

"That's different. She agreed to marry you? After knowing you for two weeks? That doesn't sound like the Isis Montgomery Zoe told me about."

Darius hesitated. "She does not know."

"Does not know!"

"I did not tell her the full import of the ceremony. And you will not either," he hastened to add. "Nor will you mention this to Zoe."

Simon lifted his hands. "You're going to be in enough trouble when Isis finds out. I won't add Zoe to your woes. In fact, I'm hesitant now to even give you what I brought."

"What?" Darius glanced over at Isis. Her arms were crossed over her chest, her foot tapped, and her look was decidedly annoyed at being left out of the conversation.

"Simon has brought something he needs to show

me." Darius switched briefly to English to speak to Isis. "We shall be back soon. Come, Simon."

Laughing, Simon shook his head and followed Darius to a private room. "Have you got a lot to learn."

Darius didn't like hearing about troubles he might have with Isis in the future. "What did you bring me?"

Instantly, Simon sobered. "I continued to look for information about the line of Abregaza, as you asked, and I found this." He handed Darius a sheet of paper. "The tablet in that picture was dug up at Susa, although nothing has appeared in the Terran texts about it. Apparently the person in charge of the dig was afraid it would be taken from him if he publicized it. It seems to be a prophecy."

Darius looked at it. It was a copy of a photograph of a clay tablet. There were words dug into the tablet. "How did you find it, then?"

"The man and I have corresponded for some time through the Internet. He considers me an expert in ancient languages, since I've translated a few things for him. He trusts me."

Darius peered at the grainy picture. He could just make out the writing. It was the prophecy as he had read it. Then he looked again. There was more! There was more to the prophecy than the torn parchment he'd found.

A fist clutched his stomach. Had he missed something in the prophecy? Something that had led him to misinterpret the divination?

Darius looked up sharply. "What did you say?" In his dismay, he'd missed Simon's last words.

"Do you know what you're doing, Darius?"

Darius look at the paper. "I thought I did. I am sorry, my friend, there are things I must—"

Simon lifted a hand in understanding. "I'll be going then."

After Simon left, Darius deciphered the blurred

picture. When he finished, he sat back, stunned.

The prophecy was of Terran origin, from the time of Abregaza. Somehow, the ancient copy he possessed had been torn, leaving only part. The entire prophecy read:

In the time of chaos,
When the powers run wild and free
Strong shall you grow or strong shall you fall
One united with the line of Abregaza,
Both willing and free.
Air and fire, balanced by water and earth, will restore.

In the time of chaos,
When the powers run wild and free
Strong shall you grow or strong shall you fall
One stands alone in pure strength
Unbound by caring
Air and fire, with power supreme, will reign.

Two paths to choose
Balance
Power
One choice to be made at the final divergence
No other choice succeeds, no other path remains.

Acid etched through his veins. There had been not one path, but two. The divination had only shown him Isis because he had not known to ask about the other path. He read it again.

If he read it right, the other way was one of unlimited power in the *Ma-at*. Highest strength under perfect control.

With that, he would surely defeat Pari.

And the only cost was caring. Feeling for others. Harbad. So emotionless that his cruel training made bitter enemies of two djinn who should have been closer than any. So powerful that he could create the *halifa* flower.

Harbad had faced this choice and had chosen the second path, abandoning Isis's ancestress with only the perfume. That was why Harbad had been so powerful, the most powerful Protector the djinn had ever known.

If Darius chose that path, he would rival, maybe even surpass, Harbad in the legends of the djinn.

The cost of that power would be Isis. Darius's gut clutched at the thought. He could not give up Isis. But could he turn his back on his people?

There would be a point when he had to make the final choice. At that point, the other path would be forever closed to him. He was not there yet, Darius sensed.

So, the question arose: Had his union with Isis fully restored his control? Enough that he could hope to defeat Pari?

Yes, it must have. The divination had shown him a path, and the prophecy confirmed it was a true one. Darius felt the tension inside recede. His choice was a good one. It was time he underwent the trials of the 1001 Circles of the Adept, but he was confident of the results.

There was just one more thing he must do: an ancient ritual, its origins lost in time, and one not often observed by djinn. Yet he was determined to omit nothing that would strengthen the ties between him and Isis.

Darius returned to Isis.

"Where did the two of you disappear to? Where's Simon?"

"He left." Darius stroked her soft cheek. "I must ask your help once more with a simple ritual. Will you?"

"I guess so."

He fetched a small tray holding a tiny but sharp knife and a single pomegranate, then led her by the hand to the side of the pool. They knelt beside it, facing each other. With deft movements he peeled away the pomegranate's thick skin, and then sliced the fruit into two pieces. He handed one to her.

"By the law of the ancients, be forever joined," he said, eating his fruit, and then he nodded to her.

"By the law of the ancients, be forever joined." She ate her piece.

"The circle completes, the rites are fulfilled, two are one," he said. When he nodded, Isis repeated the words. He joined their hands, lacing their fingers together, and leaned forward and kissed her lightly. She tasted of the tart fruit and of her own sweetness. "All is finished."

"All is finished."

The Ceremony of Closure, the final step in the joining, was done. A surge of pleasure raced through Darius. The last tie had been woven and could not be cut. His control was returned.

Slowly he loosened her hands and took a deep breath. "I must leave you for some hours. I request that you stay here, in my home, until I return. There is sustenance enough for you. Will you do this?"

"I'll wait."

Leaving everything except his turquoise tablet behind, Darius transported to the Tower Lands. It was a wild and unforgiving place, but the harsh conditions were needed for the test.

Hours later he had his answer.

At Circle 986, his control slipped. At Circle 987 it failed.

Darius dropped to his knees, dizzy with fatigue, blood dripping down his arm. Sweat and dirt coated his skin. He closed his burning eyes and fought the utter desolation.

He pulled in a ragged breath, his throat clogged

with unshed tears. His chest tightened until he thought his heart might stop from the pain.

Noooooo, he shouted silently, unable to give voice.

Joining with Isis had not restored his control. Not fully.

He must tread the other path.

Chapter Twenty-one

The dragons hissed.

"Yes, my pets, I have found it." Pari stroked each of the two dragons with her long fingernail and laughed. "I searched so hard, even resorting to seeking clues on Terra, and the answer was here, in my possession, all along. Is that not amusing?"

After giving the dragons a final scratch, Pari closed the carved wooden box. It had held the flacon of perfume she'd used to lure Isis, and finally she had thought to search it. In it, she had found a brittle paper.

"I know how to defeat Darius now. I was right, you know; the woman is the key."

Pari smoothed out the paper and read it again. It was a prophecy, with a few cryptic notes by Harbad at the edges. The prophecy told how those who grow greatest in strength must face a choice between balance and power in order to control that strength. *That* was what she had sensed in Darius when he

297

rescued that annoying child. A loss of control.

"The fool chose the woman. He could have had absolute power, and he chose the weaker path. Now all I have to do is destroy that path."

She was too late to prevent their joining—that had occurred four days ago—but if she could separate them . . .

Pari fingered the prophecy. She knew just what to do. "There are matters to attend to, my pets. I leave you now."

The dragons hissed.

Four days later, Isis threw down the dropper and rubbed her eyes. Enough! She couldn't tell six drops from nine, and her patience was at an end. Thrusting away the mortar containing her latest skin creme formula, she pushed to her feet.

There was a limit to the hours she was willing to spend blending oils and drawing up plans for Dream Scents while waiting for the *halifa* to flower and for Darius to come to his senses.

What had happened to her tender lover? What the hell had Simon said to him? Whatever it was, it had brought a haunted look to his eyes when he emerged from the conversation.

After Simon left, Darius had vanished for almost an entire day, and when he'd returned, Isis had feared for him, he looked so exhausted and in such pain. His beautiful body was bruised and bloodied, but he had not allowed her to tend him. Far worse, however, was the flat, emotionless mask that had replaced his haunted look. Isis shivered, cold to her soul, remembering those dark, passionless eyes.

For the hundredth time she tried to figure out what had gone wrong.

Since his return, he'd shut himself up in what Isis termed his workroom, a locked sanctum she was not allowed to enter. His haughtiness and arrogance returned, cold and sharp as a scalpel. He hardly even looked at her, much less talked to her.

Only at night did she glimpse the man she'd fallen in love with, when he emerged to join her on the pillows. He did not come to her with open arms or gentle teasing or infectious smiles. He made love to her urgently, almost primitively, with a raw-edged passion that seared her to her bones, and then held her tight until morning.

Whatever drew him away from her, he was fighting it. A primal part of him still desperately needed her. That small knowledge, and the fact that he still used the perfume she'd given him—daily its scent clung to his skin—were her only hopes.

Last night, however, he hadn't spent the entire night with her. After taking her twice, he'd left, going to that infernal locked room, and she hadn't seen him since. She was losing the war, and she didn't even know the enemy.

Isis didn't like to lose.

To that end, she pounded on Darius's workroom door. Subtlety, she'd learned earlier, didn't work. "Open up," she shouted. "I need to tell you something."

The door opened abruptly, and Isis stumbled forward. An unseen force stopped her, shoving her backward. Isis rubbed her skin. "Ouch, that stung."

Darius stood in the doorway, hands tucked into the sleeves of his blue robe, the planes of his face in stark relief against the shadowy room behind him, no expression on his face. "Cease. I cannot concentrate with your shouting."

Her temper flared. "I will not! What the *hell* is the matter with you, Darius?" she challenged, her chin outthrust.

"It does not concern you."

"I think it does, since I'm stuck here with you."

"You would not understand."

"Try me."

"No, a human cannot know." Calmly and coldly, he shut the door in her face, adding at the last second, "I shall come to you tonight."

Isis slammed her fist against the door, kicked it for good measure, and then stalked away. What had happened to him? Why was he acting this way? She loved him, but it didn't mean she had to tolerate such shabby treatment.

"Don't even think of coming to my bed tonight," she shouted over her shoulder. "I'm leaving."

A hot wind blew around her, and then Darius stood before her, glaring, hands on his hips, sparks shooting from the ends of his hair.

Isis swallowed. Well, she'd wanted a reaction.

"You will not deny me your pillows, *zaniya*."

Isis matched his arrogant pose. "You can't ignore me, treat me like a serf, and then expect me to want to go to bed with you."

He moved closer, lifting one brow, responding to her challenge. "Oh, you shall want me," he said smoothly.

"Oh, yeah?" Something in her kept baiting him.

"Let me erase your doubts."

He gathered her into his arms and kissed her. It was a kiss intended to dominate, to assert his sensual hold over her. A hard, overwhelming kiss strengthened by his mind whispering inside her, his hands stroking her, his *ma-at* tingling across her skin. In the dim recesses of her mind, Isis was aware that he took care not to hurt her. She was also aware that there was no tenderness in the kiss, only expertise.

Instinct told her that if she gave in, if she acquiesced to his sensual demands, then he would fall deeper into whatever it was that held him, and he would take her with him into that cold abyss. Only if he cared enough to fight against losing her would she have a chance, and he wouldn't fight if he thought he already had her.

It took every bit of her willpower to stand quiescent in his embrace, to force the air in and out of her lungs in an even rhythm, to not respond to the seeking pressure of his tongue. Her trembling hands gripped her shorts as she fought the urge to run her palms over his smooth chest. Desperate, she spelled every word she'd ever missed on a test, anything to keep herself remote.

Thank the Lord his telepathy didn't work on her.

He groaned softly, angled his head to deepen the kiss, and then dipped toward her again.

She couldn't resist much longer. "Is it to be rape then, Darius?" she asked against his lips, praying she didn't reveal the effort it took to speak calmly.

With an oath, he flung away from the kiss and glared at her. "I do not *ever* force a woman."

"Don't start now." She turned and walked toward the door.

He blocked her way. "Where are you going?"

Isis thought she heard desperation in his voice, but she could not let herself go soft. "Out. For a walk. You may be able to stand being locked away for days at a time, but I can't."

His lips tightened. "You will not leave here by yourself. I will not permit it."

"Modern tip number six, Darius: That is definitely the wrong argument. Besides, how are you going to stop me?" she goaded. "Your *ma-at* doesn't work against me, does it?"

She'd suspected that interesting tidbit after putting together a couple of remembered facts, and now his frustrated look confirmed her guess. "I keep telling you, I'm not stupid," she told him.

Of course, he was still bigger and stronger than she and didn't need *ma-at* to stop her, but deep down she still trusted that he would not hurt her physically.

"I know you are not stupid, so you should know that you cannot go alone. You do not know our customs."

"Are you going to take me?"

"Not now. No, I cannot."

"Bye." She turned back to the door.

He blocked her way again. "You will get lost."

Isis shrugged. "I've been lost before."

"You cannot go." His voice echoed with anger, as though it came from a long tunnel, and the sparks around him became a nova.

At last she'd broken through that emotionless wall. Isis fit her hands to her waist. "You're missing the point here, Darius. I'm going out for a walk. You have no input in that decision. Your only choice is whether you come with me or not." She held her breath, hoping he would say he would come with her.

She was not to know his answer.

Sand blew in a disorganized whirl around the courtyard. Isis gaped in amazement as a young boy materialized in the middle of it. He appeared to be about twelve and wore baggy shorts barely hanging onto his hips, an oversized T-shirt emblazoned with a soccer ball, and a New Orleans Zephyrs baseball cap, on backwards. Portable earphones hung around his neck, with a cord leading to a CD player attached to his jeans. His hair appeared to be shaved close, and a yin-yang symbol hung next to the turquoise tablet strung by a leather cord about his neck.

"Jared!" exclaimed Darius.

"Yo, Darius. It's been twelve days, by Terran time. You said I could come back."

At last, a djinni besides Darius who spoke English. Was this Darius's son? No, it couldn't be.

Darius's astonishment was palpable. "Mary has corrupted you," he said between clenched teeth.

"Nah," answered Jared. "I did this myself. Mary

302

just gave me a couple of suggestions. Rad, huh?"

"Rad?"

"Radical," offered Isis.

Jared looked at her. "You must be Isis. I heard Simon mention you, said he never thought Darius would take a *zaniya*, especially a human. But, hey, I think it's fine." He lifted a hand. "I'm Jared, Darius's apprentice."

So, not a son. Isis slapped palms with him, giving him a high five greeting. Already she liked this infectiously good-humored youth.

"Apprentice?" asked Darius, his gaze skimming across Jared's outfit. "That remains to be seen."

Jared glared back. "You promised, Protector."

Protector?

"Well, I'd say you two have things to discuss," Isis said brightly, recognizing a perfect chance to make her escape. "See you later." With that, she walked away.

"Wait!" called Darius.

Isis ignored him.

"When can we start training?" Jared asked eagerly.

"When you have donned a proper robe," Darius snapped.

Their voices faded as Isis let herself out of the house, grateful for the child's appearance. Jared had broken through Darius's recent aloofness with such ease. The thought that perhaps she'd been unsuccessful because Darius didn't care enough about her was a frightening one.

Protector? She mulled over the title Jared had given Darius. And what had he meant about Darius never taking a *zaniya*? The suspicion she'd buried after meeting King Taranushi, suspicion that she'd been working under a few misconceptions and that there were a few questions she needed to ask, rose again in Isis.

Outside, she halted, entranced by her first good

look at Kaf. It was a beautiful place, as Darius had said. She drew in a deep breath of fresh, clean air. No pollution here, only natural scents from cedar and orange trees, swaying grasses, and pockets of flowers. The sun was well past its zenith, but it still beat hot against her skin, undimmed by the few clouds that scudded overhead. If she stayed here long, she was going to need some good SPF 30 sunscreen.

If she stayed here long. When had that thought taken root? She couldn't stay here. In a world where everyone met his needs by magic, she was less than capable. She could do nothing. She would have no purpose beyond being Darius's lover, and that was a situation she could not tolerate. Her life, her work, her family were on earth.

She'd always known there was no future for the two of them, that their time together would last only until the flowering of the *halifa*.

Why was she fighting so hard to reclaim Darius? Why didn't she just leave and come back when the flower bloomed?

Isis sighed. Because love wasn't always rational. Because she still hoped that, if he loved her, there could be a way to work out the dilemma.

He never spoke of love, but he had to have *some* feeling for her. Why else would he want her here?

Darius's home sat a short distance from what looked like a city, judging by the jumble of buildings and the people scurrying about. At the center of the city, two spires gleamed under the sun, and a large marble building, probably King Taranushi's palace, was set into the recesses of a near by mountain.

The city was not big. On earth, it would be considered no more than a village, albeit a graceful, elegant one. Many of the homes looked more like tents than buildings, with colorful silken walls that swayed in the gentle breeze. Palm trees and massive bushes she couldn't identify provided spots of green. Overhead, a flock of birds soared.

There was no identifiable road—when people could just transport from place to place and the culture was definitely low tech, there was no need—but the sand provided comfortable walking for her bare feet. Isis looked around, trying to locate a landmark that would allow her to find her way back. That clump of cedar trees would be a suitable marker.

In about fifteen minutes she reached the edge of town, and for a moment Isis hesitated. This was a foreign country, a foreign world, and Darius had been right about one thing: She knew little of djinn customs. Suppose she accidentally broke some local taboo? Isis took a deep breath. She'd come this far; she wasn't ready to turn back. What harm could she do just walking around and looking?

What she hadn't expected was the attention generated by her mere presence. It wasn't unfriendly, but neither was it welcoming. No one approached her, but she could feel the curious looks and hear whispered conversations when she passed.

Robes or loose trousers and tops seemed to be the wardrobe of the day. Isis tugged the hem of her shorts down, feeling decidedly underdressed.

The feeling of being on display, of being judged, intensified when she happened upon a large open square that served as a common area. There were no permanent structures that could be construed as stores, but individuals intent on bartering conducted business. A few enterprising individuals had set up tents or display tables. One was roasting vegetables—peppers, eggplant, and a root she didn't recognize—on shish-kabob sticks over an open brazier. The pungent scent made her mouth water.

Seeing her interest, the proprietor offered her a stick. Isis turned her pockets inside out and held her hands up, palm out, showing she had nothing to trade. "I'm sorry."

"*Lafatan. Da-nat zaniya e kalane-tari.*" Solemnly, the woman offered the stick.

"Thank you."

The woman bowed, her two hands pressed together in front of her chest. The vegetables were delicious, and it seemed that the small gesture had served to at least lessen her scrutiny.

An ancient man scraping a pestle inside a mortar drew her attention. When he nodded at her, Isis knelt on the rug beside him, watching. He was grinding up some small seeds that released a scent new to her, part fresh camphor, part woodsy, part cardamon. When the seeds were a fine powder, he carefully poured them into a glass vial filled with oil, stopped the vial, and gave it a vigorous shake. He waved a hand over his collection of oils, motioning her to pick one.

Isis sniffed several bottles, then selected one she thought would complement the aroma of the seeds. The man nodded and added a few drops to his mixture. "Oh, I wish I could ask you what you're doing," Isis said.

"Darius chooses to keep you ignorant of our language," said a feminine voice behind her. "I wonder why that is."

Isis whirled around and saw the sleek, beautiful woman who had fawned over Darius at the palace. She looked magnificent today with a robe that glittered like yellow diamonds under the setting sun and her dark hair cascading down her back.

"You speak English!"

"I decided it would be amusing to learn."

"What do you mean, Darius chooses to keep me ignorant of your language?"

The woman shrugged. "He could have given it to

you at any time, yet obviously he has not. He even stopped Arsaces."

The djinni at the palace. Isis sat back on her heels, stunned. Why had Darius done that? Around Isis, with the sun setting, the djinn began packing up their wares and drifting away. The ancient perfumer rolled his supplies in a cloth and left, murmuring something to the woman and giving Isis a friendly pat on the hand. Small fires flared to life at the edges of the square.

"If you wish, I can give you our language," the woman continued.

Suspicion made Isis wary. "A bargain? What's your price?"

"No price. Call it a gift for the *zaniya e kalane tari.*"

It was a phrase similar to one the old woman had used. "What does that mean?"

The woman stared at her for a moment, then broke into a trill of laughter. "You do not know? Oh, that naughty Darius. I think you had better accept my offer."

"Why are you doing this?"

The woman gave her a smile full of malicious mischief. "Because Darius obviously does not want you to know. Call me Leila, by the way."

Isis looked around the square. It was nearly empty. She didn't trust this woman, but the temptation to be able to speak to Darius in his own language was too strong. Normally, learning foreign languages was virtually impossible for dyslexics; they had so much trouble with their own. There was no cost but knowledge. *Said the serpent to Eve*, Isis thought. "All right."

Leila drew one of the braziers closer. She knelt before Isis and pressed her forefingers hard against Isis's temples. Pain, like streaks of lightning, raced through her skull. Isis winced and tried to retreat, but Leila did not lessen the pressure or let her go.

Kathleen Nance

She chanted a few lines then said, "Repeat after me. 'By the fires and winds of Kaf, grant me the knowledge I seek.'"

"By the fires and winds of Kaf, grant me the knowledge I seek."

"This boon I ask, great Solomon. This boon freely given."

"This boon I ask, great Solomon. This boon freely given."

"Now, think about what you want, Isis. Think about taking in the voices of Kaf."

Isis didn't quite understand, but she tried to comply. Suddenly, a thousand voices bombarded her. A cacophony of words and songs raced through her mind. She jerked away and moaned in agony, pressing the heels of her hands against her pounding forehead. "What did you do?" she shouted, trying to hear her own voice over the clamoring inside her.

"Do not whine," sneered Leila. "It will be over soon."

Isis got the distinct impression the djinni could have used a far less painful way to transfer the knowledge. But, after a moment, the pain did subside, as Leila had promised, leaving Isis with an aching head and a strong wish for some ibuprofen.

"Do you understand what I say?" Leila asked.

It was strange. Isis knew the djinni spoke another language, yet she could understand it.

"Yes, I do," Isis answered in the same language.

"Good." Leila smiled a cruel smile, then stood and lifted her arms, preparing to depart. Her scornful voice rang inside Isis's mind with one final, mocking taunt. *Darius, Protector of All the* Ma-at *has joined with an ignorant, powerless human. You cannot really think it is because he cares, do you?*

"Good-bye, *zaniya e kalane tari*," she said aloud.

Those were the words she said, those were the

words that faded on the wind. Isis heard them, and knew their meaning.

Good-bye, wife of our Protector.

Protector. That was what Jared had called Darius. My *zaniya*, Darius had called her. My *wife!*

Damn him! Damn, damn, and triple damn. He had lied to her! That wasn't a balancing ceremony, as he had claimed.

It was a wedding ceremony.

Chapter Twenty-two

Darius had married her by his customs without telling her.

Why? Numb and unseeing, Isis wandered from the djinn city as she tried to make sense of it. From the little she'd seen, he was obviously well respected by his people. He could have chosen anyone. Sure as sulfur stank, Leila would have volunteered for the job.

So why did he marry me? Why so quickly and with such mystery?

Sure, the sex was great. All right, the sex was fabulous. Well, to be truthful, Isis knew she'd never share anything like it with anyone else.

An affair was one thing. But . . . marriage? Leila's last words rang in her mind. *Darius, Protector of All the Ma-at joined with an ignorant, powerless human. You cannot really think it is because he cares, do you?*

Isis dropped onto a flat rock and brushed the sand off her feet. In the red twilight, a nearby copse of trees became twisted shadows, and a lone bird soaring overhead emitted a plaintive call.

No, unfortunately, she didn't think it was because he cared. The pain of that knowledge came so sharply that she flung her head back with the agony. Her arms wrapped around her waist, as though to hold pieces of herself together. It wasn't because he cared.

That ceremony had been his final bargain. He must have known about it all along, planned on it from the very beginning, just as she had wanted the perfume. He'd planned to marry her before he'd even met her.

Perfume was one thing. The intimacy they'd shared was something else entirely.

He'd used her. She didn't know for what purpose, but she knew he'd used her as surely as Ben Fontenot had.

Only difference was, she hadn't really loved Ben.

Isis rested her forehead on her knees and shut her eyes tight against the tears. Shuddering breaths wracked her, and she bit her lip until she tasted blood. Anything to hold the wrenching sobs inside. She wouldn't cry.

"Well, the little human has wandered far. And so sad, too."

Oh, great, just what she needed now. "Go away, Pari. I've had enough with the djinn sisterhood for today."

"What if I've come for my favor?"

"What is it?" Isis asked dully.

"No, I don't think I'll free you yet."

Isis looked up. Pari leaned against one of the gnarled trees, her paleness a smudge against the ebony wood. The evening had gone utterly silent—not a cricket chirped or a leaf rustled—but Pari's gray robes undulated like a slithering nest of serpents. She looked younger, Isis noticed; the lines of her face were smoother and the gray in her hair darker. Good facial or a plastic surgeon? "If it's not the favor, why are you here?"

"Sharing a few truths?"

Isis snorted in disbelief.

A frown flashed across Pari's face, then instantly smoothed to a gentle smile. Isis wasn't fooled. It took a few raving blunders—like not realizing she was attending her own wedding—but she was learning. Never trust a djinni.

Pari fingered the black tablet resting between her breasts. "I thought I would share a little information with you."

"Is this going to be as helpful as the information that only a genie could get the perfume for me?"

She shrugged. "You needed the flowers, and Darius is the only one who knows where they grow. It's not my fault they won't bloom for another twenty years."

"What? Darius said—You're lying!"

Pari smiled. "You mean he did not tell you? I thought perhaps not."

It seems there was a lot Darius hadn't told her. "Why should I believe you?"

"Why would I lie? It's easy enough to check. Just ask Darius to take you there."

"And if he doesn't?"

"Is that not its own answer?"

Isis's eyes narrowed. "Why are you telling me this?"

"I thought you should know. Rather than wasting your time here, you could be tending to your affairs on Terra. I'm afraid things are going rather badly in your absence. Rumors of instability."

A stone lodged in Isis's stomach. "Darius said he would take me back to the time we left, so no one would know I'm gone."

Pari gave her a pitying smile. "I've got nothing

against you. If it hadn't been you, it would have been another. You were just a convenience to me."

"To bind Darius?"

"Ah, so you figured that out."

"I'm not stupid."

"No, I don't suppose you are. But, as I said, my argument is with Darius. Verify what I have said. For your own sake."

She disappeared, and the beetles began clicking again.

Isis sat, unmoving, thinking, until the sky turned dark with night. She'd been a gullible fool once before; it was time she stopped being one now. That meant not blindly trusting Darius again, but it also meant not accepting as gospel everything Pari or Leila told her, either. She doubted that their actions were motivated by a desire to help Isis Montgomery.

She'd give Darius a chance to explain before she asked him to take her home. His explanation had better be a damn good one.

Not being a gullible fool also meant accepting that she'd deluded herself in thinking Darius might be falling in love with her. To him, she was nothing more than a willing bed partner to while away the time.

Her mind made up, Isis got to her feet and stared around, finally taking closer notice of her surroundings. Where was the clump of cedar trees? She shoved a hand through her hair and swore. Great, a perfect end to an otherwise lousy day. She was lost.

The *Ma-at* consumed him. The winds of Kaf carried to him a thousand whispers, traces of her living connections—plant, animal, djinn. He spread his mind deeper inside her, expanding his talents beyond the boundaries that had held him before. Flames inside him roared eagerly: watching, knowing, learning.

But these flames of power were cold, not hot. Darius, sitting cross-legged before the fiery Circle 997, the Unity of the Adept, felt nothing but the satisfaction of his *ma-at* under exquisite control.

That was enough. That had to be enough. It was necessary for the Protector, all the Protector could use. It was all he ever wanted or needed.

All, that is, until Isis blazed into his life.

With a roaring whoosh, primal heat consumed him and the *Ma-at* flared beyond his control, shattering a glass shelf and sending a dozen books tumbling to the floor. They knocked over a vial of sandalwood-scented oil, which spilled into the Circle. The fire blazed up and ignited a nearby pile of dried moss, which turned to ash in seconds, leaving only a smoke tinged with sandalwood and the stink of burnt civet-moss.

Darius looked at the shambles and pressed his hand against his aching head.

When had he last eaten? He'd lost track of the days, but desperation made him push himself hard. Time was running out. Pari would attack soon, and he must be ready.

This path, this route to remastery by letting only *ma-at* into his life, had to be the correct one. Sometimes, like now, when the *Ma-at* was his, part of him, but stronger and more beautiful than it had ever been, he wanted never to let go of it. He was so close to regaining the control he must have.

All he must do was let go of Isis.

Another part of him howled with loneliness at the thought.

He had tried. He struggled to remain focused, to keep thoughts of Isis from distracting him, but too often he failed. Her scent, her smile, her tenderness, her brilliance had all taken residence within him, and he could not seem to exorcise her.

Probably because when he fought against her, it was a battle against himself, and he was no closer to winning this one than the one with Pari. In the depths of the night, he had to be with Isis, holding her and making love to her, listening to her and inhaling her essence.

Earlier today, when she shouted that she was leaving, a panic had arisen in him like a *tsuahnam*, a wall of sand raised by mighty winds that obliterated all in its path. He had thought she returned to Terra, though he did not see how that was possible. None of the djinn would displease their Protector by taking her back without his permission or knowledge. Only because he'd learned she intended to go no farther than the city, and because Jared had distracted him, had he allowed her to go.

Besides, she did not speak the language, and djinn, other than the king, would observe the ritual moontime for a new *zaniya* and leave her in silence unless she spoke first.

Darius relaid the stones of the Circle, quietly reciting the Twelve Mantras of Unity to achieve the detachment he needed to start Circle 997 again. It was not to be. This time, Jared disrupted him by flinging open the door, bursting through the locks of *ma-at* as if they were no more than parchment.

Jared rubbed his arms. "Geez, Darius, you should have warned me those were up. That hurt."

"I did not invite you in."

"I didn't figure I needed an invitation, since we're studying together. Darius, you've got to—What happened here?" Jared stared at the tumbled books and shattered glass. He waved his hand in front of his nose. "Whew, and what's that smell? Burnt civet moss? But who'd be so foolish as to burn that?"

"Go back out and enter the proper way, Apprentice." Darius sought the control. No emotion, only *ma-at*.

Jared stared at him. "But—"

315

"Go!" There was no mistaking the command in his steely voice.

Jared scowled and disappeared. A moment later, a voice sounded in Darius's mind. *Protector, your Apprentice bids entrance.*

Come.

Jared landed inside the room, at the farthest point from Darius. He had changed into the gray robes of the Apprentice. His palms were pressed together before him, and his head bowed.

Approach, commanded Darius.

Jared demonstrated his control by transporting the minor distance in seven increments. At each he paused, for the Teacher could find any one unmastered and send his Apprentice away.

Although the child did not transmit his thoughts, Darius's telepathy caught snatches of Jared's true opinions.

This is so bogus. He's worse than Darth Vadar. At least Vadar breathed hard. What's the point to all this?

Jared was rebelling against the necessary discipline, but at least he obeyed.

Permission to speak, Protector.

"Granted."

"Isis has not returned, yet. I thought you should know."

Darius shot to his feet. "What? Where is she?"

"No one has seen her since the market closed."

"Why was I not informed?"

Jared shot him a disgusted look. "I tried. If you hadn't made me do all that Approach of the Apprentice crap, I could've told you sooner."

"Stay here."

"Like, I'm going anywhere dressed like this?"

Darius ignored Jared's complaints. Instead, he touched his turquoise tablet and pictured Isis. Their joining would allow him to transport to her side. In an instant, he had found her, trudging through the

316

sand. At his arrival, she halted, brushed a hand across her face, and glared at him.

Solomon, why had she gone so far from the protection of the city? His chest tightened with fear. There were dangers on Kaf: the basilisk that slayed with a look, the Fire Streams, a rampaging *hamid-el-halad*. Dangers from djinn, perhaps, too.

"You are a long way from home. Why do you go so far?" he demanded, worry harshening his voice.

"Yeah, a real long way." She seemed unharmed, if a bit dusty and weary. Her foot began tapping, always a bad sign. "Why didn't you tell me? For God's sake, why didn't you tell me?"

"Tell you what?"

"That we were married!"

Darius suddenly realized she was speaking the language of the djinn. "How did you learn our language?"

"Leila taught me, and it was real interesting learning what *zaniya* meant." She spun away from him. "I was such a fool."

"I shall deal with Leila," he said tightly.

She spun back. "Don't you dare. At least *someone* was honest with me."

"Leila has her own reasons for what she did."

"And you don't? How long were you going to keep me in the dark about it?"

His veneer of control began slipping. "You had no need to know."

"No need?" she screeched. "It was my wedding! Or doesn't that mean anything to you people?"

"It is sacred to us. But you are human and the ceremony was not done according to your customs." Desperation crept to him. Said aloud, the explanations seemed so thin.

"So you figured you could have a few days of fun, then drop me back on earth none the wiser? God, Darius, that's despicable."

"It is not like that!"

"Then how is it? Why? Why did you do it? I need explanations, reasons. Something."

He could not tell her. Knowledge of his lack of control, his weakness, was dangerous. If it became known, the djinn would be thrown into chaos, panicked at the loss of their Protector. Pari would not hesitate to move at once.

"The divination led me to you."

"Modern tip number ten: We like to be *asked!* And number eleven: We don't find it flattering to discover some arcane ritual acted as matchmaker."

"I . . . want you to stay," he said, as close to pleading with a woman as he had ever come.

Her chin lifted. "Why should I?" she asked softly.

"Because of this?" He leaned down and kissed her, drowning in the taste and scent of her. When he lifted his lips, she was clinging to him, and his heart was pulsing in time with the beat in her throat.

Isis drew a ragged breath. "Sex isn't enough, Darius. I need more."

What more could there be? If he continued down the second path, that was all he could give her. There would be no other place for her.

She would not accept that, he knew. Not his Isis. She would not be a distant second to his *ma-at*.

A maelstrom of emotions whirled inside him, battering him. Confused thoughts pounded at his head. He could not let her go. Losing her would cause more pain than the loss of his *ma-at*. Yet his duty forced him down the other road.

In the end, Darius said nothing.

"I thought not," she muttered; then she turned and trudged away. In the wrong direction.

"Our home is that way."

"Your home," she corrected, but she turned the way he pointed.

He laid a hand on her shoulder to transport them.

318

She shrugged off his hand. "I'll walk." Sand swirled about her ankles, and she kept her gaze firmly forward.

Darius kept pace with her, eyeing her closely. She had been gone some time, and her lips looked parched. The heat on Kaf could be dangerous.

"I expect you are thirsty," he said, conjuring up a glass of cool water and holding it out to her. She shook her head.

"And hungry?" He offered a pear.

She shook her head again, but the rumbling in her stomach belied her motions. She swiped her hand across her face, and then, because she wasn't looking, she stumbled across a large stone, her bare toe scraping across the rough surface.

"Ouch!"

Darius caught her before she fell and picked her up in his arms. He cupped his hand around her sore toe, drawing the minor pain into himself and then dissolving it to the winds. He set her on her feet, but his hands lingered around her waist.

Isis brushed his hands away. "Stop that."

"Stop what?"

"Being nice." She crossed her arms over her chest. "You can't treat me the way you have, then think you can brush it all away with a few simple treats."

He matched her pose. "I was not doing that."

Her lifted brows told of her disbelief. She started back home, then stopped abruptly. "When does the *halifa* bloom?"

The change of subject made him wary. "Soon."

"How soon?"

He shrugged. "I do not know exactly." Too soon. He did not even want to think about it, for it meant she would be gone then. "Before the Festival of Mingara."

She lifted her chin. "Pari said it wouldn't blossom for another twenty years."

319

"Pari? Pari was here?" Had she set a trap? Darius searched for his enemy, but he detected no sign of her.

"She's gone, but she told me the *halifa* was nowhere near blooming. I know you said you'd return me to the moment when I left Terra, but don't you think someone will notice I've aged twenty years overnight?"

"Pari lied," Darius said tightly.

"Prove it. Take me there."

Darius's temper flared. The Protector did not have to prove himself.

"She also said if you didn't, that would be an answer, too."

Darius bit back an oath. He grabbed Isis's hand and transported them to the distant grotto.

There was a moment of utter stillness and silence.

Oh, Solomon, he'd forgotten what the near-blooming *halifa* looked like.

Chapter Twenty-three

The grotto was a place of fantasy. With a muted roar, a waterfall tumbled into a deep pool of scarlet-tinted water. Green ferns surrounded the secluded area, and the sand and feather grass underfoot were soft and fragrant. It smelled like . . . Eden, just right, like Darius.

Where was the flower? Isis looked around eagerly, but she saw no green buds, no blossoms on the verge of opening, only dried, brown petals—some still on the plants, most littering the grass. She gasped and pulled her hand from Darius's, then bent to one flower still on its stem. No, this couldn't be it!

Isis drew in a long breath. For one sweet second, she caught the erotic scent of the *halifa*, and then it faded like the last ray of a setting sun. The brown petal dropped to the ground.

This flower was not going to bloom in a few days. Darius had lied to her. Isis pressed her lips together, fighting betrayal, accepting only anger. "You bastard!" she hissed.

Kathleen Nance

"It is not as you think."

How could he sound so calm? "Oh, yeah? Tell me, what's your story this time?"

He knelt before her and tilted her chin so she looked at him. He wasn't calm, she realized, for a wild pulse beat in his throat and a red aura vibrated around him.

"The *halifa* is unique, a flower of *ma-at*. When it blooms, it bursts into full blossom. Slowly the petals turn brown and drop, and then, when the last has fallen, it is time for it to bloom again." He waved his hand around the grotto. "See, the petals are almost done. The *halifa* will bloom in a few days. At its opening, you can collect the single drop of oil contained in the heart of each flower. Each drop will be enough for many bottles of your perfume, and there are thousands of blooms. In just a few days—" He touched her cheek.

Isis shoved his hand away. Did he really believe she was that stupid, that naive? "Save it. I'm not buying what you're selling anymore, Darius."

"What do you mean?"

"Save the fairy tale for your kids." She rose to her feet and walked away from him, her hand spearing through her hair. The knot in her belly grew to Gordian proportions.

He was at her side. "Only you can bear my children."

Oh, man, that was a low blow. "Well, too bad I started on the pill last week," she shot back, fighting the treacherous idea of bearing children with Darius.

"What is this pill?" He stuck his hands on his hips and glared at her. "Children are a blessing."

Glad for the annoyance replacing her hurt, Isis rolled her eyes. "You're missing the point here. What I meant is, I don't believe you. You've kept too many things from me, told me too many half truths. Just a few days until the *halifa* blooms, just a few days

322

until the Festival of Mingara. Seems your definition of a few days and mine are a bit different. In the meantime, I've got a business that's going to pot."

He stood before her, and she saw the sparks in his hair. Well, too bad; she was angry, too.

"Are you saying I lied about this? The Protector is not doubted so."

"You may be their Protector, but to me you're just Darius."

He touched the turquoise tablet at her throat. "You wear my protection, my *zaniya*."

"I'm not your wife!"

"But you are my *zaniya*," he said a bit smugly.

"Are you saying you never lied to me?"

He had the grace to flush. "Not directly."

"Just a few sins of omission and misrepresentation. Not correcting a few mistaken assumptions. Sorry, Darius, in my book that's not the truth."

"I tell you the truth here."

"But how am I to know the difference?"

The sparks faded, and he looked away from her. "I had hoped, perhaps, you had come to know me."

"I thought I had. Now, I don't know. How am I to trust you? A man of magic with the power of dreams? I can't tell what's reality and what's illusion."

And that was the whole crux of the matter. She believed in the powers of his magic and loved the man who wielded them, but if she couldn't trust him, trust that what they shared was more than magic, then any hope for a future together was no more than a mirage.

"*Ma-at* is my reality, Isis, my only reality. Feel it." He guided her hand to a thick vine and wrapped her fingers around it. "Feel the powers of Kaf."

He stood close behind her, his arms encircling her, his hands covering hers. She felt surrounded by him, his masculine scent and heat. Isis struggled, but he held her firm.

"Feel my reality, sweet Isis."

The thin layer of air between them vibrated with blue and yellow, and electricity danced across her skin, then dug deeper, to her tissues and bones. It sparkled inside her, until Isis felt it expanding, going beyond her.

The vine was connected to the depths of Kaf in a way she had never realized before. It spoke, not in words, but in centuries of life, so slow and foreign she could only feel it, not understand it. And beyond it were thousands more, filling her with an exhilarating power. She could do anything.

"Is it not beautiful?" he whispered.

But where was love? And contentment? Joy or sadness?

With effort, Isis let go of the vine. "It is beautiful, Darius, but it's the remote beauty of a distant mountain or a carved canyon. It's not what I need." She turned in his arms to face him. "Is it all you need?"

His arms dropped and his jaw worked. "It must be," he said emotionlessly. "It is all I have ever had. What else is there?"

At least she had an answer, although it was like a knife blade to her gut, slicing her raw. Isis lifted her chin. "Take me back, Darius." The words echoed inside the hollow ache that spread through every part of her. Her chest felt so tight, she struggled for breath. "I want to go home, to my business, my life."

His golden skin paled and he flinched, as if her words had been a blow.

"You do not have the *halifa*. You said you needed it for your business." His voice was hollow.

"I'll manage without it." She could turn her business around without magic. Somehow, she'd succeed. "Take me home."

He grabbed her hand and, without another word,

transported them from the beautiful, lonely grotto. They landed outside his home on Kaf.

"I said I wanted to go home."

"This is your home."

"No, it's not. To earth. To Terra. Take me back, Darius," she spat.

"No!" His jaw clenched, and his breath came in short pants. "You cannot go. The bargain. You said you would stay until the *halifa* bloomed."

"Uh-uh. That wasn't part of the bargain. It took a few times, but I finally learned something about making deals with a djinni. I said I'd do the ceremony and then collect the oil. There was absolutely nothing about my staying here in the interim."

He was silent, obviously remembering the bargain; then he swore pithily. "You must—"

"Take. Me. Home."

"No. You are my *zaniya*." His chest heaved, and the sparks blinded her. "I cannot let you go."

Isis stared at him, fury mounting. "You're keeping me prisoner?"

He closed his eyes, pain written across his face. "I cannot let you go. Please, a few days—"

Isis flung herself away. "Then I'll find someone who will."

Isis was up early the next morning, making her way to the city. She had realized last night that she couldn't go around knocking on doors, or whatever the djinn equivalent was, in the middle of the night. At least Darius had had the sense not to come to her last night while she tossed on the pillows.

The nerve of him, keeping her here. Why? What did he want?

She found the first djinn stirring in the market, and with her newly acquired skill with their language, she had no trouble making her wants known. They were all unfailingly polite; a few were shyly friendly; a couple of the older women were embarrassingly frank. Isis, however, had not realized the full extent of their regard for their Protector.

"If the Protector says you must stay, then you must. He has his reasons."

"It is the Protector's will with his *zaniya*."

If she heard those words one more time, she'd be sick. She'd say they were afraid of him, except the tone was always respectful, even full of admiration for their Protector.

Nobody, however, ever called him Darius.

At last, frustrated, Isis stood outside the tent of the old perfumer, Gaspar she'd learned his name was.

"May I enter?" she asked.

Come in, my child.

The dark interior of Gaspar's quarters were as fragrant as her workroom. It gave Isis an immediate sense of home. Here, at least, she could find comfort in the familiar amid the foreign.

Gaspar, wearing a striped robe and sitting crosslegged behind a low table, motioned Isis to sit. "You are troubled."

"I want to go home." Lord, she sounded like a petulant Dorothy in *The Wizard of Oz,* unable to appreciate the wonders surrounding her. Hey, she even had an evil witch lurking around and a mysterious wizard giving her commands. Except, in this case, the wizard was no fake.

"Is this not your home, now?" He picked up a small packet of white crystals and sprinkled a few on a brazier that glowed on the table between them. The soothing odor of melitot—a mix of honey and carnation—permeated the room,.

Isis shook her head. "My life is on Terra."

"Yet you are *zaniya* to our Protector." Gaspar held a cruet between his hands, warming it slightly, then poured two drops of oil—citrusy bergamot—into a tiny vial. "What would you add to this for acceptance?" he asked.

"Clary, a little rosewood," Isis said.

Gaspar nodded. "I would have chosen thyme, but clary is better."

"I didn't know what the ceremony meant." Isis returned to their original discussion, while Gaspar concocted his potion.

"That does not change the fact that you entered into it willingly, and the Protector is bound by it."

That thought bothered her more than she cared to admit. She didn't want to feel the fetters of marriage when she returned to earth, and she didn't like the thought of Darius remaining alone here. He was too alone as it was.

Isis hardened her heart. "That's his problem. He should have thought about that before he tricked me."

"I imagine he did. Our Protector does not act without thought and strong purpose."

Again, Isis refused to listen to the praise. "Will you take me back to Terra?"

Gaspar stoppered the vial, then with a wave of his hand magically fused it to a chain. "No, I will not. Cease this fruitless quest. None will risk the displeasure of the Protector, nor will they think to alter his decisions. If our Protector promised to return you, then he will."

He handed her the vial. "For you, for your peace. If you wish to study with me, I would welcome you."

Apparently she could expect no help from the djinn. In fact, she'd probably just made herself look foolish by asking. Isis slipped the chain over her head. "Thank you. If I were to stay here, I would enjoy spending time with you, but I cannot."

His only answer was a fatalistic shrug.

On her walk back to Darius's home, she was surprised to see Jared lounging against a tree. He was

obviously waiting for her, for when she drew opposite him, he straightened and joined her.

"Didn't find anyone to take you back, did you?"

"You knew about that?"

"I heard you when you came home last night. And
heard a few rumors this morning."

"I probably made a fool of myself."

"Yeah," he answered with the honesty of youth. "If
it comes to a choice between the wishes of a human
and the desires of the Protector—"

"I get the picture. What is this Protector thing, Jared?"

They walked through the sand, their steps slow as
they delayed their return.

"The Protector is second only to the King, and in
some ways more honored, for he battles against
forces that threaten or corrupt our *ma-at*, the very
heart of our being. The title goes only to the strongest
of the djinn, and it is usually obvious very early who
will be next."

Isis remembered Zoe telling her that Darius had
been taken from the school. "That was Darius?"

"And now me. I wanted to be Protector more than
anything, to train with Darius and become like him,
but now—" He stopped abruptly and faced her, arms
akimbo. "I don't want to be like him the way he is
now. He's different. He was always—"

"Arrogant? Haughty?"

The boy shrugged. "That's the way of djinn; Darius
has more reason than most to be so. He does what's
necessary to protect our *ma-at*, but before it seemed
like . . . he cared. Now he is only power."

Zoe had also told her that Darius had been trained
by Harbad, an emotionless djinn. "Perhaps that is
the way the Protector must be."

Jared glared at her. "No, it isn't! I would not be
that kind of Protector. Something changed Darius,
and the only thing I can see that is different is *you!*"

Isis stepped back, surprised by such vehemence in one so young. Or, who knows, he was probably older than she was by a few dozen years.

"Keeping you here against your will is wrong. It is against all we practice. If you go back to Terra, Darius will return to who he was."

"I can't go back by myself," Isis said.

"I will take you." He grabbed her hand. "We must go now, while Darius is still involved elsewhere."

"Wait!" This was all happening so fast. To go without a good-bye, without ever seeing him again? "I don't want you to get in trouble with Darius."

"He will be glad once he is no longer under your spell."

Well, that was a different way of looking at it.

"We must leave now." Jared looked anxiously at Darius's home.

"Can you take me back to the point when I left?"

"I can go back only to the time when I left, no sooner."

"How far different is that?"

"I don't know."

The whirlwind started at her feet, hot and sandy, and moved up her legs. A dizzying disorientation swamped Isis.

At least I think I can go back. Jared's voice echoed faintly in her mind. *I've never actually tried that spell before.*

"What?"

Just give me the location of your home. We should land close.

Oh, damn.

The sand and mountains, scent and breezes of Kaf disappeared, replaced by a swirling vortex of gray.

It was night on earth when they landed, and the air was hot, humid and perfumed with the scents of night jasmine and lilac from her garden. Streetlights gave an eerie yellow cast to the sky, and red airplane

329

lights winked above. She hadn't realized how used she'd gotten to a true black sky.

"Good-bye, Isis Montgomery." Jared lifted his hands and disappeared, leaving only a sharp whirling breeze that soon died to nothingness.

Isis turned in a slow circle. She was home, yet the familiar surroundings seemed foreign. The turquoise tablet hung heavy upon her chest, like the lifeless stone it was.

Her magic was gone. Darius was out of her life, though he would never be out of her heart.

Darius jerked up his head. A glass wand shattered in his palm, bringing bright welts of blood. The pain in his hand, however, was nothing compared to the sharp agony in his chest. It felt as though his heart had been ripped from him. Wind whipped about him. He flung his head back. Silent denial welled in his throat, demanding release in a howl of loss.

Isis was gone.

Chapter Twenty-four

Isis gave up attempting to sleep when the night gave up holding back the sun. Staring at the morning newspaper, she rested her throbbing head in her palm. Two weeks. The reality pounded her numb brain. How had she been so foolish as to believe she could be gone and no one would notice? She'd been gone two weeks.

Vulcan jumped on her lap and gave her a baleful look.

"Sorry I didn't tell you I was going," she told him and held out her hand. After a moment, he butted her with his head, forgiving her, and Isis scratched him behind the ears. "At least Aunt Tildy's been taking care of you and Khu."

"Meow," answered Vulcan.

"Now, I have to get to Dream Scents and find out what's happening."

Isis threw on a gauzy flowered wrap shirt over a short yellow skirt, then swiped on her makeup. As soon as the ferry started running, she sped through the gray morning, her bright yellow a false beacon of cheer.

How had Dream Scents fared during her absence?

Inside the shop everything was familiar—the colors of the bottles, the smooth feel of wax candles. Isis paused in the doorway, drawing in a deep breath, reimprinting each scent. She walked over to the fountain and turned it on.

It sounded like a waterfall in a magical grotto.

Damn, she was not going to be one of those lovesick fools mooning over memories and mementoes.

There was a stack of newspapers on her desk, each one folded to a story about her or about Ben Fontenot. There were more of the latter—all trumpeting Ben's new success—than the former. So, her family had kept her disappearance under wraps. For the first time, Isis was grateful for the protection afforded by her four brothers and by the Montgomery name.

Impulsively, she dialed Ram's number. She hadn't wanted to disturb anyone last night. No, be honest. Last night, she'd been exhausted, and coward that she was, she hadn't been able to face their questions. They'd be worried, though, she knew, and she needed to let them know she was back.

While she waited for Ram to pick up, she glanced at one or two of the articles on Ben. She didn't have time to decipher them before Ram's answering machine picked up.

"Hi, Ram, it's Isis. I'm—"

"Ice!" Ram picked up the phone. "Are you all right?"

"I'm fine."

"What the hell happened to you?"

Isis heard a woman's sleepy voice murmuring in the background. "Catch you at a bad time? I can call back—"

"No! Wait! Just a minute." Isis heard Ram speaking to the woman, the woman's annoyed reply and Ram's soothing response. It was the same voice he used with skittish animals. After a few minutes of silence he returned. "She's gone. We can talk."

"It wasn't nice to throw your companion out this early."

"I promised to make it up to her later. Where—"

"Not even chivalrous enough to drive her home?"

"She had her car here. Where—"

"Do I know her?"

"No!" he exploded. "Quit asking questions. Where the hell are you?"

"In the Dream Scents office."

"Then where the hell have you been? My God, Ice do you know how worried we've all been? I hope there's a damn good explanation for this."

How about, I just got back from a honeymoon with a genie? "A good one; just one I'm not sure you'll believe."

"Try me."

Isis sighed. She owed them an explanation, and maybe it would be better to say this when she couldn't see Ram's expression.

"I was with Darius."

"Where is he?" His voice lowered with deliberate male menace.

"Not here."

Ram swore with pithy crudity. "So help me, Isis, the man will answer to me. And to Thomas, and Jack, and Beau, and Dad."

"What are you going to do against a genie?" she asked softly.

There was a telling moment of silence. "Oh, God, Ice," he said gently. "Not again."

"He's real. I don't expect you to believe that, but I thought you deserved the truth."

"Ah, look, I know you've been under a lot of pressure. Maybe you need to talk to someone."

"I don't need a psychiatrist. Don't worry, I'm not going to go around spouting fodder for Jimmy Ray's column or getting another page in the mugshot book. I've learned my lesson. I have too much work to catch up on."

"What happened between you and Darius?" Ram asked, softly and implacably.

I experienced the most tender and glorious lovemaking, sex beyond my wildest dreams.

I got married.

I fell in love and he didn't.

None of that was for her brother to know. "Whatever it was, it's over now."

Something of her pain must have tinted her voice. "Did he hurt you?"

Yes. "No."

"You're lying."

"And it's for me to deal with."

"I'm here if you need me, little sis."

Isis blinked back tears. "Thanks. Will you call Dad and the others for me? I'm not up to explanations times four."

"Especially not that explanation. Sure, I'll call them. We'll see you at dinner tonight."

It wasn't a question, and suddenly she found that being surrounded by her loving, if stifling, family wasn't such an unpleasant prospect.

"Fine. And, Ram, I'm sorry. For worrying you. I was gone longer than I expected."

"At least you're home."

After he'd hung up, Isis glanced at her watch. One other call, and it probably wasn't too early. Aunt Tildy picked up right away.

" 'Morning, Aunt Tildy. I'm back. Thanks for taking care of Khu and Vulcan."

"You're welcome, dear. Although Vulcan did sulk a bit." She paused delicately. "Did you return alone?"

"Yes."

"For good?"

"Yes."

Aunt Tildy's sigh sounded across the telephone lines. "Ah, I had hopes. He showed me a technique for enhancing the senses, and I think I felt something last night. Some real magic. The power, for one moment, flowed through me like a deep river. It was beautiful, Isis."

Is it not beautiful? Darius's words haunted her. "I'm glad, Aunt Tildy."

"I shall miss him."

"So will I." She replaced the phone and got to work.

"Ah, love, you're back!" Marc burst into the office a short time later. He picked up her arms and spread them, examining her closely, settling on her face. "You exude radiance and shadows. Darius exceeded the promise of his magnificent body, and he will not be back."

"Got it in two." She took a shuddering breath.

Marc enfolded her in his arms and patted her on the back. "Now you're back in the bosom of your loving family and friends, Ice. Rest and repair. Let us comfort you in your woe."

Isis looked up at him, and then burst out laughing. "You are so full of it. 'Comfort you in your woe'? Where did that come from?"

"I read it in a book years ago," Marc sniffed, "and have been waiting for the perfect time to use it."

"Well, now that you have, let's pack in the sympathy. How much damage did my absence do?"

"Nothing that can't be repaired. Your family kept a lid on it pretty well—claimed you were on vacation—despite a column by that detestable Jimmy Ray."

"What'd he say?"

He waved an airy hand. "A glum story questioning your silence, rehashing the old discords between you and Ben, hinting at weird happenings. People will be watching."

Isis crossed her heart. "I'll be a model of deportment."

"Please, I hope not."

Isis grinned. "Nah."

"It's good to have you back, Ice," he said seriously.

"It's good to be back. Now, is Ben's expansion hurting us?"

"We've noticed a tiny drop-off, but your regular customers are still loyal." He picked up a paperweight on her desk and fiddled with it. "You have to make a decision, Ice. Are you going to go for broke, try and wrest that top spot from him, or are you willing to stay small?"

"You have to ask? We're going to be bigger *and* better than Ben Fontenot ever dreamed." Isis was surprised when Marc didn't immediately join in her enthusiasm. "You don't agree?"

"I kind of like small and cozy, where we can pay attention to each person who walks in the door. I thought you did, too." He set down the paperweight and gave her a grin. "But, hey, it's your store and your call. Let's have at him." He retrieved a bottle of perfume from a drawer. "I just happen to have here a sample of Whispers, his new perfume."

"How did you get it?"

"Don't ask. Its aroma is supposed to be top secret until the bachelor-bachelorette charity auction this weekend."

"This weekend!" Isis grabbed her calendar. "Oh, damn it is. We've only got five days."

"Say, aren't you up for grabs at the auction?"

Isis made a face. "Yeah, I agreed." It had sounded like fun at the time, but now . . . How could she go on a date? She was a married woman.

Not on earth. Not by her laws. Besides, it was for a worthy cause.

Why did it seem wrong?

"Let me see that perfume." Isis unstoppered it and sniffed. "That slime! It's *my* Whispers. The perfume I created." She sniffed again. "No, wait, it isn't quite. He's changed a couple of ingredients. Changed the proportions on another. Mine was better." She closed the bottle. "That's what that complaint about the break-in the other day was about, the one that got Jimmy Ray breathing down my neck again."

"What?"

"He was coming out with this, and when you, uh, obtained a sample, he reported a break-in. That way, if I complained, or tried to come out with my version of Whispers, it would seem like I'd stolen his formula and just changed a few ingredients. I tell you, Marc, the man is a snake."

"You malign a worthy beast, love."

"What he doesn't know is, I've got something better." She didn't have the *halifa*, but the remainder of the formula for the perfume of her dreams was still a good, if unusual, one, and she had ideas for some minor improvements. Isis showed him the flacon she'd brought from home this morning. "Do you think we can get two hundred bottles like this before the auction? Something tiny for a sample. And another two hundred to hold Winter?"

"Maybe not exactly; it would have to be plastic." He started to unstop the flacon.

"Don't." Isis stopped him. She didn't want him smelling those last remnants of the real perfume, afraid the one she would create was a pale imitation. "I'll let you smell it when I get the final formula worked out. Let's plan on presenting our own scent at this auction."

*　　*　　*

Isis buried herself in work, hoping the feverish activity would erase the hollowness inside her and dissipate the lingering male scent of Darius that clung to her workroom. It didn't. It only served to remind her that the perfume she created, though intriguing, was not the one she wanted.

She took to sleeping with pillows Darius had left at her house, hugging them to her the way she longed to hug him. It was the only way she could get any rest. When she did fall asleep, vivid dreams accompanied her, some so erotic she awoke throbbing and screaming in frustration, some so fulfilling she awoke wonderfully warm and sated, and some so tender she awoke with love in her heart and unshed tears for what she'd lost.

Finally, Friday afternoon, the day before the auction, Isis sat rubbing her aching head, trying to decode the lines and curves on some papers. Lord, she hated this. Hated all the promotional headaches, the production questions. What she liked was perfumes, scents, aromatherapy, but she had no time for that.

"I wonder if my nose can still tell the difference between muguet oil and lily-of-the-valley?" she muttered.

Marc pushed back from his computer, took the pile from her hand, and turned her desk chair around so she faced the window.

"Look," he said. "What do you see?"

"Our courtyard. Green plants. Daylight."

"Good, you still recognize it. Now, get out, Ice. Walk on the levee. Take a nap. Soak in a tub."

"But there's still so much to do."

"And it will still be there Monday. All work and no sleep is making Isis a very tense lady. Like this, you'll be lucky if you bring in all of five dollars tomorrow."

Isis gave a short laugh. "That bad?"

"That bad."

She looked at the papers before her. "Are we making it, Marc?" she asked seriously.

He sighed. "It's touch and go. I'll be honest, Ice. You're spending a lot of money on this new perfume. If it brings in enough business, we'll be good. If not—" He shrugged.

"It will. I know it will." Isis covered the gnawing fear with bravado. She would succeed.

You are skilled with your craft. Is that not enough to bring reward? Darius's words echoed inside her.

If only she knew what success meant anymore.

"I'm sure this mysterious perfume will be all you claim," Marc said. "That still doesn't change the fact that I want you to go home."

Home. Isis pushed to her feet. "I'll see you Monday."

Just as she was leaving the shop, a middle-aged woman came in, looking for her.

"I'm Isis Montgomery," Isis said, shaking the woman's hand. "What can I do for you?"

The woman gripped the strap of her purse. "I just wanted to come by and thank you. I didn't get a chance earlier, things were so hectic. With the funeral and all."

"Thank me?"

The woman shook her head and gave a wan smile. "Sorry, I'm not as coherent as I normally am. I'm Cora Grisham's daughter."

The woman who had come seeking relief from the pain of her cancer.

"Mom died last week, but her last days were tolerable and she could make the final . . . preparations she needed, thanks to you. Her aromalamp burned almost the entire time. I know she wasn't always the most pleasant—"

Isis put her arm around the teary woman and patted her shoulder. "Your mother was a brave woman, and I was privileged to know her."

339

"I just wanted to thank you."

After the woman left, Salem came over. "It's good to have you back, Ice."

"It's good to be back." She just wished she could say the words with more conviction.

The ferry ride home was steamy, like the tea Darius had offered her one day on this same boat. Isis leaned her head against the post and watched the water foam past. One of the reasons she'd pushed herself these past few days was to avoid quiet times like this. At those times, the ache inside her grew to nearly unbearable proportions.

Resolutely, Isis pulled some papers from her brief-case.

She would not think about Darius.

When she got home, however, there was a crystal flacon sitting on her kitchen table. Curious, Isis lifted the stopper, then immediately replaced it. The potent *halifa*, at full strength, was unbelievably beautiful. Dreams, wishes, wants invaded her. Sitting beside the flacon was a parchment, the writing bold and elaborate. It was written in the djinn language, but Isis had no trouble reading the four words.

The bargain is completed.

Isis collapsed into the chair and wept.

"I quit!" Jared leapt to his feet.

"Sit down and do it again." Calmly, Darius undid the tangled knots of the cord and stretched it out along the row of stones.

Jared kicked the sand with his bare foot. "No. I mean it, Darius, I'm quitting."

"The Protector must master spells of dispossession. This is only the first of many. If you quit now, you will be unable to complete the others."

Jared shook his head, not looking at Darius. "I'm not just quitting this spell, I'm quitting the whole enchilada."

Darius's hands stilled. "I do not understand."

"I'm quitting the apprenticeship. I don't want to train to be Protector."

The quiet emptiness in Darius grew blacker, colder. *Not Jared, too!* Ruthlessly, he thrust back the emotions. The Protector could have only the *Ma-at*.

"You agreed to the training. A djinni does not retreat from his word."

Jared shook his head, his gaze still on his toes. "I haven't reached the age of majority. I'm allowed to freely try different paths until I make the final choice of skills."

The child was right. Darius nodded his head in acknowledgment, even though the tumultuous pounding in his temples urged him to fight against still another loss. It had taken all his strength of control to harvest the first of the *halifa*, give the oil to Isis, and not linger until she returned.

"You are strong, Jared. Versatile. Creative. You will not be happy unless you can use those powers. And only as Protector can you exercise them fully."

Jared looked at him. "I wouldn't be happy here," he said.

Words from a child should not hurt so. "May I ask why you changed your mind?"

"Who's asking? The Protector or Darius?"

Darius hesitated. "Darius."

"May I speak freely, without retribution?"

"Of course!" When had the boy come to fear him?

Jared swallowed. "Because I don't want to end up like you, not the way you are now."

"How is that?"

"Like the black mirror—powerful, cold, smooth, reflecting but not being."

Darius flinched at the boy's honesty, but said nothing.

"I thought taking Isis back would make you better," Jared continued with desperation, "but it only

341

made things worse. Now I'm sorry I did it."

"So, you were the one who took her back."

"I thought you knew."

"I did. I just wondered if you would ever admit it to me."

"Are you angry?"

Darius shook his head. Not angry, just incredibly hollow. "You were right. Keeping her here was wrong."

"So, why didn't it work?"

"There are duties I cannot shirk."

"I don't understand. You always met your duties before."

"It's not something I can explain."

"Then, perhaps your understanding is wrong. Isn't that what you tell me?"

Darius shot him a glance. Was his understanding wrong?

He did not make decisions lightly and, thus, rarely veered from his chosen path. How could he change this one?

The path with Isis had not restored his control. Now he was but one step away from total control, unexcelled power. Tonight, when he did the last of the 1001 Circles, he would take that final, irrevocable step down his chosen path. He would be ready to face Pari on the morrow, the Festival of Mingara.

You already changed your mind once, when you left the path of air and fire, water and earth.

Had that been a mistake? Was that why everything in him kept fighting, kept screaming this was wrong?

He just did not know anymore.

But he had to make his choice tonight and, according to prophecy, once this ultimate choice was made, it could not be reversed. No turning back, no opting for the other path, no matter the results.

"Jared," Darius said, "I would ask that you return to the school for the Festival of Mingara." He held up his hand, silencing the boy's protest. "Please. Do this for me."

The boy looked at him, wide-eyed. "Something's going to happen, isn't it? Something bad."

"Something I hope I can prevent."

"That ugly woman who trapped me by the poison pool?"

Darius nodded.

"I'll help," Jared offered with the eager confidence of youth. "You said I was strong."

Darius shook his head. Not for his life would he put the child into danger. "This is something I must do as Protector. I must stand alone."

Not alone, came the unbidden thought. *Air and fire, balanced by water and earth, will restore.*

"But—"

"No, Jared. There can be no discussion on this."

Jared's lips pursed mutinously as he glared at Darius; then something in him relaxed, and he nodded.

Some of his thoughts slipped into Darius's telepathy. *My friend is back.*

"After the festival, when I return," *if I return,* "we will discuss whether you wish to continue your apprenticeship. If you desire another path, I shall not stop you. Agreed?"

"Agreed."

"Now, go. There are preparations I must finalize." *And decisions I must make.*

Jared lifted his arms to leave, and then abruptly lowered them and flung himself at Darius, giving him a ferocious hug. "Take care, Protector." He chanted something under his breath and touched Darius's turquoise tablet, then stepped back.

"What did you do?"

"Just a little protection spell." Jared gave him a cheeky grin, then disappeared.

Darius stroked his turquoise tablet. A protection spell? Jared had given *him* a protection spell?

For the first time since Simon had told him of the other path, Darius smiled.

Nude, Darius sat cross-legged before the small circle of stones. In their center, a flame blazed, steady and controlled. A divination had shown him the path to start. A divination would show the path to finish.

As the sun inched toward the horizon, he sprinkled water around the edges of the fire and then, while chanting the proper words, he cast rainbow-tinted sand upon it. The flame was extinguished, leaving only thick, sandalwood-scented smoke. The faint night breeze ruffled his hair but did not disturb the billowing smoke. Around him was utter stillness.

Darius stared at the smoke, willing an answer to the decision he must make. He stared, seeking patterns, insight, guidance, until the smoke began to dissipate. Overhead an owl landed in his cedar tree and greeted him.

There had been no answer. Why? Why had the divination failed?

Because he already knew the answer, he realized. Knew it in his heart, although his mind had fought acceptance.

One lone ember, not extinguished by the sand, snapped. For one second he inhaled the scent that Isis had made especially for him, and then it faded.

He had the answer.

His path was with Isis.

It was not the path Harbad had chosen, but Harbad's path was not his. The *Ma-at* was not the only thing he wanted. He wanted Isis, wanted her more than he wanted to fly on the winds of power, more than he wanted to draw in another breath. Life with only *ma-at*, without emotions of caring and sharing, was not a life he could endure.

Darius had memorized the words of the prophecy:

In the time of chaos.
When the powers run wild and free
Strong shall you grow or strong shall you fall
One united with the line of Abregaza,
Both willing and free.
Air and fire, balanced by water and earth, will
restore.

In the time of chaos,
When the powers run wild and free
Strong shall you grow or strong shall you fall
One stands alone in pure strength
Unbound by caring
Air and fire, with power supreme, will reign.

Two paths to choose
Balance
Power
One choice must be made at the final divergence
No other choice succeeds, no other path remains.

He understood it now. His power was strong, very, very strong. It had fed on its own strength, growing until he could no longer control it. Now he had to choose his response.

One path was of absolute concentration and dedication. Through the will, the mind, the soul, power could be controlled and increased until it reigned supreme. However, nothing, no emotion, could be allowed to be more important than the *Ma-at*, the power, or it would blaze out of control again.

The other path was one of balance, recognizing that no one element could rule. Air and fire must be balanced by earth and water. The fire would not be the raging maelstrom that destroyed, but a controlled one that warmed with the power of the sun. Natural balances. Not ultimate power, no, but, like a river that etched its way through the earth when channeled by sturdy banks, a way full of deep, hidden joys.

He did not understand why he had first failed with Isis. There was something else, one tiny piece that still eluded him, but he knew he had to try.

For he needed Isis more than he needed his *ma-at*. She saw beyond the Protector, to the man beneath, and she had wanted him. She was lightness and hope and joy. She was the cooling water and the stable earth to his heated fires and ephemeral air.

He just hoped he could persuade her to give him another chance. To give *them* a chance.

It would not be easy, for he had hurt her, he knew, but he had to take the chance. This time, he swore, there would be only honesty between them.

Darius stood and brushed the sand from his skin, staring at the last wisps of smoke. There was one other thing he knew.

He was making the final choice. The other path was now forever closed to him.

If he failed, if he could not persuade Isis to care again, if he could not discover that one tantalizing answer that still eluded him, then slowly his control would slip away, and there would be nothing, *nothing* he could do to stop it.

He would be engulfed by the madness of his chaotic *ma-at*.

Chapter Twenty-five

Isis frowned at her reflection. The charity auction was a formal affair: tuxes, sequins and bugle beads, diamonds or rhinestones depending upon your budget, shiny shoes, hair lacquered until a hurricane wouldn't move it. New Orleans was a city in which dressing up was a cherished art.

So, why had she chosen to wear this? The simple, floor-length turquoise dress wrapped around her like a sensuous robe. It had one fastening holding it closed at her waistline, a loop fastened over a red stone that glowed with an inner fire. Otherwise, it fell in soft drapes from her shoulders and her hips. In the deep V neckline nestled the turquoise stone Darius had given her. Even now, she could not bear to part with it. She'd dusted her bare arms and cleavage with silver powder. On her feet she wore high-heeled, barely there, sandals.

The exotic simplicity wasn't her.

She inhaled deeply, drawing in the scent of acceptance Gaspar had given her on Kaf, which she had placed on the fragrance stones on her dressing table.

Oh, well, what the hell. Isis shrugged and slipped on her dangling earrings. It was her, because she wanted to wear it, and so what if she didn't fit the general mold of glitterati. She never had, and she had found she liked it that way.

Isis picked up the new flacon of Magic and put a single drop on each wrist.

Beautiful. Exotic. Sultry. Like the dress. It brought a flush to her cheeks and tightened her insides.

Her front doorbell rang. Ram was there to pick her up. Tonight was her night to shine.

Isis hurried from the bedroom, catching one last glimpse of herself in the full-length mirror.

The silver glow. The robelike dress. The turquoise tablet. For one brief, heart-wrenching moment, she thought she saw a djinni.

Beau clinked his glass against hers, the ice tinkling. "Cheers, Ice. Looks like you've got a success."

Royal patted her on the shoulder. "I'm proud of you."

Thomas came up beside her and wrapped an arm around her. His tuxedo strained across his shoulders. "All I've been hearing about tonight is your samples. Everyone is raving about Magic." He stepped back and ran a finger around his neck. "Damn, I always did hate ties."

Isis laughed. "You look very dashing."

"Ice, you're headed straight to the top." Jack joined them, scowling briefly at Beau who wore an identical tux, even to the studs. "We're proud of you. Tonight, you've shown everyone you're a true Montgomery."

Isis's smile faltered slightly.

"She's always been a Montgomery," Ram said, coming up and giving her a kiss on the cheek. "Just a different kind of one."

Jack rubbed a hand across his neck. "Sorry. That didn't come out the way I meant."

Isis laid a hand on his arm. "It's okay. For once, you and I understand each other. I wanted to show you I was capable."

"You've done it." Beau tipped his glass in salute.

So far, the charity auction was everything she'd dreamed of. After last night's annoying bout of the weeps, she'd worked frantically through the rest of the night, creating the perfume she knew as Magic.

Her perfume, a gift from her grandmother and Darius, was a huge success.

The shadows of the past had been banished, and Isis basked in her new-found status as media darling. A dozen requests had come her way—interviews, franchises, new products. She'd be so busy with promotion and growth during the next months, she'd barely have time to breathe.

She had shown them all—she wasn't awkward, gawky, slow-witted Isis, she was capable and talented. She'd laughed, flirted, drunk just a wee bit too much champagne, and had a wonderful time.

She was a success, just as she'd always wished to be.

If she could wish for one thing more, it would be that Darius was here to help her celebrate.

Her brothers drifted off, until only Ram was left at her side in a rare moment of solitude.

"Magic," Ram said. "There's a reason you named the perfume that, isn't there, Ice?"

She nodded. At the dinner with her family after her return, neither she nor Ram had mentioned her assertion that Darius was the djinni he claimed to be. She told the others only that she had been with Darius and things had not worked out and he was gone. After assuring them that she was fine—and not pregnant—the subject was dropped.

Ram, however, had not forgotten.

"It has the essence of the *halifa* flower," Isis told him. "The flower of dreams. It's very diluted, only enough that it smells like an ideal perfume, whatever your version of ideal is."

"Mmmm," Ram murmured noncommittally, then nodded toward a knot of celebrants. "Ben's perfume is popular, too. Not as big as Magic, but it will do well for him."

Isis gave a grin. "It should. I created it, too."

"Without magic," Ram offered.

"Yeah."

There was a pause. "I've heard a lot of offers for you bandied about tonight. You're going to be a busy girl the next few months. No more tinkering around the shop."

Isis refused to think about that. Not tonight. Tonight she would savor her triumph. "Be glad for me, Ram," she whispered.

He hugged her. "I am. If this is what you want, what gives you happiness, then I'm glad for you. Hey, it looks like they're about to start the auction."

"Promise me none of you guys will bid on me, Ram. I'd rather go for the low amount of the evening than have one of my brothers bid on me."

He laughed. "Your wish is my command."

Isis glanced away quickly, afraid he'd see the brightening in her eyes.

Invisible, Darius watched Isis. She talked and laughed with those around her, so much at home in this crowd. She glittered and gleamed and seemed so happy. This was where she belonged. This was the success she'd craved.

Darius rubbed a hand up and down his arm. With the increase in his Kafian strength, the alien streams of earth magic prickled against him, making him edgy and slightly nauseated. He should leave.

How could he leave without his *zaniya*?

How could he take her away from this, her home, her dream?

It was the first time he'd wondered that. Always before he'd assumed Isis would love his Kaf and his people as much as he did. Maybe she felt as alien there as he did here. Had he ever asked her?

He was about to leave, without ever making his presence known, when she turned.

She still wore the turquoise tablet.

Just then, her name was called and she went up to the stage. The proceedings, which he'd mostly ignored while he concentrated on Isis, suddenly came into focus.

His Isis was to be offered for a "date." His English was not so bad that he did not know what *that* meant. He'd seen television. Seen the kisses—and more—when people went on a "date."

His spine stiffened. She was his *zaniya*, he her *zani*. That was a bond not easily broken. There would be a way to settle this between them.

There had to be.

Even if it meant staying on Terra.

When it was her turn to be called up on stage, Isis was surprised by the way she trembled. Why was she nervous? The auction was supposed to be fun. Whoever won her, even if it was Ben, they'd go on the date she'd planned, have a few laughs, unless it was Ben, and that would be that.

Her brothers had each sold for a substantial contribution. In fact, they had a friendly family bet going. Whoever was won with the highest bid had to buy the others a round of drinks. So far, Beau was ahead, but she was enough of a Montgomery to want to beat them all.

She stumbled once, at the foot of the steps, when a fleeting, brilliant flash of silver caught the edge of her vision. She spun around—Darius—then shook

351

her head at her foolishness and mounted the steps.

Hiding her nervousness, Isis gave the crowd a jaunty wave and acknowledged the applause with a big smile while she strolled over to the emcee, one of the local newscasters.

"Now, here's the lady who created those lovely scents we received tonight. Put your hands together for Isis Montgomery." A few wolf whistles joined the applause when Isis struck a pose. "And listen to this creative date she has planned." While the emcee rattled off the date she had put together for the auction, Isis swallowed, trying to moisten her dry throat.

Her turquoise-tipped nails dug into her palms when Ben Fontenot opened the bidding at one hundred dollars, but her smile stayed glued in place, even when Ben topped each subsequent bid.

"Well, we're at five hundred," said the gleeful emcee. "Do I hear anything else?"

Isis saw Ram open his mouth and start to raise his hand. She glared at him, and he retreated.

"Five hundred. Going once. Going twice."

"Six thousand of your dollars." A deep voice rang out from the back of the hall.

The emcee coughed. "Ah, excuse me, sir? Did I hear you say six *hundred?*"

"No. I said six thousand."

There was a ripple of movement in the back, then the mass of revelers parted as easily as the Red Sea. Darius strode through, looking neither to the right nor the left, only at Isis.

Dear Lord, he looked magnificent. Isis's heart leapt into double, then triple, time. The sculpted lines of his face seemed a bit leaner but were still beautiful. His dark hair and long lashes gleamed like polished onyx, and his golden skin glowed. His lips were pressed together, not in disapproval but in determination. Her breath caught halfway up her throat.

He wore not the robe she was accustomed to but

a tuxedo, like the other men. Except his fit him without a wrinkle and was made of a material that looked so soft, Isis yearned to stroke it with her hands. And he wore a brilliant red vest, shot with silver.

The sandals were also a unique touch.

His natural air of command carried him through the crowd. Darius paused only once in his steady progress, and that was to throw a quick glare at Ben Fontenot. Involuntarily, Ben covered his groin in a protective gesture, before he flushed and dropped his hands. Whatever had passed between them Isis didn't know, but she suspected she would not be having any more problems with Ben.

When Darius reached the stage, she finally saw her *zani*'s eyes. Deep and black, but not the cold emotionless black she'd seen when she left. Tonight his eyes glittered with passion and magic.

Soundlessly, Darius came up the steps and stood before the emcee. "Six thousand dollars." He dug into his pocket and carelessly handed the man a large wad of cash, then turned to Isis and kissed the back of her hand.

"I await our date, Isis." *My* zaniya.

Isis could only gape, until Darius closed her mouth with one finger, then bent over and kissed her, very briefly and lightly on the lips.

A cheer erupted from the floor.

Darius tucked her hand into the crook of his arm.

"You conjured up that money, didn't you?" she asked from the side of her mouth.

"There are a few advantages to being a djinni," he said amiably. "Now, shall we dance?" He led her down the steps.

She supposed she should be grateful he hadn't just transported them off the stage.

At the foot of the steps, they met a wall of Montgomerys—all with matching crossed arms and frowns.

"Well, I guess I won the bet," Isis said brightly. "Drinks are on me."

"I think we need to ask a few questions and get a few answers first," Thomas said, watching Darius.

She supposed they did, from their point of view. She clutched Darius's arm. "Darius, no tricks with my brothers."

"I told you when we first met, I do not do tricks."

To her surprise and relief, he didn't seem angry—no sparks, no echoing voice.

"I did not keep our bargain as I should have, returning you so they did not worry," he continued mildly, "so your family has a right to their protectiveness." He looked at her then, and the heat from his gaze seared her. "I would do no less for a *zaniya* or a daughter of mine."

Damn and double damn. When he spoke like that, with that beautiful, melodious voice, and looked at her with that soft gaze, she had trouble remembering she was supposed to be angry at his deceptions.

He turned to her brothers. "I shall set any fears to rest, answer any questions you have."

Uh-oh. Maybe that wasn't such a good idea.

"You asked me to dance," she said hastily. "I accept." Tugging Darius onto the dance floor, she shook her finger at her brothers. "And you four—five," she amended, seeing her father heading toward them, "find a quiet corner. We'll join you when the testosterone has had a chance to settle."

Isis had to chuckle at their dumbfounded expressions, but at least they didn't stop her when Darius took her hand and led her to the dance floor.

The band was playing a rocking tune while dancing couples gyrated to the driving beat, but as soon as Isis and Darius walked onto the floor, he gave a small motion with his hand, and the tune shifted into a graceful, moody piece that caught the dancers midjerk.

354

"How did you—? Never mind."

"I wanted the magic of holding you in my arms once more," he said.

With that, he threaded his fingers through hers, then brought her arms down and behind her, so he could encircle her with his embrace. "Lean on me," he whispered. It was a strange position for dancing, but a pleasant one, and Isis found she could follow the unusual steps as he moved effortlessly through the crowd. Whether it was simply his innate grace or whether he used a bit of his *ma-at*, she wasn't sure, but there was no awkward bumping against other couples while they danced. They were in a world alone.

Her cheek resting against his soft shirt and the firm muscles of his chest, Isis drew a deep breath. He was wearing the scent she had created for him.

"Why are you here?" she asked.

A breath stirred the short hairs on top of her head. "It is a long story and one not suited to be told here." He reared back slightly, so he could look into her face. "Will you listen to it?"

His action pressed his lower body more firmly against hers, and Isis realized he was semi-aroused, as she was. The sensuous dance was affecting them both.

She still loved him. She'd never stopped, never would, but she was still very wary. She would listen to his explanation, but that did not mean she would give control over to him. Tonight she had proven herself capable, and she would not go with a man, or djinni, who expected anything less from her. When she listened she could not afford to be anything other than clearheaded.

Abruptly, she stopped dancing. "Let's go placate my family, and then I'll listen. But not on Kaf. I won't risk going back there."

His eyes closed briefly; then he opened them and

released her from his embrace. "I understand. It shall be as you wish."

She started off, but Darius stopped her with a hand on her shoulder. "Let there be honesty tonight. Between us and toward your family."

Isis paused, then nodded. "Honesty."

Royal, Thomas, Jack, Beau, and Ram were sitting at a table set in a far corner of the ballroom. A single candle in a glass holder created the only illumination for the shadowy confrontation.

Honesty. As soon as she was seated, Isis took a deep breath. "Darius is not from here."

"You said he was from Morocco," Royal answered.

"He's from much farther, a different dimension he calls Kaf. Darius is exactly what he told you he was at Aunt Tildy's party. He's a djinni, or genie, as we would say."

Her family gaped at her.

"Oh, Isis." A world of disappointment filled her father's voice.

"Aw, Ice." Jack shook his head. "We'll get you help."

"No," said Beau, "she's just joking, but it isn't very funny."

She'd known this wouldn't be easy. "I'm telling the truth."

Ram leaned back in his chair and steepled his fingers. He looked not at her but at Darius. "She is, you know. Telling the truth."

"What!" Four voices chorused astonishment.

"Remember what happened at the party? And I've been talking to Aunt Tildy. Darius can prove it, can't you, Darius?" Ram suggested with a hint of command.

"Do that mind talk thing," suggested Isis. "Tell them you're a djinni."

The chorus grew quiet, as Darius's distinctive voice echoed in her mind. *I am Darius, Protector of the* Ma-at *of Kaf. We call ourselves the djinn. You know us as genies. And I do not live in a lamp.*

"He said he was Darius, Protector of the *Ma-at*—that's magic—and that he didn't live in a lamp. You all heard it." Isis looked around the table, which was as silent as death. Royal had turned pale.

"Please, Dad, tell me you believe me."

After a tense moment, Royal sighed. "I believe you."

It was as if his capitulation released a flood.

Thomas leaned back in his chair. "So that's why she disappeared without a trace for two weeks, despite our not inconsiderable efforts to find her."

"And why there's no record of Darius coming into this country," added Beau.

Her family had been thorough in their search, but then she expected nothing less from them, which was why she'd known she couldn't keep the truth from them.

"You won't take Isis away from us like that again," Ram said, "with no warning and no seeing her."

"I will not." Darius hesitated. "There are items Isis and I need to discuss. In private. This weekend."

"Did you agree, Ice?" Beau asked.

"Yes."

In the ensuing silence, Isis got the distinct impression that Darius added something else, something she couldn't hear.

"Then we'll see you Monday morning," Royal said eventually.

Darius took her hand and assisted her to her feet, and she bid her father and brothers good night.

On the way out, she asked, "What else did you say to them?" ·

He grinned at her. "You were not supposed to figure that out."

She lifted her brows. "Honesty, Darius."

"I told them you were under my protection and I would guard my *zaniya* with my life."

Isis rolled her eyes. "You're as bad as them at their worst. I sure hope you didn't tell them what *zaniya* meant."

"Ah, no. I thought that much honesty was unwise."

"Smart choice."

Sitting on the sofa, Isis curled her bare feet beneath her and sipped a cup of peppermint tea. She still wore the turquoise dress—it was so comfortable—but she'd shed the heels and nylons as soon as possible. She tried to relax, but every rebellious nerve ending clamored for Darius's touch again, and the feel of his skin against hers.

Darius stood before her, hands stuck in his pockets, tie loosened. Vulcan was winding around his legs. He rubbed his hand across the back of his neck, looking very much the picture of a floundering human male—until his mug of tea floated across the room to his hand.

He took a sip, then left it floating. "There are a few things I did not tell you prior to the joining ceremony."

"Just a few? Let's start with the fact that I had no idea I was getting married."

"Are you going to let me tell you this in my way?"

"Sorry."

Darius paced around the room, alternately rubbing his arms and scratching his chin. The whole story came tumbling out of him so fast, Isis could barely make sense of it.

Divinations, prophecies, his wild *ma-at*, two paths to control, a vengeful djinni. Okay, the last one she could understand. After all, she'd met Pari.

Isis honed in on the most important part. "Why didn't you ask me? Why all the deception?"

Darius sent her a look of disbelief. "Would you

have agreed to a joining ceremony—a marriage ceremony—in order to restore my control if I had come out and asked?"

Probably not, Isis admitted.

He interpreted her silence correctly. "I thought not. Later, I wanted to tell you, ask you. If it had just been my powers at stake, I would have."

At her raised brows, he gave a rueful grin, then rubbed absently at his arms. "Then again, maybe not. But I'm Protector. I had to regain control for the sake of Kaf and my people. Regardless of my own desires, I could not risk that you would say no and jeopardize their safety."

"So I was just a means to an end?"

"In the beginning."

Isis winced at his honesty, then shook her head. "You married me because a face in a fire told you to?"

He halted his pacing and stood, arms akimbo. "A divination is a sacred rite for guidance, entered into with great care. It is not a 'face in the fire'"

"Sorry." It had sounded that way to her. "Why me? Why would your divination pick me?"

"Because you are of the line of Abregaza," he answered, as if that explained everything, and resumed his pacing.

"And?"

"And my *ma-at* does not affect you. We are balanced."

She supposed that made some sense. Darius was so naturally overwhelming and commanding, he would engulf anyone who didn't stand up to him.

But she had. This was a night for discovering all kinds of successes.

He roamed to the window, then back to his floating mug, then back to the window.

His edginess was destroying the calm she fought for. "Would you find some place to light? You are jumpier than Khu when Vulcan starts to forget they're friends."

"I cannot! The Terran magic here, the forces pluck at me."

"There's magic here?" she asked, momentarily distracted.

"Of course. All around. It is different than mine, foreign to me, but just as strong."

He flopped down on the sofa beside her, his arm outstretched across the top; however, his foot continued to jiggle.

"It's just the magic making you edgy?"

"Yes. No." He looked at her. "I am . . . edgy because of you."

Isis looked away. "Did you have to sleep with me, make love to me? Was that part of the divination?"

"Yes, I had to make love to my *zaniya*."

Isis bit her lip. God, she hadn't wanted to hear that.

"But, no, it was not part of the divination." He cupped her cheek, urging her to turn back to him.

When she did, she saw the sheen of desire in his eyes, saw the faint colors of beginning arousal, and her heart leapt in response. Whatever else they felt, or didn't feel, this was still between them, as powerful as any *ma-at*.

"I made love to you because of this." He lowered his head and kissed her, slowly and tenderly. When she didn't pull away, when she began to respond with a tentative touch of her tongue, he groaned and gathered her closer, with his arms and with the sparkling energies of *ma-at*.

Isis sighed and settled into the embrace, understanding and forgiving, but unable to forget.

When he lifted from the kiss, he did not release her, and Isis was content to lie in his arms, wondering if it would be the final time.

She traced the straight line of his brow with a turquoise nail. "Why did you come back, Darius? What happens now?"

"I do not know. I only know I ache to hold you, to feel you move against me, to be inside you once again."

His words sent a shaft of desire straight from her head to her groin, piercing her heart in its mad rush. However, this time she must know why. "Are you still using me? Using me to regain control? You spoke of two paths."

"One of power, one of balance."

"You chose the one of power briefly, didn't you? After Simon came."

He nodded. "It is not an interlude that gives me pride."

"So now you choose me, balance. Did you come merely to persuade me to go back with you? To complete the restoration? For your people?"

"I came back because of the *Ma-at*, yes, that was part of it." He must have seen the flash of pain, for he laid a finger on her lips and traced them. "It was not just the *Ma-at* that brought me back. I missed you, in my home and my heart. There is an emptiness inside me that only you can fill. A need for you in my arms and my life. *You*, not just a woman from the line of Abregaza, but Isis, who fills my odorless world with sweet perfumes. I hoped you would come back with me, yes, but after seeing you tonight—" He let out a puff of air. "Your ties to your world are strong, your accolades well earned."

Isis drew in a long shuddering breath. "And if I do not choose to come back?"

He gave a tiny shrug. "Then it will make no difference to you what happens."

Isis wasn't stupid. She could read between the lines of what he'd said. "You'll lose control again," she said flatly. "Dammit, how can you give me such an untenable choice, knowing that if I don't come back with you I'm responsible for your *ma-at* going haywire? How can I, in good conscience, refuse?"

"You said you wanted honesty. You are not responsible. I am. It is my *ma-at*. Mine. And my choices." He got to his feet, then turned and glared at her. "I do not want you coming back out of a sense of obligation or pity or belief that you must save me. I only want you to come back because you want *me*, Darius," he thumped himself on the chest, "as much as I want you, Isis. The *Ma-at* has nothing to do with that choice."

Isis blinked, unsure what to say.

He held out his hand. "Come with me. Come back to the grotto. Let me make love to you in the place of your fantasy, with the *halifa* scenting our dreams."

Red, green, blue, purple, yellow, a whole rainbow swirled about him. Her skin tightened in response, yet she hesitated, recalling how he had refused to bring her back.

"I will bring you back whenever you ask; this I promise."

Still, she hesitated.

His eyes closed in pain. "So, trust is yet to be earned."

In two strides he reached her. He picked up her turquoise tablet and held it between his hands, then chanted strange words she couldn't understand, even with her acquired djinn language skills. His words grew in strength, until at last he shouted. A bolt of electricity shot from his hands, into the tablet and around the cord that held it, and then up the back of her neck.

Isis started, then settled down as she realized it hadn't hurt, had merely surprised her. "What did you do?"

"I have given you the gift of transporting. Hold the tablet tight in your hand and say these words: *Abhn-*

ma-el. By the great Solomon, I command thy winds transport me."

"I can't do that."

"Certainly you can. Try the words."

"*Abhn-ma-el.* By the great Solomon, I command thy winds transport me."

"Perfect. Now, when you say that, you must hold the picture of where you want to go fast in your mind, as tight as you hold the tablet, and keep it until you arrive."

Isis stared at her turquoise tablet. He had given her an unparalleled gift of magic and freedom, though it must have gone against every bone in his arrogant, dictatorial, possessive body. She leaned over and kissed his cheek. "Thank you."

His hands clenched at his sides. "And now? I want you, Isis. Shall we take one more night before the decision of the morning must be made?"

"Yes," she breathed, unable to resist him any more than she could resist the siren song of a magical perfume.

"You choose where we will go. Use your *ma-at,* my sweet Isis, and transport us both."

She picked up his hand. "*Abhn-ma-el.* By the great Solomon, I command thy winds transport me," she whispered, holding tight the image of a fantasy.

Chapter Twenty-six

She had chosen the grotto. By the grace of blessed Solomon, there was hope.

The spray from the waterfall dampened his cheeks and left diamond droplets in Isis's dark hair. Darius kissed her fingers. "Very good. Most djinn land on something other than their feet the first time."

She gave him a cheeky grin. "I had a good teacher." Letting go of his hand, she spun around. A soft "Oooh" escaped her.

The *halifa* was in full bloom, its waxy white flowers perfuming the air with their rich, exotic scent. Isis knelt before one of the huge flowers. "It's beautiful." She threw her head back and inhaled deeply. "This is as close to heaven as an aromatherapist can get."

As he moved to her side, Darius ran his hands down the length of his human clothing, changing it back to his familiar blue robe and getting rid of the trousers. The sandals he stepped out of. "There is more essence we can harvest in the morn. I only took from the first blooms."

"More? I'll be set for life."

Darius plucked a small purple flower nestled among the *halifa,* not wanting to think about her leaving after she had gathered the remaining oil, and knelt beside her. He tucked the tiny flower behind her ear.

"This is a *folietta.* Its delicate scent is lost among the *halifa,* but it is a flower of constancy. For where the *halifa* is showy and lasts but a few days, the *folietta* is here always.

And may we stay as the folietta *together always.* He was careful not to send her the thought, for he wanted no decisions tonight, wanted nothing she might think of as pressure to sway her. She smiled at him, and he could resist her no longer. His hand cupped her neck; her silken hair brushed against his fingers. Darius leaned over and kissed her.

Her lips were soft and full beneath his, and the sweet fragrance of jasmine wafted from her, more perfect than the *halifa*'s exotic scent, for it was her scent, not the *halifa,* that fueled his desire. Beside Isis, all else paled.

She wrapped her arm around his shoulders and pressed against him. "It's been too long since I shared your pillows, my *zani.*"

"We have no pillows here, only the feather grass beneath and the sound of the waterfall. It is night, as in your fantasy, and I give you music." He waved his hand, bringing them the sounds of lute and harp. "And a gift I make for you."

He cupped his hands and intoned the soft words. A fire bloom appeared in his palms, the strongest and most beautiful he'd ever made. Others had been practice, flawed before this one. Rich in blue and orange and red, with green petals, it glowed in the dark night. As Isis had come to glow in the darkness of his night.

"Oh, it's beautiful," she sighed. "Thank you."

"Hold out your hands," he told her, and when she complied, he laid the bloom in them.

"I'm holding fire." The colors danced across her awestruck face.

"The fire bloom is a gift only a male djinni can make, and it is an ephemeral thing."

Her wide, sexy smile teased him. "That day I went into the city . . . now I know what that old woman meant when she nudged me and asked me if your fire blooms still lasted hours."

"What did you say?"

"I told her yes, that I expected nothing less. She cackled and said I made a worthy *zaniya* for her Protector."

"You do."

She grew serious. "It's not the fantasy I need, it's you."

"As I need you, *zaniya*." Darius bent to her lips again. With a deft twist of his wrist, he undid the single fastening at her waist. Her soft robe fell open, and he cupped her breast. Ah, she felt so good, so right.

His emotions sparkled about them, brilliant shades the red of fire, the green of earth, the white of air, and the blue of water. He caressed her with mouth, with hand, with fantasy, with mind, with *ma-at*. Inside and out, he throbbed with her rhythms. She reached for him, met him with her fevered touch, brought him soaring with her.

He trailed kisses from her mouth to her breast, and she gasped when he took it in his mouth. "You give me starlight."

"And you are my sun." He lowered her to the grass, then settled himself between her legs. Reaching up, he ran the edge of his hand along a branch loaded with *halifa* blossoms. They cascaded down, showering them with a soft white fragrance. Petals fell in her hair, on her chest, and when Darius hugged Isis to him, crushing them, they released a bloom of perfume.

Hot days, sultry nights, cool waters, perfumed gardens, these dreams were all Isis, only Isis.

She reached down and touched him intimately, and the fire in him exploded, its white-hot center burning away all doubts and barriers.

"I cannot wait," Darius gasped.

"Then don't." She lifted against him.

She was ready, so ready. With one thrust, Darius was inside her, seated to the hilt, joined to her with primal forces of body and *ma-at*.

He was engulfed by the inferno, with no thoughts of holding back, watching for her pleasure first. There was no need, for she matched him—motion for motion, stroke for stroke. Together, they climaxed, wrapped in the perfume of dreams.

Darius collapsed against her, the final elusive piece of the divination now clear.

She was his *janam*, his soul, his love.

I love you, Isis Montgomery. His mind spoke the words to her, but that was not enough.

"I love you, Isis."

I love you, Isis Montgomery.

The soft words blended with the fragrant oil that coated Isis's skin. Another fantasy, she thought.

"I love you, Isis."

Drowsy satiation disappeared in an instant. Isis's drooping lids popped up. "What—"

Darius, shifting his weight to the side while holding her tucked close to his body, rested a finger across her lips. "Shh, say nothing. Just lie here with me, love. Sleep, let our hearts beat together."

A cover, soft and warm yet weightless, drifted down, encasing them in a sensual cocoon.

At his crooning words, Isis quieted, unsure of what she would have said, unable to confess her own love in the shadow of an uncertain future. She snuggled against him, hugging him as she hugged his words close. His strength held her safe and his so-right scent, more precious than the *halifa* oil, bathed her as she watched the night sky fade. A red glow reflected against the blackness. The first fires of the Festival of Mingara; she'd heard djinn in the city talking about it. Maybe Darius would take her to it. She would ask him.

Tomorrow they would have time to talk and decide. Her eyes drifted shut. Soon it would be daybreak.

At daybreak they ran out of time.

"Well, now, isn't this cozy."

The pleasant sensation of slow arousal—Darius's fingers trailing across her belly from her breasts to the curls below, making her feel like sun-warm honey—dissipated at the intrusion of the mocking feminine voice.

Isis opened her eyes.

Pari had come. The confrontation had begun.

For a long moment neither Isis nor Darius moved beneath their concealing cover; then she felt a robe materialize around Darius and heard the swish of silk as her turquoise dress settled about her. Holding hands, they stood.

Pari, her hands tucked into the sleeves of her gray robe, stood before them. The grotto had become eerily silent—not even a tiny breeze set the vines chiming—yet Pari's silver hair blew back from her face. The odor of the *halifa* became cloying, making Isis's teeth ache.

"Holding hands. How very droll, Darius. You're losing your edge."

"How did you find us?" he asked.

"She's a human obligated to a djinni. Of course I could find her."

Darius nodded, as though that made sense. "So you come to complete your bargain."

Pari smiled. "I come to destroy you and take my place as ruler of the djinn. The favor she owes me is minor." Her hand began stroking the black tablet at her throat. It was an ugly hand now, wrinkled and spotted, as though all the age and poisons taken from her smooth skin had been channeled to her hands.

Pari saw the direction of Isis's gaze, scowled, and tucked her hand back into her sleeve.

"So, what is the favor?" Darius asked.

"A simple one, really. That she leave this grotto at once and never return."

Darius slowly nodded. "It is acceptable."

"Now wait a minute," Isis protested. "I'm the one who made the bargain. I have a say about granting the favor."

"Of course," Pari answered. "You heard it. To leave this grotto and never come back. What is your decision?"

A simple enough favor, easy to grant at no cost. So why did Pari want it? Isis had learned a few things since she'd first encountered her, and one of the big ones was to delve below the surface of any bargains with djinn.

She looked at Darius. "You want me to go?"

"Yes." *You may transport to the city and bring help,* he added with silent communication.

Her thoughts raced. All she had to do was leave; even Darius urged her to go. It sounded like a good course of action, except for one thing: Isis doubted very much that Pari would ask such a thing without a damn good reason, and any reason that benefitted Pari was bound to be detrimental to Darius.

What was going on here? She wasn't stupid. *So, think, Isis. Use that brain you know you've got.*

Isis had an excellent memory for spoken words. As a child, she would persuade her brothers to read her a book aloud, then proudly "read" it back to them, reciting from memory. It had fooled them for a while.

What had Darius said last night when he told her the whole story? That he alone must face Pari.

Something else she'd learned was to take bits and pieces, little parts that she could read and understand, and put them together to understand the whole.

If I leave now, I won't be able to come back, and I'll bet none of the other djinn will either. Maybe there would be some kind of barrier that prevented it.

Darius was a Protector; he was protecting her, too, Isis realized. He wanted her to go because he believed it would be dangerous.

How could she leave the man she loved to face danger alone?

Especially when the one incontrovertible fact was that Pari wanted her gone. Isis didn't know why exactly; something about that prophecy and about her giving him balance. She just knew that if she left right now, Darius would be weaker.

"What happens if I don't leave?" Isis asked Pari.

"If you don't uphold your end of the bargain?" Pari shrugged. "Then I can extract a penalty from you."

"Your immunity to negative effects of *ma-at* will not protect you in this case," Darius warned, "and neither can I."

"What kind of penalty?"

"One of my choosing." Pari tapped her nail against her chin. "I'm thinking, perhaps your business. I could destroy the *halifa* essence, turn your oils rancid, set the gossip tongues wagging in endless rumor. A total failure."

Her business? Her success? Everything she'd worked for? Lose everything? Go back to being the not-too-bright baby of the family?

No, even if she lost the business again, she was not

that. She was capable. She'd proved it; not to them, but to herself, and that was all that mattered

She'd been caught in her family's definition of success, and she didn't need that anymore. She could still do aromatherapy, one on one, smaller and more intimate. Her business wasn't the most important thing; her love for Darius was.

"What's your decision?" Pari said impatiently.

"I'll stay."

Pari smiled, a cruel smile that froze Isis to her bones. "I don't think you want to say that, so I'll give you a chance to reconsider."

"Isis, do not. Please leave," Darius pleaded.

She caressed his cheek. "I ran out on you once, didn't believe in you. I won't leave you again." She turned back to Pari. "I'll stay. You can destroy Dream Scents."

Pari gave a little *tsk*. "I didn't actually say that Dream Scents would be your penalty."

What else? What else could the woman ask?

"No, I wouldn't bother with your petty little business." Pari smiled again. "The cost, Isis, will be your sense of smell. Here's a sample of what it will be like."

Pari thrust her finger forward, and an arc of blood-red electricity jolted from the tip of it to Isis's nose.

And Isis's world turned gray.

She could smell nothing. Nothing! Not the potent *halifa*. Not even Darius. She rubbed her nose, rubbed it until it hurt, but still she could smell nothing.

The inside of her mouth turned to ash. Without smell, she could not taste.

She felt herself crumbling, dying inside. Silent tears streamed down her cheeks. Throughout the humiliations of growing up, she'd always had her sense of smell, her love of perfumes to sustain her and give her hope. How could she survive without smelling lavender again? Or angelica? Or spruce? Or anise?

Darius folded her into his arms. "Go, Isis," he said gently. "Do not pay that price, my love. I shall come to you when this is over."

My love. He would not come to her when this was over, not without her help. If her sense of smell was the price she must pay for loving this beautiful man, for keeping him safe, then pay it she would.

"This is all nauseatingly tender and sweet," Pari said, "but my patience ends. Your decision, Isis Montgomery."

Darius dropped his arms and released her from his embrace.

Isis picked up his hand with hers. "I'm staying with my *zani*."

"You fool. So be it. *Shali-el-shalamat*."

The arc of scarlet electricity struck Isis again, spreading from her nose across her face. Pain lanced deep, through her sinuses, to the very base of her brain. Blinded by tears and agony, Isis fought to stay on her feet. She would not weaken. Darius's hand tightened on hers, and he laid his other hand upon her chest, bracing her. His strength held her upright.

With a final crack, the electricity exploded before her. Isis felt *ma-at* ripple from Darius's hand and along her throat to meet it. "This price shall last a lifetime," Pari intoned. "*Shali-el-shalamat*." Both powers faded.

Isis inhaled deeply. Nothing, absolutely nothing. Never again would she smell the sweet fragrances of life.

Darius's hand caressed her cheek, catching the tears with his thumb, and kissed the tip of her abused nose. "Ah, my sweet Isis, why?"

She met his gaze squarely, shedding the last bits of wariness. "Because I can't let you face her alone. Because you need my balance. Because I love you." She was no longer afraid to admit it.

Because I love you.

372

The words rippled into Darius like the flow of the eternal tides, and something inside him settled into place. The prophecy was fulfilled, the divination complete, his mastery restored.

It was not joining or the balance of *ma-at* and magic he had needed, but love. Love for a friend, for a child, and ultimately the love of a man for his woman, and a woman for her man.

Harbad had not chosen to tread that path, but Darius had been so much luckier. First, in his friendship with Simon, which taught him more than the wielding of power, then in the divination, which sent him to Isis, his soul.

No sooner did those thoughts flit through his mind than he was hit with a bolt of *ma-at* so malevolent and ugly it made his flesh shrink.

The battle with Pari had begun.

He fought back, staggering under the withering, frigid onslaught. The war of *ma-at* was not one of changing shapes or clever tricks. It was pure and simple: the strength of mind and will to wield, direct, and match the powers of nature.

Air crackled and smoked. Thunder boomed. Gray, black, red and yellow flashed in blinding strobes. An acrid scent of electrified hair mixed with the sweet *halifa* in a odor that confused the mind. Only those senses beyond the five guided him.

His control was exquisite, his strength at its peak. The fires of Kaf raged through him. Darius ignored the pain of their blazing course, which sapped the force from his muscles.

He pushed Pari to the brink, burning her out with a wild power. "Surrender," he gasped. "Do not make me destroy your *ma-at*."

"Never," she hissed. "You will be destroyed." She spread her arms. "Come to me, Powers of Dark. Come to your servant."

A black fog, poisonous and choking, rose from the

earth in long fingers that circled around Pari in a hideous tornado. She thrust her hands forward, and the fog, with sinister glee, shot from her to Darius.

It clouded his mind, filled his lungs. He choked and coughed, each breath edged with knives, and he heard Isis gasping. Gathering the winds, he dissipated the fog, but Pari countered, raising more from the sinister forces that gave her new power. Acid etched his skin in burning rivulets.

These sinister forces—he did not have the power to fight their combined might. He was not strong enough, powerful enough. He was losing. He would lose.

Beside him, Isis bent over, coughing and retching.

"Your tablet," he gasped. "Transport. Leave."

Blindly she clutched his hand. "Use me," she rasped. "Use the balance."

What did she mean?

"Use the magic of Terra."

Air and fire balanced by water and earth.

"Concentrate on your Terra," he commanded, barely able to give voice. "Her rivers, her mountains. Think of nothing else."

Isis grew still, her eyes closed. Her harsh breathing became shallow and slow. Connected by their love, she became a conduit through which he could feel the magic of Terra. Only through her could he harness it and not be overwhelmed by its alien nature.

To his fire came the cooling water. To his air came the stable earth. Yet water did not quench and fire did not boil. Air did not create a whirlwind of earth and earth did not stop the air. All four together. Balanced.

Through Isis, he wielded the *Ma-at* of Kaf and the magic of Terra. Complete mastery, perfect control. Slowly, the sinister forces retreated, then turned on their mistress.

Pari screamed in agony. Darius forced them from

her, back to the darkness that spawned them. She bent over, gasping, glaring at him, nearly drained of her power.

"Do not continue," he told her. "Do not force me to take your *ma-at* from you forever."

"You shall never take what is mine." She rose to full height and pressed her hands against her temple. *Ma-at* arced from her fingertips and into her head. She gave one, last keening wail, and then collapsed.

Darius stared, dumbfounded, then rushed to her side. Despite everything she had done, he did not wish this for her.

"Oh, Pari." Once, they had been close, and he had always hoped she could be turned from her path of destruction.

Pari lay still and silent, and he touched her cooling skin, knowing there was no hope. The breath of life had been taken from her by her own hands.

Isis knelt beside him. "Is she dead?"

He nodded. "Yes. How could she do such a terrible thing? Djinn do not kill, not even themselves." His voice cracked on the words.

Isis laid a comforting hand on his arm. "She was too far destroyed for anyone to save."

He closed Pari's eyes, then chanted the djinn prayers for the dead, sprinkling her with the petals of the *halifa* and the spray of the waterfall. A flame, white and hot, encircled her, and the wind whistled, fanning the fire until it consumed her; then both died out.

Only an indentation in the grass showed where she had lain. Pari was gone. The fires of Kaf had reclaimed their daughter.

Darius was exhausted, drained to the very core of his being. His hands shook, so he could grasp nothing, and vision blurred before his eyes, yet there was one more thing he must do.

"Shalamat-le shali," he whispered, touching Isis lightly on the nose, and then collapsed on the grass.

Isis gathered him in her arms, clutched her tablet, and transported both of them home.

Chapter Twenty-seven

When Darius awoke, he was surprised to find himself
lying on his own pillows. He had been dimly aware
of Isis taking them both from the grotto, but he'd
thought she had returned to Terra. Perhaps she realized he would recuperate better on Kaf.

He stretched, feeling oddly invigorated and light-
headed. His innate sense of time told him he'd slept
for almost a whole day, while Kaf worked its healing
on him. How strange to feel his power purer and
more perfect, stronger and more controlled than it
had ever been, when he knew he must lose it.

During his sleep, he had come to a decision. Isis
deserved to be able to stay on Terra and enjoy all that
she had worked for, and the strength that came
through her family. However, he could not ask her
to accept a *zani* who must leave every time a message
spell came or every time he needed to revitalize. He
had used Terran magic in the fight against Pari, yes,
but only because he could channel it through the fil-

377

ter of Isis. Never could it be a part of him, as it was with Simon. It was simply too foreign to his *ma-at*.

Therefore, to stay on Terra with Isis, he would have to rid himself of all his *ma-at*. Become an ordinary mortal. Trust that Isis's love would stay true.

Something inside him shriveled at the thought, but it was not as impossible to contemplate as it would have been a moon's cycle ago. There were still things he could do. He and Isis had visited museums, and since he had seen most of the ancient histories firsthand, he could contribute there. He had a facility for languages and a strong knowledge of the arcane.

He had never realized he had so many talents beyond *ma-at*.

The ritual involved was a complicated one; he must start at once. He left a message for Isis, then lifted his arms to transport. Bittersweet emotion clogged his throat. This was the last time he would feel the hot rush of the vortex.

With that thought, Darius disappeared into the whirlwind.

Isis tiptoed into the bedroom, thinking she'd heard Darius stirring. Good. She'd been so worried when he lay still for so many hours, his breathing barely audible, his skin pale.

The room was empty. Isis looked around, astonished, until she saw something flickering by the bed.

It was writing, done with fire and hovering in the air.

Trust Darius to come up with a unique love letter, she thought, smiling, but her smile faded as she read the note.

He had gone to make himself human so they could live on Terra? What the hell did he mean by that?

Dread swelled through her, shrouding her insides. He'd always said he couldn't live on earth. Damn, he was going to do something dangerously foolish, she knew. She had to stop him.

Isis clutched her tablet, visualized Darius, and chanted the words. Nothing happened. She tried again, holding him firmly in mind. Still nothing.

Damn, damn, and triple damn. It only worked for places. She had to know where he was before she could get to him.

Her sense of anxiety growing, Isis paced the room. What should she do? She had to do something soon, before it was too late, but she didn't know where he was.

Maybe he was at her house; his note said he would wait for her there. Tablet in hand, Isis said the needed words. Within seconds, she was at her house, but when she raced through, it was empty.

He must be on earth somewhere. She tried again to reach him through her tablet but stayed maddeningly in place.

Dreams Scents. Again Isis gripped the tablet and stepped into the whirlwind, but he wasn't at Dream Scents either. Where could he be? She was running out of time.

A card propped against her desk lamp caught her eye. Zoe's card. Simon! Simon might know.

Because Zoe worked from home, Isis had been to the house when she'd talked to Zoe about using ZEVA. What had the place looked like? Isis closed her eyes, recalling the scent of computers, printer ink, and daisies in the room, bringing the scene to her mind. She held tight to it.

"*Abhn-ma-el.* By the great Solomon, I command thy winds transport me." Hot, swirling wind engulfed her.

She landed in Zoe's computer room. Zoe whirled around from her monitor. "Isis! How did you—"

"Is Simon home?" Isis interrupted in a rush. "I have to see him now."

"Sure, he's in the kitchen." Zoe opened her computer room door and motioned. "Go on back."

Simon was sipping a cup of tea when Isis found him. "Good morn, Isis." He looked around. "Where's Darius?"

"I don't know. I hoped you might tell me. He left this morning without a word, leaving only a message that he was going to make himself human so we could live together on Terra."

"Did you ask this of him?" Simon thundered.

"No! I want to live with him on Kaf. He just didn't stick around long enough to find that out. What does that mean? Make himself human? Is that like what you did?"

"It's not the same for Darius. I substituted the bonds of Kaf with bonds to Terra. I'm still djinn, but I use the powers of Terra."

"Is that what he's doing?"

"No. I was able to transfer bonds because of my unique situation, but Darius cannot."

"But he's so strong."

Simon shook his head. "His strength works against him here. His bonds to Kaf are forged to hardness in her fires and cooled to steel by her winds, and he has grown even stronger in the past days. Terra is very foreign, very alien to him."

She remembered the night of the charity auction. The way he had fidgeted and seemed almost distressed. He'd said the Terran forces plucked at him. At the time, she'd taken it to be simply nerves, but perhaps it had been something else. Something more fundamental to him.

"So what is he doing?" she asked.

"He's draining himself of *ma-at*. The only way he can live on Terra with you is to become mortal. No *ma-at*. No magic."

Isis dropped into the chair, her knees unable to hold her upright. She drew in a shuddering breath and pushed a trembling fist against her mouth, trying to contain the horror. "He can't do that. I have to stop him."

"Can you not care for him if he has no *ma-at?*" Simon asked, his voice cold.

Isis's stricken gaze flew to his. "Of course I can! I'd love him no matter what, but this is wrong for him. It's like asking a man to rip out his own heart. Darius is so much more than his *ma-at*, yes, but it's such a vital part of him. I won't have him give it up. I have to find him, stop him. Do you know where he would be?"

"He'll be on Terra, probably nearby, because he will be unable to transport when he finishes, but I'm not sure where."

Isis's stomach turned to iron.

"However," continued Simon, "I don't need to know where Darius is to transport to his side."

"How come I couldn't do that?"

"You are new to your power and your love," he said gently. "In time, it will come."

Isis scrambled to her feet. "Then let's go. We won't be too late, will we?"

"The ritual is an involved one. With Solomon's grace we will be in time."

He took her hand and for the fourth time in less than twenty minutes, Isis disappeared into the vortex.

She landed in a swamp. It was a hot and muggy bower, surrounded by emerald vines and leaves. Mosquitoes swarmed about her head, and the damp ground squished between her bare toes. She had no idea where in Louisiana she was, and it didn't matter. All she cared about was the man before her.

He sat hunched beside a fire, his back to her. His low chanting reverberated in the clearing, keeping him oblivious to her arrival.

"You are in time," Simon whispered. "He hasn't finished."

Isis took a deep breath, pulling in the scents of decaying loam and stagnant water. Darius was so stubborn once he had decided what he considered to be the correct course of action. She had to do this right.

She strode forward across the damp grass. "Modern point number fifteen, my *zani*," she called. "Life-changing decisions are supposed to be discussed."

You make my friend a worthy zaniya, *Isis Montgomery, and I shall be proud to call you friend, as well.* Simon's words echoed inside her, and then he was gone.

At the sound of her voice, Darius whirled around. He didn't greet her, but at least he stopped that infernal chanting. "Your numbers are mixed up. We should be on modern point seven."

"I have trouble with sequencing." Isis knelt beside him. He looked well, recovered from his ordeal with Pari. His gaze was shuttered, not cold, just . . . distant. A frayed rope defined the ritual area, which contained colored stones and a small fire. "Are you almost finished?"

"Another set of incantations; then I must douse the fire with the earthy water from the swamp."

Isis grimaced at the green-coated water in the wood bucket. "Nasty-smelling. And after that?"

"The *ma-at* will be sucked from me," he said simply.

Her insides twisted. "Don't do it, Darius."

"It is the only way." He turned back to the fire and lifted his arms.

"No, it's not. I want to live with you on Kaf."

He paused, then lifted his arms again. "I will not force you to make that choice. Not again. When I asked you to come back before, you said I put you in an untenable position, that in good conscience you could not refuse to go with me. You were right, and I will not ask that of you again."

He started chanting.

"Stop it!" she shouted. She dislodged the rope and threw the stones into the swamp, taking care not to douse the fire, hoping that disturbing his circle would stop him. "Did you think what I said in the grotto was all a crock? I love you. *I* won't ask this of *you.*"

He turned to her. "I believed it, and I know you will stay on Kaf if I ask. That is why I cannot. You were willing to sacrifice everything, even your sense of smell, that vital part of you, for me. I love you. Can I do anything less?"

"But I don't want this sacrifice," she said between clenched teeth. He ignored her and replaced the rope in a circle. Damn him, he was so stubborn, and she'd done a too-good job of convincing him she wouldn't stay on Kaf.

"Speaking of my sense of smell, how come it returned this morning?" Anything to distract him, keep him from completing the spell, while she marshaled whatever arguments she could think of. "I thought the penalty was for my lifetime."

He shook his head. "Pari's final words were for 'a lifetime' not 'your lifetime.' When she died, the spell could be reversed, which I did before we left the grotto. It just took a while for your nose to recover."

Isis remembered the faint *ma-at* coming from him, and knew he'd somehow caused that tiny but important change. "If you hadn't had your *ma-at*, I'd still be without a nose."

He smiled then, for the first time, and tapped her nose. "You would still have a very nice nose. It just would not work as well."

"Did you know Gaspar asked me to work with him?"

He gave her a startled glance. "No."

"I think it would be interesting. Your people—my people now, too, I guess, since I'm your wife—have different oils. I can't wait to start trying them. A woman even asked if I could develop a perfume for her." Okay the last was a bit of an exaggeration but she wasn't above fighting dirty. Not when it was so important.

"She did?"

"Scout's honor." She'd never been a scout, so she figured it wasn't too bad a vow to break.

"You think of my people as yours?"

"I could come to. I liked many of them. Except Leila." She frowned at him. "Just what went on between the two of you?"

"Do you really want to know?" He lifted one brow.

"Nah, doesn't matter. After all, I'm the one who married you." She picked up his hand and kissed it, much as he always did to her. "That means you have to get over this annoying habit of making decisions without my input. Like this idiotic ritual."

"Idiotic ritual?" His eyes narrowed.

Good, the sparks were coming. "Yes idiotic. Have you thought about what it will do to your people to have a Protector without *ma-at?*"

"There is no danger looming. Another will be found."

"Yeah, but it won't be you. Will the substitute be able to train Jared the way you'd like?"

Darius frowned.

"You know," Isis continued relentlessly, "I was looking forward to having Jared hanging around. I've got four older brothers; it'd be like having a younger one, too."

"But your business? Your family?"

"That confrontation with Pari made me realize something. When faced with the loss, I decided I didn't need that success. Oh, it's great to have, but I don't *need* it anymore. You once told me helping people was a reward, and you were right. *That's* what I really enjoy about what I do."

"What about your family?"

"I don't have to abandon them. I can still come back for visits. If you were from Morocco, as we claimed, I'd be far away, too." She tapped her chin thoughtfully, "Actually, getting back and forth from Kaf is easier than coping with airline schedules."

His hands stopped fussing with the rope and he really looked at her. "Is it so important to you that I have my *ma-at?*"

"Nope," she answered promptly, gratified by his startled look. "I'll love you with or without the *ma-at*, but it's important to *you*. Doing this ritual is tearing you apart, right?"

Involuntarily, he started to nod, then caught himself and scowled at her.

Isis laughed. "Your *ma-at* is part of who you are. The best part of who you are, however, is the man who's willing to give it up for me. I love that you're willing to make the sacrifice, but it isn't necessary. I was looking forward to living with you on Kaf." She tilted her head. "Unless you *want* to live on earth."

"Solomon, no!" The words came out in a rush.

"Then I guess it's decided. Kaf is our home."

He smiled at her. "Kaf is our home." He leaned forward and kissed her hand, then her cheek. "There is one condition, and one thing I must ask you."

"What's that?"

"The thing I ask you is whether, since you will live on Kaf, you wish me to change you, so you are tuned to her rhythms rather than those of Terra?"

"What's that mean?"

"It would mean that you would not be able to live on Terra again permanently. You would be like the djinn, needing to revitalize on Kaf every twelve days."

Kathleen Nance

"But I could still visit my family, just popping back to Kaf for that revitalization?"

"Yes. It would also mean that you would age with me, rather than by the faster times of Terra."

"I can image nothing better than growing old, slowly, with you. What's the condition?"

He smiled. "You have performed the djinn ritual of joining. You married me by the laws of Kaf. I would also join with you by the marriage rites of Terra."

She grinned at him. "Covering all the bases, huh?" At his confused look, she waved her hand. "Never mind. I'll warn you it's bound to be a lavish affair when Montgomerys are involved."

"As long as it makes you mine, *zaniya*." He captured her and held her tightly.

Isis kissed him. "I already am."

Darius stood and lifted the bucket of water.

Isis shrieked and grabbed his arm. "What are you doing?"

"I cannot leave the fire burning."

"But it will suck out your *ma-at*."

He laughed gently. "You broke off the spell when you threw the stones away. I knew I would not go through with it, then."

"So why all the discussion?"

"I was curious why my *ma-at* was so important to you."

She scowled at him. "Get the answer you wanted?"

"Yes, my sweet Isis." He doused the fire, then swung her up into his arms and kissed her.

His kiss was sweeter than any fantasy of the *halifa*, stronger than any magic. It left her breathless and filled with the fires of desire.

"You know," Isis said, tapping a nail against her tooth, pretending to ignore Darius's wandering hand and the warm touch of his *ma-at* along her breast. "I wasn't quite truthful when I said your *ma-at* didn't mean anything to me. I was wondering what it might be like to make love while you—" she whispered into his ear.

Darius laughed with delight while the whipping whirlwind of djinn *ma-at* descended and carried her off with her lover.

Some months later, Darius was in his workroom studying a crumbling manuscript he'd found in an ancient ruin on the far reaches of Kaf, marveling at the unique spells he'd thus far decoded, when he discovered a handwritten note Isis had tucked in his work. Between her mixed-up handwriting and creative spelling, the note was not easy to interpret, but Darius soon discovered she wanted him to meet her at the grotto.

She still did not like to write, but she had finally gotten over the expectation that he would find her attempts amusing. Instead, he treasured each note, because they were so rare.

He transported at once to her side.

She was kneeling, spreading out a blanket beside the pool of water. Darius grinned, heat traveling at once to his groin and making him hard. As many times as they had made love since their Terran wedding—a lavish and crowded affair, as Isis had predicted—he still had only to look at her, smell the womanly mixture of jasmine that was his Isis, and he wanted her anew.

He knelt behind her, his legs on either side of her, his arms wrapped around her waist. "I love you," he murmured.

She leaned back, resting her head on his shoulder and exposing her vulnerable neck to his kiss. His hands cupped her breasts, gently teasing the nipples in a way that he knew she liked. Djinn love sparkled around them.

"Making love in a rainbow," she sighed. "I don't think I'll ever take it for granted."

"Make sure you do not," he growled with mock seriousness, nipping at her neck, then added, "I got your note. Were you going to tell me something?" His hand drifted to her lightly rounded belly.

She stilled. "You know? About the baby? How long?"

"Probably before you even did. A djinn male is very sensitive to the nuances of his mate's body." A fierce wave of protectiveness welled up inside him. A djinn child was precious and rare, but no more so than its mother. He would care for both the mother and child with everything inside him.

"I've been here months, yet you guys still keep throwing me magic curves," Isis grumbled.

Tenderly he kissed her again. "Are you content here?"

"Yes," answered Isis. "Content and happy."

She was happy here. The djinn were like humans, most nice, some less so, and they didn't seem to view her lack of *ma-at* as a weakness, valuing instead her skills as a perfumer and aromatherapist. She'd learned from Gaspar and had taught him a few things, to their mutual delight.

Darius made no secret of his pride in her. Oh, they still argued on occasion—his commanding nature hadn't mellowed that much—but the making up was so much fun. And, to his chagrin, his *ma-at* still didn't work on her when she refused.

She went to Terra often, visiting her family and Dream Scents. She had paid Aunt Tildy back, then made Marc and Salem full partners. With their expert guidance, Dream Scents rivaled Fontenot's By Nature, and she planned to turn the business over to them, along with the rights to Magic and Winter. These days her successes, more and more, were on Kaf.

Jimmy Ray Frank still sniffed around on occasion, but with the closure of Madame Pari's shop, Isis's departure to "Morocco," and Marc and Salem's lack of interest in magic, his story had fizzled, and he moved on to other targets.

Her family had grown accustomed to her choice of husband and had even found some areas of common interest with Darius. Her father, Beau, and Ram had even come to Kaf a couple of times, although so far Thomas and Jack had refused.

Aunt Tildy was a frequent visitor, especially since she had found and perfected an ancient method of transport involving mirrors. Aunt Tildy, the debunker, had finally found her magic.

Jared took up residence with them, training with Darius. He spent a lot of time on Terra, with Simon, Zoe, Mary, and baby Lillie, and also with Tildy.

"Yes, I'm very happy," Isis repeated softly. "Are you pleased about the baby?"

Darius tightened his hold on her. "Ecstatic."

He never regretted his choice. He was not the most powerful Protector, would never reach Harbad's heights of *ma-at*. The final Circles of the Adept were beyond him without Isis and the magic of Terra, but he found it did not matter.

"Maybe the baby will be a girl," Isis suggested.

Darius shook his head. "Not this one."

She didn't ask how he knew. "I'd like to visit my family and tell them. Will it be safe to go?"

"It will be fine. We can go tomorrow."

"You don't need to come."

"Yes, I do," he said firmly. "Besides, I would like to visit Simon and his family."

"Lillie is only six months old, but I hear she's all djinn. Maybe Zoe will have a few tips about coping with a djinn baby."

"You will cope wonderfully, my love. But now—"

With a deft movement, Darius turned Isis around

and laid her down. He sprawled next to her, kissing her, stroking her.

"Oh, Darius," she moaned, her arms holding him tight as his hand stroked her belly.

An insistent chiming intruded. With a groan, Darius rolled off of Isis and glared at the message orb.

It was only a pale yellow, not urgent at all. With a wave of his hand, he sent it spinning away. He bent down, savoring his *zaniya*'s kiss and her fervent response.

After all, some things—like love—were worth more than magic.

J • KATHLEEN NANCE

Jigsaw

A car following too close, too fast, left Bella Quintera wrecked by the side of the road. The identity of her rescuer confirms Bella's fears. Years before, Daniel Champlain had been her lover, but the relationship was one she strove to forget. The NSA agent's rugged good looks still haunt her—as does his betrayal.

Now Daniel demands Bella listen. She is in danger. He wants to know about her new creation, about its implications for national security. What she's designed is worth killing for; but is a master criminal truly after her—or is Daniel again pursuing his ambition, thoughtlessly flipping her life upside down? The peril is real, no game like the jigsaw puzzles she makes in her spare time. And this puzzle has missing pieces: the ones that show whom she can trust.

Spellbound
KATHLEEN NANCE

As the Minstrel of Kaf, Zayne keeps the land of the djinn in harmony. Yet lately, he needs a woman to restore balance to his life, a woman with whom he can blend his voice and his body. And according to his destiny, this soul mate can only be found in the strange land of Earth.

Madeline knows to expect a guest while house-sitting, but she didn't expect the man would be so sexy, so potent, so fascinated by the doorbell. With one soul-stirring kiss, she sees colorful sparks dancing on the air. But Madeline wants to make sure her handsome djinni won't pull a disappearing act before she can become utterly spellbound.

Enchantment
KATHLEEN NANCE

The woman in the New Orleans bar is pure sin and sex in a stunning package. And for once, hardworking, practical-minded Jack Montgomery lets himself be charmed. But no sooner has he taken the beautiful stranger in his arms than he discovers his mistake: Lovely, dark-haired Leila is far more than exotic; she is a genie. When he kisses her, heat lightning flashes around them, the air sparkles with color, and a whirlwind transports him out of this world. Literally. Trapped with Leila in the land of the Djinn, Jack will have to choose between the principles of science that have defined his life and something dangerously unpredictable and unsettling.

Burning Tigress

JADE LEE

Charlotte Wicks wants more. Running her parents' Shanghai household is necessary drudgery, but a true 19th-century woman deserves something deeper—her body cries out for it! Through a Taoist method, her friend Joanna Crane became a Tigress. Why should Charlotte be denied the same?

Her mother would call her wanton. She would label Charlotte's curiosity evil. Certainly the teacher Charlotte desires is fearsome. Glimpses of his body inspire flutters in her stomach and tingling in her core. The man had a reputation among the females of the city as a bringer of great pleasure. There is only one choice to make.

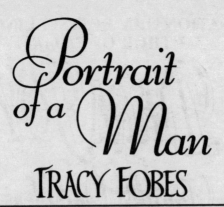

Portrait of a Man
Tracy Fobes

In a world where only the wealthiest man has the price of a bride, Rourke of Calandor holds no hope of knowing a wife's gentle touch. But this rebel dares to travel into the past in order to defy the established order. Only by painting the likeness of a very special woman can he open the doorway between Blackfell and Philadelphia....

Alexis Conner has been fascinated by the macabre all her life. She's made a career of verifying the paranormal. But the image materializing before her is no ghost. This is a real man. And the first thing he does is crush her into his arms and blow all her scientific cool with a kiss....

Rejar

DARA JOY

Lord Byron thinks he's a scream, the fashionable matrons titter behind their fans at a glimpse of his hard form, and nobody knows where he came from. His startling eyes—one gold, one blue—promise a wicked passion, and his voice almost seems to purr. There is only one thing a woman thinks of when looking at a man like that. *Sex*. And there is only one woman he seems to want. *Lilac*. In her wildest dreams she never guesses that bringing a stray cat into her home will soon have her stroking the most wanted man in 1811 London....

_52178-4 $6.99 US/$8.99 CAN

Mine To Take

DARA JOY

He is full-blooded and untamable. A uniquely beautiful creature who can make himself irresistible to women. With his glittering green and gold eyes, silken hair, and purring voice, the stunning captive chained to the wall is exactly what Jenise needs. And he is hers to take . . . or so she believes.

___4446-3 $6.99 US/$8.99 CAN

Dorchester Publishing Co., Inc.
P.O. Box 6640
Wayne, PA 19087-8640

Please add $2.50 for shipping and handling for the first book and $.75 for each book thereafter. NY, NYC, and PA residents, please add appropriate sales tax. No cash, stamps, or C.O.D.s. All orders shipped within 6 weeks via postal service book rate. Canadian orders require $2.00 extra postage and must be paid in U.S. dollars through a U.S. banking facility.

Name_____

Address_____

City_____ State_____ Zip_____

I have enclosed $_____ in payment for the checked book(s).

Payment <u>must</u> accompany all orders. ❏ Please send a free catalog.